MW01175032

the portable conundrum

[signature]

Liane Keightley

conundrum press · Montreal · 2006

the portable conundrum
© 2006 the respective creators

Edited and designed by Andy Brown
Cover illustrations by Marc Ngui and Billy Mavreas
First edition

Library and Archives Canada Cataloguing in Publication

The portable Conundrum / edited by Andy Brown.
Includes bibliographical references.
ISBN 1-894994-14-0

1. Canadian literature (English)–20th century.
2. Canadian literature (English)–21st century.
I. Brown, Andy, 1968-

PS8251.1.P67 2006   C810.8'0054   C2006-901639-9

Dépot Legal, Bibliothèque nationale du Québec
Printed in Quebec on Enviro paper which is 100% recycled and
ancient rainforest friendly.

conundrum press
PO Box 55003, CSP Fairmount,
Montreal, Quebec, H2T 3E2, Canada
conpress@ican.net   www.conundrumpress.com

conundrum press acknowledges the financial assistance of the
Canada Council for the Arts toward their publishing program.

**Canada Council
for the Arts**   **Conseil des Arts
du Canada**

INTRODUCTION   5

CATHERINE KIDD–Niagara Falls   11

ANDY BROWN–from *You Are Lance Blomgren*   24

AMANDA MARCHAND–Holed   31

GOLDA FRIED–Liela Tov   40

BILLY MAVREAS–Seven Prophesy Bunnies   51

PETER PARÉ–Read 'em and Weep   59

LIANE KEIGHTLEY–Inlet   70

DANA BATH–from *Death by Sky*   76

HOWARD CHACKOWICZ–Cartoons   86

MEG SIRCOM–Dream Apartment   95

LANCE BLOMGREN–Four Household Paintings   100

VALERIE JOY KALYNCHUK–Mouth Froth Promise   108

VICTORIA STANTON–Dee-Dee the Epilator   113

VINCENT TINGUELY–Jackie   117

MARC NGUI–Playing Noisy   127

COREY FROST–Genji, the Shining One   139

MARC TESSIER–Into the Light   149

HÉLÈNE BROSSEAU–Totem   159

SUKI LEE–One Night in Bangkok   166

JULIA TAUSCH–Crazy Jane   177

JOEY DUBUC–Drawings   182

CHANDRA MAYOR–Bridget, Barbie, and Me   186

STÉPHANE OLIVIER

    & GILLES BOULERICE–Lacustrine things   193

SHARY BOYLE–Tempere 2005   202

MAYA MERRICK–from *The Hole Show*   207

JOE OLLMANN

    & WAYNE GLASS–Three Ladies and Jesus   219

NATHANIEL G. MOORE–from *Legends of Welfare*   227

ELISABETH BELLIVEAU–How to lead a double life   239

MARC BELL–Ten Drawings   249

ROBERT ALLEN–from *The Journals of Irony Jack*   259

RICHARD SUICIDE–Monsanto II   272

JILLIAN TAMAKI–Sketchbook Drawings   283

APPENDIX–Posters   292

BIBLIOGRAPHY   301

CONTRIBUTORS   305

Introduction

From my vantage point here in the smoking room at Conundrum Towers I can see the unpaid interns fixing the open sewer below. They pack up for the day and leave me to my mansion, the gold-plated door knobs, the armoury, the battlements, the inventory. I scan the property not believing my good fortune. The hobby farm in the back yard is really underway. The maple tree, given as a gift, is about to bud. The stableboys are grooming the horses, the chauffeur is on red alert.

Spring comes to Montreal in a jolt. Suddenly it's here. Like a new traffic light on a well worn road. Unexpected. There is a moment, just a few days really, before the heat sets in, when you notice how dense the neighbourhood has become due to the winter construction of condos; when the bicycles smashed by the Bombardier machines finally emerge from the snow; when you retire your longjohns but not your gloves and wonder if the tamtams are back. It's that time right now.

Ten years ago I was living in a crumbling apartment not far from here, in the depths of post-referendum Montreal. Having finished with treeplanting after seven grueling years, and done with school, I was wondering what all this talk about 'desktop publishing' was about. After a few kind souls took pity on my attempts I was scraping by. There seemed to be something going on with 'chapbooks' and 'zines' and there were psychedelic posters on every lamppost advertising 'spoken word' events. I stumbled over one such group after interviewing Corey Frost and Colin Christie for an article about the chapbooks they were producing through something they were calling ga press. These chapbooks seemed pretty simple to make, or so I thought. Soon I was working with these folks and their friends writing for *index* which had taken to the streets as a free litzine. We distributed it by driving borrowed cars around the city. I moved into a high ceiling eight-and-a-half in Mile End with a bunch of roommates paying insanely cheap rent. One of those roommates was Catherine Kidd.

Catherine was talking into a hand-held tape recorder every time I saw her around the apartment. She seemed to be repeating herself. We shared avocados because all I ate were sandwiches. She was memorizing with that device. Soon I saw her perform what she had been mumbling all month. She wore a bloodied butcher's apron and blew everyone away. So this is what they call 'spoken word'.

The shiny new sewer pipes glisten in the early evening sun. Surveying the Conundrum Towers estate I observe the heli-ski returning from patrol. My drink is beginning to warm so I add more ice. Just another day selling wildly innovative, nostalgia inducing yet trendy books to the masses. Time to check on the inventory. The golf cart picks me up in front of the fountain and off we go. Ten minutes later we reach the warehouse. I give the warehouse manager an Easter bonus and send him on his way. I want to be alone.

Lying here, the boxes stacked up all around me, surrounded by the overwhelming smell of ink, I remember those days as if they were ten years ago. I approached Catherine to do a book of her writing; I barely knew QuarkXpress, how hard could it be? I came up with all kinds of elaborate schemes for the book which eventually became *everything I know about love I learned from taxidermy*. While I was knocking myself out cutting every page and hand printing every cover, Catherine worked with DJ Jack Beetz at The Swamp on the sound. We launched the book and cassette (before CDs!) at a loft and sold beer (see appendix). The book kept selling and I had to make more. Even though I figured out to adjust the size so I wouldn't have to cut every page it was still labour intensive. On one of those print runs (on the photocopier of course) I used the excess trim and made a book of one of my own short stories. Then I thought to make it $1 and have a series. Remarkably, writers with whom I had been associating were happy to have me make their stories into little books. Soon I was drawing, cutting and folding, taking photos; it all went into the books. A group calling themselves Fluffy Pagan Echoes seemed to be everywhere I looked. I realized all those very trippy posters were by the same guy. I contacted the poster artist who turned out to be Billy Mavreas. We made a book of his posters. Then he moved into my big cheap apartment and started introducing me to comic artists. A whole new world opened up for me. Soon after, I was approached by two of the Fluffies who had done seventy artist interviews and wanted to make the resulting oral history into a book. It was with Vincent Tinguely and Victoria Stanton's massive tome *Impure* that I really discovered the amount of work necessary to publish books, but I took the plunge and went into debt.

After Hollywood came calling, however, I was able to move into the Towers and expand the estate. That's what paid for the second Jag. One simple mention of conundrum press in an Academy Award™ nominated movie was enough to get me a ticket to the big time. Oh sure, I had to hire a staff of fifty (although the cook is only freelance) but it was worth it to be able to get unique Canadian books into the hands of the billions around the world starving for the conundrum brand of culture.

Time to come clean. I only have one Jag. Actually, I'm sitting at a desk filled with empty lobster shells and the traces of diamond dust writing this ridiculous introduction. *The portable conundrum* is a dream fulfilled for me. I wanted to see if I could do an anthology and get work from everyone I had published over the past ten years. Could I find everyone and get something from each of them? I think the results speak for themselves. I am impressed that this all came together and disappointed that I'm the last one to get my submission in. But it means I have had time to go over these pages again and can have the last word, which is all I've ever wanted.

In this anthology are essays, comics, a photo essay, drawings, a translation, and short stories. Some can not be put into any of these categories. This reflects the mandate of the press. We are now publishing fiction, graphic novels, and art books from people we've never met in cities we've barely heard of. For the com-

plete list of every title conundrum has published turn now to the
bibliography in the back of this book. The pieces here are
arranged in chronological order, the order in which the contributors were published. The final few submissions come from
those who have books coming out this fall, books which are
being put together by the worker droids on the ninth floor of the
Towers even as I write this.

Appropriately enough we start this anthology with
Catherine and a story she wrote ten years ago, when I was first
putting together her book and forming the press. So, a nostalgia
trip right off the bat. The next thing I notice about these contri-
butions is the frequency of the theme of becoming a parent.
Times have obviously changed and ten years later many of us
have new priorities but are still plugging away on 'upcoming'
projects. This is proven by the number of novel excerpts featured
here. Obviously these people are not slowing down.

Here at Conundrum Towers, where the certificates and
awards are so numerous that they have become the new wallpaper in the mezzanine, we are honoured to be represented by so
much talent. The contributors to this anthology are the reason
for any success conundrum press may have had. They are our
inspiration as we move into a new decade. Perhaps in another
ten years the 'Conundrum Wing' of the new Super-hospital will
finally be complete.

– Andy Brown, March 2006

the portable
conundrum

CATHERINE KIDD
Niagara Falls

Ihave realized that everything about you is flammable. I persistently imagine you lying in a grey heap in the ashtray on the varnished pine desk. I believe that you would understand this, as Douglas would not, if I were to say the same sort of thing of him. He says I am unflattering. He means I am unhappy. If I were to murmur my vague dissatisfaction with waking up every morning to the same face, my face, in the mirror, while other things like the dining room rug and the bookshelves swell and gather dust, slowly advancing like a forest, he would stand behind me, shaving, and say that I could be thankful if I didn't show my age. This would not be what I meant.

I would have meant that it is ridiculous and rude to be confronted with the same face day after day, as though I am the same person now that I was ten years ago, or twenty. Perhaps I am. And I *do* show my age, Douglas, I *do* notice how much more I resemble my own mother now, than I did in a previous life. And yet the face is the same, or else changes so gradually I hardly notice it, while everything else gathers perceptible dust or is accumulated in boxes marked with black felt.

This morning I'd been going through stacks of envelopes, vinyl over-night bags, purses I haven't carried for years – laying hands on every letter and photograph I could wish to recall except for the one I am looking for. I'd recognize it if I saw it, although I'm no longer sure when it was written, from where, nor the pictures on the stamps. Loons, possibly, which mate for life. Or leaves, which reduce to compost over time. Letters sent to me from within my own city, the various lodging houses where you camped out until you moved away permanently. I'd recognize the hand-writing, though – careless, loping, back-handed. Scandinavian-looking, with the dots anticipating the *i's* several characters too soon. I would skim through your humourous middle-aged complaints and your stories of mis-identified bones until I found it: the premonition, the confession.

But because I wake up with Douglas, my daily inventory mostly touches him: the red corduroy dressing-gown was his Christmas gift from two years ago; the Niagara Falls ashtray was bought to commemorate our ridiculous excursion to the place as well as the gag, which Douglas keeps running, about our basement sink, the pipes of which perennially burst and cause a dark stain to spread beneath the brown low-pile carpet like a dirty puddle beneath a layer of ice. It is certainly no cascade. I experience it only as a sopping spreading stain discovered in the morning. I peel back the carpet and sweep the water out the back door, let it dry, sprinkle on baking soda, sweep again, cover it up. Douglas repairs the pipes cheerfully, purposefully, a comfortable annual event like decorating the tree or an anniversary waltz, but the smell lingers year round.

With you, it was the pilot-light in the furnace going out. Our historical gags, if we had had them, if we had pretended to care about things which did not function properly, would have concerned mastodons and creeping glacial masses forcing us back to the primitive warmth of our bed, playful, squealing, mock-fighting, excited. All our life together, the successful part of our life together, it seems, was games. Maintenance, we pretended, was unimportant. The rest of the world could go to hell, for all we pretended to care. But at least you, Richard, would have been able to tell me whether or not the same water – the very same molecules – plummet over the Falls only once and for all time, or whether they follow some circuitous route undergound and back, in a loop, to fall again and again incessantly. It is possible that the conventional portrait of Niagara Falls – like the one at the bottom of the ashtray, always appearing rudely and humourously the same – is in fact entirely accurate.

Whenever I am in one of my panics about some unavoidable mishap, or even one which could have been avoided (such as the loss of Douglas' wedding ring at the Toronto Greyhound station, or the death of people to whom I have neglected to write),

Douglas, after a respectful interval, will shrug his shoulders – *Water under the bridge, Dolores.* This he says kindly, and means it kindly, but his short-sightedness makes me quietly furious and embarrassed for him. As though the features of a life could be washed out and left abandoned like terminal morrain. As though a lost thing ceases to have being simply because it is lost.

Douglas' son, Trevor, is more interested in such things than is Douglas. He comes into the kitchen with a modest stack of photo albums and spreads them out on the table, offering them to me, like a housecat depositing a bird at my feet.

"Is that you, Dolores? How *old* are you there? That's Richard, right?"

Richard and I are standing in front of a camel. Richard has one hand on the animal's neck as though it were a great salmon he had caught. His shadow almost eclipses the small, dark man who stands on the sidelines, holding the reigns, waiting for Richard to open his billfold and pay him for the ride. I am wearing a preposterous hat, a safari hat, a present from Richard.

"I suppose I'm about nineteen, there," I say, but surely I was older. I'm trying to apologize for the earnestness of the hat. I squint at the photo, falsely, as though I can barely recognize it.

"And that's Richard, yes, he was thirty-three. It's not a very flattering picture of him, really."

Richard looks paunchy and red-faced, but not unattractive. I would prefer Trevor to imagine Richard as having been an attractive man, I don't know why. Perhaps so that it might come up sometime, in conversation between Trevor and his father, that my previous husband had been an attractive man. I would never point this out to Douglas myself, of course, but I might allow Trevor to say it for me. This is how I am unkind to Douglas – in quietly indirect ways.

"Is this from when he found the skull?"

Trevor knows about the famous skull, alas. There was once a hologram of it on the front cover of a glossy photo magazine concerned with the global environment. Douglas still renews our subscription every year, as a Christmas gift to Trevor, an offering to me.

"No, Trevor, he found it in Mongolia. We were already divorced then. This is in Egypt, which was really only Richard escorting a group of archeology students on an international field-trip." I realize as I say this how unkind I have become, to Trevor as well as to Douglas.

"Didn't he do a dig?"

"Yes, I suppose Richard did do a dig. He mostly dug up kitchen utensils, some dolls I think, some bits of clay pots..."

I don't finish telling Trevor about Egypt, he'd heard the story before anyway, various versions of it. I think it was the fragility of *clay pots* – I thought of tea-sets and elderly ladies baking pies, and I thought of my sister – which made me not wish to continue. I was caught suspended, felt Trevor watching my throat as it trembled. I'm certain it was *this* – suspense – which Trevor was looking for. A proof of my dissatisfaction, or evidence that Richard had been, and was still, a torch-bearer of sorts.

Trevor seems to be almost as in love with Richard as I was, and for similar reasons, though certainly they've never met. Trevor apologizes for Douglas, his father, in tiny, secret ways – like bringing me the photo albums, bringing me drinks, reading books which I have read and which Douglas has not, nursing my melancholy.

But Trevor is mistaken there. I am grateful to Douglas, I am accustomed to and soothed by him. When we moved into this house, just before Trevor came to live with us, the walls had been excessively pock-marked with nail-holes and putty-stains where pictures and shelves had been hung by the previous tenants. There were so many holes that I could almost reconstruct, in my mind, the previous interior decor. Douglas had patiently filled in all the holes with plaster, smoothly and evenly, and repainted most of the rooms, except for the bedroom, because I once had said the blue floral paper looked like the Falls seen quickly through the slats of a barrel. Douglas thought this was smart, anything about the Falls seemed smart to him, or dependably clever, because the Falls are so huge, and so easily recognized. The Falls, to Douglas, are like an inside joke which everybody knows, with no risk of being excluded.

The bedroom now resembles the dusty blue Niagara ashtray roughly set down amid the eggshell-white and sand of the other rooms, which look clean and uninhabited. I can scarcely recall where the holes had been at all.

Trevor brings me a glass of wine and then goes up to his room.

Egypt. There had been a wedding parade along the river, with hired musicians in red jackets like ushers. We had followed the parade to catch a glimpse of the bride. I might have actually said, "Look, Richard! There she is! Do you think that's her?" — excited to discover something exotic and mysterious about being a bride. There were several women I'd thought could have been her, I didn't know a thing about Egyptian bridal costumes. I spent much of my time wandering in the bazaars, visiting the excavation site once or twice, a young wife. I chatted with the students and asked whatever questions I supposed they'd be able to answer.

Then Richard broke his wrist. He'd taken a short-cut into the excavation-pit, down the slope like a skier, and had fallen. It was quite dramatic. Richard got an Egyptian cast, which looked like any other cast, really. But when we got back home, his university newsletter printed an article with a picture of Richard looking like a noble wounded soldier.

But in truth, Richard had been required to fill out the same application forms the students had, and had paid the same fees, which included the hotel but not meals. I'd been slightly disillusioned to learn that Richard and 'his Egyptian correspondent' had not even met before Cairo, I saw them shake hands in the lobby of the Hotel Ibis as polite embarrassed strangers. I'd been envisioning them as old colleagues, of course, reunited after

years, delighted at the opportunity to finally descend together
into the earth and rattle ancient bones. I have even wondered
since then if Richard was chosen for the trip primarily because
he was one of the only faculty members who didn't have children at home to support, or any real responsibilities.

I drink Trevor's glass of wine standing at the kitchen window, watching the neighbour scrape ice from his windscreen
with a plastic shovel. Then I go back into the bedroom.

Small boxes and envelopes are still cast about on the bed, the
dresser, some on the floor. The space-heater has been left on, the
smell of heated dust and cold coffee. I take off my dressing-gown
and sit down on the bed. The mirror over the dresser is too high
for me to catch a full reflection of myself from this position. I can
only see my puzzled, colourless face, like a face reflected in the
mirrored side-board of a dining booth, seen over the shoulder of
somebody else. I know that below the frame of the mirror, my
body is naked, tired, soft. I put on my dressing-gown again and
lie down on the bed.

It is obvious when someone is well suited to being looked at,
and Richard was. I had seen him teach, and seen him at parties,
and knew that this was so. He would grin in a bemused and
vaguely lupine way when students asked him questions, girl students. He would drawl his replies over centuries of buried bones
as though he'd been there himself to see them committed to dust.
The irony was supposed to be his seeming much older and more
experienced than he looked, than he actually was. He had stud-
ied long and diligently to fit in anywhere, any time or place. Like
American dollars, possessing the same indevaluable currency,
presumptuous.

In the early days we pretended to revel in voluptuous poverty. We read *Down and Out in Paris and London,* and you smeared
shoe-polish on your ankles in lieu of socks, as though it were
socks that we could not afford. My typewriter would collect dust
quite happily, in a corner, as I believed that those lost evenings

would eventually resurface like sapphires, to be set and polished later on. The most beautiful things to us, back then as now, were things theatrically saddened by time. We scoured second-hand shops for antique baby carriages, taxidermy raccoons, rare and yellowed books, for a song.

I sat across from you in a red vinyl booth at a bus station diner near Kelowna. It was the first time you expressed any concern, for my own sake, that I was not writing. We did not get back on the bus, but stayed in the local motel for three nights in a row, with the idea that we wouldn't leave until I had completed a story. You phoned to cancel your lecture in Calgary, as though you could afford to do that. Of course, I still did not write, how could I?

Perhaps there is no need for writers to lead exquisite, depraved, scintillating lives after all. Perhaps no one ultimately cares how many lovers you've had or how much you drink or whether you are dying of a beautiful disease. Or maybe it's simply that I never really cared about these things. You loved archeology, you often said nothing really matters until after it is dead.

Richard would be an excellent subject for biography, not because his life has been any more remarkable than anyone else's, really, but because of his talent for being looked at. I suppose I did love him for this.

I take off my dressing gown again and put on a green turtleneck, a brown plaid skirt, the silver thistle-pendant Douglas had given me some anniversary ago. In the mirror I brush my hair up from my temples with my fingers, attempting to do it briskly like an actress. The same face. I put on lipstick and boots and leave the house.

I thought about visiting my sister, Phyllis, who now lives in a mustard-yellow duplex above the paint store at 14th and Fraser. There is still a piano in her apartment, now covered up with doilies and vases and that same tawdry lamp, painted china base and pleated cherry shade, held out at an extravagant angle like a hoop skirt. On her kitchen table is the sewing machine at which she perennially sits. I envision her sitting, bent over some meticulous work involving her fingers, the tension of strings, and her eyesight, which is failing prematurely. I think of her repentantly playing the church organ behind some maroon-robed choir, or sewing rosettes to someone else's bridal train.

Phyllis has collected the most wonderful and various supply of canned food I have ever seen, stacked in her kitchen cupboards like decorative tiles, although of course she lives alone. Over the coming weeks, she will go through them all and arrange colour-coded Christmas hampers for local church charities.

My sister does not speak about Richard and I, nor about Douglas and I, though she asks after Trevor. She speaks about funerals, generally, how she has been to two this week. How she has baked a lemon loaf for the Ladies' Auxiliary luncheon, and a pumpkin pie for the social following Sunday service.

"There seems no end to baking pies," she says tiredly, as though she might easily have said, "There seems no end to funerals." She shakes her head disappointedly and looks down at the backs of her hands. "Other than that, oh, well I've been doing various things I guess, there was the Rebeccas' supper, I made a salmon pie for that, oh and I drove Alice Beaulieu downtown for her eye-appointment." Phyllis touches the back of her head, touches her hair, which is now short permed, light wispy brown. "She has cataracts, *in both eyes,* imagine."

"You shouldn't be driving at all, Phyllis, with your eyes," I've told her. "Why can't Mrs. Beaulieu take a cab? Wouldn't do *her* any good if you were both killed in a car accident, would it, blind leading the blind."

"I'm *not* blind, either. Besides, well it's actually a blessing to have Alice or I would have had *another* funeral to go to, in the same after*noon,* imagine – Mr. Drummond, poor man, away out in Burnaby."

Phyllis will not let me believe she ever reflects on the things she does, except to punctuate her sentences with that word *imagine.* I don't know what I am meant to imagine, if it is not what she says. I only find myself growing peevish at this dishonesty, my own dishonesty, when in truth we both could be split open like piñatas and a thousand reprimands would pour forth like bonbons, like water, but neither of us betrays even a trickle.

I know perfectly well that Phyllis has an excellent memory; she claims this is only true for poetry and recipes. *Other* people's words, what *other* people have made.

"Oh, I could never write a poem or a story like you do, Dolores," she tells me. "Me, *imagine!* I haven't got the first clue what I'd write about, I really don't. I haven't had that sort of life." *What sort of life, Phyllis?* I have wanted to ask, *Your own life or a borrowed one?*

It used to be that we could sit together quite happily, on the porch of the house on Clarke Street, in folding lawn chairs. Richard would have been there too, of course, it was our house, mine and Richard's. Phyllis only came to stay after failing her nursing exams. But we would sit on the porch in the evening, the three of us, and listen to Richard tell stories about Egypt and bones. Or Phyllis would sometimes recite the various poems she'd made a point of memorizing. Richard would make gin and tonics. She would sip hers sparingly, deceptively, while we got rather drunk in the purple dark.

We. In fact, I'd begun to no longer think of Richard and myself in terms of being a single artifact – a change, I'd thought, which greatly improved things between us. It was an easy balanced *we,* I had thought, like two leonine bookends with volumes between. I lay back in my lawn chair, my gin and tonic in one hand, the other resting lazily on Richard's thigh.

Phyllis seemed to be another artifact unto herself. The concern I felt for her was like what one would feel for a daughter, perhaps, though I don't know. Her offerings were gentle, tentative – she would hold up one gracefully curving finger as she recited, as though following tinily-written words on a page.

I tried to draw my sister into our goings-on, encouraged her to grow her hair long enough to wear in the style fashionable back then, shoulder-length and flipped up at the ends like fish-tails. Phyllis wore terrible glasses with thick black frames which monopolized her face.

"Phyllis has quite nice legs. She should wear her skirts shorter," I would say to Richard.

"Too muscular. Too athletic," he'd say.

This was true. Although Phyllis was never athletic, her body seemed to be held in solid tension; the muscles of her calves like the dormant nest of elastic bands at the centre of a golf-ball.

"She should grow her hair," I'd say to Richard.

"She does have hair growing. On her face."

"What a mean thing to say."

"I didn't pass judgement on it, I just stated a fact," he'd say. Phyllis did have a soft down growing in front of her ears, at the corners of her mouth, along her cheeks like a fawn. She had the face of a fair freckled twelve-year-old boy. Alert, bony in a delicate way, often embarrassed. There is something attractive about Phyllis, I would say to Richard, and he would say, Yes, Phyllis was just the sort of woman about whom other women say there's something attractive. And *why* did they say that? he'd ask, *because* she was no threat.

No threat. Why is it a surprise to find that people other than ourselves are able to tell lies?

When Richard's colleagues came for drinks, I would keep one eye open for prospective suitors – men who were as shy, ingenuous, invisible as Phyllis – men who, like Douglas, would be content to spend evenings hunched over textbook or drain-pipe or body of woman whose present dishevelment could occupy all their cautious, myopic attention. There were a few such men, but they never seemed to speak to Phyllis, nor Phyllis to them, each standing against opposite walls sipping their drinks self-consciously like teenagers at a prom. Phyllis wore a pink polyester suit with ruffled sleeves, and peered out at the gathering like a puzzled owl from behind her glasses.

It never once occurred to me that *I* could be threatening to

Richard in any way whatsoever. I'd be there, in my dark blue Tunisian caftan with silver embroidery at the throat, sweeping by with a tray of drinks or sausage rolls – yet would still half-envision myself as a sort of accessory, in the context of these gatherings at least.

But what a dishonest thing to say. It had been *his* fantasy, apparently, while I, for my part, pretended not to recognize the deep familial trench I so easily fell into. But neither was I any longer an accessory, in the pliable, domestic sense of a lamp or a chesterfield, or that so ridiculous hat Richard had bought me in Egypt, which I so ridiculously had worn. We were both proud, yes, and we fought, about Phyllis, about the pilot light, about whether or not to have a child, about money. I would often stay at home and read articles in women's magazines. Case histories about stay-at-home wives, and jealousies, and restlessness of various types. When my faith was intact and riding high, I would skip over these lessons superstitiously. When it was low, and very low, and gone, I read them for comfort, because it is a comfort to discover that one's own case holds no particular agony, only some shopworn, recognizable pain.

I admit, I'd once thought that if it were to be either of us, it would be me. After all, I was at home while he was away at the university, or very occasionally at a dig. And Phyllis kept to herself, so I thought. I had the whole day to do with what I wanted, did I not? You Richard, were too much in the sun. I didn't think your particular entrenchment offered such convenient escape routes, such secretive release.

Eventually I unburied my typewriter again, began writing articles for women's magazines, even used a different name. I thought you would have appreciated that, sincerely. Phyllis would sometimes come downstairs in the morning, and make herself a cup of coffee in our tiny kitchen. I would ask if she wanted any brandy in it and she would reluctantly take just a little, for her throat.

"Brr-r! How can you *stand* it down here? If there was space

for your typewriter up in my room, well I'd just move you right in there with me." Phyllis would be perched on the edge of the bed, rubbing her stocking feet together nervously, sipping her second coffee and brandy. "As it is, oh well you know, I have barely enough room to swing a cat, imagine!"

Swinging a cat had been Richard's expression. Richard woke up early every morning because, according to him, there was not enough room in our kitchen to swing a cat, if anyone else was in there with him. Later, there seemed to be not enough room in the entire house to swing a cat, so Richard spent more and more time working in his office. I never phoned him there to check, why should I have?

Richard and Phyllis swinging a cat. Richard and Phyllis going through my closet to find a nice dress that was small enough to fit her, so she would look pretty and eligible at our next party. Richard taking Phyllis to the hippodrome to get her out of my *hair* for the day. Richard offering to move my typewriter up into Phyllis' room so I could work evenings in peace. Richard and Phyllis being very, very quiet, for my sake. All of this with my consent, of course, but listen to the lies, the half lies, the absurdities.

I get as far as Phyllis' front door before something just sort of bursts, or snaps, and I cover my mouth with my hand, with my whole arm, to stifle the sob. The howl, amazingly, I never would have thought. So it can come just like that, and all of a sudden. I realize I had given myself the three weeks just in case it might, I really thought it would take that long, if it came at all. Plus one week to get things in order again. Now here it is already, on only second day. It was pushing things, I suppose, to come here. I wanted to see what would happen, whether anything would fall.

It was not as awkward as I might have anticipated to get the time off work. I simply said that I was thinking of taking a trip to the city associated with your name, no questions were asked, and none will be asked. Everyone at the Museum is at least familiar with you, of course, some like to speak of having known you well. A few of them, I know, knew you intimately. Only one of the other custodians, a man my age who has long believed in some tragic untimely sympathy between us, asks me *Why, Dolores?* for which I have no answer, except to make a gesture with my hand meaning I am tired of something – or that some object is floating downstream. I am not sure what I mean myself; but expect that he will understand. This man might have been the one I could have retaliated with, years ago, but you would have found something to say to make my transgression seem even more disgraceful, more humiliating, than your own.

"Surely, Dolores, you could have done better than that."

"Really, Dolores, you've sold yourself a little cheaply this time."

But there is even a room at the Museum, though not on my floor, which is named after you – The Richard Hammett Exhibit of Primitive Culture – with an aluminum plaque outside the doorway bearing your name and a little blurb about the Mongolian skull. The skull itself is not, and has never been, part of the local exhibit. It was bought by the American Museum of Natural History in New York City, where it has sat these last thirteen years like an expensive impractical gift.

This story was written ten years ago. A few sentences in it are grafted from a short story by a well known Canadian author. See if you can guess. The experiment was to see whether a phrase or two from a different tissue sample would sprout a different voice.

ANDY BROWN
from You Are Lance Blomgren

The woman doing the presentation looked as if she had once worn braces on her teeth. A small-scale model of a building was at her side. She asked the audience to use their imagination. In the front row Lance Blomgren was dreaming of blowjob pants. Could he make any money from this idea? He had been called an 'idea generator' in the press release for his second book, *Money is No Object*. The woman produced a baton from somewhere and began to describe the architectural wonders inherent in the building represented in miniature. Lance Blomgren looked around him at the others assembled. They were a motley crew of artists. Painters, poets, performance artists, the biographers of the insane. Lance Blomgren popped a couple maca pills, for virility, although there was no one to impregnate in his life. However, this presenter had nice teeth, what was she doing later?

Lance Blomgren had won the competition with his idea for a public sculpture based on German scheißenporn. He did it as a joke but the joke took off. When he was filling out the application he realized he was on to something. Naw, blowjob pants were not going to work. Perhaps the female presenter was on the jury; did that mean she was into the erotic possiblities of excrement? To Lance Blomgren this was a perverse idea and he suddenly got a boner. Nice teeth he thought.

After the success of his breakout first book, *The Tell Tale Boner*, about a massage therapist, Lance Blomgren had gone into seclusion. This was his first public appearance in five years and he was incredibly bored.

"Please notice the elegant lines on the dormitory windows," the woman was saying. He would be spending the next three days behind those windows, where he was expected to 'work' on his project. Did they choose him for the artist's colony because of the success of his first book? Or for his idea? Surely a scheißenporn statue in the town square wouldn't be taken seriously. How can those feisty Germans top scheißenporn? Diarrheaporn? The idea made him flaccid again. Oh, for those blowjob pants right now.

The introductory seminar for the artist's colony was almost over. There were a number of people asleep. Lance Blomgren looked down at his name-tag which read *Lance Blomgren*. Would this carry any weight?

"You are Lance Blomgren," said a spindly man with gel in his hair and a Western shirt. He said this as a statement and not a question. His name-tag read *Joey Dubuc*.

"That's correct," said Lance Blomgren.

"I enjoyed *Money is No Object*, I disagreed with the critics who called it sophomoric."

"Thanks, but it really was intended as a joke. Of course it's an object."

"Well, after your first book was such a big hit it must have been difficult to follow up. Can you give me the number of your masseuse?"

"What's your story?" asked a bored Lance Blomgren.

"How do you mean?"

"Why are you talking to me? What's your big proposal?"

"Oh, I see. I'm writing the world's longest Choose Your Own Adventure book. Really, it'll be in the *Guinness Book of World Records* when it is finally complete."

"Wow," said Lance Blomgren, trying to hide his complete lack of interest.

"Let's be roommates."

Thus began the relationship that was to shake the foundation of the art world for the next decade.

The Tell Tale Boner was a cult success. In it Blomgren had used the Poe story as a backdrop for his theory of eroticism. A young nubile masseuse has a string of rich clients. She gives the men handjobs and later blackmails them. Blomgren had created a complex plot which really did not end in any sort of redemption. When his agent told him the movie rights had been picked up for a disgusting sum Blomgren did not even ask if they changed the ending.

"How could you let them change the ending?" asked Joey Dubuc.

In the Poe story a man hides a freshly murdered corpse under the floorboards of his house and confesses his crime when he believes he hears the heart still beating. In *The Tell Tale Boner* the masseuse does not confess her crimes. Her victims all pay her and she buys an island in Nova Scotia which she keeps untouched, virgin, away from the millionaire jet ski crowd. The novel ends on this island. She pitches a tent on the rocky beach and listens to the lapping of the waves, their rhythm, which Blomgren makes painfully obvious, is like the beating of a heart.

But in the movie version the masseuse cuts off the member of one of her clients after he threatens to tell the police about her blackmail campaign. She keeps the article under her bed. Later she meets the man of her dreams and when she takes him back to her apartment and things get hot and heavy they find themselves having an encounter in her bed. Just before climax she hears the throb of the dismembered penis from under the bed and confesses. The man, who let's not forget is her soulmate, feels sympathy for her and they escape to live on an island in Maine. She takes the blackmail money and builds a huge mansion on it. She spends the rest of her days redecorating.

"I really didn't have a say in the matter. I did use the money to buy an island however."

"Really?"

"No. Actually I invested in a maca distributor." He produced a pill bottle with an illegal unilingual label and offered the spindly man a taste of his investment.

Elsewhere at the introductory seminar Leah was also popping

pills but these were to reduce the anxiety of her even being there. She was not good with people. More than once already an artist selected for the colony had told her she reminded them of the Carrie Fisher character in *Star Wars*. She got this a lot because of the way she wore her hair, like two dinner rolls on her temples. For this reason she had never seen the movie. She took a long drag on her cigarette. Her paintings of feet sold well to the acupuncture crowd.

The artist's colony had a reputation. Those who had participated had gone on to do great things. There was the infamous sailboat made out of broccoli. The movie of an underwater drive-thru. In fact Lance Blomgren had felt a great surge of pride at his application being accepted. There was no money in it of course but money was no object to Lance Blomgren.

Lance Blomgren called his agent on an available pay phone. His agent spoke into the phone like he was about to jump out of an airplane.

"The producer is considering the movie rights to your second book."

"Why would he do that? It's a book of poetry and not really very good. I meant it as a joke."

"You shouldn't keep saying that."

"Okay, how does he propose to do this?"

"I don't know. If you wrote the screenplay you could double up on the cash. Would that be possible?"

"I'll think about it. I gotta get through this next three days first."

"What exactly are you doing there?"

"I'm too embarrassed to say."

"Well think about The Money screenplay." That's what he called the book. The Money.

"I promise I'll try."

After he hung up a waif-like brunette scuttled past him and

plunked in a quarter. Her name-tag read *Leah*. No last name. *Must be a performance artist*, thought Lance Blomgren. He loitered near the phone smoking a cigarette. She lit one too as she talked. They had so much in common. She looked like that actress in that movie. With the hair and the stance. Like she was going to pull out a phaser at any moment. She was describing an art project to the mouthpiece, although presumably there was someone at the other end.

"No. It's a perfect yellow cube. The blue paint is inside. Sealed…. That's right…. No one can ever see the blue paint. That's it. It will just seem as if it's a yellow cube. I'm going to call it Sweden."

Lance Blomgren put out his cigarette on the sole of his shoe. He was once a shot putter. He'd tried out for the junior national team once. If only his coach could see him now. Lance Blomgren took a final look at the waif before searching the dorm, the full-scale version, for his room. Watching her smoking, talking about hidden blue paint, Lance Blomgren knew he was in love. *This is a woman with something to hide*, he thought.

The Money was a book of poems on the themes of commerce and regret. Lance Blomgren had regretted ever publishing it but the publisher of his first book, the successful one, was desperate to rush something into print. Lance Blomgren scoured the depths of his hard drive, his long lost scraps of paper, the back of receipts, phone messages. He searched his tax returns for the past decade looking for anything. It all went into The Money. The publisher was unsure how to approach the material but was a good sport.

"We'll just do an initial print run of ten thousand," said the publisher. Lance Blomgren considered how many trees would need to die. In making this consideration he understood the purity of linking the two themes of commerce and regret and briefly thought he might be on to something.

For the screenplay he considered a story about a stockbroker who becomes a treeplanter. No. A treeplanter who becomes a stockbroker. No. What this movie needs is sex. Germans and sex. No. Not commerce *and* regret but the commerce *of* regret. Yes. A character who trades in regret as if it is a stock. Regret was up today by three points. Regret closed at a loss. Yes. Now he was onto something. The black market of regret.

"If you wish to use the bathroom turn to page 76," said a voice behind him. Lance Blomgren turned to face his roommate and potential stalker, Joey Dubuc.

"What's that?"

"Do you need to use the bathroom cause I'll be in there a while. Helps me think. And we're all about the thinking here."

"Go ahead."

Lance Blomgren looked out the dormitory window onto the compound below. From their sixth floor vantage point a lake could be seen in the distance. What would a millionaire of regret do with it all? Build a mansion out of poor materials so that it collapses? Could he sell his regret and feel reborn? Lance Blomgren wished to swim.

"I'm going for a swim," he said to the closed bathroom door.

"Whatever helps," came the voice. Separated from his body Joey Dubuc's voice sounded like a power tool on the lowest setting. It was not an unpleasant voice. It could be tolerated for three days. But no more.

The sun was setting over the lake. The reflection in the water of the dormitory tower was actually quite beautiful. Nothing like the miniature mok-up created by an architect. No. This was fluid and real. At least a reflection of reality. Leah was standing on the shore smoking. She looked out into the dark water and held her arms over her chest. *She is chilly*, thought Lance Blomgren. *The chivalry routine is imminent.*

"Would you care for my coat?" asked Lance Blomgren.

Leah turned quickly. Too quickly, losing ash. "No," she said and turned back.

When he returned tired to his room Lance Blomgren was surprised to find a map covering an entire wall and a closet filled with Western shirts. The map was more of a web of lines and points, a connect the dots which, when completed, would reveal a colour-coded map of an underground transit system for a city with a population of one billion. This was possible in this day and age. Each of these points had a word and a number attached to it, some of them question marks. *Cliff / 33. Discman / 894. Treasure? / 2456.* As wallpaper it wasn't very attractive. But he supposed it served some purpose. Joey Dubuc was nowhere to be seen.

That night Lance Blomgren dreamed of an old girlfriend, one who he had treated cruelly. In compensation he offered her a bond of regret. "It's valid in some countries," he said to her. "But it will increase in value after the movie comes out."

The next day Joey Dubuc woke him with his stare.

AMANDA MARCHAND
Holed

Alice was listening to a song in her head and it went like this:

Oh, just me
Just me
Just me and my pretty
Little cunt.

Alice had no idea where the tune had come from and wasn't really giving it much thought, the song hadn't been lifted from the radio or her iPod, but it might have had something to do with her doctor. He had promised, as he stitched her up, that he would make it look 'pretty'. That's why, he had said, it was taking so long, not because of the number of stitches. She remembers, at the time, feeling relief mingled with disinterest. How could it ever matter? It would become just a cunt, in exile, of sorts, in the end. A pretty little forlorn thing (she liked the sound of that, it spoke of martyrdom). Now and forever.

Forever is a long time. Too long sometimes. But not long enough when you are a new mother. Because forever is only, after all, just a lifetime. So short! A scratch on a piece of paper.

Just me
Just me
Just me... Alice hummed, looking out her window.

The reason for this song (and the many others like it) was that Alice suddenly had a lot of time at home. Albeit with hands full, she suddenly had a lot of time to think – but only muddy thoughts. The songs were a kind of doodling, for Alice, without a pen. The truth was that Alice had arrived at a strange place, a place of wonder, with bizarre events unfolding, non-sequiters. Alice found herself, quite unexpectedly, a part of a club, so to speak. While this meant that she now belonged, it also meant that she was now 'the same', a blade of grass in the largest field. The redundancy didn't feel bad, necessarily; it just didn't quite feel good. She was somehow (now) 'over there', having stepped through the glass door of youth. She was beyond the remote possibility of normalcy, or regular conversation, or even regular meals, and certainly, it goes without saying, regular sex. Her body felt weird, not her own, like she was twelve again. It responded like a stranger's: new, delicious, peculiar.

Milk spraying her clothes, sweet and warm, never souring, but spraying, actually spraying half a foot sometimes, from where she sat. Milk soaking her shirts so that she had to pad her bra. This body, her body, almost a new lover in the way it handled. She would wake in the night in a pool of milk, like drool, as though having kissed for too long.

And it was, sometimes, a little like that. A love so large, she didn't know where to put it. It didn't fit in her heart. It didn't fit in her head. It felt as though she had to store it up outside her body as though stuffing were spilling out, in grave danger of getting stepped on; this vulnerable contraption that tangled around her and trailed behind the rooms she left or at the bottom of staircases, unattended, like a phantom tail.

Your mama loves you, she whispered over and over again. *Your mama loves you.* He was in her arms, a grunting thing awake at 5:00 AM, the time of day she liked best, groggy, still under covers, in the dim light of pre-civilization. *Your mama loves you,* stroking his furry head. This was her favourite thing. It smelled of him. It was so round and so small, so perfectly formed. Alice had been shy, hadn't wanted to move too fast. She hadn't ever kissed his face. She hadn't yet nibbled his tummy, kissed the crease of his neck. She thought, *He's been inside me all this time, and here he is and I don't even know him. I don't even know a tiny corner of him.*

It was nothing that should have taken her by surprise. This was, it could be argued, the Love of all Loves, part of her cellular cocktail, rooted in eternity, shared among penguins and apes and dogs and humans and probably even some fish (certainly dolphins, though they were not, technically, fish). TRUE LOVE. She wanted to turn down the volume (oh, but she didn't really, she didn't really want to turn it down at all). Alice finally knew what it was to love without measure or question. His body, his surly wail, the smell of a full diaper (one mother down the street had confessed!). *Your mama loves you.*

It thrilled Alice. It also embarrassed her, worrying that anyone could glance her way and see how much this saccharin love undid her. Alice was a little girl again, in the way she could not buffer emotion, the dizzy way she had felt early on, for a teacher, her mother and father, the older girl on the block. *You have no resources,* she thought, looking out the window and up at the sky. *You can't build up defenses. Or be ironic. Lack of sleep breaks you down, and hormones, and the endless nursing, and lack of sleep – oh, she'd just said that. . . . It's like a game of snakes and ladders where you think you're getting to the number 100 at the top, but you keep sliding down bigger snakes, all of them smiling.* Alice stated this in her head as well as she could, not entirely sure what she was referring to specifically, and then noticed the clouds sailing past, gusting, as though a high speed projection – like in an old war documentary in which the film cuts away from marching troops to a hurtling sky and overexposed sun – and the next moment it seemed as though this thought had been stated by someone else in the room talking to Alice, and she caught herself agreeing, nodding her head, about to answer. But there was no one else in the room, except the little turnip, as she liked to call him, and she looked down at him and he smiled, for the first time. With his eyes. And she smiled back.

Alice was on the other side of the camera lens, as though traveling backwards through the aperture to find oneself looking at oneself being looked at. Through a different aperture, her son – born, like plants, to suck up the light of day. Born to eat light, the way plants eat light, born to love light and everything it embodied. And even at the beginning, so early on, this fact was obvious. He would bathe by the window with his mouth open, contentedly sunning himself, his jaw wide for hours at a time, eating the warm light of early fall.

It revealed itself to Alice in many ways, but all of these were really one and the same.

The mother no longer feels safe near railings or windows.

The mother fears planes, cars, and food poisoning.

Afraid of meteor showers in the Western Hemisphere, the mother makes her child wear a hockey helmet in summer.

The mother exchanges physical fitness for nail biting.

The mother worries constantly about the heat and the cold and wind and rain and loud noises in the street.

The child, on the other hand, is fearless, a force of pure energy. His naïve sense of immortality translates to the mother's total paranoia and lack of hard edges. When the child cuts his finger for the first time, she sobs. When the child rolls off the bed, she sobs. Each time she cries long after the child has stopped, feeling sick, feeling anguish. Every scrape is a blow to her own physical self. For each mother behind each carefully purchased stroller, fear remains the primary mode from which she secretly operates. Mothers all over the world, everywhere, in factories, libraries, swimming pools, checkout lines, all singing the same refrain, *What if....*

A time of beauty and magic and promise. A threshold state. But, in truth, those first few weeks everything hurt. The body was secondary, everything hurt for the child. For Alice, every passing minute was an hourglass, the sand measuring her child's eventual growing away from and leaving her. *Beside her baby on the bed. Beside her baby* – how surreal, in the beginning to say that. *Her baby. Her baby.* And still surreal. If she whispers in his ear he will quiet. If he smells her, she knows, he will quiet. To have him in her arms. To cradle him, hold him, to rock her own infant, swaddle him in her arms.

Alice had entered a twilight place where the Hallmark sentiment was, all of a sudden, 'so true'. Maybe she was the only one who had traded sanity for this servitude to a love that usurps everything. She never asked any of the other mums about what she had come to think of as 'the change'. The change, for Alice, was a little like a change of outfit, only on a much larger scale. *If you've ever thought about how you feel in flannel pajamas,* remarked Alice, *or how you feel in heels and a dress and chandelier earrings…* and then realized that her little turnip could not fully grasp this distinction for many reasons, one of them being, he was a boy, and another being, well, he was a baby boy. *It's like this, Turnip…* she started again. And she picked him up in her arms and kissed the places where the light poured from his face, and she began to sing a song that she had once heard the little cartoon girl, Pebbles, on The Flintstones sing.

You are my sunshine
My only sunshine
You make me happy
When skies are grey…

Alice never spoke of her inability to find pleasure in old habits, her newfound zeal for all child related products (she could read about the merits of cloth diapers on-line for hours), or the encroaching sugariness like a snow in the world she now moved through. 'The change' had occurred in a precise instant lost to her now, but there was no question, Alice was a different person from the girl she had been. The night before labour Alice had gone to bed watching *Kill Bill*, falling asleep with judo kicks, samurai swords, and blood baths dancing like sugarplums in her head. Afterwards she was no longer able to watch violent films. They cut her. Even benign dramas offered something too hard to bear – loss, neglect, hatred. Even, and she found this a little hard to admit, but even *March of the Penguins* was too much (when the penguin egg cracked in the minus 80 degree weather and the tiny heartbeat inside stopped!). Alice could hear her own mother's words, "I just want things that make me feel good."

Every now and then, an evening out with another new mother. An escape hatch, is what it felt like. Floating up, up, turning upside down, her skirt lifting, she could almost begin to remember what once had been.

The lovely dragonfly
Is attracted
To the sky
Take me away
Take me away

Alice was absent in dishwater feeling very sleepy and stupid. She had sour milk all over her nightgown, she hadn't eaten anything yet that day or bathed all week, and the Little Turnip had been up at two hour intervals all night. He doesn't belong to me, she realized with a shock. He didn't belong to her — *she* belonged to *him*. As she washed plates and rubber nipples, she began to imagine that she was standing on a precipice and that she was being given a chance to jump to save her baby's life. *Take me away. Take me away,* the child band crooned on the stereo, and Alice knew with absolute conviction that she would jump if it meant he could go on living forever.

This is all Alice really wanted now; for him to outlive her. It was a very simple thing and, in some ways, a small thing. But it was also a huge thing. And it consumed her. She wondered if it consumed the others too, but no one ever mentioned it. The mothers talked about everything else, 'poops', hours slept, inches and pounds, nannies and nurseries, but they never mentioned the one subject that had become the cornerstone to her every day.

Alice knew she had to do something to protect this new life, more than she was doing as a mere mother. She had stopped watching television altogether. She began to play her own films out in her head. These were not light, fluffy films about basking in motherhood. They were films whose main theme was: Without Question The Worst Thing in The World.

Your mama loves you, breathing this now into him, into his mouth, his hair, pressing these words into his flesh, mouthing them into his neck, rolling with his tiny body on the bed, falling asleep and waking and falling back to sleep together, sweaty under too many blankets. To think that somewhere in the world right now an unloved child was crying. It seemed the biggest possible evil. Bigger than war. A crying baby. A baby who just wants to be picked up and held.

And so Alice killed her own child over and over again – in her head – in order to assure him the one thing no mother could, that he would always be safe. She made up films of torture, death, abuse. Films no sane person would watch, never mind dream up. Alice imagined her son drowning in a swimming pool, no one there to save him, the water entering his lungs, his eyes open wide underwater, the little movements his hands would make. After reading newspaper headlines she pictured him raped. She imagined him falling from a high window, seven stories, landing on a car below. She saw him suffocating in his crib, silently, while she slept in the next room.

Alice played these scenarios out, never speaking them, but pushing herself as far as she could to vividly *see* each scene, testing whether she could bear it (she never could allow herself to imagine it through to the end.) All this, in order to save him. Walking to the store Alice would see the pit bull and her infant's mangled face. Making coffee she would envision him scalded from boiling water. She waved goodbye to the babysitter who was taking him for a walk one day, and knew that was the end; she would never ever see either of them again. Over and over she ran these shorts. In this way, she believed, she was casting small safety spells. The rule in life: if you imagine a thing, it never happens. It was Tuesday and mid-morning and Alice added to the list; death by car crash, death by tsunami – chalk circles into which her child would one day step and remain forever safe. *Oh please, oh please, oh please.*

The words rolled out, words with little meaning. Alice was

skimming a magazine, not really bothering to read past the first
sentence or two on each page. A call for entries: No submissions
with clouds or bunnies, please, it read. *Clouds or bunnies! If only,*
thought Alice, looking over at her sleeping child, *if only I could
embroider happy faces, bunnies, ice cream cones on socks, on towels, embroider everything, wrap those edges in protective coverings, the fabric of grand-
mother tea-cozies, anything that might cushion against all this, this, this –*
and with the sentence dangling in mid-air, the Little Turnip
stirred and began to cry and Alice was unable to finish articulat-
ing her thought. The thought was abandoned for more pressing
matters, a diaper change, a feeding, a cleaner kitchen counter, a
stroll to the park, dinner preparations and a bath. But what Alice
meant to say, as the remainder of her sentence fizzled and spurt-
ed, a deflating balloon, was: This responsibility. This weight.
This enormous everything.

   Happy. Yes. Alice was tired but happy. In its mischievous
way, happiness had tagged her and hunted her down. Her heart
had melted. Like the Wicked Witch of the West she was now liquid. Love like a storm of wet love, gusting through her small
home. Tears and sweat and blood, and milk and more milk (a
whole fridge full). Alice knew now there was nothing on the
inside of her anymore, nothing but liquid anyway, no brains, no
spine or bones, just a white milky heart. Her infant and all his
paraphernalia consumed her; onesies and tubes of cream, and
cloths and bottles, and all the rituals that continued round the
clock. To succumb, to be pliant. To dive down deep and come
up a kind of soggy, soft thing, smelling strong and tasting like
sugarwater.

   It felt better than 'not entirely bad' – it felt, incredible. Alice
was 'over there' looking back at everything as though through
thick, blown glass. She could see friends and acquaintances
doing the same old things they always had, party going, leisure
lounging, and buses to work or dinners out, but from over here
it seemed like all of that had never really happened. Or that it

might have happened, but to a distant cousin. It was as though she had never really given any of it up. It was as though she had always been right 'here'. In this room. In this storm. (On the other side.) With her son and her new, pretty little cunt.

Just me,
Oh, just me,
Just me and my
Pretty little,
Pretty little,
Pretty little cunt.

You know it will turn out pretty, she thought. But you don't know it will be this pretty.

GOLDA FRIED
Liela Tov

Her parents had named her Liela Tov which meant 'night' and then 'good' in Hebrew, as in 'goodnight'. Why did they call her this? She felt like it was a name that shrouded her in a dark cloud. Her Mom, when asked, would mumble something about how she wanted Liela to have restful sleeps.

In Calculus class in her last year of high school, Liela's teacher rolled around in his chair like David Letterman and was constantly reminding them that Calculus was not that hard. She liked school because the teachers were the closest thing to entertainers. It would not be that way in university when the professors stood like ghosts in front of the students, not really there at all.

In front of Liela was Jennifer – a long-time patient of her Dad. Jennifer had been going to Liela's Dad for her allergy shots once a week for years. He had asked Jennifer to look out for his daughter, to be friends with her. He had probably said, "Liela needs a buddy; can you help her out?" like how they pair you up with swim buddies when you're younger so you won't drown.

Jennifer and Liela weren't eat-in-the-cafeteria-together friends or go-out-Friday-night friends; they were walk-over-to-the-bus-stop friends. Jennifer attracted everyone with her no shame personal questions and storytelling ability. She also had a laugh that was like running down halls.

Jennifer whipped her ponytail around. "Jeff's asked me out Friday night."

"That's so romantic," Liela said. The class was supposed to be working on math problems and Liela was slouching down behind Jennifer's frame so the teacher wouldn't see her.

"I don't know; he pumps gas at a gas station for a living."

"That's so romantic," Liela repeated.

On the other side of the classroom, in the second desk from

the front, sat Mike Singer. He wore New Balance tennis shoes. His elbows jutted out beyond the desk like butterfly wings. He was quiet but self-assured. He had a laugh that didn't wonder if it was okay to laugh. While the Calculus teacher went over the same Calculus problem for the fifth time for the girls in the front, who wore Roots clothing and had big hair, Liela would stare at Mike Singer and know that he was 'all good'. There were many signs which pointed to this fact. Mike Singer always wore white. He had a permanently calm facial expression. And his name 'Mike' rhymed with 'bike' which was child-like and hurt-free, she decided.

Mike Singer had his head bent over his notebook trying to figure something out. His tongue hung out the side of his mouth like a loyal dog.

When Liela got home with her snow-covered boots that always muddied up the front walkway, she found her mother frantically making dinner. "Shoot, I didn't put enough sauce on the steak. I am so stupid," she said to the air. Her mother flitted between the den, the laundry room, and the kitchen.

"There are donuts on the table," she muttered to Liela over her shoulder. Liela took a honey-dew donut out of the white cardboard box – they were all honeydew. It was like her Mom didn't want to venture out into Hawaiian sprinkle or cream-filled or maple-glazed or all-chocolate.

The donut tasted good. It was Liela's first meal of the day. She couldn't stand breakfast because she found cereal soupy, and then she couldn't eat the sandwiches her Mom had made her for lunch, because she found the bread had become soggy from whatever her Mom had spread in the middle. Liela chewed on the donut and snuck downstairs to watch *General Hospital*.

Liela's brother Dove was also 'all good'. She had taken him to see *The Rocky Horror Picture Show* when he was probably too young to handle it. But he looked like all the other eleven-year-olds on the outside. Her Mom was always reprimanding Liela

for walking too fast when her younger brother was beside her.
"Can't you see he has a limp?"

Six years ago Dove's right leg had gotten crumpled in a car
accident. Her Mom was driving. Her Mom had quit everything
to focus more on her family.

"I'm not an asshole on purpose," Liela would mumble. "I
don't really think about it. I walk fast. It's like I'm going to
explode."

"Stop mumbling," her mother would beg and then answer
the phone in a nice cheery voice.

Liela couldn't wait to go away to university. It was already
decided that she was going to go to Montreal to McGill. She had
seen a TV movie where the main character was in a dorm and
had clothes on the floor and music posters on the wall. She wanted that.

Liela stared a lot at Mike Singer in Calculus class. And when
he caught her staring, she didn't look away. She wondered
what he would do. She trusted that since he was 'all good', he
wouldn't do something mean and he didn't. He smiled sweetly.

She got his number from her friend Jennifer who spent every
night on the phone and had everyone's number. She took it from
Jennifer's fingers like coaxing a ladybug off of a sweater.

Leila climbed on Dove's bed when she got home. He was
reading *The Lord of the Rings* and didn't flinch when she bounced
up and down beside him, having that exploding feeling again.

"I'm going to call a boy," she said. No response. "Can I bor-
row one of your stuffed animals?" Since Dove was only five
when the car accident happened, he had gotten about thirty
stuffed animals from everyone her parents knew. No one knew
what else to do while he lay in a coma for two weeks.

"Take a big one," he said without looking up. "You're going
to need it."

She took a big bear with a never-been-sad expression on his

face. She brought her phone down to the floor and sat leaning against the bed and almost strangled the bear with her left arm while she dialed with her right hand. She tried to loosen her grip on the bear as the phone rang. She looked around her room and was embarrassed at how messy it was.

He answered on the third ring. She had to make up some bogus excuse that she needed to know what the Calculus homework was.

"You've already done the problems on page 86?" she asked amazed.

"When were you going to do them?" he said. "They're due tomorrow."

"I usually end up doing my homework in the car on the way to school, giving myself a heart attack wondering if I'm going to finish it in time."

"And then you get an A," he said. "Most people hate people like you."

Mike started lingering by the door in Calculus class so that he could walk out beside her. Soon he asked her to dinner and a movie.

"Dinner and a movie?" She said to Jennifer. "Do you think that's pretty unoriginal?"

"What do you want? A helicopter ride? We're in high school. Come on, Liela." Jennifer pushed Liela with her elbow. Liela was such a waif that she hit the lockers on the side with a big thud.

When Mike came to her parents' door, it was like someone had stuffed her in a locker and she was finally getting out. He had even brought some red roses.

Liela wished they were anything but roses: wildflowers, daisies, calla lilies. She felt like an asshole from the beginning.

Her father shook his hand. Her mother followed them out to the car.

Finally, Liela was in the passenger seat. "Put on your seat belt," her Mom started screaming through the window.

Mike Singer and Liela Tov Bloom drove in silence for a while and then Liela said to him, "You know, I have a rock 'n roll heart."

He smiled.

That was the only warning she could think of to tell him that perhaps she was not 'all good' despite her middle name which meant good.

She started checking out what tapes he had in an open arm rest between the two front seats. The Cowboy Junkies. She thought that was okay. Van Morrison was good. Supertramp was iffy. Steely Dan was iffy too.

"Steely Dan is a fine band," he said.

She kept looking.

He drove so calmly, so differently. Since her brother's accident, both she and her parents drove on the defense with their eyes constantly going back and forth like every car was going to ram into them at any second. His eyes stayed straight ahead, not shifting at all. Alert, but relaxed. He even did that drum beat hand thing on the steering wheel.

The restaurant he picked was the Rosedale Diner. Her eyes widened as he perfectly parallel parked out front. A pink rose dotted the *i* on the sign and she skipped under it. The first room of the restaurant was decorated like a library. The second room had floral wallpaper which made her feel like a Southern belle. He kept walking her through the kitchen to get to the back patio where there were colourful patio lanterns. Mike let her pace through the whole place a few times before deciding where they should sit.

She picked outside because she needed the fresh air.

There was silence. There was hunger as they waited for the food to come.

"Let me see your wallet," she said.

He handed it over. Brown leather. A gym card. Driver's

license. School ID. He posed in all the photos like he was a no-monkey-business FBI agent.

"Serious faces," she commented.

"I don't smile for photos." He had really nice skin, green eyes, lanky arms, no jewelry. "My Dad had this great trick he'd do with me and his wallet when I was a kid. I hope I remember to do it when I have kids."

When I have kids reverberated in her head. "How can you be so sure you want kids?"

"I just know," he said. "Like I know I want ketchup on these fries." There was no doubt about it. "My Dad used to give me his wallet to look through," he continued. "To distract me. And then when I was really into his wallet, he'd rip off a Band-Aid."

She gave back the wallet.

The movie was the dark romantic comedy *I Love You To Death* and she kept her eyes straight ahead. About twenty minutes into it, he stretched an arm over her head that landed on her right shoulder. His hand felt as big as King Kong's.

On the drive home, she got more and more nervous. No one had told her that dating would be scary as hell.

He walked her up to her front door. He leaned toward her and she closed her eyes. She could feel the soft whiskers of his upper lip. When she opened her eyes, he was already walking away.

Her locker turned out to be around the corner from his so they were destined to meet again. But when he took his paper bag lunch and started toward the cafeteria, she couldn't follow him. Her right leg actually felt frozen.

She had always eaten by her locker.

Mike grabbed her hand and they sat at one of the cafeteria tables with many of his friends. The noise was deafening. Some girls were staring at her. She quickly looked at her hands. Then at Mike. Mike was talking about basketball when she clued back in to him. To her horror, she realized he was a jock.

The next day at lunch, he invited her over to his house. He lived nearby; they could walk. She was animated beside him, sometimes twirling. At one point, she tried to push him into some hedges like Jennifer had done to her by the lockers but he hardly shifted.

In the entranceway of Mike Singer's house, there was a large round marble table with nothing on it except a vase filled with over-sized flowers. You had to walk around the table to get to the other rooms of the house. On the way to the kitchen, they passed a white grand piano. When he took her into the kitchen, there was a little wooden-topped brush with bristles that looked like a mushroom, by the sink.

"That's to wipe dirt off mushrooms," he explained when she picked it up.

At his house, they sat on the couch and watched episodes of *MASH* – his favourite TV show. He wanted to be a doctor like his Dad, who was a heart surgeon. "I don't get this show," she said to the TV. "Just give it a chance," Mike said, not even able to look away from the TV set. Mike loved how doctors on the show would joke about how bad dinner was or about girls, as they operated on people and blood splattered all over them.

She would close her eyes and cuddle up beside him. She loved how he smelled, all lemony and clean. Finally, she found out that it was the smell of Sunlight detergent. She asked her mother to start using it, but her mother refused, saying it doesn't really get out the stains.

It didn't take an emergency for her to run over to Mike's house. Her mother could have made a slightly sarcastic remark. She'd find any excuse to see him with eyes that looked at her like a butterfly had perched on his knee.

She showed up on Mike's doorstep soaked through.

Mike gave her an umbrella. When he handed it over, it was all black and she stared at it too long, probably being rude and not thankful. But black was the colour of funerals. Her mother was always reminding her of that fact whenever she tried to wear the colour.

Liela took the umbrella and put it in her closet. Gifts were always welcome in her world. When she walked around the block with her brother to exercise his leg and it was raining, she tried the umbrella out. It felt goth. It felt like it kept the dark clouds around her head from floating up to the sky as much as it kept the rain out.

Then Liela started calling Mike at all hours of the night, just to talk. If his parents answered, she'd hang up, but she had to talk to him. His parents quickly got him a second phone line.

Once at three in the morning she said to him, "This relationship is only going to work if you have a dark side. Do you have a dark side?"

"What are you talking about? Our relationship is working. I am really happy."

She was quiet for a few seconds. "But do you have a dark side?"

She pictured the skeleton's head in the basement. It was her father's from med school.

"I have a dark side," he said in the most serious of tones. "I could tell you but it's very personal. You have to promise to always keep it a secret."

"Okay," she said.

She started going to his basketball games with headphones and a Walkman. And he would accompany her through Kensington Market's strip of thrift stores waiting for her by the curb with a newspaper under his arm.

He came with her to her cousin's bat mitzvah. They slow-danced in the basement rec-room, her cheek on his shoulder as the DJ played Pink Floyd's "Mother" and helium balloons shifted on the ceiling.

"Do you think your mother likes me?" she asked him.

When Liela and Mike were in her father's car, she said, "I can't do that in my father's car. He might smell something tomorrow."

Mike didn't get mad. He put his arm around her neck and said okay.

She took a red bandana out of her school bag and made him wear it rolled up and around his forehead and then tied up in back. She was obsessed with his ear and kept sticking her tongue inside it even when he said it was too wet.

They talked about college a lot. They would go to McGill. She would get those glow-in-the-dark stars for her ceiling.

It was April, five months after they had started seeing each other, when his mother officially invited her over for dinner for the first time. Liela chose to wear a tie-tied T-shirt. She knew somewhere in the back of her head it might not have been the best choice but it was confirmed when his front door opened and his mother was there in a beige pant suit before her.

She had made a dish called *coq-au-vin* for the occasion. His Dad was quiet.

"Aghh, this chicken is so good, Mom. It just falls off the bone," Mike said.

"So what does your Dad do?" she asked Liela though Liela was sure she must already know.

"He's a general practitioner."

"And your Mom?"

"She was a nurse."

"So Mike says you're going to McGill. We're so happy, he's going to Western. McGill's a great school but Western's smaller and I've heard the classes are more intimate."

Liela looked over at Mike.

"I was going to tell you," he said.

"I have to go," she said. Mike followed her out.

Liela dropped her keys on the pavement more than once trying to open her Dad's car door.

"Liela," Mike said.

She couldn't even look at him; she felt so abandoned. "What the hell are you thinking? Western? Every snob in our school goes to Western." And what about us? She was really saying.

He put a hand on her shoulder, "It's going to be okay."

After that, things were not okay. Liela took on an insane friend named Christy and started bringing her along on dates with Mike. At least Christy was going to McGill.

Mike put his hand on Liela's knee as they waited for Christy to get ready and Liela felt like moving his hand. They were going to watch the Benson and Hedges Symphony of Lights show at Ontario Place where there were fireworks set off to classical music. Liela hated classical music.

Christy came downstairs zipping up her designer jeans and started struggling with a black leather belt, trying to get it in the belt hoops. Christy put her face in front of Mike's and said, "I'm going to put my booger in the ice cream so no one else will eat it. You want some?"

When Mike didn't respond, Christy took the leather belt and started whipping it on the couch an inch from Mike's face saying, "Answer me, boy." Liela just felt empty.

Mike took Liela to the prom. He played "Desperado" by the Eagles for her on the grand piano when his parents were still at work. He bought her glow-in-the-dark stars for her future dorm room at a hobby store. But September was approaching.

Mike came over to say goodbye. It was so weird how they never said they were breaking up – they just knew it. He didn't even say goodbye. He kissed her on the cheek, a small flesh wound, and said, "Goodnight." She could handle it.

Liela had been settled in her dorm room for a month and

hadn't put up the glow in the dark stars. Mike hadn't called her either.

She called him up and stammered, "You know, you're really lame."

"Whatever," he said to her and they both hung up.

His indifference hurt so much she gasped. She stared at the phone for a good ten minutes. She did not know if she should have tried harder, switched schools, done something. It felt like someone had ripped a Band-Aid off of her heart.

She jabbed at the phone, calling her brother Dove. "Don't ever be lame," she said to him.

"Okay," he said. He was used to her one-liner advice statements with no further explanation.

An hour later, she did not think Mike was lame. She knew that he was probably the closest thing to something 'good' she would ever meet.

She ripped open the bag of glow-in-the-dark stars and they spilled out onto her jeans. She stuck them one by one on the inside of the black umbrella that Mike had given her.

Liela couldn't believe that she had still not walked around the city of Montreal, never leaving the square that was the university campus. She reprimanded herself as she stuck on each star. She was scared. She would do it now.

She walked out of the dorm with the umbrella above her, the stars glowing in the night air.

BILLY MAVREAS
Seven Prophesy Bunnies

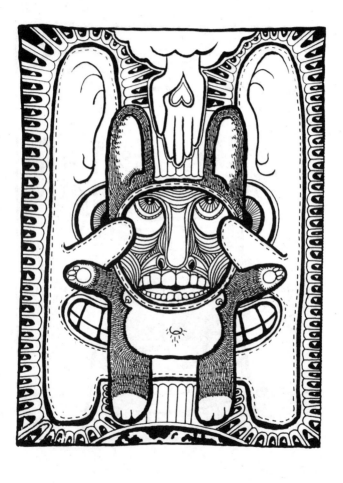

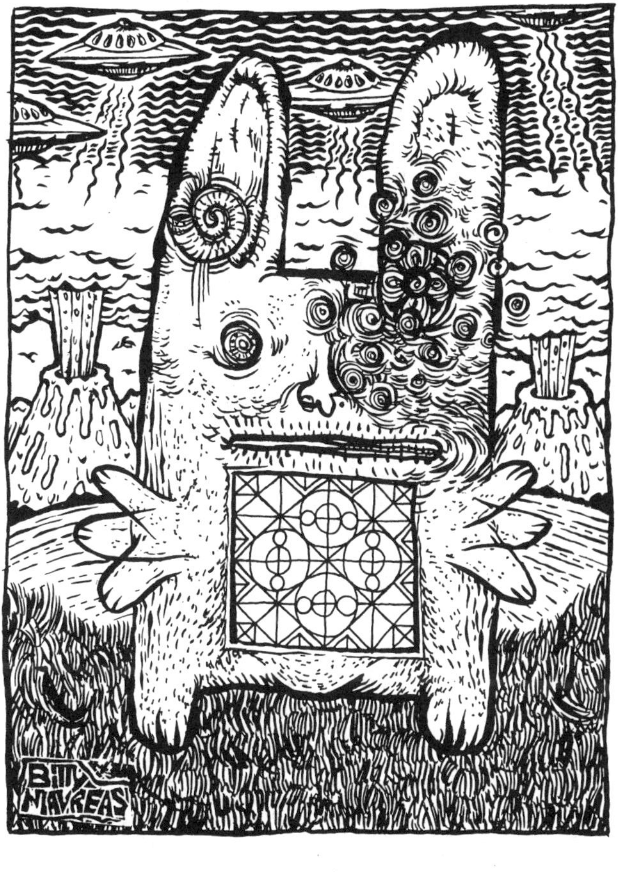
BILLY MAVREAS

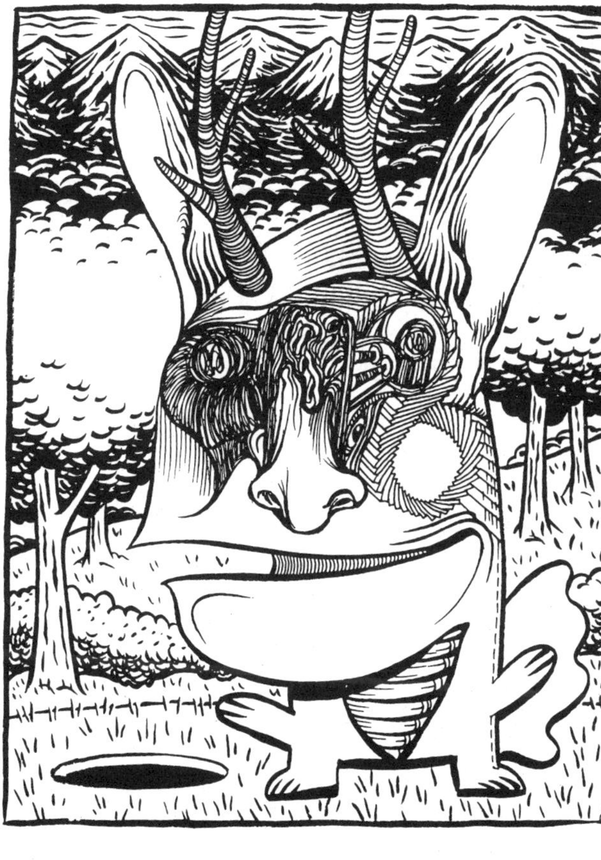

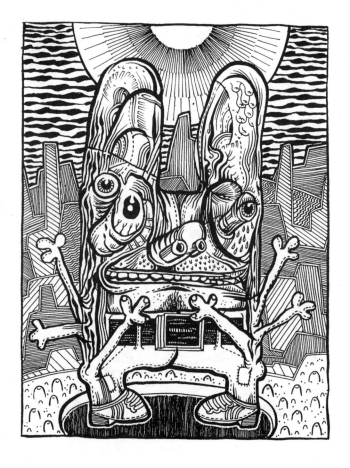

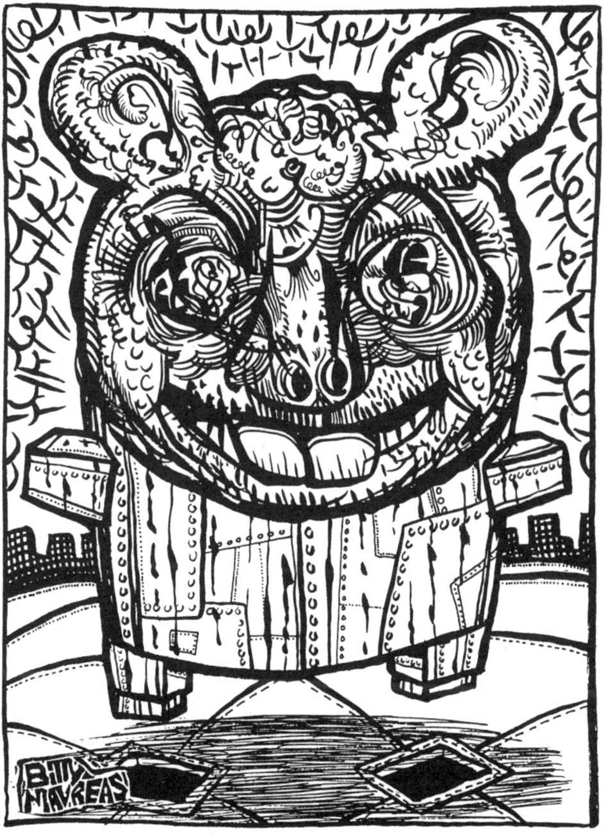
BILLY MAVREAS

PETER PARÉ
Read 'em and Weep

I sit down at 8:20 PM. A little later than I normally start on a Thursday evening. The game is mostly regulars – Chai, Lucky-Larry, dhroller are playing – but there are a few players I don't recognize. I like to sit at a table for a while before I begin playing. Get a feel for the flow. About three hands in some kid, calling himself juniortj, spikes an ace to take a few hundred from Larry. Larry isn't happy about it, I can tell, but he doesn't say anything. The kid's play was bad, and I can tell Larry wants to keep him around for a bit.

In the game of poker bad players are referred to as fish. When you have a fish at your table you don't want to discourage or scare him / her off. There is a saying – don't tap the aquarium – which essentially means leave the fish alone. Don't tell fish they played a hand badly. Don't belittle or intimidate them. In fact, after a hand they play particularly poorly most good players say, "Nice hand sir." A thinly veiled insult amongst the seasoned players. Bait.

I watch another seven hands before buying in. I buy in for the maximum. $400 in this game – 2/4 no-limit hold-em. There are eight of us at the table. Chai asks how my kids are sleeping. I say, "Angelic." He asks if I saw the end of the $200 tourney last night. "JohnnyBax was unstoppable. He finished it off with his signature 79 suited." I hadn't seen it, but am not surprised. There are a handful of players that play well above the rim. JohnnyBax is one of the best.

My first five hands are junk. I fold all of them. My sixth hand is an ace queen suited. A strong hand. I raise to $15 before the flop and get one caller. The flop comes ace, six, four rainbow. I bet $25 at the pot. And get called. I have not played with this player before so I don't know his tendencies. I have a penchant for slowing down the betting when I don't know the player, so when a jack comes on the turn, I check to the other player. He bets $25. A strange bet. I still think it quite likely I am leading the hand, but I just call. I am either way ahead or way behind, and if it is the latter I didn't want to turn this into a monster pot. So there's a little over $100 in the pot. The river card is another ace. This is a great card for me, but I still check. I might raise if he bets, but I'm hoping he'll bet. And then he does a very strange thing. He bets all his money – $600. Into a pot of $136. So it's going to cost me my entire buy-in to call here. And now I'm not so sure I'm ahead. Maybe he has a pair of sixes, or fours, and that ace made him a full house. Maybe he has ace, jack – again a full house. I get a sick feeling in my stomach. Exhilarating and sickening at the same time. And I think. I go into the tank. I have learned never to make too quick a decision. I go over the hand in my head. If he really has the full house, wouldn't he want a call here – wouldn't he have bet less, extract a few more dollars? I finally call, close my eyes, and push my chips in. He turns over pocket tens – a pair of tens. "Nice call," he says.

The way I played it, he must have assumed I didn't have the ace – maybe a pair of queens or kings – and when the river brought another ace, another check from me, I think he was quite sure of it. So he tried to push me out. "Nice bet," I say. And mean it. I would have folded a pair of kings or queens in a heart-beat there. Hell, I almost folded my ace queen.

It makes for a good start. I doubled my money in less than ten minutes. But the next hour passes without many interesting hands for me. I hover between $700 and $900. Win a small pot, lose a small pot. Chai cleans out juniortj when he turns a straight. Junior isn't sophisticated enough to lay down top two pair. He quickly leaves and Larry starts in on how Chai has Larry's money. Joking with him, only a hint of bitterness.

ManicMike sits down. The guy can flat out talk. He launch-es into a story about a prop bet he made with two strangers at a McDonald's two nights ago. Apparently he bet them he could eat six Big Macs in a minute. Got three-to-one odds. Did it with six seconds to spare and ordered an apple pie to chase them. Walked out of the fast food joint with $600. He says his favourite line when he's ordering fast food — and apparently he uses it every chance he gets — is when the cashier says, "That'll be $6.47." He pulls all his cash out of his pocket and slams it down on the counter. "I'm all in," he says. And then he says to us, "They usually fold." Mike's new girlfriend is unhappy with Mike's poker-centric lifestyle. She's given him an ultimatum. Her or cards. All this despite the fact that he claims he supports her by playing poker. He says she had an uncle who was a gambling addict. Destroyed his life. He's tried telling her that poker isn't gambling, but he says he ends up feeling like a junkie defending his gear. He's proposed cutting back. Scheduling a weekly time slot to play, but she isn't budging.

Dutch Floyd sits down. Dutch is eating breakfast. Black coffee and black toast. Marmalade today. He says he always has the same breakfast. I glance at the clock. 10:44 PM.

When I look back at the table I've been dealt two red aces. An unknown player to my right raises to ten dollars. I consider my options, and decide I want to play only against this one player if possible. My pocket bullets have been getting cracked lately, and it's been costly. I reraise to $30. It folds back around to this guy. He just sits there blinking. The dealer finally gives him fifteen seconds to make a decision. He calls.

The flop comes down queen, ten, five. Two hearts. He checks to me. I bet 50, just looking to win it right there. He raises me another 50. Hmmmm. Could be a set. Could be a pair of kings. Or ace queen. I make the call. The pot is already $266. The guy to my left has a bit less than $200 left. A three of hearts comes off the deck. My opponent checks, and I smell weakness. I think I likely have him beat already, but even if I'm behind here, another heart on the river gives me the nut flush. I push all in for the second time in the evening. This time I'm not risking it all; he only has $188 in front of him. Again, he shuts down. Now I'm sure he has ace queen. The dealer gives him another

warning. He calls. Flips up the ace queen – queen of hearts. I
smile, and then a queen comes off the deck. His three queens
beat my aces and queens. $642 dollars moves from the middle of
the table to his stack. I'm left with a touch more than my initial
buy-in. $446. "Nice two-outer," says Floyd. The guy sits out and
leaves. "Hit and run," says Mike. I don't feel much like talking
just now. A great night just turned into a break-even grind with
the turn of a card. On cue my one-year-old wakes up crying. I
move my mouse to the 'sit out' button, click it, and hurry
upstairs to comfort my baby boy.

I play on-line poker a few nights a week. I play with people
all over the world. People from Europe, Asia, South America,
Australia. I have the perfect poker face. Even when I'm sitting in
front of my computer in only my underwear. It is a unique and
unusual culture. I 'know' people I play with. We discuss poker,
sports, books, family. We criticize bad play and applaud the
good. People I have never laid eyes upon. People whose voices I
have never heard before. Just interpreted nuance from the typed
words, from a timed click of a mouse, from betting patterns. It is
a powerful on-line community. And it is growing.

Some people play multiple tables at once. At sixty hands an
hour per table they are getting dealt a thousand hands in a four-
hour stretch. This exposure to hands has exponentially
increased the speed at which people learn poker. Final tables of
major tournaments are seen on TV nightly. Hole card cameras
have given us a window into the thought process of top poker
players. A virtual library of poker books has been published over
the last decade. Because of this influx of information, of players,
there are more games, more money can be made, and there are
many, many more good poker players than ever before. Is the
glass half empty or half full?

Weathervein played high stakes poker for twenty-four years
before ever playing on-line. He traveled the country gravitating

to the big games, especially the big no-limit and pot-limit games. He was never a grinder, his bankroll oscillated from made-in-the-shade to cashing in free casino meals he accumulated when his cards were running hot. In the fall of 2002 he was running hot. Coming out of the Mirage casino one night a player he respect-ed told him the easy money was all moving to the Internet. "On-line poker is taking over," he said.

Weathervein let it ruminate for a week or two. He asked some other players he knew and liked, and when they agreed, he proceeded to the nearest CompUSA to buy himself the newest, fastest, sleekest laptop available. He had someone from the store come to his hotel room to set up the wireless router, and get him on-line. He signed up for an account with an on-line poker room and deposited a large chunk of his bankroll.

Weathervein found a lively high-stakes no-limit game that night, and tried running the table over. He raised and re-raised for hours and got little respect. He found it frustrating, but as a player who had played poker for years he knew there were long-term advantages to being seen as a maniac. He logged off that night down, having lost half of what he deposited.

The next evening he sat at the same table with many of the same players. He understood they perceived him as a loose aggressive maniac and was prepared to exploit that understand-ing. He raised a few hands early just to make it known that his play hadn't changed, and then he sat back and waited. As luck would have it he hit a number of monster starting hands. As luck would have it he was outdrawn over and over again. Finally when his flopped top set was beaten by a runner runner flush, Weathervein stopped playing. He calmly unplugged his new computer and took it to the balcony of his hotel room. And then he threw it. Twenty-two stories down into the hotel pool — for-tunately closed at the time.

The next day he ran into the friend who had recommended on-line poker. He told his friend the story of buying the laptop, of losing on consecutive evenings, of the rather steep decline of his bankroll. "Seems like a waste of money, throwing away a laptop like that," his friend said.

"I think it saved me thousands," replied Weathervein. "Maybe tens of thousands."

Weathervein eventually bought himself a new computer and plays more on-line poker than live these days. He is one of the winningest and most feared on-line players around. I know he is married. I know he drives a silver Porsche. I know he'll lead out on a flopped nut flush just as fast as a stone cold bluff. What I don't know is his real name. No idea if he has brown eyes or bad breath. If he shakes when he has the nuts. He's an on-line poker celebrity. A moneymaking card calculating intellect.

Gigabet is another colossal figure of on-line poker. As close to a poker philosopher as there ever was. He talks about virtual poker chips in the framework of a tournament as blocks of winning potential. Stairs to victory. He talks of negative re-raise fold equity. Game theory.

One of the current largest on-line poker sites holds monthly Tournament Leader Board (TLB) competitions. If you win in any given month you play one of the site's sponsoring pros heads up in a freeroll for $5,000. Gigabet has won this monthly contest multiple times. One evening in the spring of 2005 he was discussing strategy with a few friends and they got into a conversation about the TLB. Gigabet said he could win it any month he put his mind to it. One of his friends —sheets — said he could get Gigabet action on that bet. Hours later nip/tuck took him up on it. Gigabet went so far as to give nip/tuck two-to-one odds that he could win the contest. And they bet $10,000 on it. nip/tuck made it clear from the beginning that he would not keep quiet about the bet. Gigabet didn't mind, he welcomed the competition. They decided on August.

nip/tuck knew that if he could post this bet on some of the on-line poker forums that other people would be more interested in beating Gigabet. nip/tuck improved his odds by broadcasting the wager. Then he sweetened the pot. nip/tuck offered $5,000 to the winner of the August TLB. The race was on.

It was the talk of the on-line poker community. Some players swore that Gigabet would win, others disagreed vehemently. While playing at Turning Stone Casino in a live game mid-August, two on-line superstars discussed the wager. BigSlick789 claimed Gigabet would win. Thorladen wasn't so sure. BigSlick789 said he'd put a thousand dollars on it – straight up bet. Thorladen thought a thousand was chump change. "How about a hundred thousand," he said, "make it one hundred K and I might be interested." They both decided to think it through. Thorladen logged onto his poker account to check the current status of the TLB. Gigabet was outside the top ten. When Thorladen met with BigSlick789 again they agreed to the bet. $100,000 was put on the line. Thorladen assembled a team of top ranked on-line players to play on one account. They would play around the clock, any and every tournament. Since the TLB is calculated by averaging a player's top twenty tourney results this didn't make Thorladen's team a lock to win, but it certainly gave them an edge.

Thorladen's team immediately moved towards the top of the leader board. sheets was in the top five. As was Gank – self-professed best on-line poker player alive. And Gigabet was gaining ground. He was fifth at the end of the third week in August. And right on top of the TLB was JJProdigy, a lesser known, but obviously gifted player. It is questionable as to how much any of these players or player teams slept in the last week of tournaments, but when the month was up JJProdigy remained the leader. Gigabet had given it everything, but fallen short. It didn't hurt that his month's winnings eclipsed his $10,000 wager; he was a gentleman in defeat.

PoBoy plays almost exclusively multi-table tournaments. One night in the fall of 2005 he was leading a $200 buy-in tourney with only forty players left. First prize paid $126,000. His stack stood at

115,000 chips. The closest player had only 75,000. PoBoy was feeling pretty good about his chances of making the final table. He was hoping to win the whole thing.

When he had arrived home from work that evening he had decided to go for a run. He returned home forty-five minutes later, showered, put on his robe and made a quick dinner. At 8:00 PM he settled himself in front of his computer with a glass of red wine and began to amass chips. At 11:45 PM, leading the tournament, his Internet connection died. He tried rebooting his computer to no avail. He tried calling his service provider – no one answered. He phoned a few friends who played on-line and might be able to finish out the tourney for him – no one answered.

Finally, more than thirty minutes after losing his connection, PoBoy decided to grab his laptop and head out in the car in search of random wireless Internet access. He marched out his front door wearing only his frayed light blue terrycloth robe, a laptop under his arm. It was almost 12:30 in the morning. PoBoy got into his Chevy Valiant, started it and put it in gear. He opened his laptop and placed it next to him on the passenger's seat. He opened the Wireless Network Window and monitored the connection listings. He found three hotspots before he was finally able to connect to the Internet. Two and a half blocks from his home. The connection was tenuous and required that he be parked directly below a flickering street light. It was 12:39 AM.

PoBoy opened the poker site he played on and logged in. Immediately he was taken to his seat at what was now the final table. One player had already been eliminated. He and eight opponents were all that was left. The first thing he noticed was that he was almost out of chips. In fact, the first hand he played turned out to be his big blind, and the large size of the blinds at this final table meant that having paid his big blind he was essentially all in. The blinds were 2500 / 5000 with 300 chip antes. Once his 5000 chips were in and his ante paid he had 1150 chips left.

PoBoy proceeded to double through on the next three consecutive hands. By the end of the third he stood fourth in chips.

One by one players dropped away, were busted out. Finally PoBoy was heads up. Just him and someone called buzzymozzy. They were about even in chips. It was 1:07 AM.

PoBoy noticed the tap at his window before he even saw the flashing red and blue lights. At one in the morning, sleep deprived, totally focused and parked beneath a strobing street light his long range sensors had all but shut down. Someone had called the police to report a suspicious male parked in a Valiant. PoBoy's honest explanation didn't seem to win him any points with the policemen. "So you're gambling on-line in your robe in your car at one o'clock in the morning?" they asked. "Poker is hardly gambling," replied PoBoy. "Step out of the vehicle sir." And then, with a certain finality, the battery in his laptop failed. His screen went blank.

PoBoy took second place in that tournament. In doing so he earned $67,000. But all he could think of was how bad luck had cost him $59,000 (the difference between first and second place). He spent four and a half hours at the police station. Finally at around 6:00 AM he returned to his house. His wife was just waking up. He relayed his crazy tale and lamented his bad luck. "What bad luck," she said, "if you hadn't lost your Internet connection you would probably have donked off your stack bluffing into a calling station. That lousy Internet connection just made us almost $70,000." There are two sides to every coin.

SkateBored was sixteen when he started playing on-line poker. He 'borrowed' his mother's credit card to set up an account. And when he lost that money he 'borrowed' it again. Until he got caught. When his ability to redeposit vanished SkateBored had $23.55 in his on-line poker account. He went on a heater and ran his bankroll up to $2,000 over the next few weeks. His play seemed to improve in the absence of a safety net. Early in August 2005 SkateBored won a $2,500 entry into the main event of the WCOOP (World Cup of On-line Poker). The day before the tournament his father discovered him playing poker on-line. His father disconnected SkateBored's Internet connection. Early on the day of the event, SkateBored found a friend to loan him a laptop with wireless.

SkateBored knew his neighbours had a wireless Internet connection, he had heard his father say it was unsecured. He found he could only get a steady signal when he held the laptop out his window. He ran an extension cord out the window, crawled onto the roof and started playing. Nine and a half hours later SkateBored won the main event of the WCOOP along with over $600,000.

SkateBored's parents went on to condone his poker habits. He bought himself a car, a games room, and a stack of designer tracksuits, which he can allegedly pile from floor to ceiling in his room. SkateBored got a bracelet for winning the championship, and augmented that with a few pounds of other bling. He is an on-line teenage legend, with an ego to match.

When I arrive back at the table having soothed my son back to sleep, the complexion has changed again. Larry and dhroller are still playing, as is Mike, but the others are all new. I notice I have notes on one of them. Most on-line poker sites allow you to make notes on players and attach the notes directly to the player. That way if a player you have notes on sits down at your table there is an icon above his name, which indicates the notes. Rancher1984 is his name. My notes claim he pushed all in pre-flop with 78 unsuited for over $200. He is sitting directly to my right. Perfect spot for a loose cannon.

I find myself folding whenever he raises, not willing to mix it up with a maniac without a solid hand. Finally after three rounds of cards and Rancher1984 raising and reraising everything I catch two black queens. As usual Rancher1984 raises. He makes unusual raises, and this one is $27. I decide to call and see what the flop brings. Everyone else folds. The flop is a beautiful queen, ten, five. Three different suits. Rancher1984 comes out firing. He bets $50 into a $60 dollar pot. I call. The turn pairs

the five, giving me a full house. Rancher1984 immediately pushes all in for $324. I call just as quickly, and he flips up an ace five
for three of a kind. One out in the deck, the last five. The pot
stands at $808. The last cards comes a...

LIANE KEIGHTLEY
Inlet

From the top of the steps, the water looked unwholesome. The sun had dipped behind a large, dense cloud that looked a little like an elephant on its knees. There was no breeze at all, and the tiny lake sat before them like a large muddy puddle, the surface a dull and uninviting brown. Cottages and docks were tucked up all around the edge of the lake like desperate children gathered at a third-rate circus.

"You could drink that water," Ber said to reassure Lola. "Seriously." Lola had only remarked on the colour of the water, knowing it didn't necessarily mean anything. His confidence seemed to falter. "Maybe," he said, thinking about it a little more. "You could maybe drink that water." He tugged absently at the waistband of his shorts. "I don't think I would, though."

"Where's the inlet?" Lola asked. There was no sparkle or movement to the water, though she didn't doubt it was clean enough to swim in. This, after all, was cottage country. Ber stared at the water in front of them. He looked vaguely to the left, then to the right. "The inlet?" He wore his swimming trunks hiked halfway up his meager chest, like an old man with an axe to grind.

It was intimate, but it was also claustrophobic, this little lake. So small there was no room for assumptions. They stood on the dock side by side. Ber was still wearing his shoes and socks. "I'm living the retired life," he said, as they watched a canoe paddle past twenty feet in front of them. It was something he often said, even in the city. He thought it was funny. But it wasn't far from the truth.

Up close the water looked only marginally better. Lola kneeled down to look at it. Beside her Ber did a little vaudeville two-step, then quacked. He raised his chin in the air like he'd come up with something brilliant and quacked again, louder this time, followed by a rapid series of loud, enthusiastic quacks. "Think they'll come?" he said, looking up into the sky expectantly. Lola undid his shoe laces and pretended to tie them together. She leaned closer and sniffed at his shoes, then fell back onto the dock in a dramatic swoon. "I think you need some new Odour Eaters," she said, looking up at him from where she lay.

Ber looked happy for a moment.

"I make no demands," he said, extolling what he thought was one of his virtues. He looked down at her with renewed expectation.

"Why is that good?"

Suddenly he was angry. "Why don't you trust me?" he said, but it was an accusation rather than a question. "We could get married. And −"

"And what?" They'd already had this conversation on the drive up.

"And," Ber looked around him in frustration, "I don't know. We'd be married."

The sun emerged from behind the cloud, and everything lost its focus. The neighbour's flag drooped on its flagpole.

"Let's swim," Lola said.

Ber flipped his sunglasses down over his eyes and said nothing.

He could look so sullen. Lola stood behind him and rubbed his shoulders. She pressed her face into his back and felt him soften. "Come on," she said, coming around to face him again, "Let's swim for a while, then we'll go fire up the barbeque and open a bottle." She rubbed her hands together and smiled at him. "You can practice your quacking," she added. He smiled back tentatively. They were friends again, for the moment.

Two docks away, a middle-aged man with a deep Florida tan was working on his motorboat. He spotted them and waved. Ber waved back, smiled and nodded several times, hoisted his shorts up even further. "Everyone's always so friendly up here," he said.

"Who's that?"

"I don't know. You just wave back out here." He reached for her index finger and fondled it for a moment. "People like to keep to themselves." Two ducks came into view overhead and dove towards the lake, flapping and skidding onto the surface of the water. Ber raised his eyebrows at Lola and shook his finger at the ducks wildly, like a demented old man. "It worked!" he said.

Lola was still looking at the neighbour. "He looks like the guy who does the news on TV," she said. Ber suddenly looked surprised, and turned his head towards the man with the Florida tan. "Oh yeah," he said. "It is the guy who does the news. My parents go over there for barbeques." He looked back at the ducks. "Ap-parent-ly." He did another little two-step.

Lola glanced at him and kicked off her flip-flops.

"I forgot my towel," Ber said, doing something with his face that was halfway between a smile and a grimace. The sound of someone hammering echoed across the little lake. Some industrious neighbour was building an addition onto their cottage. Lola thought it could be fun to paddle across and offer to help for a couple of hours, then afterwards sit and drink beer with them by the lake, pointing back to where they stood now and saying, Look, that's where we are. But Ber would never want to do that. She waited, looking out towards the sound. Ber looked at the water without making a move towards the house. He shifted his weight to one leg, while giving the other one a tentative shake, pantomiming pain from when he had banged his foot on the door stoop earlier that morning.

"Want me to get it for you?" Lola said, still looking out across the lake.

"No, no, of course not," he said, giving his foot another slight shake and twisting his face into a minor grimace.

"I'll get it," she said, and turned to look at him briefly. He gave her a guilty smile.

"Thank you!" he shouted after her as she headed back up the hill towards the house.

The house had that genteel cottage feel, all wood and windows, with carved ducks on the side tables and floor-to-ceiling windows looking out over the lake. Antiques magazines were laid out on the coffee table beside a thick glass bowl filled with coloured marbles. The house had a funny smell.

Two large, pink Post-It notes on the fridge bore one of the few living signs of Ber's parents. It was a list: a list of tasks to be performed while Ber and Lola were up there. "Hi kids!" it said at the top. Ber's mother was responsible for this.

It wasn't simply a list of things that needed doing, but ways that regular things were meant to be done. "Double-bag the garbage!" was the first one. "Don't leave anything perishable in the refrigerator!" came next. The third one was interesting. "Don't put any utensils in the toaster!!!" Lola could only assume that Ber's mother thought a) that Ber was still nine years old; or b) that he was an idiot. It was sad to see such a bald lack of faith in a son. Lola had read it aloud in disbelief when they'd arrived, but Ber seemed unperturbed by it. "She means well," was all he'd said.

The Post-It list was an interesting artifact, the kind of thing you could take to a psychoanalyst and have him tell you where your life had gone off track. In fact, Lola herself could slip it in her bag and show it to a shrink. She could have him read it like tea leaves in the bottom of a cup, tell her what a future with Ber would hold.

She opened the fridge door absently. It was full of the food they'd brought, but also the stuff that Ber knew she loved. He had run into the country store on their way up here to grab a newspaper, and emerged with a paper grocery bag full of fancy cheeses and artichokes, black olives and Alphaghettis, two things of Jiffy Pop and a bottle of cheap bourbon to make up for the one she'd forgotten to pack. She looked at the bourbon sitting on the counter. As the fridge door swung shut, she caught the words "Lock the door!" down at the bottom of the second Post-It. She reached for the bourbon and drank it straight from the bottle.

Ber's painting lay on the kitchen table. He'd started it that morning in a fit of enthusiasm. It was the starkest thing she had ever seen. Next to the painting lay all his paint things, nothing closed up properly, the brushes tipped out of the murky dish of water and onto the wood of the table. The chair cushion had fall-

en onto the floor. She picked up a brush and added a stroke of
blue to the water. She painted a tree onto the horizon, suggesting
land where there had only been a wide-open expanse of ocean
that went on and on. She added another tree, and a stick man
standing beneath it. She added a small platform of land. It was
done before she could stop herself.

In searching for Ber's towel, Lola discovered a turquoise bag
of moist wipes sitting on the floor in the front entrance. This was
where Ber had unwittingly dropped them.

"I can't find them," she'd called to him from outside the bathroom door the evening before. "Take a shower if you can't manage to clean yourself the old-fashioned way."

"But I need them," he'd whined through the door.

"You'll manage."

She heard muffled sounds of movement through the door.

"My ass is my bread and butter!" he shouted.

"Funny," she shouted back. "What do you want from me? I
can hose you down if you'd like."

She'd thought he was making a joke of it, but he didn't talk to
her for a good twenty minutes after emerging from the bathroom.

She was still carrying the bourbon around. She took another
swig and put it down on the table. Looking out the big window,
she could just see Ber from here, standing motionless down on
the dock. It was like looking at a photograph. She tried to imagine him gone from her life. She managed it, but it hurt. She
stripped off her clothes and dropped them on the floor. She
didn't want to be alone anymore in this house.

From the balcony overlooking the lake, Lola called to Ber.
"Anyone in sight?" Standing way down on the dock, pale-
skinned with his shoe laces undone, dwarfed by the distance
between them, Ber did a quick scan then shook his head. A
breeze had come up, and the lake was rallying. It sparkled a little in the sunshine.

Lola jogged down the steps with Ber's towel wrapped around

her. As she got closer to the dock she picked up speed. When she hit the dock, she dropped the towel.

"It has to be done!" she shouted, streaking past Ber and canon-balling into the water.

The water was icy. She hadn't expected that. Her skin burned for a few moments, before it began to numb.

Ber was laughing. She watched him. When she made him laugh, she was happy.

"It's okay," she said, gasping a little as she spoke, her body trying to adjust to the cold. "It's just the first shock"–she could hardly catch her breath–"that hurts."

Ber paced the dock like a caged dog. She knew it was hard for him. But she wanted him to try.

"Just come in," she called, "come in with me, and we'll swim." She turned in the water, her hands like the oars of a small craft moving her roughly, but pointing her in the right direction. She raised a hand out of the water, causing the rest of her to sink a little. She was determined to try. "There," she said pointing across the little lake. "We'll swim to that cluster of trees, and see what we find."

"You'll find another dock just like this one," Ber said, "and people who don't want you on their property, particularly if you're naked."

Lola continued to tread water in front of the dock. She was getting cold, and would soon need to either start swimming or get out. "Maybe we'll find the inlet," she said, looking across the lake. She didn't want to get out.

Ber was frustrated with her. His face had crumpled in on itself like a wounded animal's, and she could see that he was unhappy.

He looked down at her treading water in front of the dock. "We could go to Vegas," he said. "We could." But still, the water was too cold, and he wouldn't come in.

DANA BATH
from Death By Sky

Sarah meets Leon through a telephone dating service. She calls him because his profile says he owns a cooking school. On their first date, at a coffee shop, he says, "When I was a child, I thought adults were bears in people suits."

She smokes, and he frowns.

Leon has bad table manners. He chews with his mouth open, and farts. But he knows how to begin a conversation and how to prevent it from ending. He likes to take Sarah to the best ice cream shop, the best bar, the best bookstore. He likes to teach her words; yesterday it was 'halcyon', which means calm and peaceful. He's dumpy and small-eyed, so it's unlikely he will stray, although she's not sure how much it would bother her if he did. She signs up for classes at his cooking school, Marguerite Kitchens (*Les Fourneux de Marguerite*), and quickly demonstrates herself to be a natural.

*

Leon has a two-year-old daughter named Aileen. Aileen's mother died shortly after Aileen was born, of a tumour in her brain. Leon was married to her only a short time.

Aileen is a luminous, brown-skinned, golden little girl with breakable-looking hands. Her eyelids shimmer bluely, glaucous as plums; she has startling gold-flecked hazel eyes almost as big as her face.

Leon explains that when his wife was still alive, he barely allowed her to hold Aileen. He feels guilty about this now, but at the time, he was so enraptured by the baby, he couldn't put her down. He changed his daughter's diapers, and got up in the night to feed her with the milk his wife pressed from herself and left in a bottle in the fridge. As soon as Aileen could sit up, he carried her on his shoulders any time they were together, which was often. Her first word was "Leon." His wife was too tired to hold her daughter, too tired to get out of bed in the night.

The first time Sarah meets Aileen, the little girl clings to her father and frowns when Sarah tries to touch her. The next time Sarah visits, she brings a blue flannel bunny she found at a Unicef shop. She hands the bunny to Aileen, who is sitting cross-legged in the middle of the livingroom floor, scrawling with crayons on some sheets of newsprint. Aileen looks at the bunny, then at Sarah, and then at the bunny again. She puts down her green crayon and holds the bunny with two hands, looks seriously into its face, as though keeping it still while she tells it something important. But she says nothing. Sarah, impulsively, reaches to take Aileen up in her arms; Aileen stiffens a little before she relaxes. Then she leans into Sarah quietly, passively, her eyes still on the bunny. Sarah holds her for the rest of the evening, until she falls asleep in Sarah's arms, on the sofa in front of the television. Sarah looks down at the blue light on Aileen – such a strange golden face on such a small girl – and her heart clenches with something like grief.

*

Leon likes to buy books for her. He buys her everything by Patricia Highsmith, as well as Jane Bowles, Katherine Mansfield, *The Kreutzer Sonata* by Tolstoy. She obliges him by reading them, even though she doesn't much like reading any more; when she finished her English degree, she decided to stop wasting her time on books. She always feels there's something else to do – dinner, the beds, errands – until there's nothing left to do but sleep.

One day he lends her a book of stories and she finishes it in a single afternoon. It's a small book, and she isn't entirely absorbed, mostly running her eyes over the words. When she gets to his place that evening, she puts the book back on his shelf. He asks, "Don't you like it?"

"I'm finished."

"Sorry, what?"

She shrugs.

Later that evening, after a few silences, he begins to ask small, innocent questions. What did she think of the woman in the third story; did she find her sympathetic?

She shrugs again. "She was unhappy; I suppose that could inspire sympathy."

And what about the final story; didn't she find the girlfriend totally compellingly realistic?

"With her prosthetic leg and her third nipple and her hallucinations? Not exactly."

His brow smooths over and he nods. "Wow. You really did read the whole thing."

She stares. He meets her gaze impassively for a moment, but when she doesn't look away, an expression like fear drops down over his face.

A few days later, though, he gives her a copy of *Pride and Prejudice*, which she has never read. She begins it that night, and is immediately consumed. She'd forgotten what it was like to read desperately, to resent any call back to the real world. She read like this when she was a child. The day she finishes it, she tells Leon that she is going to finish with the cooking school this year, and in the meantime, she's going to apply for a graduate degree in literature. He seems to think this is a fine idea. "You need some intellectual pursuits," he says. "You insist on limiting yourself, as if you don't believe in your own capabilities."

She has no idea what he means. She suspects he isn't talking about her at all.

*

After dinner one night, Sarah says that she likes coffee better than tea because of coffee's whiff of Mayan civilization. Leon sneers. "You like coffee better than tea because of the taste. Why can't you express yourself honestly? Do you enjoy that kind of self-aggrandizement?"

Passing by Lake Ontario once in the car, Sarah and Leon see a sentence spray-painted across a cement girder: *I WORRY ABOUT YOU*. Then he teaches her the word 'eudaimonia': the state of being happy by following your demons. And then he tells her that Flaubert liked tinsel better than silver, because tinsel has everything silver has, plus pathos.

*

One night Leon comes home and tells her that as he was driving to Magog, he passed a dead cat on the road. On his way back, the cat was still there, so, hating to see it lying in undignified plain view, he got out of the car and got the shovel out of the back to remove it. When he touched the cat with the tip of the shovel, he saw that it was still breathing, its crushed ribs heaving in and out, bloody through the orange fur. He almost got into his car and drove away, but then he brought his shovel down on the head of the cat. And then did it again, to be sure. He picked the cat up with the shovel and flung it into the trees. He tells her this, and then he puts his head into her lap and cries.

*

It's early evening, and the air is damp, thick with the odour of roses. Sarah and Leon are sitting at the white plastic table on the verandah behind his duplex in Notre-Dame-de-Grace. Sarah has coffee with a splash of Frangelico in a red mug; Leon has Darjeeling tea. The Sunday *New York Times* is spread on the table in fat, gently flapping piles. Leon is reading about the Expos trouncing the Mets, his small hands stretching the pages almost flat and vertical in the air before his face, the way one might hold a newspaper-sized mirror. Sarah's bent over the Home Styles section.

She's reading about smoking rooms. She's thinking about how that small dark room in the back would make a good smoking room, with its high windows, openable only with a pole, which could let the smoke out without creating too much draft in the winter. She could suggest filling that room with low tables to hold ornate ashtrays, and easy chairs – leather so as not to absorb the smell – and maybe a little bar at the end for port and brandy. She could make a smoking room a condition under which she would move in.

Leon winds up the antique Victrola in the living room and plays records by Georges Brassens. They sing and dance through the threadbare, wobbly furniture, laughing and twirling, careful not to bump too much and scratch the record. She thinks of what her mother said to her once, about how the important thing is to choose someone who amuses you, someone with whom you can imagine having a fine conversation in twenty years. At the time, Sarah didn't believe that her mother meant that at all.

When they've finished dancing, they return to the verandah. She pulls out the Sunday Magazine, and opens it to an article about a child hip-hop star. They stay up half the night, discussing the boundaries that need to be drawn for children, the boundaries that are drawn for Aileen, and then the question of what boundaries they would draw for their children if the children were hip-hop stars, and then the question of whether they will have children, a question they don't resolve. The stars are out. Sarah's in the hammock and Leon's at the table. They hold glasses of Amaretto and talk softly through the buzz and chirp of the crickets and the traffic.

She enjoys sex for the sake of sex itself, without thinking too much about who she's doing it with.

*

She moves into Leon's duplex. It is tall and thin. The kitchen is large, all polished wood, with glass doors that face the back yard and the house behind. The kitchen is nice in the mornings, like a magazine ad for coffee, sunlight warming the wood, except for the dust and smudges the light shows on the floor, and the sink filled to the brim with unwashed dishes.

The living room adjoins the kitchen with no separating wall, so that whoever's cooking can talk to whoever's watching TV.

Leon redecorates the room off the livingroom as a smoking room, just as she asks. They strip the wallpaper together, and he paints the walls a glowing, opulent red. He refinishes the wood floor and buys Persian-looking rugs. Together they choose the buttercream leather sofas and chairs, and the gentle halogen lamps to fill the space with indirect light. They install a small bar and lay it neatly with a few bottles of brandy, port and scotch. On the far end is Sarah's desk, which soon sports a computer, sloppy piles of papers, and an overflowing ashtray.

Upstairs, a small telephone table sits below a low round port-hole window on the landing. Aileen's room is on the right. The carpet is bright, dark pink; the wallpaper writhes with fuschia, orange and purple flowers, and is peeling a little at the corners. The curtains are fluffy, white, and lacy, like a doll's dress, but old, and turning an uneven tea colour.

The road outside is lined with trees, and the houses, one after another, are all the same, sheltered by small gardens and set back from the sidewalks by yards.

She is soon coming home to Leon in the evenings wishing she weren't coming home to Leon in the evenings. She knows that if she were coming home to an empty house, she'd wish for the opposite.

*

Sarah finishes up the program at the cooking school just as she is accepted to do her Masters at the university. Leon suggests that she teach a couple of basic culinary courses for him over the summer, and the idea appeals to her.

Her first class is on the first day of June. She stands before the students and watches them shuffle. They look so young to her, the girls with their smooth hair full under their brown nets, the boys thin and defiant with sideburns that should really be trimmed. She discovers, though, over the weeks that follow, that some of them are her age or older, some of them just out of graduate school, or beginning careers they are now trying to get away from, in finance or law. Sarah is touched that this is a vision for some of them, that they've abandoned everything they have in order to chase after what she has. She sometimes wants to ask them: What is it you think you're going to find? And then she sees them, covered in flour and laughing, one smearing another's cheek with a chocolate finger, dropping a scorched pan into the sink and weeping while the others gather around murmuring comfort, and she thinks: Maybe they've found it.

Aileen sometimes comes to Marguerite Kitchens during the day, usually passing the time in the office with Leon. When Sarah walks in on them, Leon is often dancing Aileen around the room in his arms, or leaning over the edge of the playpen to hand her a toy. Aileen is generally content to stay where she is, looking at picture books or drawing with pencil crayons, although she's three now and more than big enough to climb over the walls of the pen.

When Leon needs to go out, he carries the playpen downstairs and sets it up in a corner of the kitchen so Sarah can watch her. Aileen rarely cries or makes any kind of fuss, and the students find her charming, sometimes leaving their pans too long while they coo over her and make faces. Watching them, Sarah is regularly seized by a mixture of pride and fear. She often feels, when she explains how to whisk a roux or slip the skin from a blanched tomato, that she's speaking to Aileen, who sometimes pulls herself up and peers over the edge of the playpen with her eerie, glittering eyes.

*

They're in the supermarket and Leon asks Sarah whether she wants white or brown eggs. She's been teaching soufflés at the cooking school all day, and groans. "For once, I don't want to make this kind of decision," she says.

He grows pale and rigid.

She ignores him for fifteen minutes. Then he bursts out, "I make decisions all the time. I decided we should redo the smoking room. I decided to ask you to move in with me."

They're standing in the cereal aisle. She stares at him. She tries to remember if these things are true; it seems to her that they're not.

"Is this how it's going to be?" she demands. Her voice is clear and loud enough to carry all the way up and down the aisle, and maybe beyond. "Fighting in the supermarket about eggs? I spent the day having to decide everything from eggs to butter to pans to fucking aprons, all afternoon. Why do you think everything that comes out of my mouth is a personal attack? Is this how it's going to be?"

The tension drains from him like blood from a magic turnip. He looks like a turnip, standing there, the pale colour of a rutabaga tinged with ruddy purple. His small eyes turn down to the floor.

"No," he says. "You're right. This isn't how it will always be."

This is the final decision, here in the cereal aisle. It isn't a hard decision, even if she believes it will bring her no joy, just a sort of refuge from the opposite.

*

They are married in September, just as Sarah begins school. Aileen is a resplendent flower girl in green tulle, her waves of golden hair drawing gasps from the few spectators.

*

They don't tell Aileen about Santa Claus. They don't want their child to grow up believing lies. Later, Sarah won't read her fairy tales, or talk to her about love.

They do take her to the Santa Claus Parade the year she's about to turn four, and she tells several of the children around her, loudly, that the man on the truck is just an ordinary man in a red suit. Sarah grabs her up and shushes her. Aileen is too shocked and confused to cry.

*

In the spring after Aileen's fourth birthday, Leon has a heart attack in his office at Marguerite Kitchens. He is not found until it is too late to do anything for him. Aileen, fortunately or not, is at home with Sarah at the time. In his will, everything – the house, the cooking school, Aileen – goes to Sarah.

On the summer nights after his death, the house is unbearable, huger and emptier than anything Sarah's ever been in. She lies on the sofa and watches movies on cable TV, smokes, and cries. She goes through a full bag of potato chips every night, just to feel something give way with a vengeful crunch between her teeth. Within a month she puts on fifteen pounds. This isn't so bad – she's always been too thin – but her skin starts to go.

When she tires of the television she spends night after night, after Aileen has gone to bed, in the smoking room. Leon had intended to redo the whole house. He managed to tile the bathroom, and paint the kitchen, but the smoking room was the only room he finished. The air has become slightly blue with smoke; a window high on the outside wall stays open all the time, but it is the only window, and the air doesn't circulate well; the ceiling fan is sluggish, and only operates when the lights are on.

In the mornings she's bleary and snappish, even after two cups of coffee. Once, when driving Aileen to day camp, she nods off at the wheel and jerks awake just before going up on the curb. Aileen's humming into her hands in the back seat and hasn't noticed. Sarah deposits her safely at the door and then sits and breathes, pressing her fingers to her temples.

After that she tries to go to bed before midnight, but often she can't sleep, and ends up wandering to the kitchen, wandering to the television, back and forth until four or five o'clock. Once or twice she's still awake when Aileen pads down the stairs in her pyjamas, ready for breakfast.

Sleep, when it comes, is bad, a gaping, empty room thick with white noise, through which nasty creatures — emaciated cats with claws longer than their paws, snakes dragging their half-shed skins, monkeys with beet-red eyes — occasionally crawl.

HOWARD CHACKOWICZ

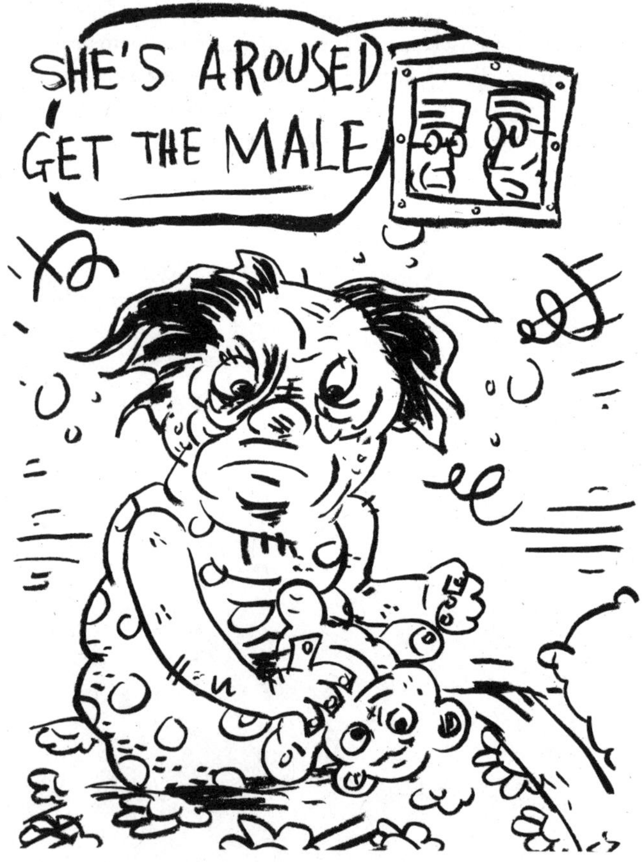
SHE'S AROUSED
GET THE MALE

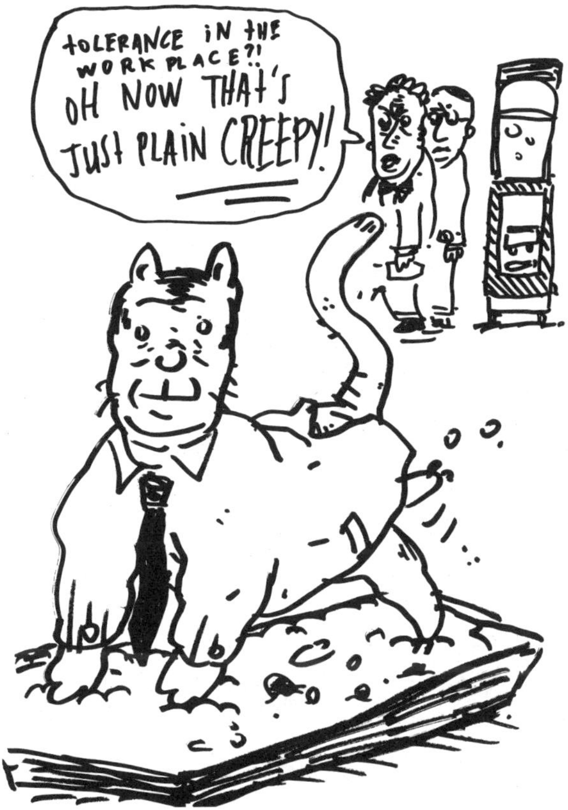
TOLERANCE IN THE WORK PLACE?!.. OH NOW THAT'S JUST PLAIN CREEPY!

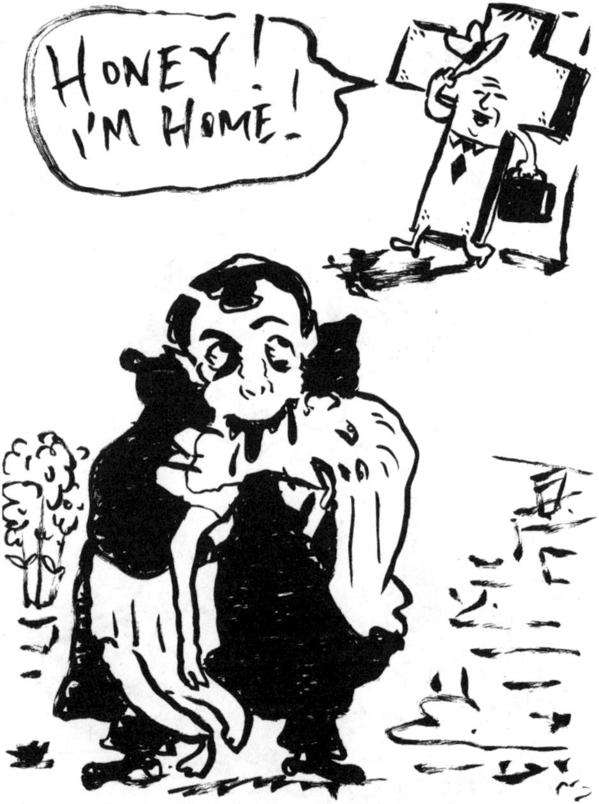
HONEY! I'M HOME!

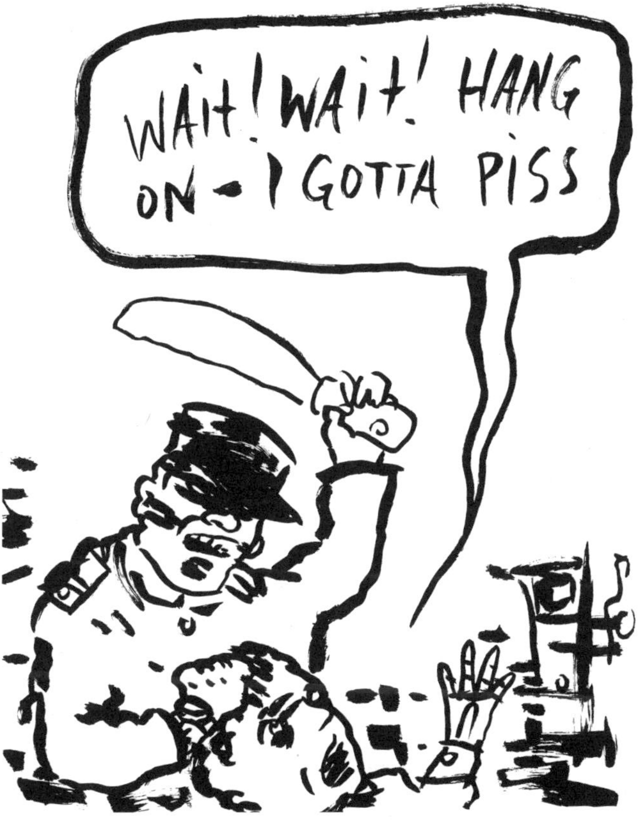
WAIT! WAIT! HANG ON - I GOTTA PISS

I - I... I ONLY HAVE ONE BALL!!

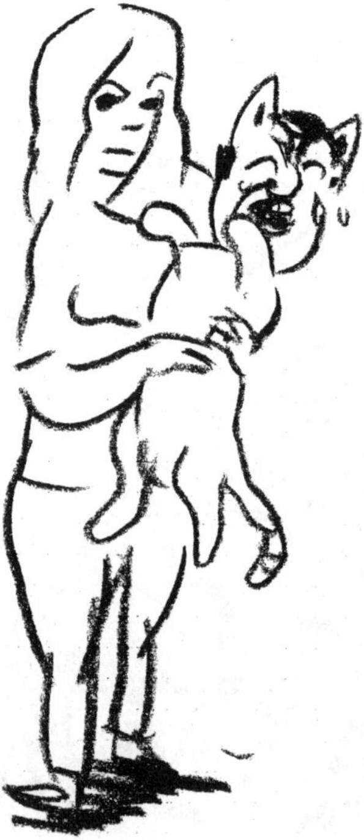

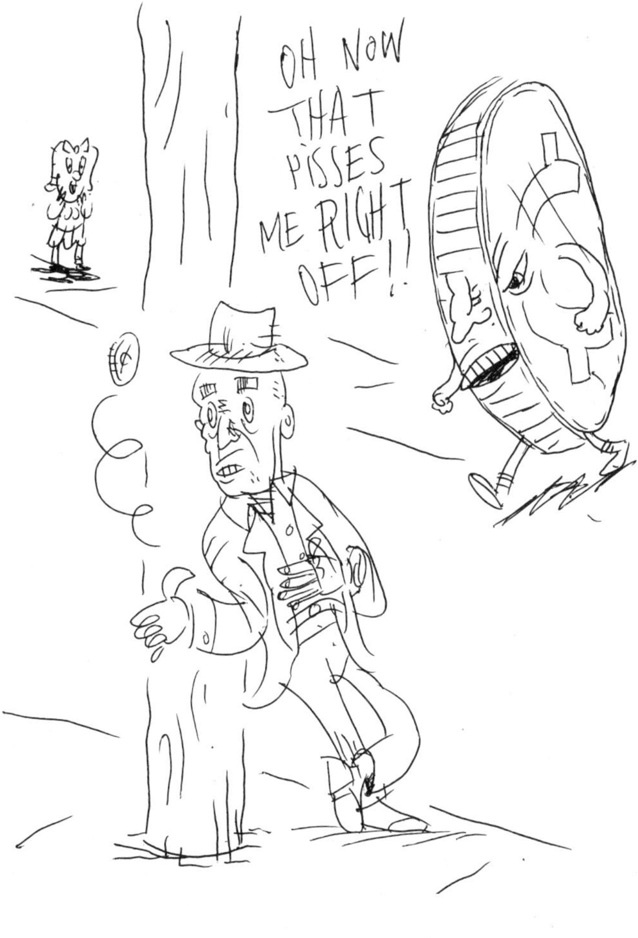
OH NOW THAT PISSES ME RIGHT OFF!!

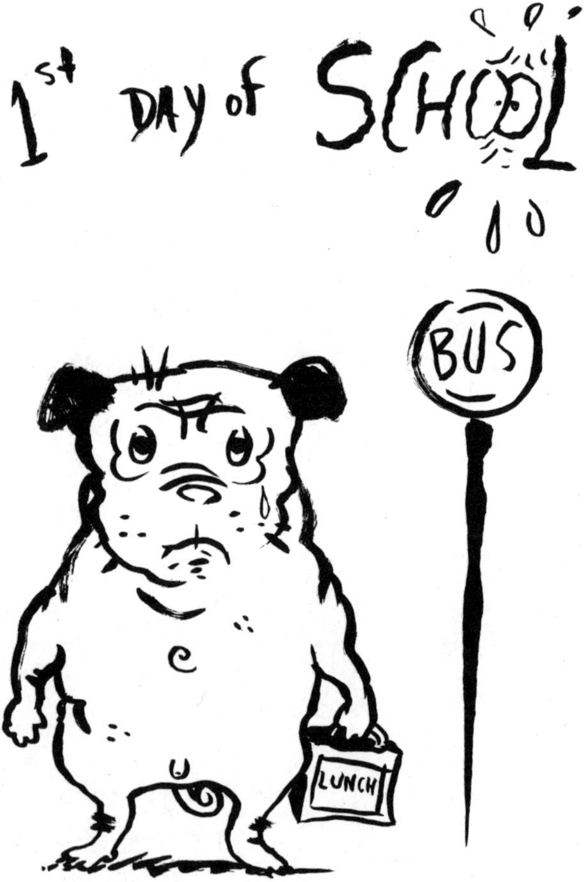
1st DAY of SCHOOL
BUS
LUNCH

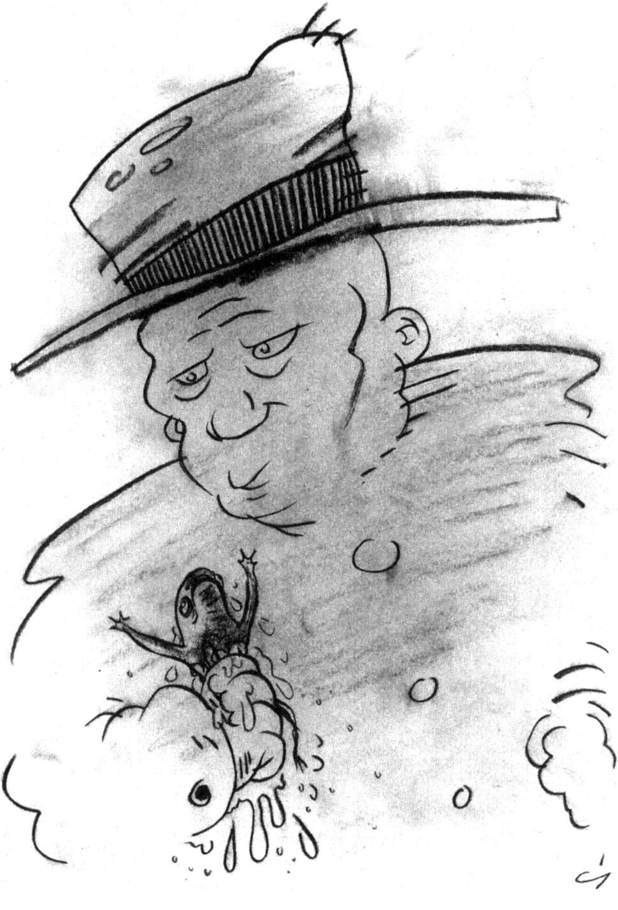

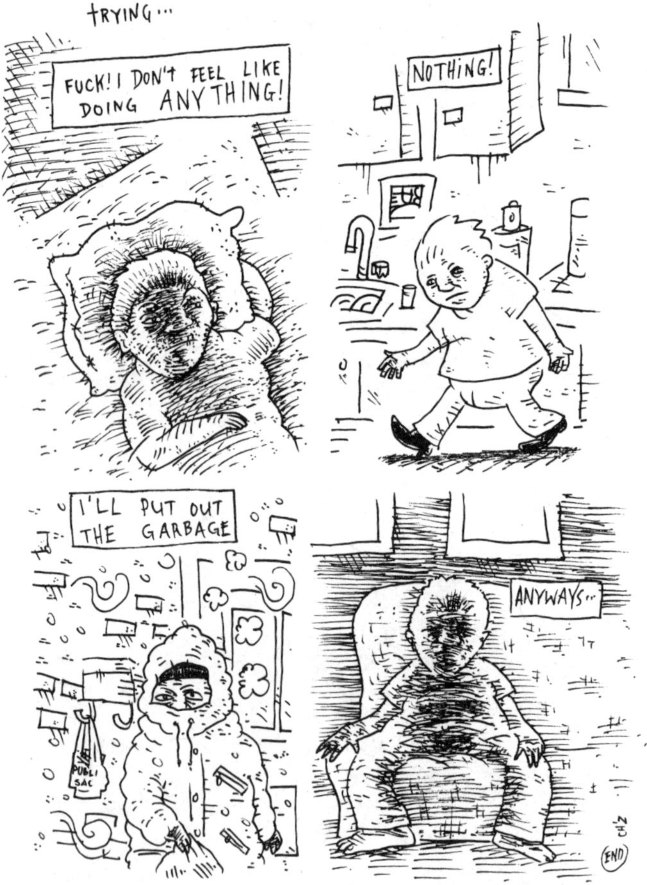
TRYING...
FUCK! I DON'T FEEL LIKE DOING ANYTHING!
NOTHING!
I'LL PUT OUT THE GARBAGE
PUBLI SAC
ANYWAYS...
END

MEG SIRCOM
Dream Apartment

She looked around feeling that they'd decorated their dream apartment for the wrong person. They'd decorated it tastefully, with white walls and real art, for someone who had dinner parties and conversations; and carelessly, with furniture picked off the curb, for someone who might drop a half-chewed slice of pizza on your front steps at 4:00 AM instead of finding a garbage can. It suited a person who didn't notice the downtown traffic noise, the smell of the downstairs neighbour's cigarette smoke percolating up through the floorboards. It was exactly the wrong apartment for this limp, blue-lidded baby who, three months into his life, slept on her lap, his chest barely rising and falling with each breath, a birthmark like a crêpe-paper strawberry over his eye.

All their friends who had dropped by had loved the apartment. "It's like a New York loft," they said. "You could have an art show in here." Friends they hadn't seen in months came by to see the new apartment and the new baby. Friends of friends came by. They brought wine she couldn't drink. At the hospital the nurses had told her to take visitors up on their offers to put a casserole in their freezer, or to do the dishes. Their friends stayed too long, drinking their wine. The glasses piled up in the sink. "What's it like being parents?" they asked.

"It's like having a hamster. Each time you see it sleeping you think it's dead. You just worry about keeping it alive," she said.

"It's not like having a baby changes your personality," said the father. "Don't forget to invite us out to things."

Once in a while the friends looked at the baby sleeping on her lap. "He's cute," they said doubtfully, eyeing the birthmark.

"He's sleeping now," said the father, pouring himself another glass of wine. "Let's finish this off, get the cat to babysit and hit the clubs."

The baby sighed and his chest stopped in mid-exhale. The mother held her breath watching. The baby's chest rose again and she breathed too. She had spent days gazing at the baby like this. The minute she put him down he screamed, and incapable of taking the father's advice to just let him cry, she held him until her arms went numb. She had begun to feel as if she were on a twenty-hour flight to Australia except she never reached Australia. She only had the little square wet-wipes, the dried-out eyes, the underlying dread of flying. "It reeks of cigarette smoke in here," the mother said. "Can't you go downstairs and ask the neighbour to smoke outside?"

"It's not like we have a smoker right in the apartment, you can barely smell it," the father reassured her. "It may even be good for the baby."

The father thought a little pollution was healthy. It would toughen a person up. Like the birthmark. It would build character. This is how he viewed any difficulty. He had a home-opathic outlook on life. It was the Finnish sauna aspect of his personality that had first attracted her to him. It had made her feel hotter, and tingly, like she was being swatted with bunches of small sticks. "Did you lose weight?" people asked her when they started going out. "You look good. Did you get a new hair-cut?" Since the baby, however, his attitude seemed like some-thing to retreat from. "Have you lost weight?" people now asked her worriedly. "Are you okay?"

The baby stirred and stretched, squeezing his eyes open and shut, lifting his tiny arms up the sides of his head.

"How do you think it feels to have arms that only reach up to your ears?" the father said. He took the baby from her, sat him on his lap and moved his arms up and down, as if he were playing baby air guitar. "I'm as free as a bird now," sang the father, "and this bird can never change...." He flapped the baby's limp arms like a free bird. He would have the baby marching in through the front door, the door that someone had painted salmon pink, the one with the speaker phone, whereas she saw the baby creeping up the fire escape and scratching to be let in at the back window like a stray cat.

She thought about telling him the dream she'd had in between the naps and feedings last night. Or was it the night before? She had taken the baby for a walk in the stroller. He slipped out without her noticing and rolled behind some garbage on the curb. She went half a block before she saw that the baby was gone. When she looked back for it all she could see was a dirty little arm sticking out from behind a stained cardboard box. Then, as she did in all these dreams, she stepped in and started dictating, predicting, like the ominous music in a horror movie. She knew that she could make a garbage truck appear, and sure enough the garbage truck in the form of a giant backhoe clanked up to the pile and started scooping the garbage, baby and all, off the sidewalk.

"I had another dead baby dream last night," she said.

The father stopped playing and leaned back with the baby on his stomach. He furrowed his eyebrows at her, the way a shrink might. She knew he liked it when she told him her dreams; it made him feel professional, even if her dreams were easy to interpret.

Her dreams were always related to what they'd done that evening. Their friends had continued to invite them to things and the father encouraged her to go with the baby. She needed to get out of the apartment! She brought the baby to video game and CD launches, to art openings, to fundraisers, to panel discussions, to wine and cheeses. The baby slept through these events strapped to her front in a leopard print baby carrier, a thin red scarf protecting him from the smoke and lights. "You look great," the father would say, coming over to offer her another glass of wine. "You don't look as if you just had a baby." She took only one glass of wine and pretended to sip it throughout the evening. "A drink or two isn't going to do any damage," said the father. If the music was too loud, which it almost always was, she held her hands over the baby's ears. When they had gone out to a bar one night she dreamt that she'd left the baby with a drunk babysitter, who stared at them over a bottle of vodka slurring, "Baby, what baby?" when they came to pick him up. They'd taken the baby to a hockey game and she dreamt that they'd driven off a bridge and into an ice-covered lake. She'd woken up trying to get the baby out of the car seat.

"Why are you always so happy when I tell you my dreams?" said the mother, catching his look. "Don't you remember we share the same baby?"

"I'm not happy," he said, "I'm helpful. You always wake up before the baby actually dies. I'm here to supply the happy ending, to make it funny." He cupped the baby's hands behind the baby's ears. "Come on, the baby wants to hear your dream. It was about bowling, right?"

Last night they came home after a birthday party of day-glo bowling, the baby damp and dazed, she exhausted with public breastfeeding and worry.

"That's it," she said. "No more outings. From now on the baby and I are going to stay in, put our feet up and watch TV."

"If you won't tell me your dream, I'll tell you a joke," said the father. "What's the difference between a truckload of bowling balls and a truckload of dead babies?"

She stared at him. He suddenly looked a little too eager, as if he needed to confess something. "I can't believe you're telling jokes. Our baby really could die of SIDS. Secondhand smoke is one of the only known causes." The mother put her nose into the air and took a deep sniff. "Anyway, I bet he smokes in bed down there. This place would burn down in five minutes if he caught his mattress on fire." She thought about the neighbour. He was shaky and frail looking, as if he'd have a seizure if you addressed him directly. They saw him coming back from the store with a six-pack every morning, his shoulders hunched under a too-thin jacket. "He probably smokes *and* drinks in bed. We'd actually have about five minutes to get out." She pictured the baby crawling around in clouds of black smoke. "We should put a bucket of water next to the baby's bed. I could dip his blanket in it and wrap it around his head. Why haven't you put up the smoke detectors yet?" she said to him, listening to her voice rising with panic and hormones. "You said you were going to put up the smoke detectors."

The father reached over the baby and rubbed her arm. "I'll get you something to drink." He sounded relieved. Whenever she was upset, he offered her something to drink, but in used cups. He brought her orange juice that tasted like coffee, milk that tasted like beer. She shook her head, feeling her unwashed hair sticking to the back of her neck.

The baby panted a little and stared at her. His birthmark, more prominent than ever, made him look lopsided, like a miniature crazed clown. He arched his back, rolled his eyes and howled. The father turned him around and cradled him next to his chest. "I could eat this little strawberry," he said licking the birthmark. "You don't want to hear any dead baby jokes, do you?" he crooned. The baby stopped crying and the father looked up at her. "Okay, I'll go down and tell the neighbour to stop smoking," he said in his toothless old man voice, the one that was meant to reassure her that he'd be there beside her on a rocking chair thirty years down the road. "I'm going, sweetheart," he said, handing her the baby.

The baby made a cheerful trilling sound. She felt herself relax. The air already smelled cleaner, as if someone had just opened a window. "We're going to be happy in here," she told the baby, lightly tracing his birthmark with her finger.

When he had gone the mother got up and wandered from room to room. She would get this apartment right. She would do a little painting. The living room would be yellow. "I'll paint your room blue, with clouds. I'll make a little nest for you," she told the baby. She bounced him gently in her arms. "And I'll take down some of this art," she said, stopping in front of a huge plaster head attached to a kind of metal cage that one of their friends had sculpted. She put the baby on a chair and pulled the piece away from the wall to find out how it was attached, and of course, she could see that the sculpture, heavy with steel, was going to fall, catching the baby a glancing blow as it went down.

LANCE BLOMGREN
Household Paintings

I

The submarine world of the painting always filled the child with mystery and dread. The blue, tropical water belied a creepy, primordial danger that would seep regularly into his thoughts during the day and occupy his dreams while asleep. The gnarled fish and malevolent stingrays that swam in the kelp forest of his sleep would sometimes wake him up gasping for air. At the marine zoo tidal pool, the boy froze with terror, witnessing first-hand the insectile crabs, obscene, fleshy anemones, and slimy vegetation of the not-so-blue-at-all underwater world. The painting, which sat prominently in the TV room, remained a constant reminder of his all-consuming fear of the ocean, and ultimately the source of what would become his abnormal obsession with it.

The image of the scuba diver, slick in black neoprene, cocooned with air tubes and regulators, entered his fantasies in his teens. The thought of the thin material, barely separating him from the claustrophobic horrors of the deep, made the hair on his arms bristle. He saved his allowance to purchase a wetsuit jacket which he wore alone in his room, caressing the rubbery fabric as he diligently memorised underwater distress signals. Danger: Raise arm straight out, just above shoulder level and make a fist. Out of air: Bring hand to throat and make a horizontal cutting motion. As an adult, he fantasized about getting caught in seaweed, running out of oxygen. He masturbated to eloquent scenarios about sea snails entering his body. He began searching for a woman who shared this erotic terror of the sea.

They planned to meet at the wharf at dawn. As they agreed, they spoke only in hand signals. They poured warm water from a thermos into their wetsuits and shivered as they geared up. They hugged awkwardly, then lowered themselves off the dock and into the water. He felt his stomach tighten with fear and excitement, and could feel his erection growing. The sandy bottom was murky, brown at first, but quickly fell away into a large underwater cliff. They adjusted their buoyancy vests so they could float down the rock face with minimal effort, holding each other as they sank past the sharp drop of water temperature at 40 feet, the hideous sponges which covered the rocks at 60, the ghostly, human faces of wolf eels, peering from their caves at 80, the incomprehensible darkness of the vegetation which greeted them at 110 feet. And then the unthinkable happened. A jellyfish, four feet in diameter, suddenly appeared, its yolky innards throbbing lasciviously inside its translucent, aqueous body, and he orgasmed violently in his wetsuit. Immediately a wave of embarrassment passed over him as his arousal dissipated. He signaled to the woman, extending his thumb. Going Up. The woman was vigorously rubbing herself between her legs. She pointed downwards, looking dejected, wanting to continue. His lungs tightened as his embarrassment turned to shame and then outright panic in the sea's oppressive atmosphere. Ignoring all rules, he ascended alone, and back on the dock, was unable to even look at the woman when she finally surfaced, and lay there until she left.

2

The sisters told each other stories they already knew. And every time they began, their expectation would run ahead of them as they remembered important moments in the story that were still to come.

The painting in the upstairs hallway depicted a Venetian sunset scene of vast canals and gondolas, with the basilica of San Marco rising in the background like some sort of dream. The scene was blurry, seemingly in motion, with the buildings haphazardly sketched into being and the orange reflection of the sun smeared across the canals in a couple thick lines of paint. Few people were lucky enough to inhabit this majestic city of water: the gondola driver, the tourists embracing in the front of the boat, and the fuzzy outline of the two dockworkers, just visible in the lower right-hand corner.

The gondola driver is whistling an old folk song to the couple in his boat, believing he can sense the woman's attraction swell with every note. Tomorrow, if everything goes well, he will meet her in the lobby of the hotel while her husband is changing traveller's cheques in the Piazza. The lives of these three characters form the outline of this painting, acting as a quaint backdrop, but never fully develop into anything on their own.

So, almost twenty-five years later, it's the workers who once again capture our attention, here in this hotel, in another hallway. The workers, of course, are siblings, who have decided to go through life as a team, taking an oath of blood at childhood, dropping out of school together and finally taking jobs with a small shipping business on the Rio Della Veste. They go home together to their adjoining apartments, eat together, and walk around the city together on their days off. They both married at the same time and divorced at the same time. We see them laughing, as the gondola goes by, shaking their heads at the spectacle of the driver's deluded acts of flirtation and overt loneliness.

"Hopeless," they say patting each other on the back before unloading the last crates of the day.

We know now that the brothers will have an irrevocable argument over something petty, and will live out their days full of regret, hardly speaking. We know too that one sibling will become a recluse, while the other will travel extensively, both searching for something to replace the feeling of loss. But at the time, there was no way of knowing this as the brothers catch a vaporetto to a café near the Rialto to celebrate the end of the day with a glass of wine, feeling invincible in their partnership, nothing in the painting to help us predict the forces which can allow a story to change long after it has ended.

The sisters waited impatiently, barely containing their excitement, for certain details to emerge, then would quickly forget them as soon as they were uttered, abandoning them for expectation, which was already racing ahead.

3

Somewhere deep in the minds of all Danes, lurks the image of P.S. Krøyer's painting, *Two Women Walking on the Beach*. This painting, famous for its flat, 'midnight sun' quality of light, depicts a banal, yet Romantic, image of two women sharing an evening stroll and some conversation on a beach in Skagen, at Denmark's northernmost tip. All children will have seen reproductions of this painting in school, and most adults will have heard that this image is a representation of bohemian life in the Skagen artist colony in the late 1800s. Many know that the women are Krøyer's wife and her friend, the artist Anna Archer. The mixture of bourgeois manners and outdoor adventure, elegance and measured decadence embodied by this picture remains an inspirational model for the passionate, yet practical life: fresh air, exercise, relaxation, friends, family, food. And then there's that light, a haunting North Sea blue-grey that flares in the mind like an afterimage flash on the retina, a light that many Danes know eventually began to drive Krøyer into mental illness. Similar to the Little Mermaid, Krøyer's painting has become something of a national symbol and thousands of reproductions have been made by forgerists and enterprising souls worldwide.

Perhaps it's not strange, then, that *Two Women* is rarely seen in the houses of Danes. Many disdain it. The painting is hopelessly saccharine, offering little but empty nostalgia to the modern viewer. So it takes one by surprise when, in the living room of some distant relative, *Two Women* is on display over the fireplace, its outdated quaintness somehow at home amidst the teakwood furniture and minimal décor. The image is not a poster, but it has been mechanically printed onto canvas, then smeared with gesso to give it the appearance of texture. It takes one by surprise to see the painting displayed so brazenly, creating a backdrop for what was otherwise predicted to be a stiff, boring evening.

This is really the way to eat an early dinner. Textbook festivity. We share sandwiches and potato salad. We parenthesize the meal with bitters and port. The houses beyond are dark. The tablecloth is red. There is more than one way to eat rabbit and it is called roasted lamb. The great aunt stews rhubarb. Someone's children are swearing and counting money. The casual comments between a new husband and wife about an obscure news item prove significantly to the bystanders that they are perfectly suited as a couple.

After dinner we step carefully from one slippery rock to the other as we walk along the shore. The dusk is not cold, not quiet, and is hanging lustily. We can't feel our arms for the air. The laws of breathing let us gasp for air so we climb the embankment before discussing unrequited love, and finally turning in.

And this is unrequited love. We are sick with it. We either sleep it off, or find suitable distractions. We are modern viewers and nostalgia is being offered – we'll take it. Isn't the far off sound of traffic on the highway the sound of fortune? Of warning? The evening is like a dog, awaiting its reward for lying still. I am a woman smelling of a soap called melancholy. I heard today that my friend Fred Douglas had died.

4

The people of this small town on Vancouver Island look constantly at the forest, which rises into mountains around them. There's a single logging truck rolling up the winding incline into the mid-morning light. Smoke drifts from the chimneys of the houses. The people of this town drive trucks to work and their children walk to school. They get letters from banks. Store clerks pay attention to them and generally treat them with politeness. Every noon, at lunch, they read their newspapers in cafés. They are able to remain calm in most situations, but sometimes they explode.

The boy is the same age as the other kids, but almost twice as tall. He runs around the lawn in his filthy socks and is always pretending to punch people in the face. Nobody likes him, but for some reason he's always around. The children agree on a plan to lose him in the woods. At the edge of the forest, they scatter, running about two hundred meters into the trees, then falling to the ground to hide. The boy runs past and disappears into the bush, calling to the others in confusion. Five minutes later, the boys meet back at the clearing, collect their bikes and ride off, peddling fast down the dirt road, turning into the trails that lead back to town.

From this point of view we turn to consider the nature of passion and commitment among friends. Noticing the way the fog slowly erased the mountainside, the way the sawmill disappeared into the dark green of the fir trees, you tried to get me to talk you out of your malevolent plan, broach the issue of risk. But the complete unpredictability of the situation was its own argument to continue. The more we joked, the more it made sense. If the sound of rain were to drop away, the way a barometer drops when something goes missing, we would be able to hear the sound of moss creeping through the streets and into our thoughts. We would be able hear our breath quicken, the stillness of the woods becoming an animal in our stomach taking small, measured bites. Your face was alternately flushed or flat white. You said there was still time to be talked out of it. It's too late, I said. You'd have to kill yourself, which is why, I concluded, there is no fiction.

And this brings us to the precision of the landscape painter, the most prolific in town. It is actually impossible, at times, to distinguish his paintings from photographs. The one in your father's study, if you remember, showed the lumberjacks in action, while the one in my livingroom depicted a bear walking through a logging camp. You could almost smell the freshly cut wood. At this time of the morning, hesitation can mean losing the rhythm of creative process, wasting the whole day. We can imagine the painter shuffling through a stack of snapshots, looking for the one which will give him the spark to begin yet another painting. When the people of this small town aren't looking at the forest, we can imagine him thinking, they're looking at this.

VALERIE JOY KALYNCHUK
Mouth Froth Promise

Metro closed. Never mind about punishing it. Flower over the whole planet. Justify no appetite. Like train ride telepathy. Seven hands force the doors open and the go sound is over the warning speaker. You might hate the muffled language but it's sending you somewhere anyhow. Innate knowledge sometimes more satisfying than learning. Good of the grain. Auspicious message in morse. Going on with the thrill of headlights off. Cul-de-sac is a new direction. Never give up morning coffee. Appraise a sink in the stomach and every core organ. No one isn't listening but none will make do and push on nine to five. Rest against the mirrors pressed into the glass elevator. Books never shelved it's all right. Stacks of gesturing murmurings all tokens of being silver and red and read and blessed. Believe those who would come across the pebbled path. Coffee creamer as pseudo as you are.

Divine your rasp America. Unfold your generations, quick learners. Hover and huddle. Precipitous confession to the inlaws with their fenced in neglect. Steam scald those strangers today in the line up with their oblivious guessings. What would they have made of it had only one of them simply smiled. Slow drip passive. Peels at the ceiling in the room where a suitcase rests empty but for silk scarves perfumed with stale lavender rose or burnt vanilla and picture postcards of Venice without message, address, or caption. Wince at their insult on an evening cloaked in grey volcanic ash which keeps you from flying to those social teas and causes you to never look left for fear of seeing fallibility. Capsize the sublime. Plunge in after it. All waking life asleep. All seen through pellucid infant eyes. Sea to mountain peak. A chorus of one harmonizes in a forgotten language that has always been on the tip of your tongue. A crane to pick up this edifice erected out of a harness wish. A spot on an approaching tunnel. A cloud is a gift horse in the mouth. A split severed lip is a joke. A punch line too late is a gasp. A guess is a determined train wreck. Wane to be set up again. An honest answer to the wrong question is not a game.

Funambulist requests no net this time. Ear to ear grin waves away the short white gloved one who would spot him. No first self reproach no tease teetering. The audience is lost. He's taken their delicious vicarious fear made it spun sugar on stilts. Step over wasps nest. Disease dormant. Breed for gain or to be grilled. Soot lungs with the words iron will find out soon. Near brink collapse. A weight await to drown. Why ever negate this ease. He reaches the other side too soon. Wants to go back and do it again. Outstretches his arms, throws back his head, laughs. Does it so easy.

Flora and fauna are so spitefully entangled in and over themselves
dread locked matted. Too tightly bound to unravel. Light eyes
blur gaze before sharply back to sleep. River Nile desires true
breath. Relief cursive. There is a name which melts in an eddy of
hot blowing snow. In the countryside we are so lost, vacant land
that forgets its own predictable weather. Birds we've never seen
in these parts return. Shakes stop in time. Ocean longs to give up
its brink. Settle for more than being forever driven by the moon.
Ellipses in your argument. All those flicker lash utterings. Scope
of the future. Your own ebb retreats and always comes back
again. Want to confine you to the vast Sahara where bedouin boil
mint tea and lower their eyes in knowing half smiles.

Shot put while off balance. Forget about the Arctic diamond mines, the barren ocean, the broken forests. Will not ride will walk to bend the present history. Lie awake to melt the fever dreams of canceled cheques. Every species denied evolution. Every human heart in devolution. High and mighty will not meet half way. Scratch words into fabric not tough enough to withstand long distance human trial and error. Not some Vesuvian ideas erupting on their own. Cannot clamor. Sprint down the avenue gripping stolen gardenias. Apprehension of wild animals. Mouth froth promise. Dash through a parade of a thousand, choosing oblivious oblivion. Stragglers will finish at the ribbon.

VICTORIA STANTON
Dee-Dee the Epilator

"Ohmygod. Feel this."

It's Dee-Dee. Sitting two desks over from me in homeroom. I'm supposed to stretch my arm out, across the loose-leaf binder spread open in front of Davie on his desk that sits squarely between me and Dee.

"Quick, c'mere. Feel this!"

She's got her pant leg pulled up slightly above the top seam of her tube sock exposing a small patch of smooth olive-coloured skin. She's proudly rubbing the area with a pointed index finger. She won't give up until I've tested and verified her truth.

"*Hello*!? It's now or never!"

Bent over Davie's desk I touch her leg. "Yeah, it's smooth."

"I know. I shaved this morning. Here Davie, you can check too."

It got to the point where Dee-Dee didn't even have to say anything, she just had to pick up her pant leg and point her index finger at her calf, and we all understood: Dee-Dee shaved today. It became the national sign of our grade ten class — picking up the pant leg while passing each other in the hall. Davie, Ian and Michael started standing next to their lockers, rubbing their own legs with stubby index fingers. Not in a lewd way either. Just an acknowledgment of how obsessed Dee was with what seemed to have become her favourite pastime: shaving and showing off her hairless legs.

*

"Ohmygod. I love Mark. I love Mark *so* much."

It's Dee-Dee. Sitting at her desk behind me in Chemistry. I hear her whispering the words of a lust-struck fifteen year-old, consumed with thoughts of after school snacks. I, fresh off the mall circuit from lunchtime, rub my newly pierced and infected earlobe.

"It's not fair that we can't both have love at the same time." This is Dee-Dee lamenting the fact that my boyfriend just dumped me. She has no idea what I feel like. I feel like my whole world just collapsed. I feel like I want to go to sleep and stay in my bed forever except that when I'm in bed too long I start to hyperventilate. I feel all these things that I have no name for. But I don't want to talk about it because I'm more interested in talking about Dee-Dee.

"Mark and I started doing it." It's Dee-Dee walking next to me out of the locker room and into the gymnasium. Now she's rubbing her whole leg with the entire palm of her hand because now she's in gym shorts. She has the kind of skin that turns the perfect colour brown in summer.

"Oh, I love Mark. Mmm…. I love Mark *soooooo* much." She moans these words like she's just woken up from a valium-induced sleep.

"One day, we will both be happy at the same time." She, of course, speaking the universal language of "it is only with the company of a steady boyfriend that we will ever feel normal and complete."

And at sixteen, I know exactly what she means.

*

"Ohmygod. This is *so* weird. You call this *music?* It sounds like someone's being *strangled.*" Dee-Dee seems to share the same opinion with my mother.

I'm sampling new sounds because I know there has to be more to radio than "Like A Virgin." I hear Madonna and instantly feel nauseous, my distaste so deep as to originate somewhere in my liver. I make Dee tune in to Brave New Waves one night at her house and she can't stop laughing. I don't find it funny at all.

But she's my friend and I persist. We have listening sessions at my place and I foist one cassette after another on her. I see her eyes start to cross and it makes me agitated. I say, "It's not top-40, okay? It's called 'Alternative'." She's hating every minute of it and her distance is making me cranky. We both sit and pout.

"Alternative to what?" snaps Dee, "Listening to *real* music and being in a *good* mood?"

One such evening, I am struck with menstrual pain so severe I'm crawling around the apartment on all fours. She's convinced my 'Alternative' music is making me physically disintegrate.

*

"Ohmygod. Lisa. You *have* to hear this."

It's Dee-Dee catching up to me in the bathroom. It's lunchtime and my fifth visit in fifteen minutes. My period is ruining my life.

"Lisa. Listen to this. The Smiths found The Cure for The Cramps." She pauses for my reaction then folds in hysterics.

I want to swat her for making light of my torture. And yet, I'm impressed. She can't stand listening to my heroes whining and shriveling but has found it in her heart to remember their names.

She gives me a hug and sniffs my neck. She likes the perfume I wear. It's ridiculously pricey but she and a few of our other friends chipped in to get me a bottle for my sixteenth birthday.

"Ohmygod. You smell so good. But your hair looks *totally* strange."

Dee-Dee has a way of making me feel great and awful, all at the same time. She bounces out of the bathroom leaving me to contemplate whether Robert Smith buys expensive cologne.

VINCENT TINGUELY
Jackie

That first year Jackie and I were in separate classes, and in separate Boy Scout patrols. We both lived on the military base nestled just behind the promontory where Old Fort Henry dominated the shore of Lake Ontario, the mouth of the Rideau River, and across the river, the Limestone City. CFB Kingston's residential area looked much like any *Peanuts* comic strip suburb anywhere, with meandering roads, great green playgrounds and schoolyards, and cookie-cutter houses. The base had a poor cousin relationship with the city. The Barrifield bus, which linked the base with the town, was always the crummiest, oldest, stinkiest bus they had, a leftover from the fifties. I loved that old bus. The rounded hull, fore and aft, the worn chromium poles, the vinyl-padded old seats, the Singer sewing machine clatter of the deisel engine as we made the long grade up to the base, the damp smell of wool in winter, dark outside and not even suppertime yet, clattering up where the highway cut through a hump of limestone, jagged layers of rock ramping up on either side.

Summer days Jackie and I would sometimes wander out in the fields beyond the PMQs where he lived, through old farmers' fields long gone fallow, good berry picking country in the late summer and fall. In the spring we walked through copses of tightly clustered lilac bushes, where paths wove like a labyrinth through heavenly aromatic blossoms. We'd follow hard-packed dirt paths that led to the top of the rock cut over the highway, where we'd enact endless Everest scenarios on narrow limestone ledges, and discover the old bore holes where they'd planted the dynamite to make the cut. *We were up there and now we're down here,* I'd think after making the long descent. We'd walk down the hill into Kingston from the rock cut, testing our powers of ESP on each other – first, Jack'd hold an image in his mind, and I'd try to guess it, and then I'd do the same. We kept hitting it two out of three times, which seemed to be more than coincidence could explain. As far as we were concerned, telepathy was a reality. There was the girdered lift bridge over the river to cross, the endlessly changing waters of the lake, the islands offshore, RMC, the Martello Tower. There were Airfix models to be bought on Princess Street, Testors glue for the assembly and matte paints to adorn them. We had Panther and Tiger and Sherman and T-34 tanks to duke it out on bunk bed battlefields, tiny soldiers from five or six armies, anachronistically mustered from two or three different wars. Aimless perigrinations through the Giant Tiger and the Met, guzzling purple grape drink from the burbling lunch counter dispenser. Splurging on the photo booth and pulling a series of insane faces, splitting the results fifty-fifty. Jack had elaborately shaped eyebrows like racing stripes on a car, slightly devilish, paradoxically sleepy blue eyes, curly corkscrew brown hair, running to fat yet dynamic. His sharp mind kept mine sharp like a whetstone.

Summer days were also spent tooling around the base on our bikes – once I'd succeeded in extracting Jackie from his bed, which generally didn't happen until noon, or later. I'd been up for hours already, drawing Total Ninny cartoons and playing with Fred and Charlie, my favourite rubber monsters, and making an elastic band banjo between the two knobs of the white china cabinet until my father'd had enough of the twanging and I'd ventured forth on my green-and-white CCM standard to find my friend. Jackie's mother let him stay up late watching movies when he didn't have to go to school. I'd inevitably find him semiconscious, swaddled in blankets, maybe listening to tunes on his boxy portable record player. One fave was Arlo Guthrie making fun of the Vietnam war. We could recite the whole thing just about word for word: *"Kid, have you rehabilitated yourself?" And I said, "You got a lot of damn gall asking me if I'm moral enough to kill women, children, villages, burn bodies after bein' a litterbug."* Musing over a comic book or some object of interest, a model, an H.O. scale train engine, a particularly finely detailed boxcar.... "Geez it's twelve o'clock, let's go."

"In a minute." A minute infinitely stretched to ten minutes, half an hour, an hour.... I extended the microphone of a cassette recorder in his direction.

"Mr. Connaught can you explain to the audience your current predicament?"

"Well, Mr. Ebersohl, it would seem that I've slipped off the edge of the bed and am currently trapped, I say trapped, between the wall and the bed."

"With just the one leg still up on the bed —"

"And my arm, I'm barely holding on."

"Is there anything we can do?"

"Yes. Get the wrecker!"

The wrecker was a tow truck, but a monster tow truck that could lift the enormous vehicles of the military, the deuce-and-a-halfs and the three-quarter tons, even APCs and tanks, right up onto its back. It required a wrecker to get Jack out of his bedroom on these lazy mornings.

The base was split in half by the highway — our half, between the highway and the lake, was where the PMQs were, the schools, the gas station, and the new shopping plaza where some wag had graffitied a huge *FLQ* in black letters on the cinderblock backside of the Canex store. Further along, the military barracks and the parade squares could be found, where the soldiers marched in circles under soaring elms. On the far side of the highway were miscellaneous 'temporary' structures — buildings thrown up quickly during the Second World War and still in use these decades later. Housing, for instance, the photography club, and the old Canex annex where they set up Santa's Toyshop every year and where I'd bought my very first album, Iron Butterfly's *Ina Gada Da Vida*. One day Jack led the charge across the highway and into this dilapidated part of the base. Eventually the pavement stopped and gave way to gravel, buildings petered out entirely and we were buzzing along through the wooded training grounds. It was a drizzly day, not ideal for exploring, but not so bad we couldn't stop occasionally to take a sip from our army surplus aluminum canteens, or nibble on a cookie, or just look around at pretty much nothing.

We were on a stretch of gravel road running through a fairly spread out patch of woods when a soldier stepped out and stood waiting for us there by the road. He was wearing green combats, black boots, a helmet adorned with freshly cut leafy twigs, and a poncho. Jack pulled up by him and I pulled up by Jack, and Jack started to talk with him just like that, like it was perfectly normal and everyday that a soldier would just step out of the woods in the middle of nowhere and start talking to a couple of kids. It was while Jack and the soldier chatted that I noticed, with a start, that there were trucks, and tents, and soldiers all around us, draped in camouflaged netting and cut brush. We were in the very midst of a whole motorized platoon under cover. I grabbed Jack's arm, pointed out a TOW missile launcher mounted on a jeep. "Cool!"

"Yeah, I know."

I began to get the sense that Jack had already been out here before, maybe with his Dad, and had already seen this set-up, and he had thought to bring me here too, without saying what it was we were going to see, just so I could have that same holy secret joy of discovery.

We hadn't been friends for very long when I landed my first-ever job, a paper route for the Kingston *Whig-Standard*. I started it in the summer between grades six and seven, making my way from Paardeburg Square, where my house was, out across the huge playing fields of Lundy's Lane school, and to the point where Batoche Crescent intersected with Niagara Park. It was the edge of a plateau overlooking the clustered houses along Batoche, beyond which the PMQs stopped and the land dipped gently down toward the lake. Every day I meandered along that declivity and around the crescent to Niagara Park and then back up the hill to the intersection again.

Jackie had immediately volunteered himself as a partner in my enterprise. I welcomed the idea. Upon announcing my plan to the family circle, my brother suggested I offer Jack a buck for the privilege of doing half the route. Given that the take was a whopping $6.80 per week, I thought this wasn't very fair at all, but since my brother knew everything and I knew nothing, this was what I proposed to Jackie the next time I saw him. However, Jack's mother, no fool she, intervened at this point.

"How much do you make a week?" she asked.

"Six-eighty."

"Well, then Jack should get more than a dollar, shouldn't he? I mean he'll be doing half the work."

"Not all of it, I still have to do the paperwork," I said.

"Oh, I see."

I thought about what my brother had told me to say. "And anyway, it's my paper route. I'm responsible."

Jack's Mom nodded sagely. "Still, he'll be doing a lot of the work, it's probably worth more than a dollar."

I shrugged. "How much do you think I should pay?"

"Well, why don't you keep a dollar a week for the other stuff you do, the administrative stuff, and split the rest?"

I mulled it over. "That sounds okay," I said. So Jack became my partner for the princely sum of $2.90 per week. There was always a certain amount of friction over that extra dollar and I don't know why, but I could never bring myself to just split it down the middle. So it went for the summer, and then on into early September when we were enrolled in Lundy's Lane, a kind of junior high for grades seven and eight where all the big kids went. We were astonished to discover on our first day that we were now the big kids.

The powers that be had divided the classes at Lundy's Lane five ways, based on the grade standings of the students. Being an almost straight A student at the time, I found myself in 7E – the intellectual elite of the seventh graders. Meanwhile poor Jackie's laisser-faire attitude toward school and C average had landed him in 7B. On one level I was completely diplomatic about it because Jack was now my fast friend and I didn't want to hurt his feelings, but I probably lamented at least a little that he wasn't in my class because if he was we'd be having so much fun! But no, he was under the tutelage of the inimicable Mrs. Hogeboom, who was something like a nineteenth century matron, and I was the pet of Mrs. Galt, equally ancient but somewhat more modern in her outlook on school life. (We knew they were both incredibly old because they could remember the days when they were just starting out as student teachers, and Old Fort Henry served as a prison camp for German POWs.)

Our paper route was handy to us during school days; we'd zip on our bikes across the field between the school and the inter-section where the papers were dropped off, fill up our respective paperbags and zoom around the circuit in a matter of a half-hour. We left our bikes in the playground behind the houses, and when we finished our route it still wasn't supper time and there was nothing to do, so we played on the swings or just goofed off. One idyllic fall day I was standing on the hard wooden swing, pumping to get it up high. Because I was twelve, I was practical-ly too big to play on the swings and they were kind of stupid if you didn't try to go recklessly high. At the peak of one of these high, reckless back swings the chains suddenly went slack, and my feet lost contact with the seat and I was launched backwards into space. I instinctively threw my hands out behind me and landed hard on my back, and not suprisingly, when I regained consciousness and lifted my hands up in front of my face, my left wrist was grotesquely twisted.

"Fuck I broke my arm! Fuck!" I couldn't move, I just lay there staring at it and shrieking. "Fuck!"

"Can you feel anything?"

I looked at Jack's face hovering over me, the bright blue sky behind his halo-like curls. "No!"

"Can you get up?"

"I dunno!" I staggered to my feet with his help, cradled my

busted paw against my chest. "Fuck!"

"What're we gonna do?" he said.

"Go ask someone for help," I said. Jackie balked.

"Who?"

"I dunno. Where's the doctor live? Let's go there!" We went across the playground to the doctor's back door and knocked on it. In a minute a woman with a pinched, worried expression opened the door.

"Yes?"

Jackie blurted, "He busted his arm!" I shoved it in her general direction, hoping my tear-streaked face would get the message across. "Is your husband the doctor home?"

She shook her head. "No, he's not home yet."

"Oh."

She looked at my broken arm, and began to gently close the door. "You should go home now, I'm sure your parents will help you."

Jack and I stared at each other, flabbergasted.

"What're we gonna do now?" I asked.

"Well, I guess we better go to your place," Jack said.

"But that's like a million miles!"

"Come on, I'll help you."

"Wait, what about my bike?"

"Leave it, you can get it later."

I couldn't believe the lady had shut the door in our faces. What a pig! Jack and I cursed her as only twelve-year-olds can curse – the cursing seemed to warm our hearts and made it easier for me to make it up the hill, across the fields of Lundy's Lane, and through the meandering streets of the base to Paardeburg. We got home just as my Mom was pulling up the driveway in the Rambler from work. She took one look at me, thanked Jack for his help, bundled me into the front passenger seat of the car and drove me into Kingston and the hospital emergency ward.

Next Saturday morning I was struggling to get my paper bag strap over my shoulder, awkward with my left arm in a sling, a cast from wrist to elbow. Jack had come to meet me — we were going to walk to the route, because obviously I couldn't ride my bike. "Are you ever a dummy," Jack said.

"What do you mean?"

"Falling off a swing and breaking your arm."

"I guess you're right there."

"You're a real dummy, all round, all right. You're supposed to be so smart, but you can't stay on a swing."

"So what?" I wasn't in the mood to take Jackie's arbitrary abuse.

"So you're a dummy. Mr. Smartie who can't stay on a swing."

I suddenly knew what this was really about. "I'm a dummy eh? *You're* the dummy in 7B, almost in 7A!" 7A was reserved for 'special' students.

Jack just glared at me for a long instant, then threw down the paper bag and walked off. "No, don't!" I protested weakly. "Come back. How'm I gonna do the route by myself?" But he just kept walking. I had to deliver the whole route, broken arm and all, and then walk my bike back — it was still there in the playground, a couple of spokes busted out where I had put my hand through the front wheel. I thought it was all over between us. Suddenly the coming school year looked bleak, empty, horrid. And what about Scouts? We were in the same patrol, finally, and now we hated each other! It was a nightmare.

Sunday dragged itself by somehow, and I made my dejected way to school Monday morning. I walked into my class, 7E, and there was Jackie sitting right in the first row. He looked at me with this smug expression, and I went along to my own desk in a kind of haze of astonishment. Jackie was in 7E. A strange new light seemed to be shining in the classroom, a light full of mystery, brighter than the autumn sunshine pouring through the windows. I waited restlessly for recess, and then caught up with

Jackie in the corridor on the way out to the schoolyard.

"What're you doing in 7E?" I asked.

"Well, they made a mistake when they put me in 7B," Jack said.

"Oh." We walked along without talking for a minute. Then I said, "Are you going to come deliver papers with me today?"

"I dunno." Jackie was uncharacteristically avoiding my gaze, shuffling his Adidas in the gravel of the school yard.

"Come on. You know I never meant it."

"Oh yeah?" Jackie didn't look very convinced.

"You *know* you're not a dummy. You're as smart as me!"

"Do you really think so?"

"Yeah!"

I never figured out how Jackie ended up in 7E. At the time, it seemed to partake of the same magic as our ESP exchanges and the secret encampments in the forest. Later, I realized it was his mother, of course, who saw what had happened between us, and went to bat against the whole school system to save her son's friendship. No fool, she.

MARC NGUI

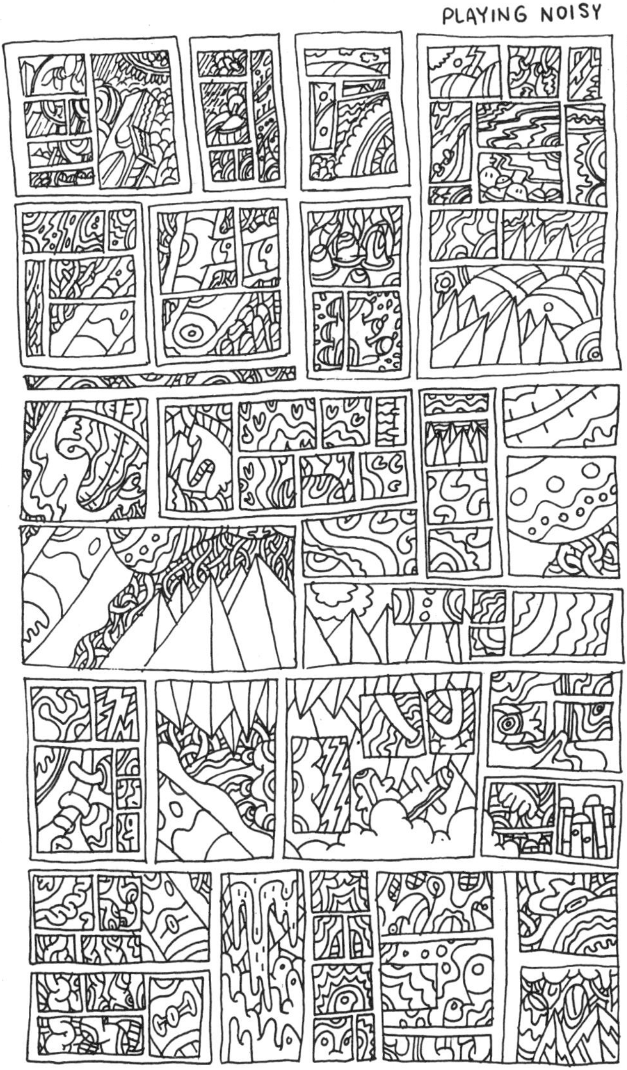
PLAYING NOISY
JULY 14 04

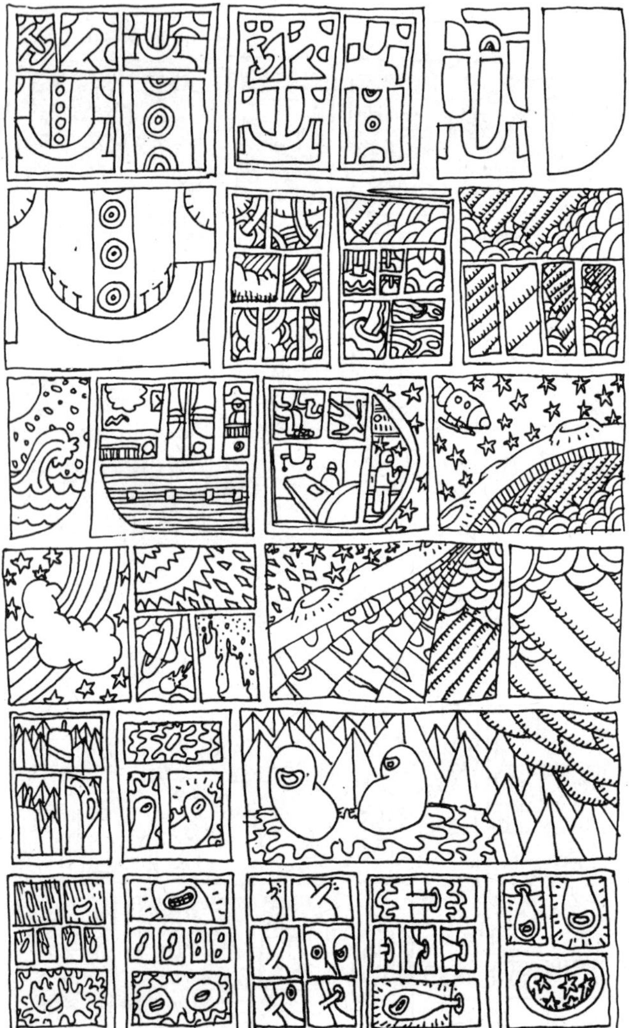

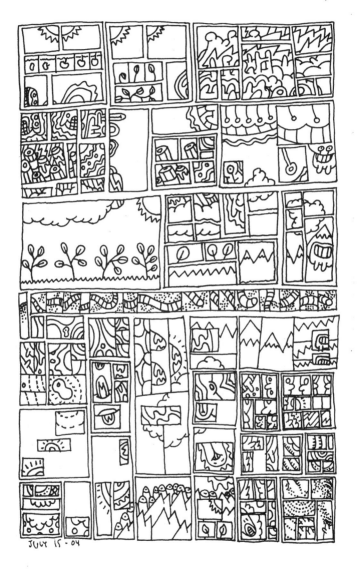

JULY 15 - 04

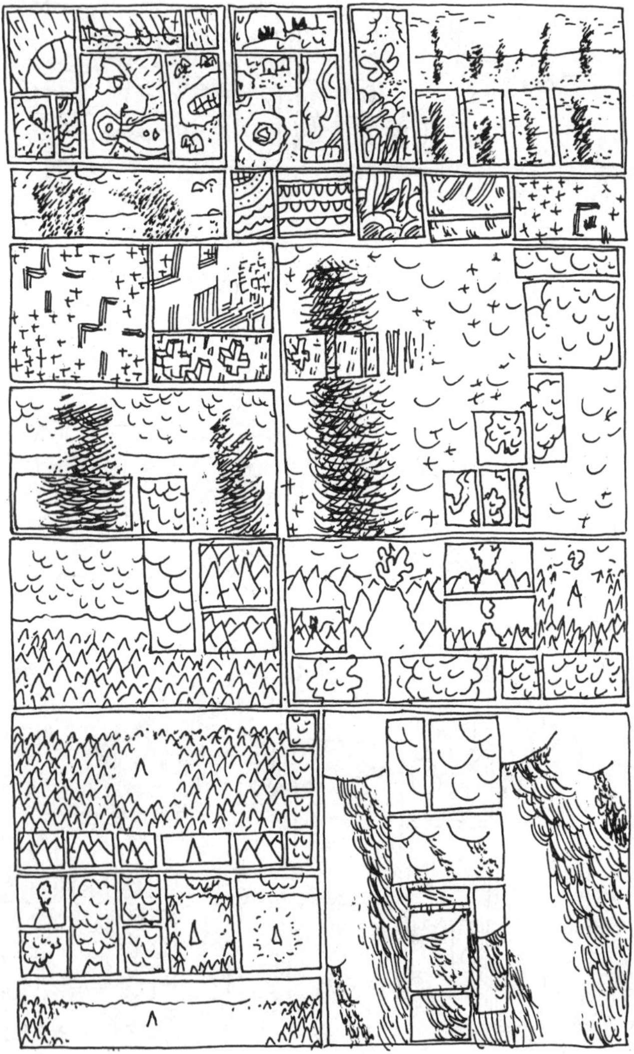

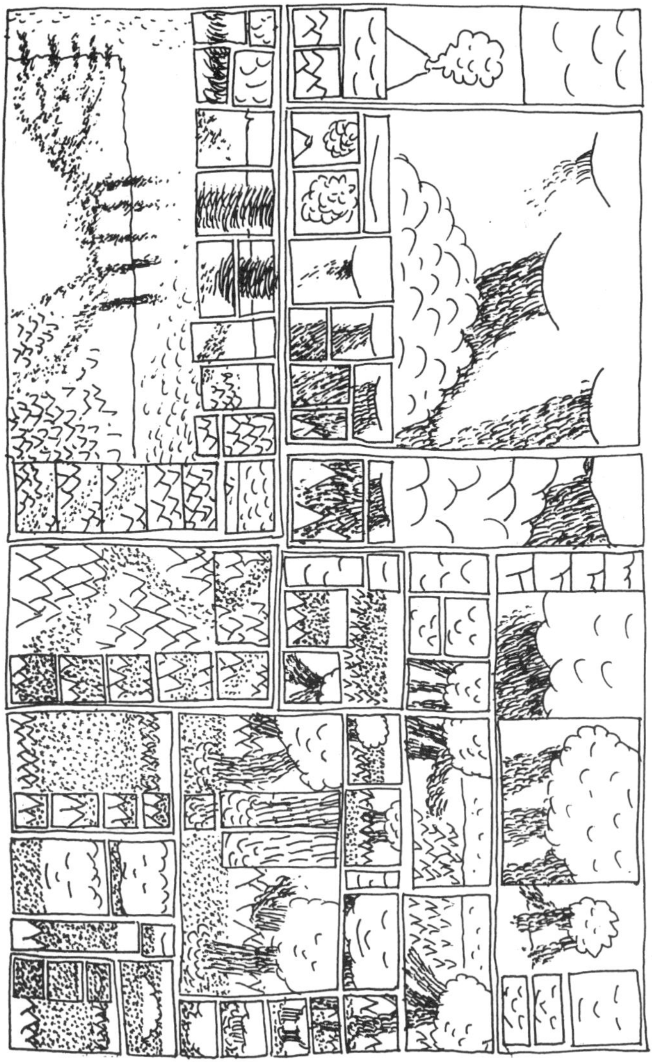

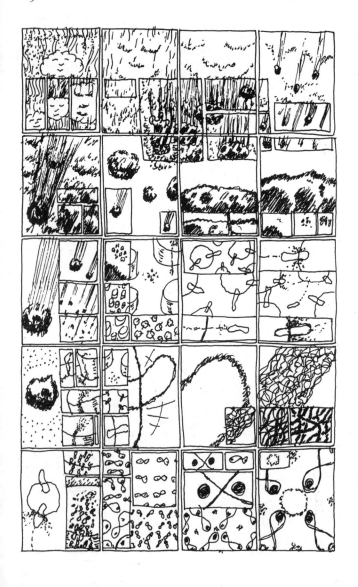

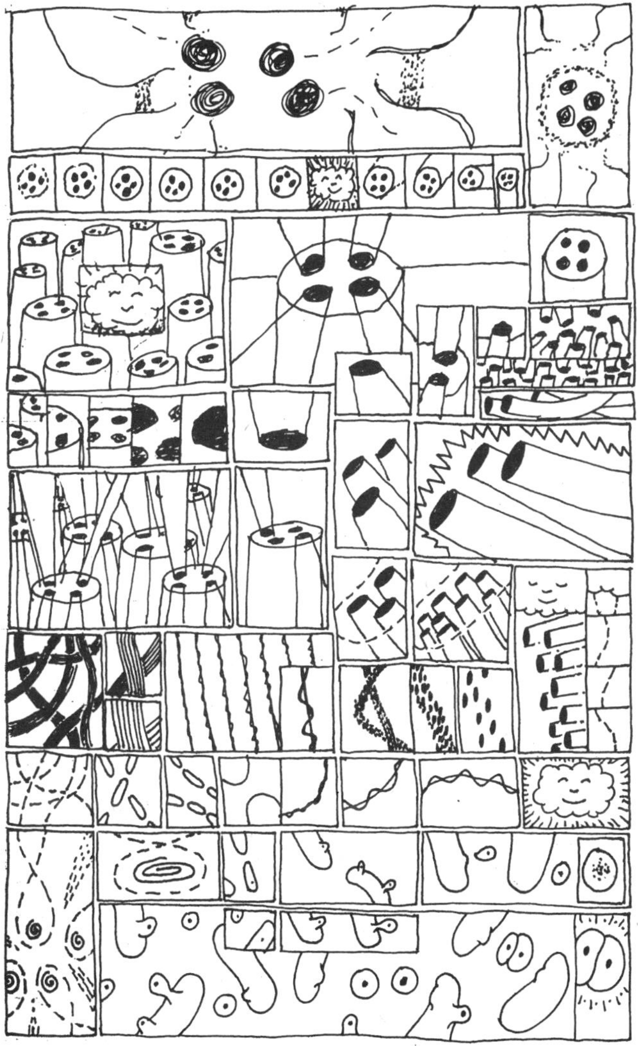

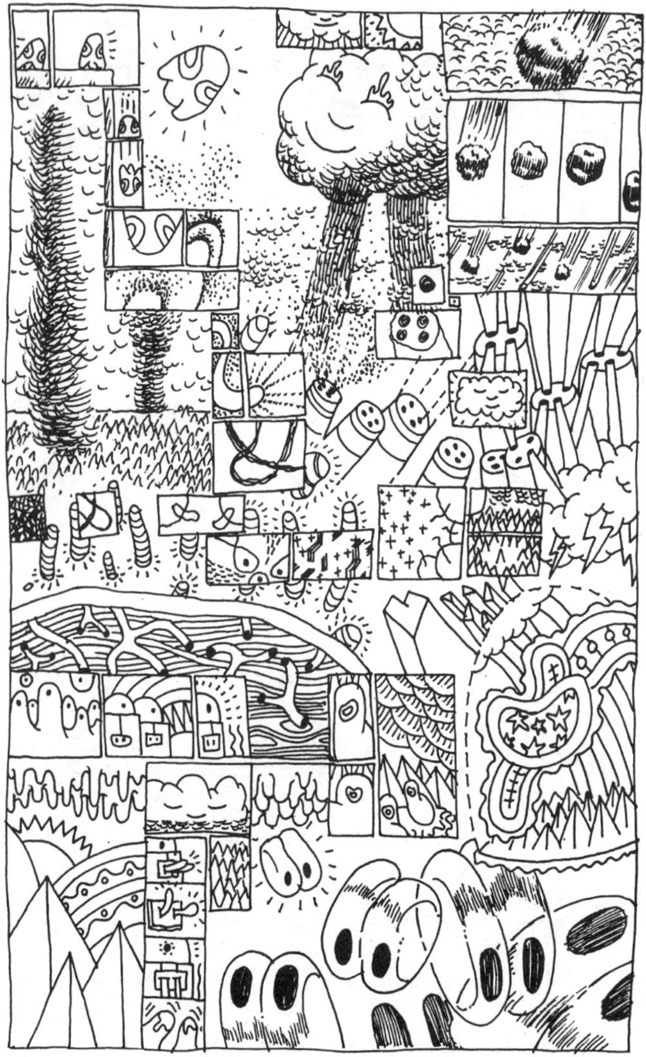

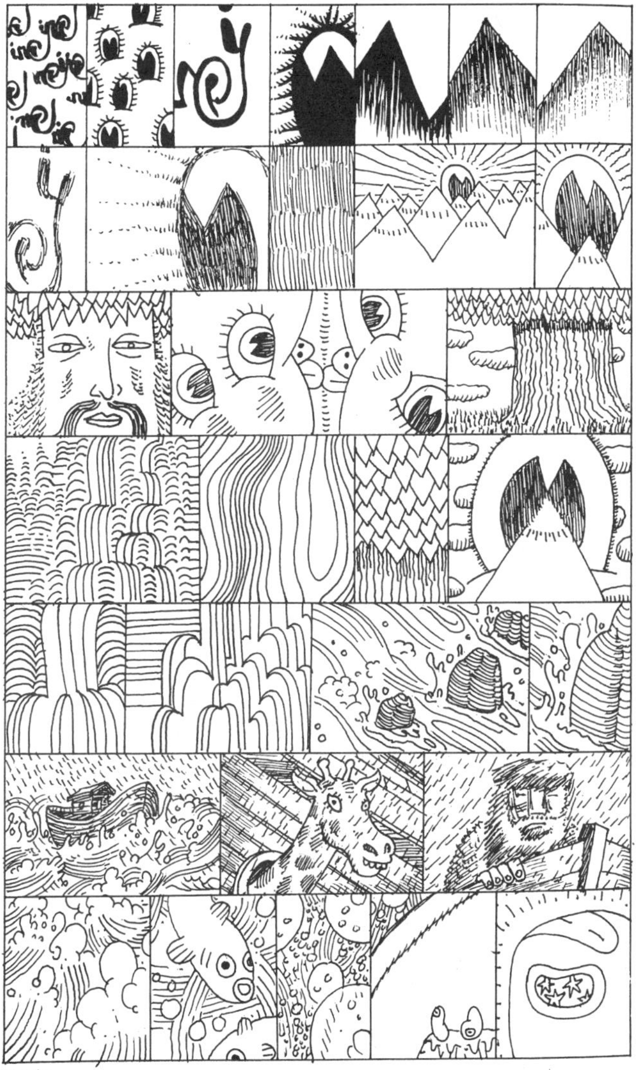

AUG 06.

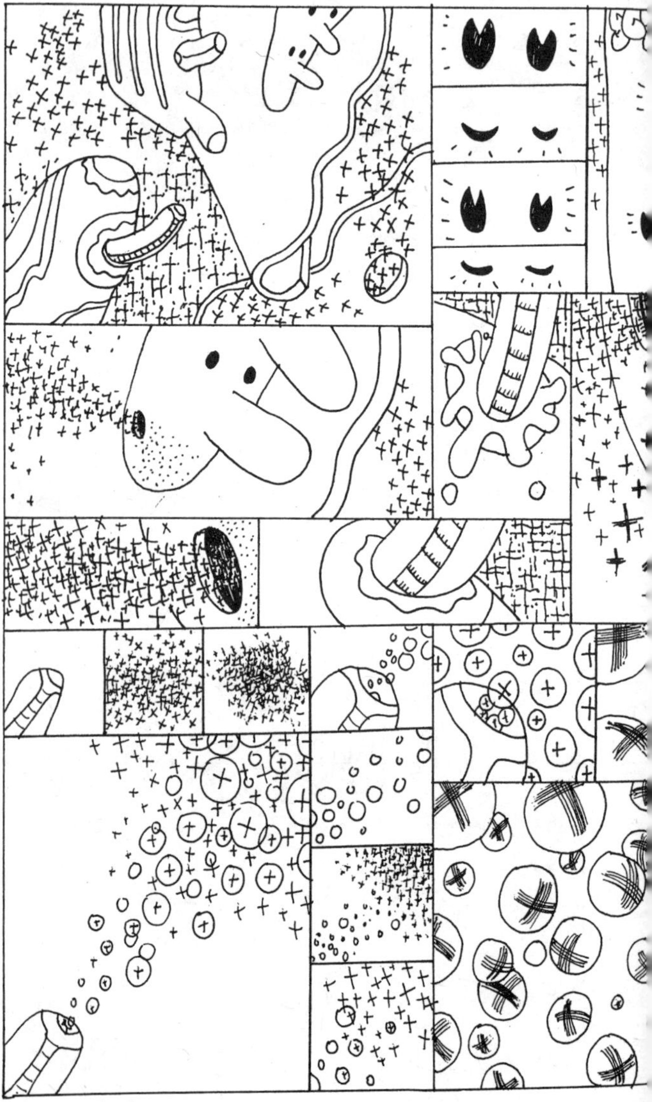
JULY 31 - AUG 4, 04

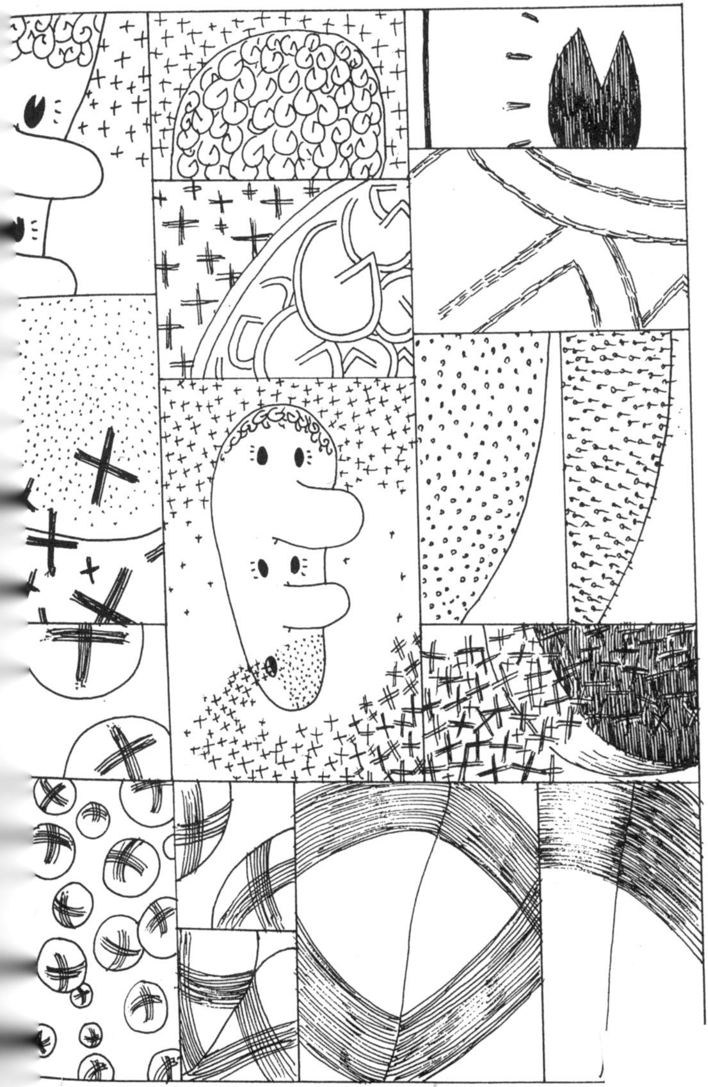

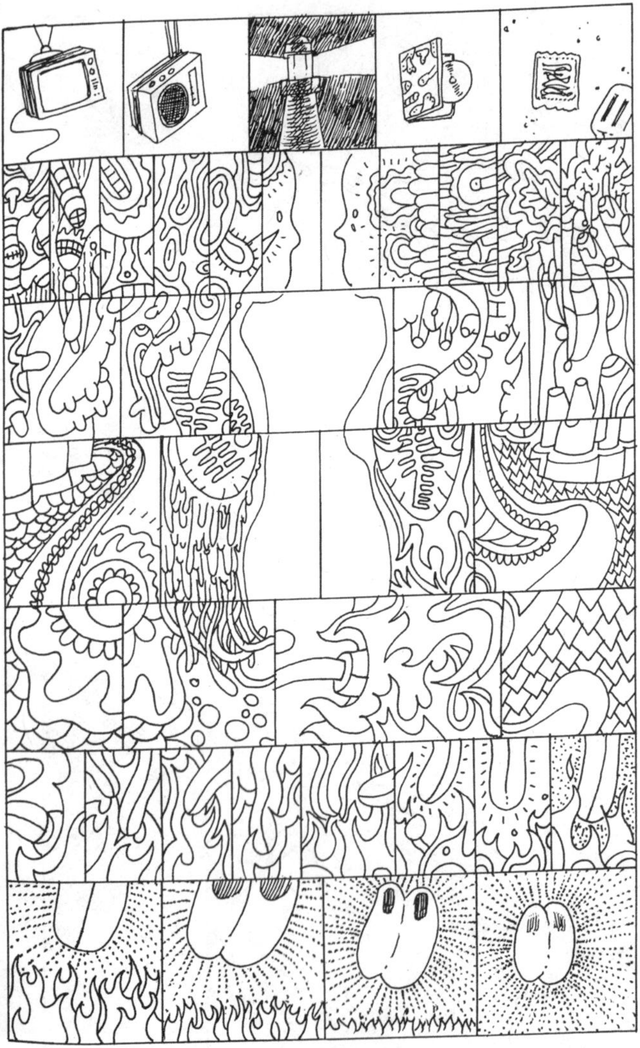

COREY FROST
Genji, the Shining One

Translator's note: *Genji Monogatari (The Tale of Genji)*, the world's first novel, was written in Japan around 1000 AD by a woman named Murasaki Shikibu. It narrates Prince Genji's haphazard and Quixotic search for a perfect love. This version, featuring the vocabulary and cadences of modern Japanese English, was written by a troubled narratologist in 2000, at night.

CHAPTER 1: HIKARU GENJI

This is just what you've been looking for. This story about young men was made by young men, for young men. For breezy, fashionable gentlemen like us. Get acquainted with it. This is the beginning of a relationship that will last a lifetime. This is super. It's the sexual escapades of Genji, the Emperor's son, who is filled with youthful innocence and vivacity. He is so handsome! that even many persons of ripe experience are astounded that such a creature could actually have been born in these latter and degenerate days. Some people say that his nickname Genji, The Shining One was given to him by a Korean fortune-teller. Who knows? Authentic elegance has an incredible power which changes the surrounding atmosphere. This story is about the dissipation of an era of elegance, and sentiment. It is full of strange occurrences. The people in the palace whispered among themselves that in the Land Beyond the Sea, such occurrences had led to riots and disorder and catastrophe. What a melancholy story. Some of the events are dismal, but once I have told the story, you won't be sad. Because, instead your faith in the logic of existence will be renewed and you will want to enthusiastically embrace life. Maybe you were afraid of misfortune in the past, but you won't be now. Let's grab the moment, you'll say. Let's get tomorrow! You will say, I hope that more suffering will soon arrive in my path, so that I can throw myself at it with zealous abandon. Bring it on, you will say. I want it. I need it. Now is a good time to begin, I think.

CHAPTER 2: THE BROOM TREE

It is the rainy season. Tonight there is a steady downpour and there are not many people around the Palace. Just the frogs, who are happy-go-lucky and always have a good time. Genji is looking at books in a comfortable chair. Its stylish and casual design has original themes for enjoyable life co-ordination. We have to live together with our interior; that's for certain. His best friend To no Chujo is playing the flute. Suddenly Genji goes to his desk and pulls out some letters. To no Chujo immediately becomes curious. It's just in his nature. I can show you some of the letters, says Genji, but there are others which I'd rather not.... But those are just what I want to see, says To no Chujo. I have no interest in ordinary, commonplace letters. What I want to see are passionate letters written in moments of resentment, letters hinting consent, letters written at dusk.... Finally Genji allows him to peruse the contents of the desk. There are stupendous piles of letters, including many like the ones To no Chujo mentioned, but of course the most revealing ones Genji has already hidden out of sight. They are from all of his lovers, and women that he wants to be his lovers. Genji is a prince and he has to keep up the appearance of respectability, and besides, the frivolous dallyings of his companions do not interest him. But when on rare occasions, despite all resistance, love does gain a hold on him, it is always in the most improbable and hopeless entanglement that he becomes involved.

Then Genji wants to see some of To no Chujo's letters. I will show you, says To no Chujo, if you will tell me about your outrageous love-life. There is no time like the present, says Genji. That is our motto.

CHAPTER 3: KIRITSUBO

Once upon a time, there lived an extremely pretty girl with
chestnut-coloured hair. Well, one night when the sky was so
clear and the stars shining so bright, she opened a window in a
dreamy state of mind and found an exceedingly beautiful bird
perched there. I am the Emperor of the Land, it said, and long-
ing to meet you has made me become a bird and fly over here to
see you. Now, I must return to the castle immediately so I shall
leave to you gifts of all my heart. No sooner had this emerald-
coloured bird flown back in the sky, the stars twinkled and then
started to fall down radiantly one after another into the hands of
the girl, and the stars were altered to abundant sweets. The only
star that remained in the sky is said to be still shining. It is called
the 'Blue Star'. The girl awoke. I have had such a strange dream,
she thought. But the next day the Emperor called for her to
come to the palace. He was crazy about her. So the girl went to
live at the palace.

But her life was miserable, because everyone else in the
palace was jealous. The Emperor lavished all his affections on
this young girl who was, besides, of a pitifully low rank, so people hated her. Once someone locked the door of a passageway,
so that the poor girl wandered back and forth for hours, in a
state of extreme distress. All the honours heaped upon her had
brought with them terror rather than joy. Then, she had a
bouncing baby boy. Lovely! It was the Emperor's son. When he
saw the boy, even the Emperor was overcome by his beauty.
Soon the young prince was three years old. It was time for the
Putting on of the Trousers.

Kiritsubo had become ill. The constant persecution by the
other ladies-in-waiting was too much. People die of hate all the
time. In this story about a perfect and enduring love, people
sometimes die because they are filled with hate, or someone else
is filled with hate for them, or else they are jealous, or they are
lonely, and they get ill because of this, and their lovers come to

their bedsides every day and send poems beseeching them to recover, asking them not to take everything so seriously, that it's not the end of the world, but they do not recover; they languish in the throes of vague, indefinable maladies and eventually they die. Sometimes is it simply because they are in love. Kiritsubo asked to return to her house, but the Emperor begged her to stay. He found her in her quarters, still beautiful, but weak, her skin wan. She scarcely seemed alive. But the Emperor lamented: we promised each other we would be together to the end. How can I let her go?

He couldn't sleep. In the night, a messenger arrived with a letter. It was a poem, the last thing she had written before dying. It said this is a dream from a sincere soul. It incorporates many romantic feelings and painful stuff. It's pure life. Please listen to my dream with a fresh heart. The Emperor sat and stared into space, motionless. The funeral ceremony took place at Atago and was celebrated with great splendour. The servants who waited on the Emperor had a miserable life, because all day and all night he cried, day after day.

Chapter 4: The Flower Feast

Genji: Did you do anything interesting today? To no Chujo: A very angry day. Very sad day. Very tedious day. And you? Genji: In the afternoon, the sunlight was really mild, so I drank tea with my friends. We always meet once a week like that. As usual. Travel, fashion, games, love, poetry, etc. We talk and talk, not being conscious of the time. And at last we had a wonderful idea. We will tell one another our dreams. It's true when they say that beautiful things are beyond time. To no Chujo: I'm ready for a long weekend of festive fun. I want to go away with a good time in my mind. I very much like to eat. So I am quite sticky about sweets. My choice is always 'this'. What is this? It is just the taste of spring, summer, autumn and winter. An erotic relationship with the proper names for everything. Please keep in mind, my first marriage was one of convenience. What feeling do you need the most in your lifestyle, right now? A trendy feeling, a natural feeling, a traditional feeling. Excitement and comfort are the basics of our living style. You can't have one without the other. I'm going to do some research into this. The flower feast begins tonight!

CHAPTER 5: CLOUD-DWELLER'S TEARS

The time of the autumn equinox had come. He sent the quiver-bearer's daughter with a message to the home of Genji's grand-mother, where Genji had lived since Kiritsubo's death. The garden was overgrown and the house in ill repair, and the grand-mother burst into uncontrollable weeping. The Emperor's message went something like this: I had thought that after a while there might be some blurring, some slight effacement. But no. As days and months go by, the more senseless, the more unendurable my life becomes. I am continually thinking of the child, wondering how he fares. The Emperor sent an allegorical poem in which he asked the grandmother to bring Genji back to the palace. The sinking moon was shining in a cloudless sky. In the grass, the bell-crickets tinkled their compelling cry. The quiver-bearer's daughter then recited a poem mentioning the bell-crickets, and the grandmother answered with a poem about the cloud-dweller's tears, because the people at court are called the dwellers above the clouds. When the grandmother died, Genji began to live at the palace.

He was now twelve years old and the time for his Initiation had come. He was also to be married, to the daughter of the Minister of the Right, whose name was Blue. The horses from the royal stables and the hawks from the royal falconry were to be gifts for him. The ceremony was to happen in the East Wing of the Emperor's own apartments. The Emperor himself had directed all the preparations. Genji arrived at the hour of the monkey.

CHAPTER 6: THE BRIDGE OF DREAMS

It is a distant old dream, says Genji. There is a blue sky and sun-shine, and the sea that goes on and on. I am on a small island as I recover consciousness. I can't remember whether I do anything there or not. I just memorize the sky and the sun and the sea. You have to understand, this isn't to say that the dream was just a dream, to tell the truth.

People who lived at court were called dwellers above the clouds, and most of the time they were engaged in poetry or sex, or poetry that slyly alluded to sex. So few people communicate by writing poems now, which makes this a sad story. Not many people communicate by sex, either. The moral of this story is that there should be more poetry, and poetry which alludes to sex, or sex which somehow conveys or alludes to poetry. The world was so different then. It was wider, and sparklier.

CHAPTER 7: UTSUSEMI

It was getting dark. The position of the Earth Star made it unlucky for Genji to return to the Palace so he went to stay with Ki no Kami. Also in this house was a young woman who was Ki no Kami's father's new wife. Genji was not given a chance to meet her, but through a screen he overheard her discussing him and he was intrigued. Late at night, he crept into her room and told her he was in love with her, and spent all night trying to con-vince her to be his lover. She was reluctant because of the obvi-ous futility of any kind of relations between them, given their respective positions. He began to write letters, which her young brother would deliver, but she didn't write back. At length he contrived an excuse to visit the house again, but she refused to see him. He gave the boy a poem to bring her, and she sent one back. It's sweet whisper time, she said. The wind whispers soft-ly, the flowers whisper sweetly, the earth is whispering joyously, here the tender colour is overflowing, in peaceful co-operation.

Genji ended up with only the boy for company, whom he found not a bad substitute for his sister.

CHAPTER 8: THE BROOM TREE

So far, the crocuses are only peeking out at the rain. A happy present from the earth! It was breezing a little as I rode here, and I thought how the air is already becoming crisp, and then I remembered my earliest days. You know, Chujo, even now when the curtains billow in the hallway I feel unspeakable happiness. Innocence, Rapture, Fatalism – this is the space where we can be willing to enjoy peaceful times. Sometimes I feel down and I want to kill myself. Then I lock myself away from the world, and my hands are given to strange flights of fancy, so that the habitual movements that most people consider trivial and routine seem to me strangely full of meaning and importance. This is it! There's no other choice, I'd say. We've reached this conclusion in our pursuit of humanity. This power has resulted from our consideration of human love. The secret is capricious ideas and steady feelings. Don't you think? This will be our proposal to new generations. I wonder where I should go, whom I should meet. What a splendid future I have!

CHAPTER 9: YUGAO

It was while he was secretly visiting a different lady in the Sixth Ward. Yugao, which means 'evening face', was not her name, but the name of the flowers on the trellis next to her house. Genji was on his way to the Sixth Ward when he glimpsed the flowers – at first he thought they were the faces of women peering over the fence to see him. He sent a servant to pick some, and a girl wearing cute informal attire came to the door and offered a fan to put the flowers on. After he had finished his visit, he examined the fan and found a poem written on it. The Yugao in their coats of dew have puzzled you. Our life with flowers is simply a dream of delight. Genji wrote a poem back, saying he would not be puzzled if he could get a closer look. This garden is a door into a world filled with many flowers, he said. Except here, all the flowers are varied and different from the others. They are here and gone beautifully and re-born one after another. A world full of bright energy will certainly give one a feeling of comfort for a while. This exchange led to a torrid romance.

CHAPTER 10: THE FESTIVAL OF RED LEAVES

Genji asks, Do you think I am emotionally transparent? You asked me that before, says To no Chujo. You always ask me that. Well, before when I asked you, what did you say? Why are you so worried about being emotionally transparent? It's not the transparency itself that worries me so much, said Genji. I'd just like to think that I understand myself at least as well as other people do. You intend to guide your idea of identity, don't you? asks Chujo. For sure, I do. Every day, in every way. The more I know, the more I grow. You are a talented poet, says Chujo. It's because I understand the value of a poem, says Genji. A poem is the only thing that satisfies that whole body hunger situation. Do you know what? A poet's responsibility is to look at the present and create the future. There is no time like the present, says Chujo. At least, this used to be true. Now, few people believe such things. Poetry is a precarious road to self-actualization. Sometimes, it seems, people will die of poetry. Just leave a tender moment alone for a moment and see what happens. It goes away somewhere and nobody knows where it is. That's a dark and lonely place. But poetry is a real life-saver. It lays down wooden bridges at all the most dangerous places in the language. You'll regret it if you fear it, says Chujo. We can experience it right now! says Genji. Let's go! says Chujo.

CHAPTER 11: FUJITSUBO

What's new? How is the world treating you?
You haven't changed a bit. Lovely as ever, I must admit.
What's new? How did that romance come through?
We haven't met since then. Gee, but it's nice to see you again.

The Emperor still missed Kiritsubo. The rustling of the wind
or the chirping of an insect could cast him into the deepest
melancholy. The people who waited upon him began to feel use-
less. At this time, there was another girl who lived in the palace,
and it was said that she looked just like Kiritsubo. The disconsolate Emperor fell in love with her, he couldn't help it. As a boy
Genji had heard that she resembled his mother, and he became
very fond of her too. He was always thinking how much nicer
she was than anyone else, and only wanted to be with people
who were like her, but no one was the least like her. He kept that
secret from his childhood clear in his mind and close to his heart.
Fujitsubo would eventually be named Empress, and she would
bear a son. But the irony is that this child would not be the son
of the Emperor, as everyone assumed, but actually his grandson.
There is nothing actually ironic about it.

CHAPTER 12: THE FIRST SNOW

To no Chujo has gone home to his wife. How does it feel to be
loved? Genji asked him as he left. Now he is standing restlessly
on a patio. When I was young, he says, the ladies at Court used
to tell me sad stories of this kind. I never doubted that the emo-
tions were real, and I would cry helplessly. But now I am beginning to suspect that some of the sentiment of those stories was
simply affectation. I don't know who he is talking to. It's late at
night and I'm half delirious because I haven't slept for two days.
Out the window in the faint gleam of dawn I can see the season's

first snow on the ground. This story was written 1000 years ago, but nevertheless I find I easily confuse it with current events. I've only made it through the first few chapters so far. Did you notice a resemblance to *Remembrance of Things Past*? That's what they say, you know. Beautiful things are beyond time, they say. What I need is a hot bath. What I want is a trendy feeling, a natural feeling and a traditional feeling. I want a new style beyond the definition of existing simplicity and casualness, which will guide my idea of identity.

When the sky is blue, and the sun shines brightly, I embark on a happy mood. To have a feeling is good, but when love is added, it changes the direction of the wind. I am flooded with that feeling, so that the past wins a victory over me. A victory of the wrong kind. Sometimes I hear a rich, natural, comfortable sound. There is no occasion to hear it in usual life, but there it is. And I am so young. It makes me jubilant for the first time. Even if I decide, I think I will immediately have a change of heart. I had that one moment of good feeling, it was here for that moment, and that was when it was most important. I'm thinking of the weather conditions now: sunny, with a few clouds. The sun will slowly go up to the sky.

MARC TESSIER

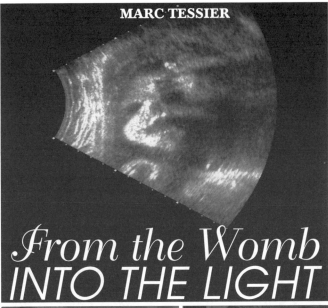

From the Womb
INTO THE LIGHT

2004

1963

Some years ago, I wrote a story about my mother and I wanted to do one about my father but coming up with tales about him stumped me. My Dad and I seemed so different. Where would I begin? Then I got married and a couple of years later my son Diego was born.

I never met my paternal grandparents. Both were born in 1892; Wellie Tessier died in 1942 and Eva in 1957. My father Marcel came from a family of twelve (three children barely a year old, died from weak hearts).

My grandparents Wellie and Eva's wedding picture, 1915

After Wellie's death, Marcel stayed with Eva and helped her take care of the family until she went blind and passed away. His dedication to helping his brothers and sisters kept him out of the loop, which is why he married and had kids later than most.

My dad at four,1928

My parents, Huguette and Marcel, met in 1957 at Molson's distribution headquarters in Drummondville, where they both worked. They married in 1961. My father was thirty-nine years old when I was born; my Mom was twenty-two. I always figured, like my Dad, I could wait to have kids until I was thirty-eight. Still it took me longer; I turned forty-two after my own son was born. When I was fifteen I challenged my Dad to a foot race, certain I would be the winner (young stud, old Dad). Of course, he passed me like he was The FLASH. My defeat humbled me. I owed him far more respect than I gave him. My father was in excellent shape. He played curling, softball and bowled. I only cycled around the block. I still had a lot to learn.

Marcel with his car, 1978

My father, at fifteen, 1939

At Molson's, 1958

My Dad learned English on his own and spoke it well. He liked to travel and every year he'd take the family to the beach in the States until my two sisters and I were teenagers. When I was a kid, going to the seaside was a yearly ritual of rebirth. We would leave at the crack of dawn and travel for days reading novels, comic books and eating candies in the car. At the beach we'd chase crabs, bury jellyfish and collect seashells. There my Dad taught me to catch the waves and body surf (which I still love to do). Next year I plan to continue the tradition by taking my own family to the sea.

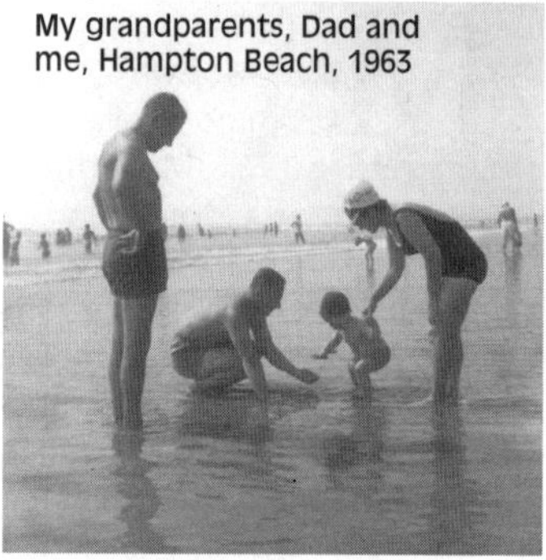
My grandparents, Dad and me, Hampton Beach, 1963

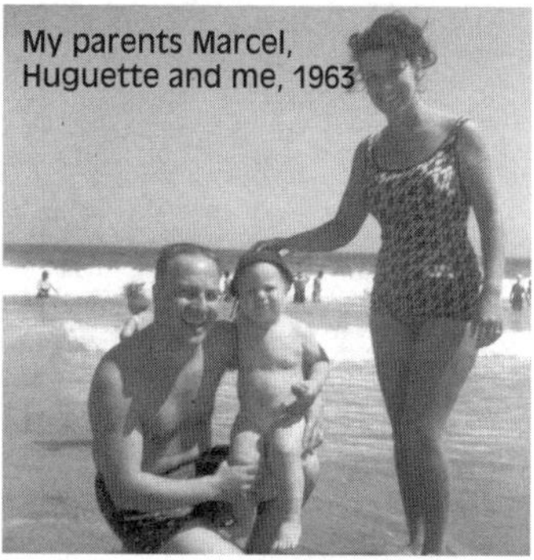
My parents Marcel, Huguette and me, 1963

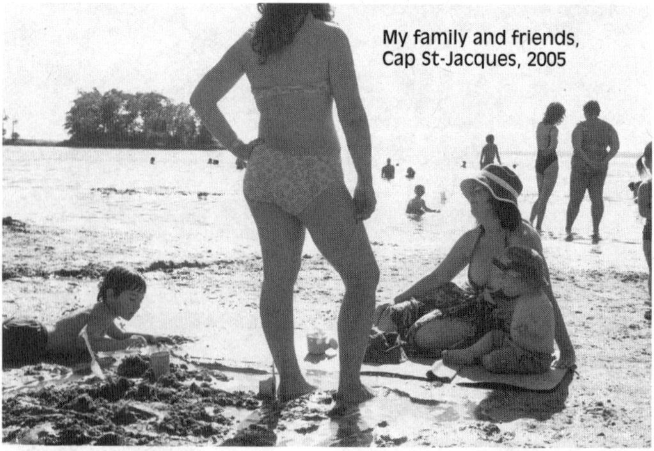
My family and friends, Cap St-Jacques, 2005

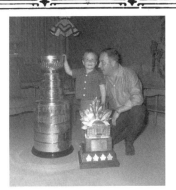

The Stanley Cup, me and my Dad, 1965

I should mention that my relationship with my Dad was strained all the way past adolescence. He loved hunting, fishing, hockey and sports, all of which I hated. It seemed our natures were worlds apart. Like many sensitive men his age, it was hard for him to communicate his feelings (he had less trouble with my sisters). Deep down, I needed his guidance and I resented him for not being able to provide it (in his defense, I must say I wasn't able to communicate my needs to him).

Holding a dead fish and crying, 1966

At seventeen, I left home to study film and photography. Years later, one of my sisters revealed to me that my Dad's dream before meeting my Mom was to move to California and work in the film industry (that's why he learned English). That floored me.

Was my passion for making movies the continuation of my father's aspirations? Is our legacy the dreams of our parents?

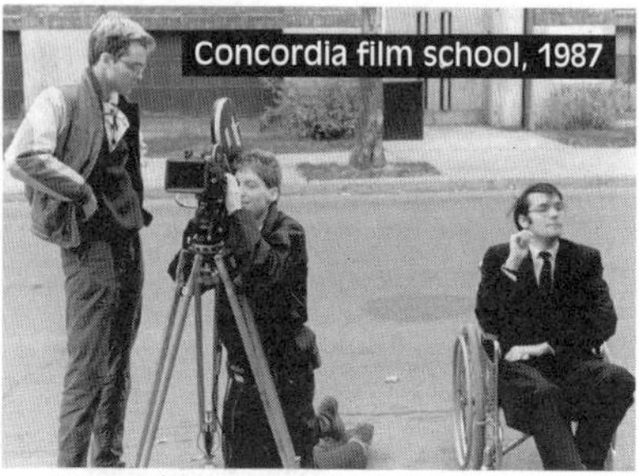
Concordia film school, 1987

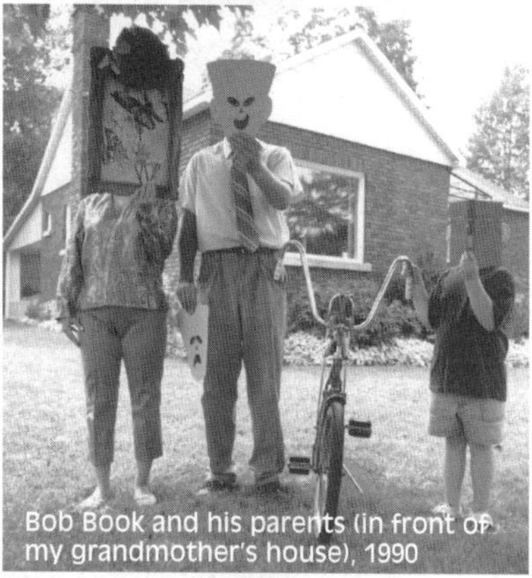
Bob Book and his parents (in front of my grandmother's house), 1990

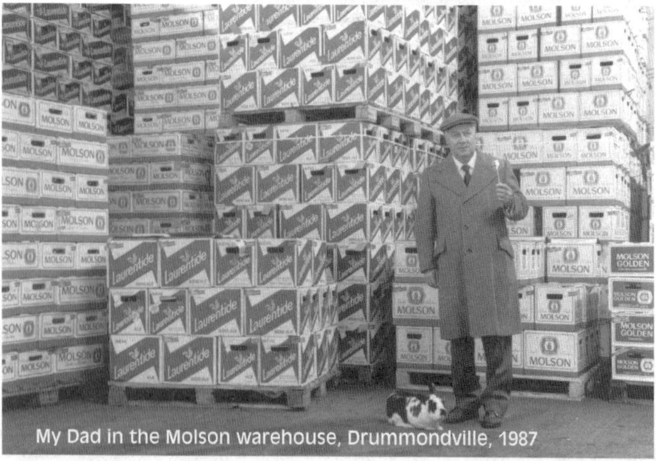
MOLSON
Laurentide
MOLSON GOLDEN
My Dad in the Molson warehouse, Drummondville, 1987

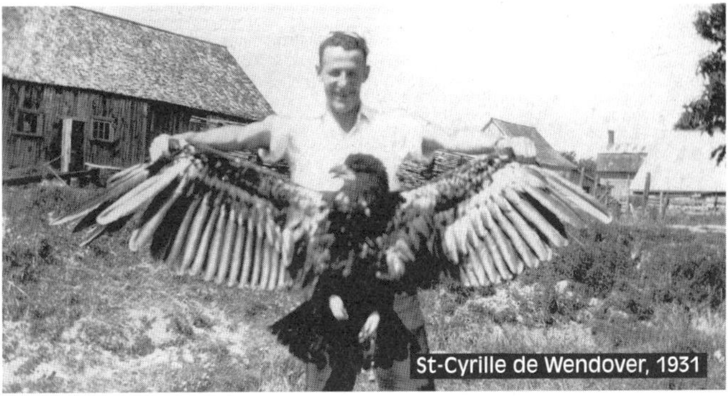

St-Cyrille de Wendover, 1931

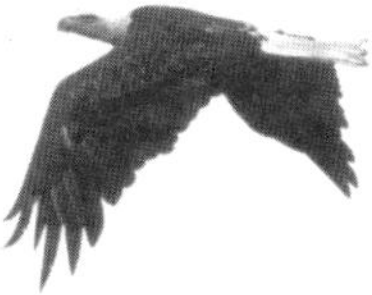

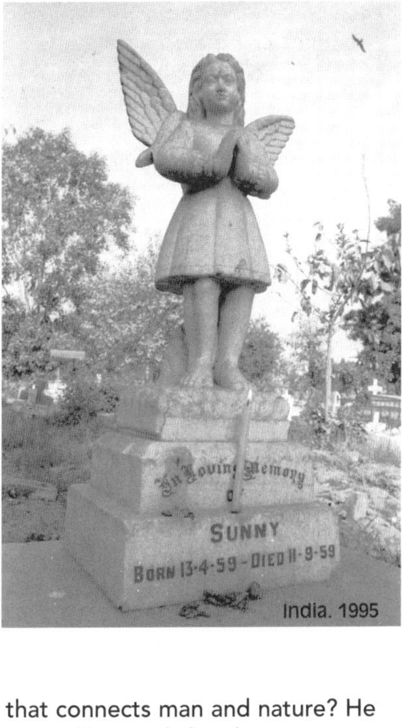
In Loving Memory
SUNNY
BORN 13-4-59 - DIED 11-9-59

India. 1995

My maternal grandfather Charles killed an eagle. He regretted it all his life. To Native Americans, it is a symbol of faith (i.e. what is above). I was taking a photo in a Hindu Christian cemetery when an eagle swooped down on me, touched my back, and flew past, letting out a cry that seemed like laughter. Did he want to remind me of the spirit that connects man and nature? He need not worry. My parents still attend church every Sunday. They have always practiced their faith by helping others, teaching us that all things are linked.

Valerie is my youngest sister. She used to star in my 8mm monster movies. She had two kids before me. As I watched my Dad play with my niece and nephew, I noticed how good he was with them, always smiling and patient. Being a grandfather suited him to a T. I began to see Marcel in a new light. When I fathered a child, holding this little wonder in my hands and feeling unconditional love for him, I realized my Dad must have felt the same way about me.

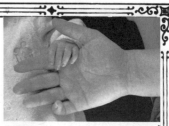

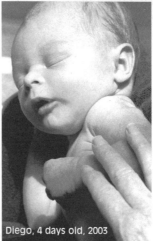

Diego, 4 days old, 2003

My Dad and his grandchildren: Gabrielle and Nicolas, 2002

My father is a man of honour: wise, strong and gentle. For years it was easy to feel the positive impact my mother had on me but after having a kid, I discovered a strong kinship with my father. Strength of character, respect for others, a sense of humour, determination and a code of ethics; the qualities that make me a good man, I owe to him.

My parents are quite a pair. My wife says, they're "normal" (meaning they're an exception because most families are fucked-up). In retrospect, I'd say they're EXTRAORDINARY! Real superheros are folks like my parents.

I hope to raise my son selflessly and guide him towards his own path like my parents did with me. I'm convinced that their legacy of help and compassion will live on in their children and grandchildren.

Photos from left; top to bottom:
1. My Dad at one. 2. The author, one year old. 3. At five. 4. At twelve. 5. At fifteen.

Photos from right; top to bottom:
1. Me at eighteen. 2. At forty. 3. My father at eighty. 4. My son, one year old. 4. My son at two.

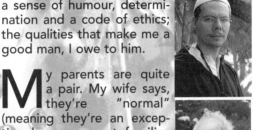

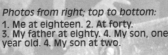

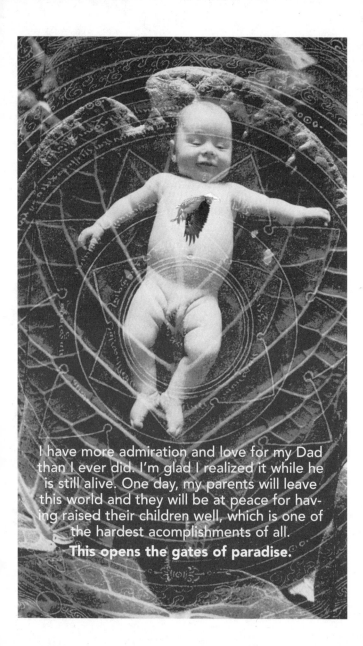

I have more admiration and love for my Dad than I ever did. I'm glad I realized it while he is still alive. One day, my parents will leave this world and they will be at peace for having raised their children well, which is one of the hardest acomplishments of all.

This opens the gates of paradise.

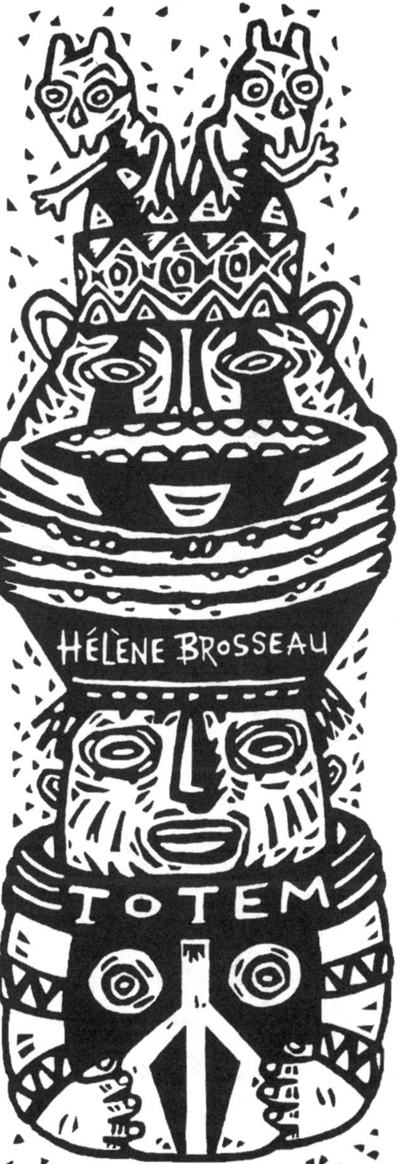
HÉLÈNE BROSSEAU
TOTEM

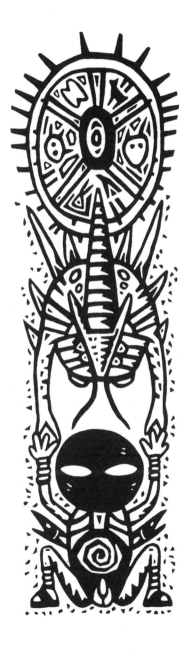

SUKI LEE
One Night in Bangkok

D an and I have been together for eight years, and he just confessed that he's not in love with me anymore. I wish I was
fully dressed to hear this. Instead, I'm perched on the edge of our
Bangkok hotel room bed, feeling awkward and undignified in
my underwear.

Dan drops his head and starts crying. He runs his hands
through his thinning blond hair, which I continue to find sexy
even now. Like a dog on all-fours, he crawls over to the bed, sub-
missive. He grabs me by the chest and starts kissing me, and
then cries into my neck. I act cold, but he takes his shirt off. I
love the look of his muscles under the fluorescent light. He's really handsome and I start getting excited. As he climbs onto the
bed and kisses me, I suddenly realize that he took me to
Thailand on a pity vacation. He must have been trying to break
up with me the entire week we were on that beach in Phuket. It
all makes sense now: his moods; flirting with our Thai waiter;
wanting to party the whole time. Dan pushes me down on the
bed. He pulls off my underwear and puts my cock in his mouth.
The metal ceiling fan whirrs above us unevenly. I wonder who
he's fantasizing about.

Afterwards, Dan lays his head on my stomach. I touch the
stubble on his jaw, and look into his eyes. They're the same light
hazel as ever, except I can't even hazard a guess at what he's
thinking. He could be bored out of his skull; he could be planning his life without me.

"You still want to go out and eat?" he asks, casually checking the time.

We were in the midst of getting ready for a late dinner when
he broke up with me.

"We can grab some pad Thai at a noodle stand," I suggest.

"I can do better than that." Dan gets up, suddenly chipper.
"How about we stick to our plan and go to that hotel restaurant

down the street? It's on me."

"We could…" I hesitate, as he rushes to the bathroom.

"We don't have to…." He turns around, disappointment on his face.

"No, it sounds great," I placate him as always.

Dan gets in the shower to prepare for our 'date'. I stand in front of the mirror looking at myself, naked. I feel pathetic, like one of those overripe pineapples that street vendors pawn off on tourists. He's probably standing under the shower head, feeling a huge surge of relief – or maybe he's jerking off to a fantasy of some guy he met on-line.

I'm suffocating. I need to get out of here. I hurriedly pull on pants and a T-shirt while Dan's in the shower. As I leave, I swipe his money from the dresser.

Once on the street, I walk past a sidewalk noodle stall. Just that morning, Dan and I ate breakfast at one of the little fold-up tables scattered around it. A single light bulb hangs over the slightly pudgy middle-aged woman who runs it. She's stir-frying a heap of garlic in a wok. It smells delicious and I stare, because I'm famished. She wipes her hands on her apron and signals me over. *Come here and eat,* her look says, but it quickly turns to concern.

"Maybe later," I mumble. I have tears in my eyes. I feel stupid.

I clutch Dan's money inside my pocket as I walk past vendors selling pirated DVDs *(You like movie?)*, green papaya salad *(You hungry?)*, fisherman's pants *(What colour you like?)*, fake university degrees *(You want teach English?)*, knock-off Tommy Hilfiger's *(What you want? Hey – I talking to you. Hey – what's wrong with you?)*.

I'm barely here. I feel transparent without Dan.

I flag down a three-wheeled tuk-tuk, and climb onto the hard cushion in the back.

"Patpong," I instruct him, without negotiating a price for the ride.

Like a frenzied mosquito, the tuk-tuk flies past Bangkok's Buddhist wats and food stalls, taking a shortcut along the city's majestic Chao Praya River and speeding past Western-style malls and hotels. Pollution surges into the open-sided vehicle. Between waves of panic are questions. Should I move to another city? Who's Dan been fucking? And then the thought over and over again: my life is screwed.

I pass the driver a hefty amount of cash after he drops me in front of a bar. I'm faced with a Thai dude whose neck is laden with bling. His pants are hanging off his ass, flashing the waistband of his Calvin Klein's.

"Come look! Live show! No cover!" He sweeps his hand down a laminated menu as if he's a waiter in a fine French restaurant.

I scan it quickly – *pussy ping pong, pussy draw picture, pussy blow birthday candles, lady lady lesbian* – and look past him into the club. Plum-coloured lighting splashes onto two women dancing onstage. One kicks hard around a metal pole in a fine show of athleticism, while the other gradually lowers herself into a horizontal split.

I look back at the establishment's maitre d'. "I'm looking for a game," I tell him.

He ushers me through a sweltering bar filled with straight male tourists. In a screened-off corner, a few poker games are in progress. The card players scrutinize me when I'm introduced, so I pull out Dan's money and put it on the table. A chair is offered; I sit down. A woman is presented; *mai bai*, I tell her – no thank you. A glass is placed; I drink from it. Mekong whisky. I close my eyes as its fire slides down my throat.

The cards are divvied out by a very good looking Thai, who deals me an abysmal hand. I carelessly toss out a stack of bills. My fellow players are all half tanked, so they match my bet even though they're not holding anything either. The guy with the greased-back hair gets three new cards, as does the fellow with all the tattoos, as do the rest of them. We show. Unbelievably, I'm the winner with only three of a kind.

I'm disappointed. I wanted to lose the game. As a way of

seeking revenge, I thought I'd blow all of Dan's money in one night. I don't even want tuk-tuk fare to drop my miserable ass back at the hotel.

The next hand I'm dealt turns up a pair of queens and jacks. I figure one of the other guys has got to have something higher. I hold, but end up winning the second round in spite of myself. My winnings are spread all over the table, so I stand to collect them. The guy with the greasy hair across from me starts talking. The others laugh. His high-pitched giggle rings in my ear. I look at him sideways.

"We all think you cheating," he slurs.

They go back to talking. The tattooed man says the word *faggot* after I sit down. When I look at him, he gives me a full-faced smile. His gold tooth glistens under the light.

Fucking Dan, I think. He got me into this mess.

As the game goes on and I continue to win, I feel a headache coming on. It's probably all the Mekong whisky I've been swilling. I massage my aching temple.

The next time I glance up, I see an unusually tall woman standing before me in a Venus pose, all polished nails and glitter. Her Thai eyes, dark and heavy with makeup, bore into me. Her red lipsticked mouth is perfectly framed by her long poufy rocker hair. Her tight sequin dress fits her body like she's a mermaid covered in silver fish scales. She shifts her hips back and forth, giving the illusion of curves. Her open-legged, high-heeled stance is obviously practiced.

"You need Cocaine." She smiles languidly at me, oozing confidence.

I lean back in my chair to take a better look at her. She's fixed herself up nicely: her fake eyelashes are set off against the hollows of her cheeks, which are carved out with blush. She's perfectly confident in her sex (fingering her hip bone, rolling her eyes). It's her hands that tell me she's a man. They're the same size as mine. Thais call her kind *katoeys*. I've seen others around, but none as exceptional as the ladyboy who stands before me.

"No, cocaine for me," I tell her, wondering how she makes her tits look so real. "Just more whisky please."

"I no offer you drugs," she leans over me, revealing a fairly muscular bicep. "I'm Cocaine – that's my name." She gestures with a fake thumbnail at her chest. "I no drug dealer, you know? I massage therapist. I give good Thai massage."

"Sorry," I tell her, rubbing my forehead. "Some other time."

"I no charge you then. I make your headache go away."

Cocaine settles me back roughly and pushes her thumbs against my forehead. She's so strong. It feels like she's going to dig right through my head. I'm released from the pain almost immediately.

She moves to my shoulders. "You feel like papaya before it ripe," Cocaine coos in my ear. "You stressed or something?"

She's all I've got at this point, so I pull her close. "They think I'm cheating," I whisper. My mouth brushes her face.

"Are you cheating?" she asks, raising a pencilled-in eyebrow.

"Of course not." I throw out my highest card to demonstrate. I'm given an ace back. I've already amassed a pile of baht two inches high, and still, the money flows to me magnetically. My fellow players are talking and gesturing at me almost continuously now.

"They say more than just you cheating," Cocaine whispers in my ear. "They call you lying faggot American. They want to take you out back, show you what real man is."

"Tell them I'm not American." Her neck is scented with citrusy perfume.

"I think maybe they not believe you." She shakes her head, doubtfully.

Next to us, another poker game is in progress at a table occupied by enormous Russian men who drink from beer pitchers. Security's loose in this place like everything's loose. There's no sign of the management. Cocaine's fingers patter rhythmically, her fake nails brush across my skin like the spiny shells of sea urchins.

I don't need a massage, I need a plan. I could fold, but that might encourage the men whose money I've amassed to take care of me themselves. It seems that my only option is Cocaine. I turn to her. Her tits rise above me like twin hot-air balloons.

"Hey," I say to her. She leans down and her long hair tumbles like a waterfall into my lap. "Get me out of here," I whisper, making it appear as if I'm nuzzling into her neck.

She raises her head and looks into my eyes. "You want outta here? You sure?"

"I'll make it worth your while."

Her fake eyelashes blink several times. "Relax and sit back," she instructs me, continuing the massage.

She presses deeply into my shoulders. Rapper tunes pound to the same rhythm as Cocaine's fingers. When she finally releases me, I feel like I'm floating. Strobe lights flicker, illuminating every second frame. In one moment, light shines like the sun on that Phuket beach where Dan and I spent the past week. In the next, it's dark and I'm lost in the haze of cigarette smoke that surrounds me like a sauna. In the stilted strobe light, I watch Cocaine pull something from her purse and thrust it into one of the men's faces. His expression turns to agony and he claws his eyes. Cocaine moves rapidly to the next man and the next and the next. They grope at their eyes in pain. The men stumble out of their chairs, cards in hands, cigarettes falling from mouths. One of them falls onto the Russian men's table and upsets their beer. It sprays through the air.

When I see Cocaine coming for me, I sit there, half wondering if I'm next. She yanks me by the wrist. Before I know it, we're cutting a swathe through the bar's patrons, running for the front door. She's tucked my money beneath her arm like a football. I look back once and see a fight erupting between the Thais and the wet Russians.

We get outside and I struggle to keep up with Cocaine as she rushes through alleyways, turning this way and that. She doesn't slip up once, but is fast and fierce like a leopard. It's obvious that Cocaine was born to wear high heels.

"What did you spray them with? Mace?" I ask breathlessly. "Sweetie, please!" she hollers back at me without slowing her stride. "That was my favourite hairspray."

Several blocks away, we stop running and enter a narrow alley. Under its shadows, beautiful men lean against the walls. They look at me; they look at Cocaine; they look back at me. Cocaine takes my hand, intertwining her fingers with my own, and drawing me close. Pretty soon, none of the alley guys bother checking me out.

At the end of the alleyway is a black cement building. We walk in. It's dark inside. Cocaine stops briefly to speak with a sleepy-eyed attendant, then tells me how much to pay him. I hand over the money without question, and he passes her a key. We walk by a locker room, and then another room with a TV showing gay porn. Cocaine struts ahead of me down the hall, her hips swaying from side to side, her heels clicking. She's taken me to a bathhouse.

After opening a door, she flicks on a light. We enter a room no larger than four by eight feet. There's a double bed, a small table with a fan on it, and a curtained window.

We sit down and something about Cocaine makes me start talking. Like a fool, I tell her about Dan breaking up with me and this pity vacation he's taken me on. While I'm talking, I notice the tiniest bit of sweat glimmering on Cocaine's skin. It goes nicely with the glitter surrounding her eyes.

When I'm done talking, she doesn't say a word. She gazes at me for a long time before releasing a long sigh to the room's ceiling. I wonder if I've bored her.

It's at this point that she decides to show me why she's called Cocaine. She pulls out a little baggy filled with white powder. With the tip of a manicured fingernail, she takes some cocaine out and drops it onto a small compact mirror. She asks me to hold it while she rolls up a baht. She uses it to snort a line. Then it's my turn. I lean down and inhale through the baht.

"You crazy," she tells me. She wipes her nose and throws her hair back. "Don't worry about this Dan. Let him go."

"We've been together for eight years. I can't imagine my life without him."

"What this Dan like that life without him so terrible?"

"He's a serious intellectual type. Very well-read and know-ledgeable. He broods a lot. People often mistake him for a snob."

"Is he?"

"Not really. He's just a good looking guy. Think of a pretty girl who knows she's pretty – that's Dan."

"A pretty boy, huh?" Cocaine says, examining her perfect half-moon nails. "You be glad you got your freedom back then."

"Yeah?"

"Yeah! Fuck this guy. Whatever! You're good looking. You have no problem finding someone else."

Her words give me a stony, cocaine-induced epiphany that sends a shudder across my head, my throat, my body. For the first time all evening, life feels like it's full of possibility.

Cocaine stares at me. Neither of us talks until I decide to fill the silence. "I'm glad you noticed that I needed a massage. I don't know how I would have gotten out of that game without you," I say earnestly.

Cocaine rolls her eyes.

"What?"

"I didn't think you needed massage." She slaps me in the leg. "I thought you the cutest boy I ever saw in that place."

As soon as she's finished that sentence, she puts her hand on mine. It's hot and makes me feel like something's just kicked me from the inside. A slow smile makes its way across her mouth. I'm held captive. She's a man, a woman, neither, both. Cocaine leans in and so do I. The taste of lipstick and the feeling of her smooth face is a woman's, but the hard body under my hands belongs to a man.

While we're still kissing, Cocaine pulls something from her

purse. It's a bottle of poppers. I've been offered them before, but never tried them. She gives me a deep snort. I immediately feel their aphrodisiac effects. Cocaine becomes blurred. She looks like a Thai version of Marlene Dietrich in the 1940s. While looking at her, I realize that I never really liked blonds outside of Dan. Cocaine hikes her skirt up, kisses me, and then lies down and spreads her legs. I'm nervous – I've been a bottom my entire life. I pull down my pants, my underwear. She throws me a condom and I put it on. I take one more snort of the poppers, and then drive my cock into her. She's got a gorgeous hairless ass that I slip right into. Nothing's ever felt so good.

Afterwards, Cocaine and I gaze up at the slow methodical spinning of the ceiling fan. I puff on the cigarette that she lit for me. She leans up on her elbows and looks into my eyes. "Ever been to a bath house?" she asks.

"No."

"Ever fucked a ladyboy?"

"No."

"See? Things better without Dan already."

When she lies back down, I realize that Dan hasn't been a thought in my head for a while. I inhale deeply from the cigarette and wonder if the night food stalls are still open.

It's dark when we leave the bath house. We say goodbye out on the street. Cocaine shakes my hand as if to say that our time together is over. She turns and walks away, all glitz, all mermaid, sparkling in the dawn. While I'm watching her, I realize that I forgot to give her something. I run over and hand her the money I made in the poker game.

"Why you give me this? I no hooker, you know," she quips, pretending to be offended. Cocaine fans herself with the big wad of cash, and admires it glowingly.

"It's yours. Keep it. I couldn't pay a shrink at home for the help you've given me tonight."

With that, Cocaine kisses me on the mouth and slips the money down the front of her dress. Wordlessly, she brings the palms of her hands together in a *wai* – a sign of respect – and bows. This time, she leaves me for good.

I flag a tuk-tuk that flies me through the city's streets at top speed. I wonder whether the exhilaration comes from the dangerous ride or the possibility of a new day.

It's six in the morning when I get back to the hotel. As I walk upstairs to our room, I plan my packing strategy so I won't awaken Dan. But when I open the door, he's facing me, sitting on the edge of the bed with an empty Mekong whisky bottle at his feet. A cigarette smoulders between his fingers.

"Oh my god! I was so worried!" He leaps up and stumbles toward me.

His breath smells of alcohol, the fly of his shorts is undone, his hair's all scruffy – he's a mess.

I walk past him, and stuff my bags with Thai fisherman's pants and the obligatory shirt and tie he made me bring. I sweep my toiletries off the bathroom counter into my bag like I'm a bartender.

Dan sits back down on the edge of the bed and clears his throat. He looks like he's going to start crying any second. "While you were gone, I realized I made a mistake."

"I'm delaying my flight home by a week," I tell him, as I close my bags. "That'll give you a head start on your packing. You've got more stuff than me. I figure the condo will be sold the same day it's put up on the market."

Dan stares at me, dumbfounded. "Didn't you hear me? I said I was wrong. I'm sorry!"

"No, I think you were right, Dan. It's been over between us for a while now."

"I'm sorry, I said!" He takes his head in his hands.

I lift my bag onto my shoulder and scan the room once more for my belongings. I don't notice anything that's mine.

As I close the hotel door behind me, the last thing I see is that bald spot on the top of Dan's head.

Outside, the new day surges with life. Motorcycles, school-children and vendors fill the streets. Thais nod hello to me. I'm the only *farang* up this early.

The woman at the noodle stall is content that I no longer look distressed. I'm her only customer. She prepares a divine offering of noodles infused with garlic, chillies and lime.

While eating, I decide that I'm going to call Stephen and the other friends I've lost touch with when I get home. Maybe I'll buy a new car, or look for another job. Thoughts spin around like a roulette table. I dream of taking up swimming again, reading that stack of books, seeing more plays. One idea skips to the next. Everything is clear. Plans come like rapid-fire. The future opens.

The woman who owns the food stall wipes her hands on her apron. "You want anything else, Mister?"

JULIA TAUSCH
Crazy Jane

"Just went out to the beach to smoke a jay, and for the first time in a long time it was just really perfect, you know? It's cooled down a lot since this afternoon, so everything's covered with this brittle layer of ice, you know, when your boots crash through the top and then kinda poof down into the snow? It's like that now, and when I got onto the rocks, all covered in ice and snow, the craggy ones just above the beach, there's this perfect little patch of light shining down, like a tiny spotlight, and I look up and it's the moon. I put my hand out, you know, and the moon's glowing in the palm of my hand, I was wearing my hunting mitts, they got these shiny leather palms. And I look over to the left of me, and there's some lights that people made, a bunch in a row, the lake winking up their beams, warm and orange, just like the snow-covered rocks are winking silver back up at the moon."

Drake and Jane were in the kitchen at the Art Centre, out on Toronto Island. They were sitting at the little table with the computer for e-mail checking, and they had the lights off so they could see the watery moonlight coming in through the ton of windows in the South wall. Drake had been having a beer in there when Jane came in, limping a little, red-faced from the cold, settled her huge body into the chair beside him, and started talking. He handed her a Stella Artois. Drake was happy to see her, he was feeling kind of twitchy from being alone all day.

"You know," she said, cocking her head and looking at him like a little girl, "I was outside for about two hours this afternoon, but I didn't start listening to the lake today until right about then, standing there in the moonlight. I start listening to it, and suddenly — and I know this makes me sound like a really blasted old hippy right now — but suddenly I feel that feeling, like I'm connected to all the people in the world in some way. I start picturing other places, you know, from what I know of other places, I guess like what I've seen in magazines and on *The Amazing Race* and stuff, hot, destitute places, droughty places, and then I picture people in green fields, like in Germany, and I picture people standing near water, listening to it lap a shore somewhere, and I get to thinking about the wee...."

Jane pressed her thumbs and fingers together on both hands, like pudgy lobster claws.

"I imagined the tiny, tiny differences between things, and how those differences build on each other on their way round and round the world, just... minuscule variations, that could be the difference between, let's say... the difference between a palm tree and the tundra if you're looking at two countries, miles apart, sure. But what would the differences be like if you made your way around real slowly, you know?" Her chubby hands snaked through the air in front of her, she bobbed her head up and down, "wending your way from plant to plant." She turned the points of her lobster claws down, lurched them up, one at a time, as if yanking a string up with her teeth, attached to the back of each hand. "If you could only tip-toe one skin cell at a time through the billions of people on this Earth, through each day of each month of each year since the beginning of time, if you could move that slowly through it all, having a close and careful look and smell and touch and taste and listen, but not really pausing to think at all – I think that's the key, just pressing on, tiny piece by tiny piece, if we could only make a journey that slow, we would know that there are no differences, not really, at all. We're just all the same stuff."

She sat quiet for a split second, breathing like Lady Darth Vader – she was actually wearing a T-shirt that her ex-girlfriend Lucy made her, with *Lady Darth Vader* ironed onto it in sparkly letters that stretched across her mountainous chest – long enough for Drake to notice the burly whir of the fridge, almost long enough for him to be embarrassed, but then she started up again in a breathy, bouncy voice, her watery blue eyes jumping and sparkling in their pale, puffy sockets.

"I wanted to get closer to the water, so I sat on my bum, shim-mied down the slippery rocks, dropped onto the beach. I walked to the edge of the water, and the tiniest little wave was getting licked silver by the moon every time it thwacked the shore, and turning black on its way back out. I crouched down and put a hand in the water and I couldn't believe how quickly it stung, like it was biting me. I imagined the people in hot countries again, and for once I actually felt Canadian. It felt so… like, exactly the way Canada is marketed to other countries, you know? The water was frigid, the air was still, my boots crunched the glassy ice shel-lacking the sand. And I felt the sand, too, rubbed it between my fingers, it was wet and cold. I touched the dry sand, a bit further up from the water, frozen solid, and it felt like stone. The whole time I'm feeling that great sense of connection, and then I looked up to the horizon. It made me think of this letter I wrote to Lucy, ages ago, ages ago, from the very beginning, where I told her about how my love for her was like a huge body of water, the kind you can't possibly see the boundaries of, no matter how hard you stare, no matter how clear the day. Looking out at the horizon, thinking about love, I find myself thinking about all those people, scientists and professors, and guys who think they know it all, who say that love is bullshit, that it's just science, some dog-and-pony show stitched together to legitimize our bio-logical needs, it's just sex, it's just survival. And I looked at that horizon, and I thought to myself —" She stopped, her mouth breaking into a wide grin, her chin-length blond hair falling like a ratty curtain around her face, as she looked down, grinning at her lap, "This is a real stoner doozy this one, Drake, Jesus!"

"Please. Keep going," Drake laughed. It was good, she was on a roll. She lifted her head and looked straight through the window.

"Science is just love, Drake. It's the opposite way. Why in God's name else would we work all day at figuring out stuff we try to figure out? Everything supposedly scientific we do is out of the desperate pursuit of love, whether you love God or your-

self or somebody you're, you know, fucking or somebody you
share a bed with or somebody you laugh with, or a dog who
leans her head on your thigh, whether you show it by inventing
the cure for cancer, or baking bread in a bakery, or being in a
gang, or fighting a war, or anything really, my point is anything,
it seems to me that all the stuff we spend our time on only gets
our time because of our ultimate belief that there is something
out there that makes it worthwhile. That maybe those moments
we're connected – to stuff, to music, to nature, to bodies, whatever, I think it's all love – those moments make it pretty worth
our while to twitter around and fight for food and make stupid
noises for years on end. Drake, I know I'm being maudlin. I'm
sorry. I just sometimes think it's a shame that we don't spend
more time in awe, dumbfounded or at the very least thinking
about the fact that the sun is a huge burning ball of gas, and it
lights our planet, a thing we live on with water and creatures and
plants. Where are the differences between things when we think
about it like that?" She was breathless, and blushing, beautiful in
the moonlight, Drake's mind couldn't help alliterating, he'd been
writing all day.

"Yeah, I really got up a whole head of steam out there, I said
'Ha,' out loud to the lake, climbed up the rocks on my hands and
knees, and started chugging back to my little room, ready to
pound profundity into the old Toshiba, determined already to
laugh at myself in the morning. I was so split in two, you know?
Real excited to go write it all down, but also busy watching
myself be this fat, old stoner, be embarrassing, be illegitimate, an
impostor, that I didn't even feel myself slip on the sidewalk till
the pain was blurry in my leg and my ass; it was only then that
I registered the thunking sound of my own goddamn body hitting the concrete, cracking the layer of ice on top into shards. I
picked myself up, and I said, 'Hm!' I said, 'My wretched self.'
Out loud! Standing on the side of the road, shaking my head,
talking to myself. Like a crazy person. I felt so free, talking to
myself like that, kept right on talking while I stumped back

through the footprints I made on my way out."

"That sounds great, Jane."

"Yup, really great. Seriously." She shook her head and patted her massive thighs.

JOEY DUBUC

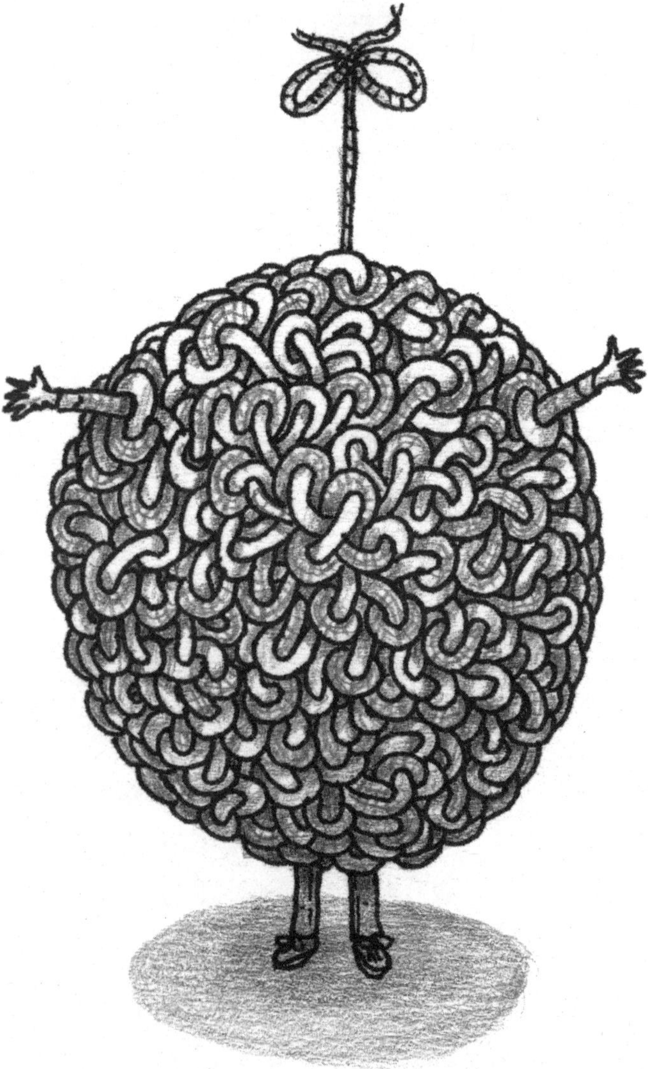

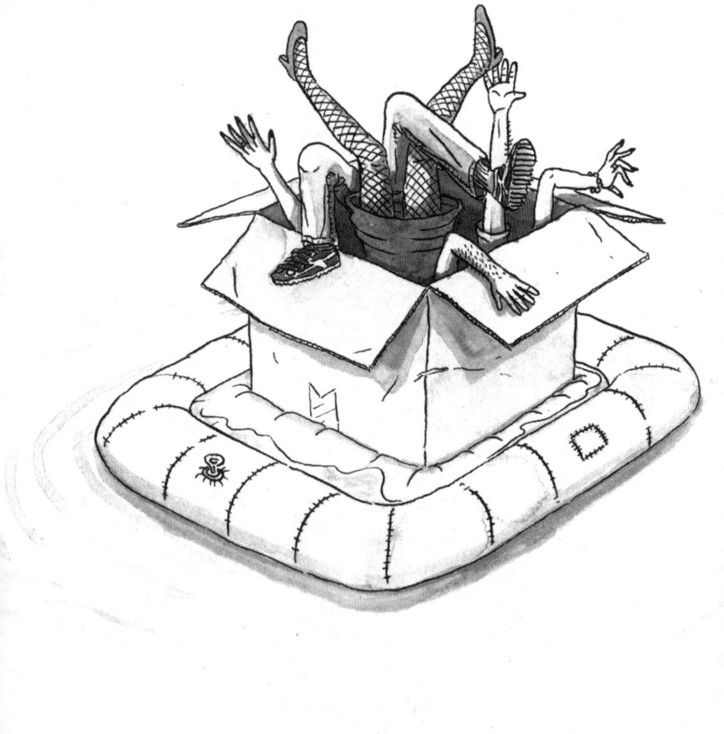

CHANDRA MAYOR
Bridget, Barbie, and Me

Bridget Jones, the arbiter of all things true and meaningful, hit the nail on the head. In the very beginning of the movie (the first one, the good one), her well-meaning and meddling mother introduces her to Mark Darcy at her annual post-Christmas turkey curry buffet. Mark seems a likely candidate. Bridget makes her usual charming fool of herself when she talks to him. And then Mark, not knowing that Bridget is standing behind him, tells his mother that the last thing he needs is a woman who smokes like a chimney, drinks like a fish, and dresses like her mother. Mark and his mother turn around to see Bridget standing at the buffet table behind them. "Mmm, turkey curry," she says. "My favourite." And she walks past the both of them, head high, spirit crushed. "That," she says in the voice-over, "that right there was The Moment." Cut to Bridget, in red pyjamas, drunk on red wine, alone in her apartment singing along to AM radio.

Bridget never explains exactly what The Moment means, but I know. Cut to myself, eight years ago, alone in my apartment in the middle of the night with my three-year-old daughter, Julika. It was not the best time in my life; I refer to it as The Winter of My Discontent. I couldn't remember why I was in university anymore, so I'd taken the year off. Which left me day-careless, penniless, and generally aimless, living in subsidized housing, and waiting for the monthly cheque to arrive in the mail. Julika, meanwhile, had ceased going to bed before 4:00 AM. No amount of singing, reading, cuddling, pleading, threatening or crying could induce her to sleep any sooner. I decided that her circadian rhythms were off and that the only thing to do was to stay up an hour later every day until we'd worked ourselves around the clock to target bedtime. Which sounds brilliant on paper but was insanity in practice. One day we'd go to bed at 11:00 AM; the next day at noon. We'd wake up at ten at night, wide awake and ready to face the day. Except that obviously, 'the day', for normal people, had ended. It's extremely difficult to grocery shop in Winnipeg in the middle of winter at 2:00 AM. It's also hard to call your friends at that hour and have them actually be willing to talk with you. We didn't even have TV — only the entire Disney collection on VHS tapes. It was like living in the middle of a nuclear winter — Julika and I were the only people still alive on the face of the planet, with our dwindling food supplies and the spectre of stark raving cabin-fever madness lurking behind every tick of the clock.

And I, of course, was a writer. Or, was desperately trying to be a writer. I wrote some poems and wrote in my journal a lot, but mostly my writing was of the manic arts and crafts self-medication kind. I had a lot of things to sort out during The Winter of My Discontent. I remembered that the road to hell is paved with good intentions. I had a lot of good intentions that had somehow gone terribly awry. One winter night I found myself cutting cobblestones out of Julika's construction paper while she was ensconced in front of Shoe Dancing (a.k.a. *Bedknobs and Broomsticks*). On each multicoloured cobblestone I wrote a small poem (I only had time for small poems) about a good intention gone belly-up. I taped all the cobblestone poems to the linoleum, paving my own paper road, snaking across my floor from the bathroom to the bedroom. Insanity. As the inimitable Norman Bates says, We all go a little mad sometimes. Fortunately Julika wasn't yet able to read, and as I said, I didn't have a lot of visitors.

What I'm saying is that the urge to write was inextinguishable. My grasp on sanity may have been precarious (and wildly fluctuating), my life may have been a bit of a shambles, and most of my time and energy may have been taken up by the joys and demands of a raucous toddler (we paid more than one visit to the emergency room that winter, fortunately located just around the corner — stitches, head contusions, fractured leg — she was a wild child with no fear and utter disdain for the consequences of her high-flying acrobatics). Still, I was compelled to write, to scribble, to have a never-ending supply of pens even when the milk and coffee and bread were running out. I was in need of an identity of my own; I was a mother of course, but I also needed to be someone on my own terms, not just an adjunct to someone else. We define ourselves in relation to those around us, but I needed an inner definition, too, something that would carry me through those long nights, something that I could hold inside myself like a shell or a feather (or possibly a rope around my waist). The only thing I'd ever consistently done (apart from screw up, I told myself on particularly long nights), the only thing that woke a fire in my belly and provoked dizzying vertigo, the only thing that gave me a sense of the possibilities of a world beyond Alphaghetti and Cinderella's dancing mice, was writing. I claimed the word poet. I am a poet, I said to myself. A mother-poet. A poet-mother.

Which leads me to The Moment. Against my better feminist judgement, I had allowed Barbie into our apartment, and Julika was temporarily fascinated by her brazen buxom blonde presence in our lives. I should also mention that my own mother, a Home Ec teacher, was a formidable force when I was growing up. Like June Cleaver on dexedrine with a bottomless pit of rage and misery. I had at least five different elaborate hand-made costumes every year for Halloween. She could knit up an Irish cable sweater in a day. Christmas meant, among other things, intricately-fashioned, homemade gingerbread trains, clumsily decorated (not to her standards, I might add) by my friends and me. It was like growing up with Martha Stewart for a mother, if Martha didn't have the outlet of an empire. Personally, she was a bit of a train wreck. But in the traditional Mom department, she set a high bar, and I'll admit to having a minor complex about it. My lopsided paper dolls festooning the walls of my apartment couldn't hold a candle to the stained glass window she hand-painted in the hallway of my childhood home. You get the picture.

Julika was still young enough to believe that I could do anything. (She quickly grew out of that, but for a few glorious years, I was her Super-Mom). And I wanted to be Super-Mom. Not just because I was a minor screw-up in most life departments, but because I loved her with that animal fierceness that mothers have, the love that chokes your throat and takes over your mind and makes you want to fling yourself in front of cars to protect her. Fortunately she never asked me to fling myself in front of a car. But she did ask me to make her a new Barbie dress. I can do this, I thought. How hard can it be? I had entire homemade seasonal wardrobes for my Barbies when I was a kid. I found an old shirt in the back of my closet that I was willing to sacrifice for The Cause. The Cause — I wanted Julika to grow up singing, without irony, that Jann Arden song about good mothers. This seemed my opportunity to prove my motherly worthiness. I didn't think I had outrageous delusions about my abilities; I wasn't aiming for sequined evening gown or smart pant suit. I thought a simple smock for the blonde beast would satisfy. This was my shining moment.

Have you ever tried to make a Barbie dress? Perhaps you have, in which case I unselfconsciously agree that you are a better woman than I. My Barbie dress was an abject, wretched failure. The stitches were loose. The armholes were lopsided. I'd cut the fabric on a bias so that the two sides didn't quite match up with each other. And worst of all, the neck hole was too small — I couldn't fit Barbie's massive head through the tiny little opening in the fabric. And the whole time that I was wrestling with Barbie and the wretched dress, my face was frozen into a smile because Julika was watching me with her big hopeful doe eyes, full of confidence in me, full of wide-eyed assurance in my motherly abilities. And I realized that I just couldn't do it. I couldn't be Super-Mom. I couldn't even figure out how to make an A-line Barbie smock. I couldn't get my life together, I couldn't keep my apartment clean, I couldn't even call a friend because it was three in the morning (about noon, for Julika and me), and I couldn't hold it together one second longer. I couldn't help it — the tears of frustration and self-loathing began to come, unwanted and unstoppable. The miserable little dress (mother failure) in one hand and the naked Barbie (feminist failure) in the other became emblematic for all my failures, ever, and into the foreseeable future.

To her eternal credit, Julika was kind and consoling and sweet in the way that only a three-year-old can be. She brought me toilet paper from the bathroom to wipe my eyes. She put her battered old favourite doll in my lap and offered to 'read' me *Sally, Where Are You?,* her favourite book. I put my arms around her warm, fierce little body and held on for all I was worth. I cleaned myself up. I made her an omelette with a smiley ketchup face on it, and she was happy again.

I sat on the couch and contemplated the situation. So I let her have a Barbie. Big deal. I had Barbies and I still grew up to be a feminist. So I couldn't make a stupid dress. So what? I had other talents, other skills, other things to offer the world. Who was I? I, I remembered, was a poet. And this was all raw, poetic material. I, I thought, was a mother-poet / poet-mother, and I would make all of this into a poem, and thus salvage my dignity. I would take life, even my crappy, unstable, arts-and-crafts-as-therapy life, and turn it into art, real art. I got my blue notebook and a pen, opened the book to a fresh page (an invitation, I thought – a promise), and waited for the words to come.

Except the words didn't come. Rather, some words came but they weren't the right words. And as soon as I got close to a good word, something happened – Julika finished her eggs and wanted me to help her build mega-blocks. Then she tripped on something I'd left lying on the floor and banged her head. Then she needed a bath. Then she wanted on my lap. Then she wanted me to read to her. Etc. etc. The day (night) wore on, and then it was time to put her to bed, an hour's worth of stories and singing and ritual.

After she was finally asleep I snuck back out to the living room, opened my notebook abandoned beside the couch, and looked at my sad collection of inadequate words, my imperfect attempt at recounting my failures, my so-not-good-enough stab at reclaiming my inadequacy as something deeper, more meaningful, my ridiculous attempt at reinventing myself as an artist – someone with an incredibly insightful inner life – a poet.

And that was my Moment. That was The Moment, right there, when all my varying failures crystallized into one perfect moment of clarity. I was too inadequate to be a good mother. I was too good of a mother (at least, too consumed by being a mother) to be a good poet. The simplicity of the equation. The despair I felt as all my illusions dropped away and I was left with scraps of fabric, scraps of words, and a tiredness so entrenched in the structure of my skeleton that the only possible, plausible answer, was sleep.

Cut to myself again, eight years on. I finally rented *Bridget Jones's Diary* one night, and when Bridget had her Moment in the beginning of the film, I felt a spontaneous surge of sisterhood, of empathy, a sinking in my stomach and a soaring of my spirit. When all your pretences and efforts drop away from you and you're left with the shards of your self-esteem, yours to piece together again however you can, it is a heart-breaking moment in life. She didn't have to explicate what The Moment meant to her. I knew.

Of course, Bridget pulls it together and makes a pretty good go of it regardless, and by the time the movie ends, she's more or less gotten it together. I did too, although not being constrained by consideration of the average audience member's attention span, my process took a little longer (and continues to be 'in process'). I am learning to negotiate the dual (and sometimes duelling) identities of mother and poet. I am learning to let go of my Super-Mom complex, though she still occasionally rears her ugly head (Julika is now old enough to just roll her eyes at me when the occasion warrants).

I never did write the poem about my Barbie / mother failure; my attempts are buried away in my Winter of Discontent notebook somewhere in the basement. I have no words of advice on how any of it happened, how any of it managed to turn around, turn out. It just did, eventually, through sheer force of will and obstinacy. Maybe when you have your Moment you'll be able to write about it immediately, with clarity and grace, exorcise it from your life. Or maybe you'll have to wait eight years too and try to tell it as the funny, breezy story of a plucky girl with authentic heartbreak. I hope it's the former.

And stay away from 3:00 AM Barbie dresses.

Olivier & Boulerice

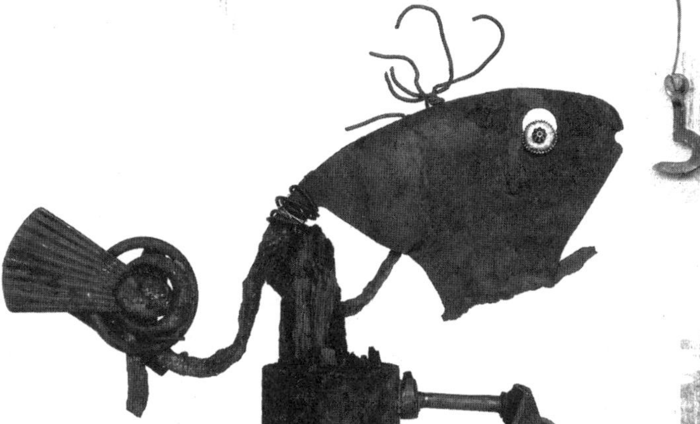

Lacustrine things

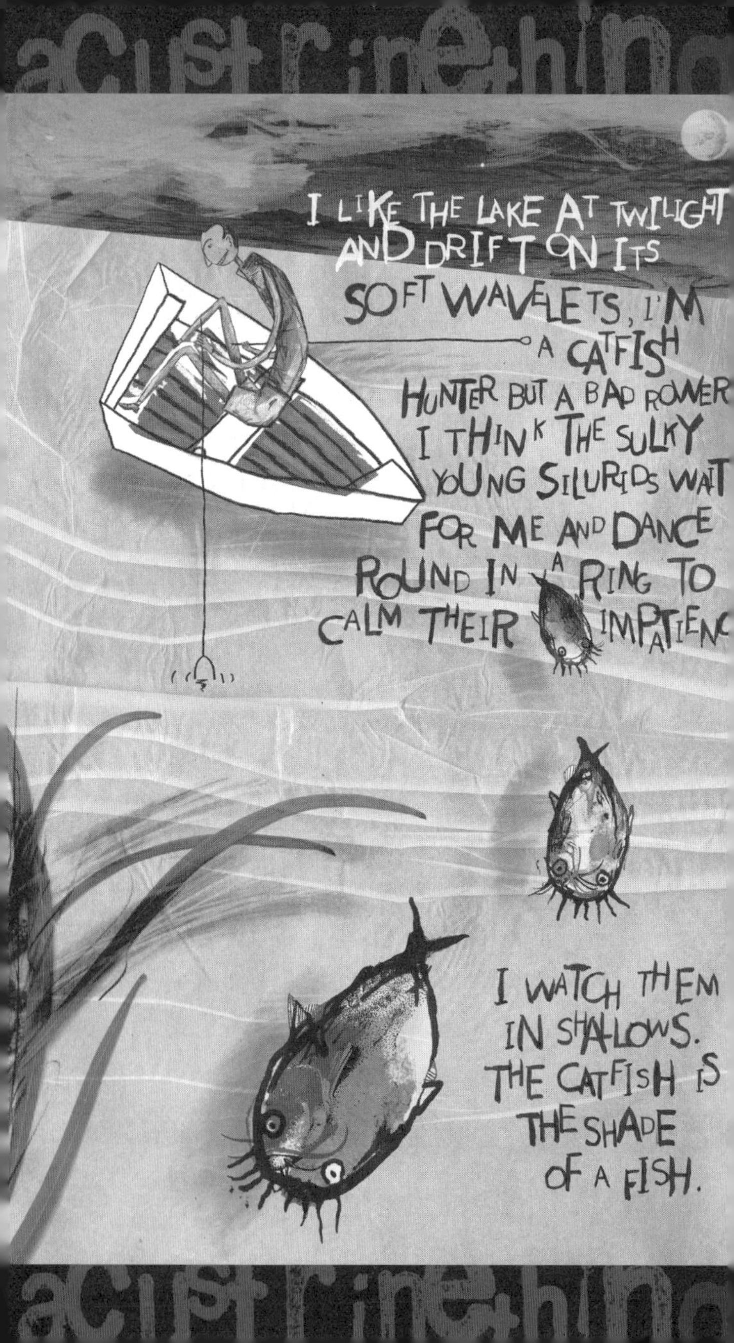
I LIKE THE LAKE AT TWILIGHT
AND DRIFT ON ITS
SOFT WAVELETS, I'M
A CATFISH
HUNTER BUT A BAD ROWER
I THINK THE SULKY
YOUNG SILURIDS WAIT
FOR ME AND DANCE
ROUND IN A RING TO
CALM THEIR IMPATIENC
I WATCH THEM
IN SHALLOWS.
THE CATFISH IS
THE SHADE
OF A FISH.

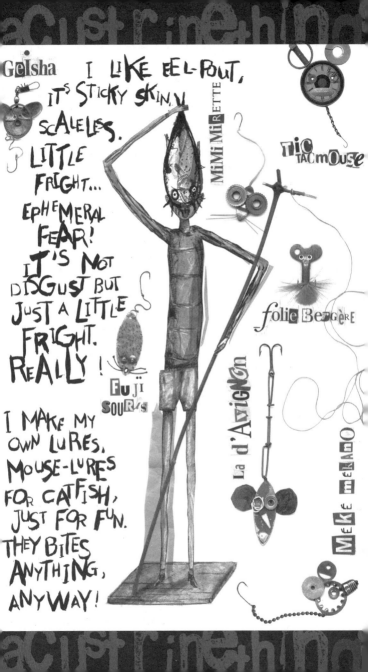

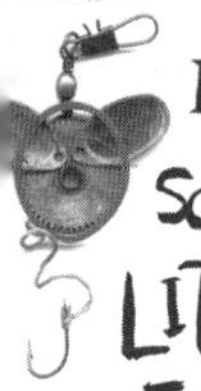
Geisha

I LIKE EEL-POUT,
IT'S STICKY SKIN,
SCALELESS.
LITTLE
FRIGHT...
EPHEMERAL
FEAR!
IT'S NOT
DISGUST BUT
JUST A LITTLE
FRIGHT.
REALLY !

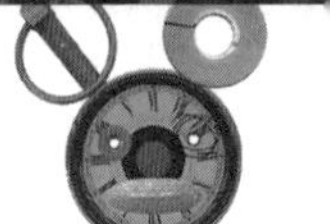
Tic TACmOuse

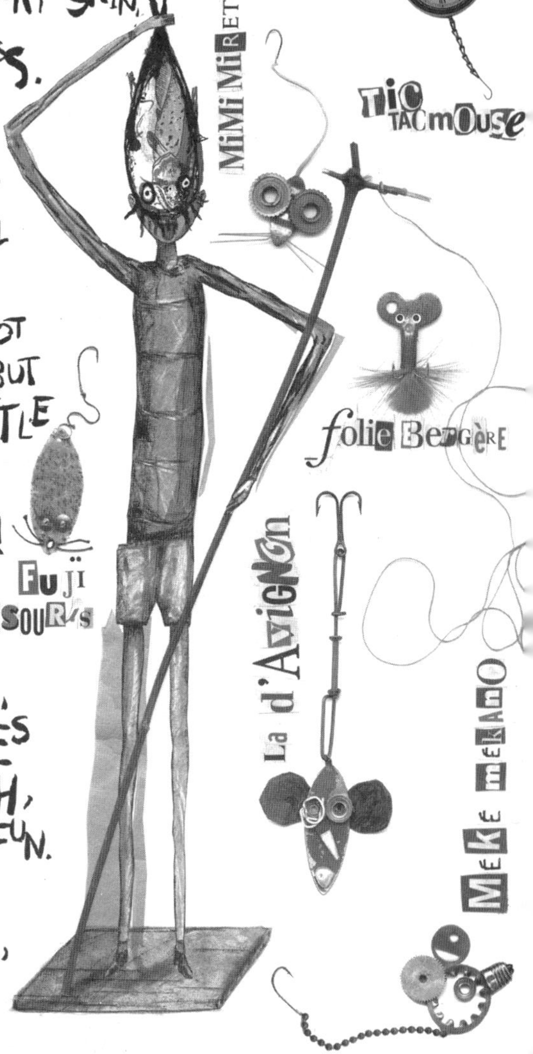
MiMi MiRETTE
folie Bergère
Fuji
Souris
La d'Avignon
Meke mekano

I MAKE MY
OWN LURES,
MOUSE-LURES
FOR CATFISH,
JUST FOR FUN.
THEY BITES
ANYTHING,
ANYWAY!

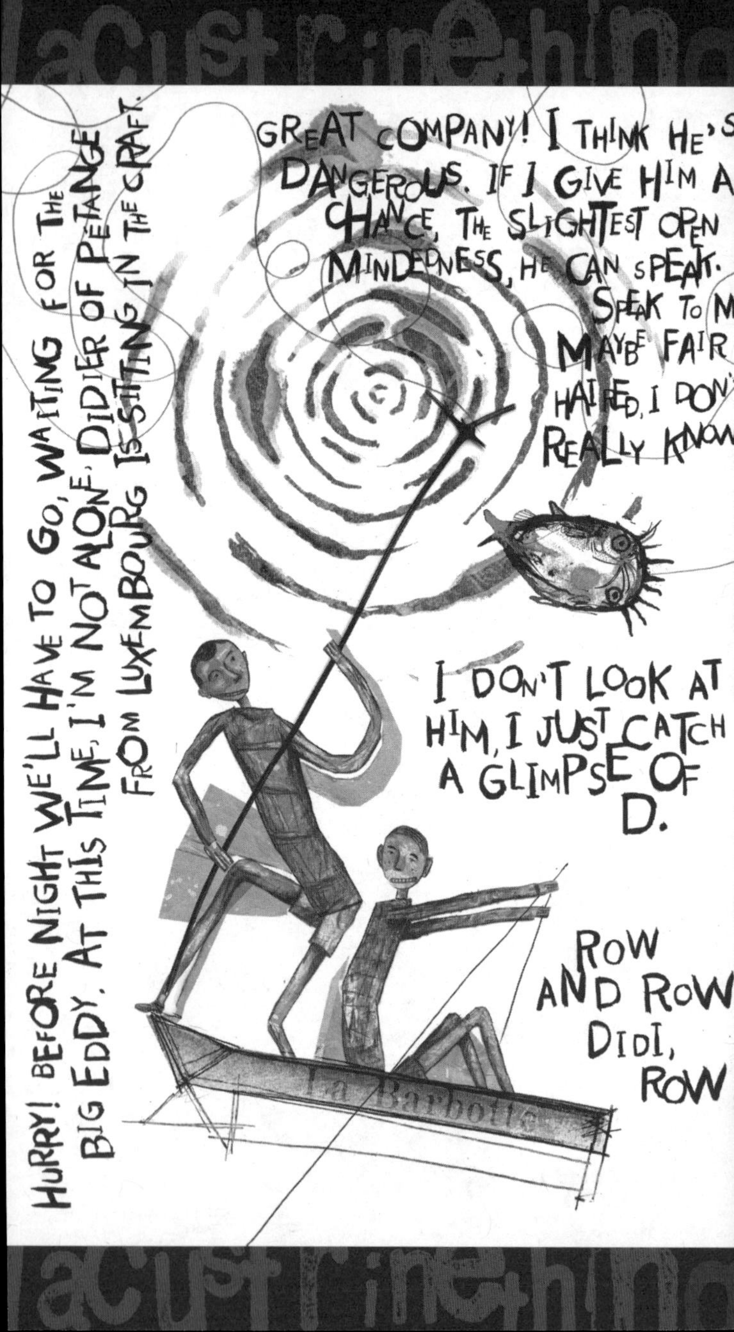

HURRY! BEFORE NIGHT WE'LL HAVE TO GO, WAITING FOR THE
BIG EDDY. AT THIS TIME, I'M NOT ALONE, DIDIER OF PÉTANGE
FROM LUXEMBOURG IS SITTING IN THE CRAFT.
GREAT COMPANY! I THINK HE'S
DANGEROUS. IF I GIVE HIM A
CHANCE, THE SLIGHTEST OPEN
MINDEDNESS, HE CAN SPEAK.
SPEAK TO M
MAYBE FAIR
HAIRED, I DON'
REALLY KNOW
I DON'T LOOK AT
HIM, I JUST CATCH
A GLIMPSE OF
D.
ROW
AND ROW
DIDI,
ROW
La Barbotte

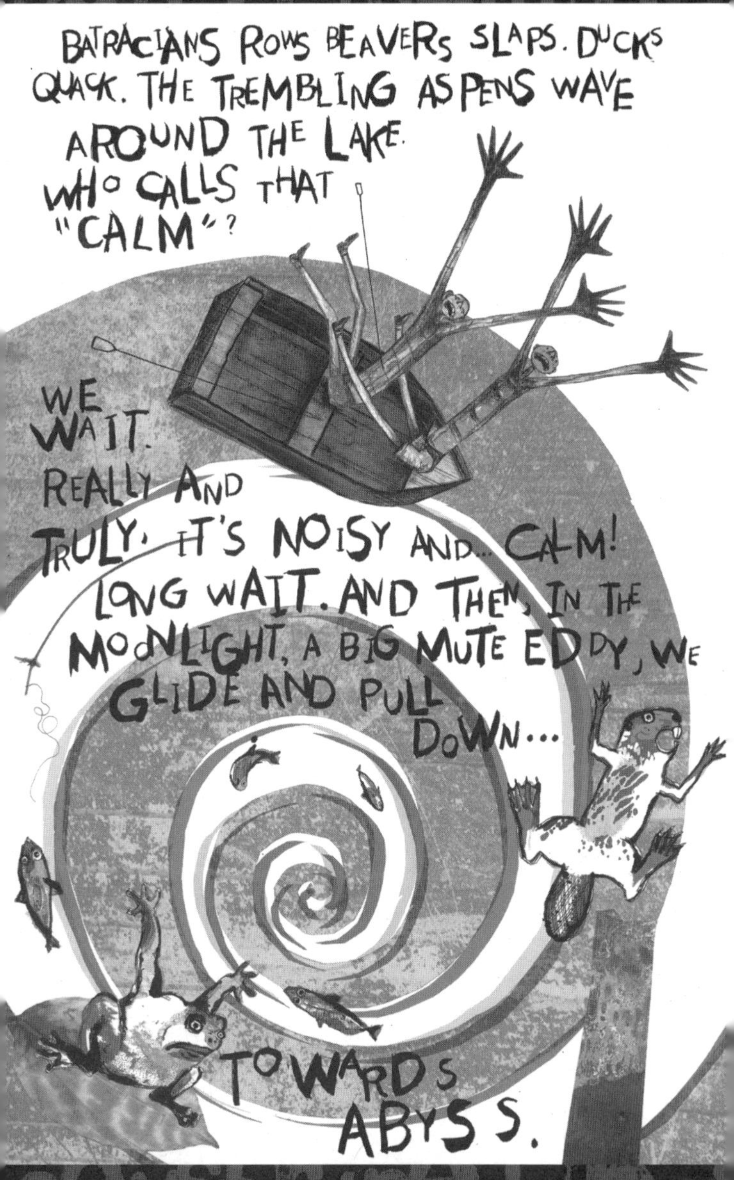
BATRACIANS ROWS BEAVERS SLAPS. DUCKS QUACK. THE TREMBLING ASPENS WAVE AROUND THE LAKE.
WHO CALLS THAT "CALM"?
WE WAIT. REALLY AND TRULY, IT'S NOISY AND... CALM!
LONG WAIT. AND THEN, IN THE MOONLIGHT, A BIG MUTE EDDY, WE GLIDE AND PULL DOWN...
TOWARDS ABYSS.

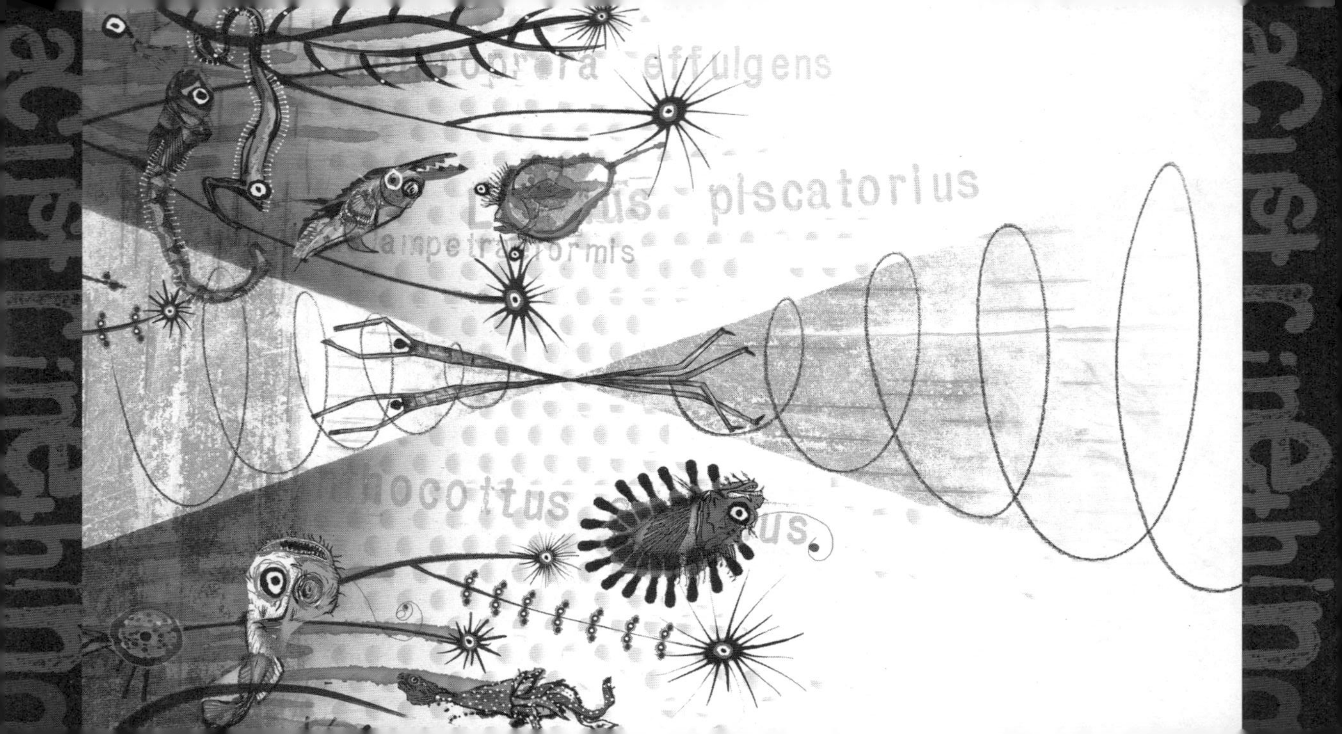
effulgens
piscatorius

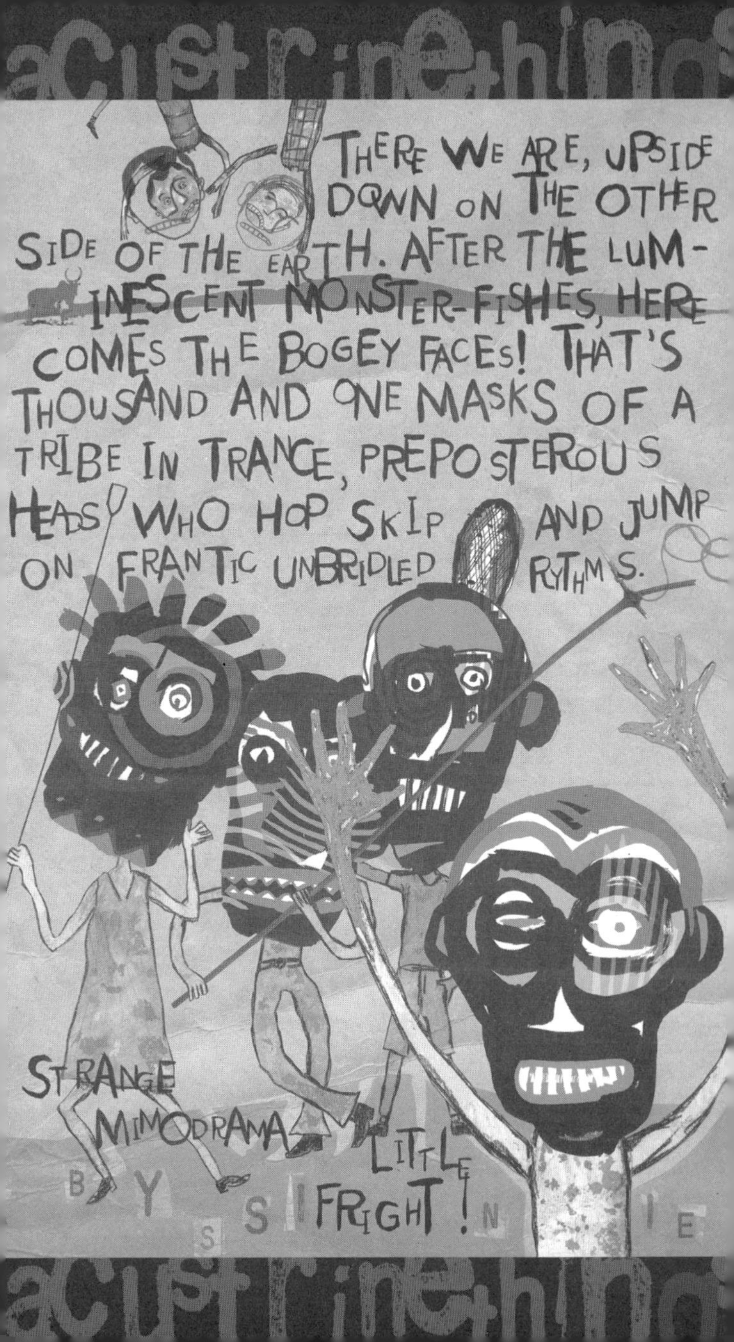
THERE WE ARE, UPSIDE DOWN ON THE OTHER SIDE OF THE EARTH. AFTER THE LUM-INESCENT MONSTER-FISHES, HERE COMES THE BOGEY FACES! THAT'S THOUSAND AND ONE MASKS OF A TRIBE IN TRANCE, PREPOSTEROUS HEADS WHO HOP SKIP AND JUMP ON FRANTIC UNBRIDLED RYTHMS.
STRANGE MIMODRAMA
LITTLE FRIGHT!

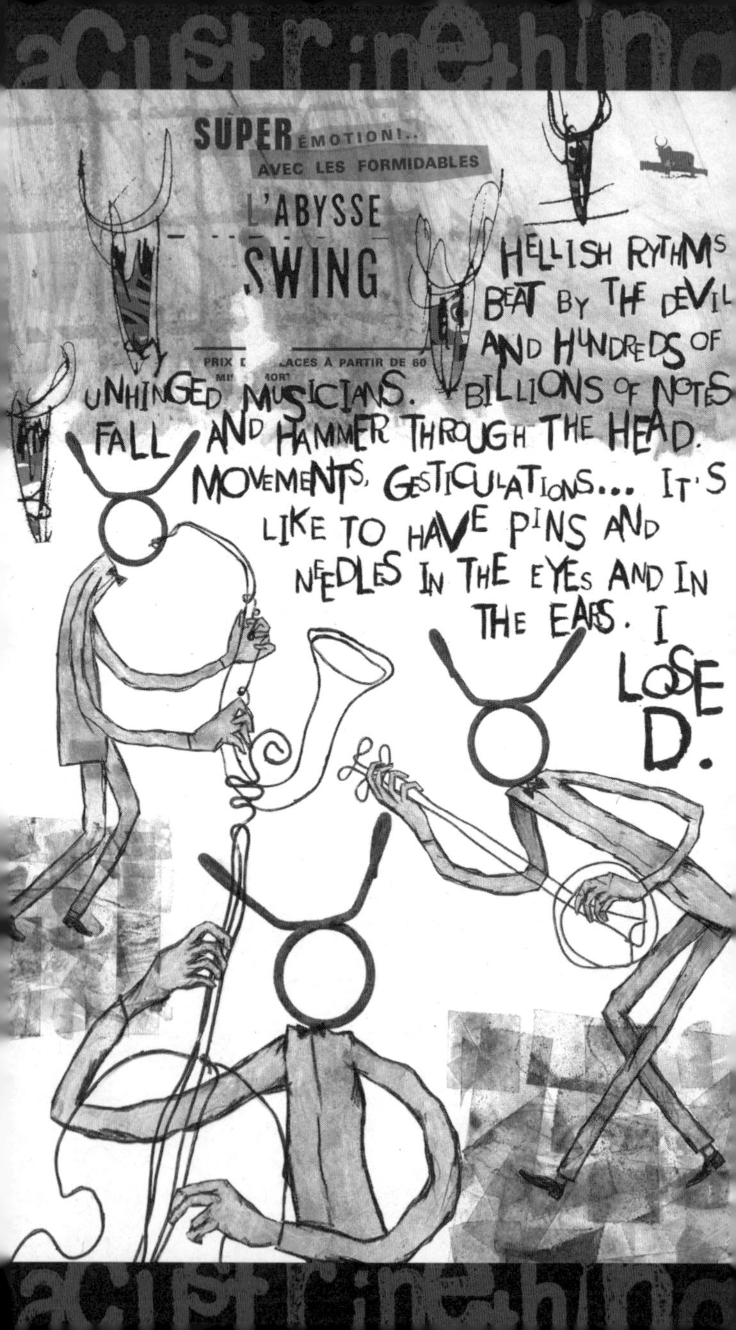
SUPER ÉMOTION!..
AVEC LES FORMIDABLES
L'ABYSSE
SWING
HELLISH RYTHMS BEAT BY THE DEVIL AND HUNDREDS OF UNHINGED MUSICIANS.
BILLIONS OF NOTES FALL AND HAMMER THROUGH THE HEAD.
MOVEMENTS, GESTICULATIONS... IT'S LIKE TO HAVE PINS AND NEEDLES IN THE EYES AND IN THE EARS.
I LOSE D.

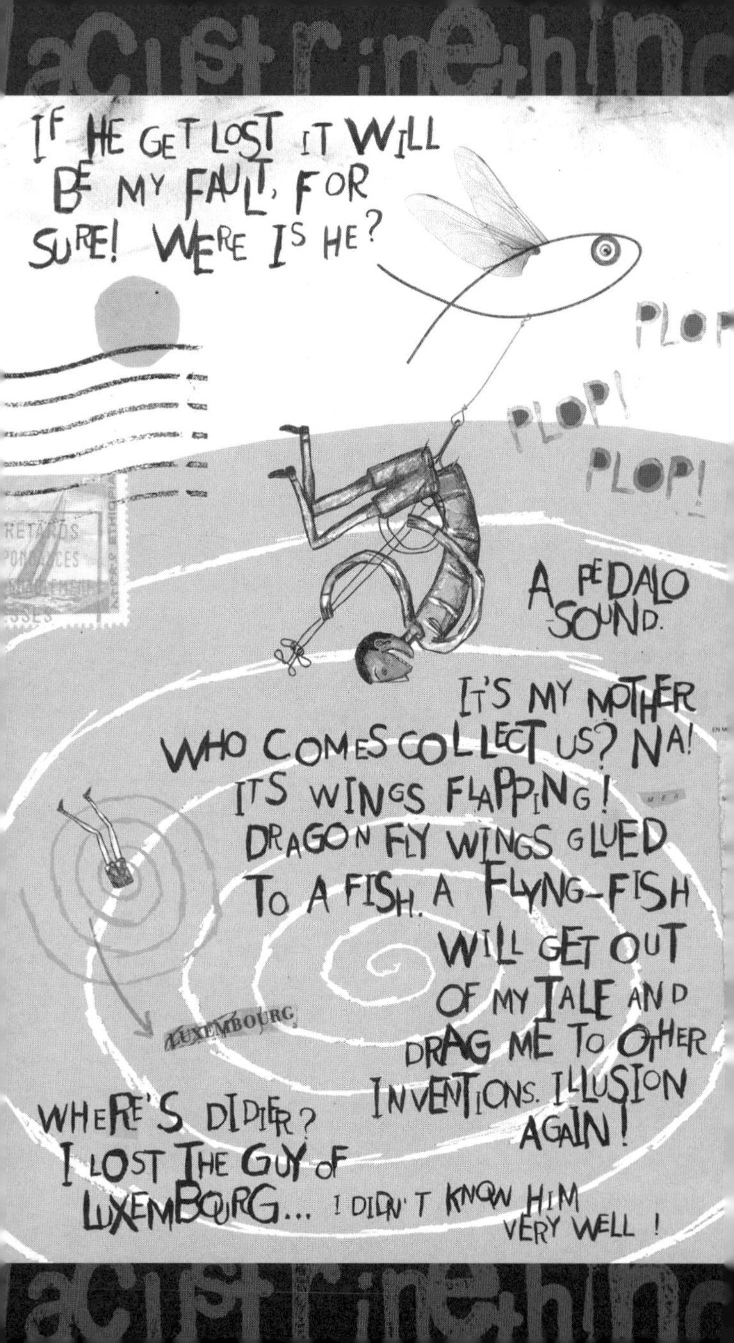

IF HE GET LOST IT WILL BE MY FAULT, FOR SURE! WERE IS HE?
PLOP
PLOP!
PLOP!
A PEDALO SOUND.
IT'S MY MOTHER WHO COMES COLLECT US? NA! ITS WINGS FLAPPING! DRAGON FLY WINGS GLUED TO A FISH. A FLYNG-FISH WILL GET OUT OF MY TALE AND DRAG ME TO OTHER INVENTIONS. ILLUSION AGAIN!
LUXEMBOURG
WHERE'S DIDIER? I LOST THE GUY OF LUXEMBOURG... I DIDN'T KNOW HIM VERY WELL!

SHARY BOYLE

Tampere 2005

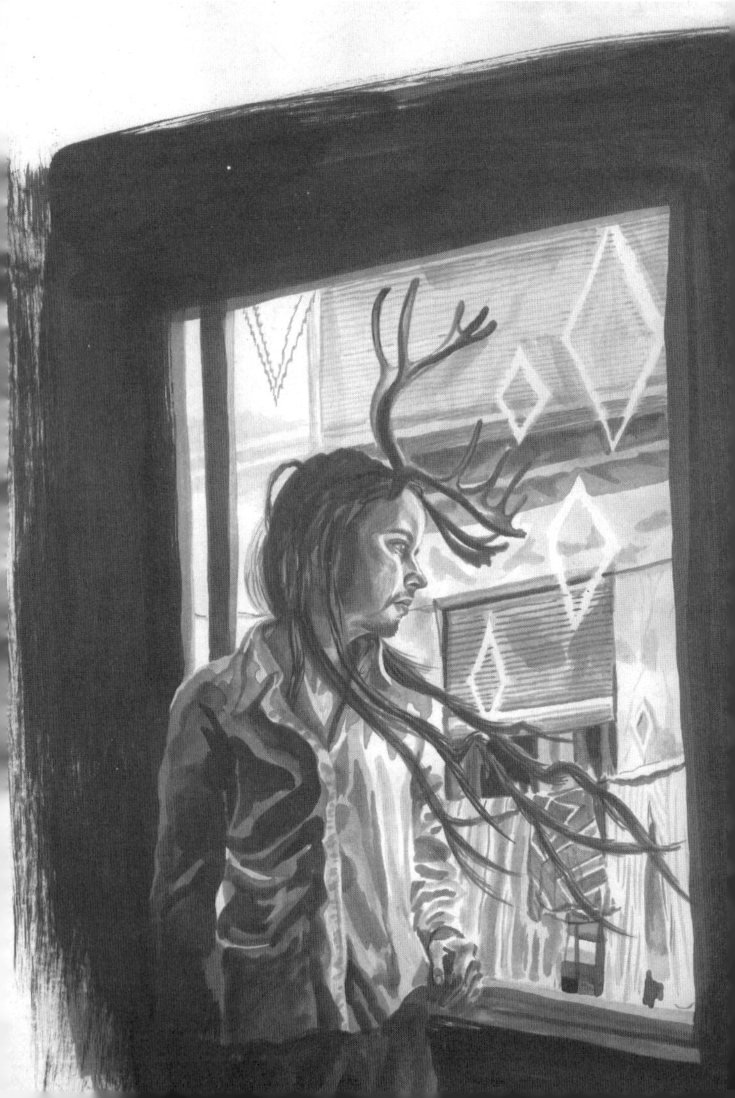

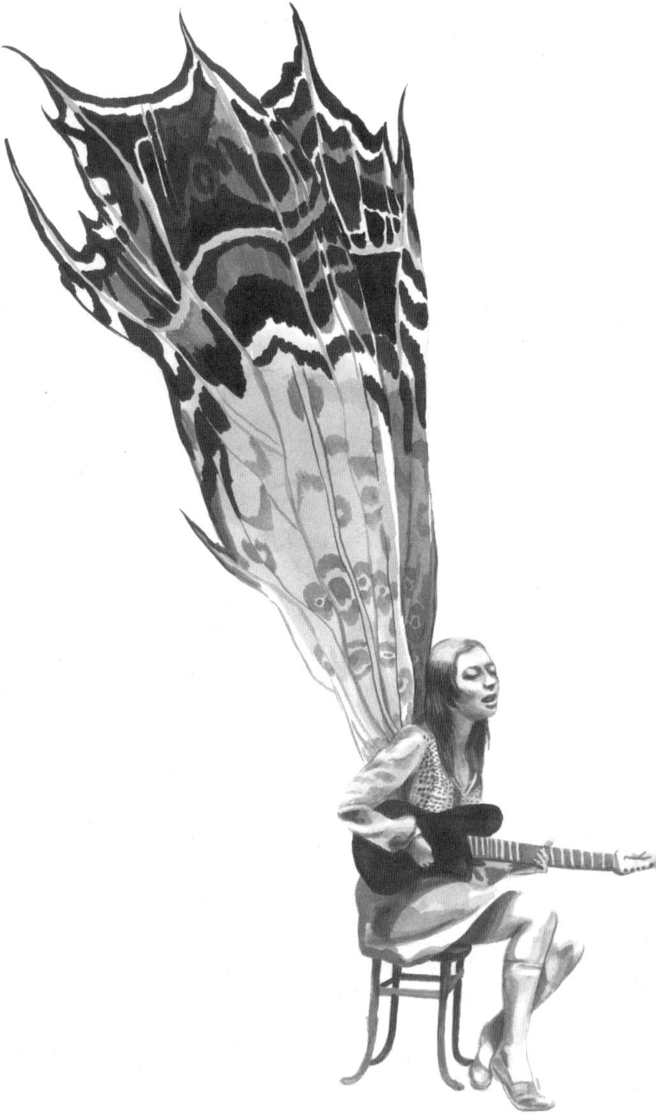

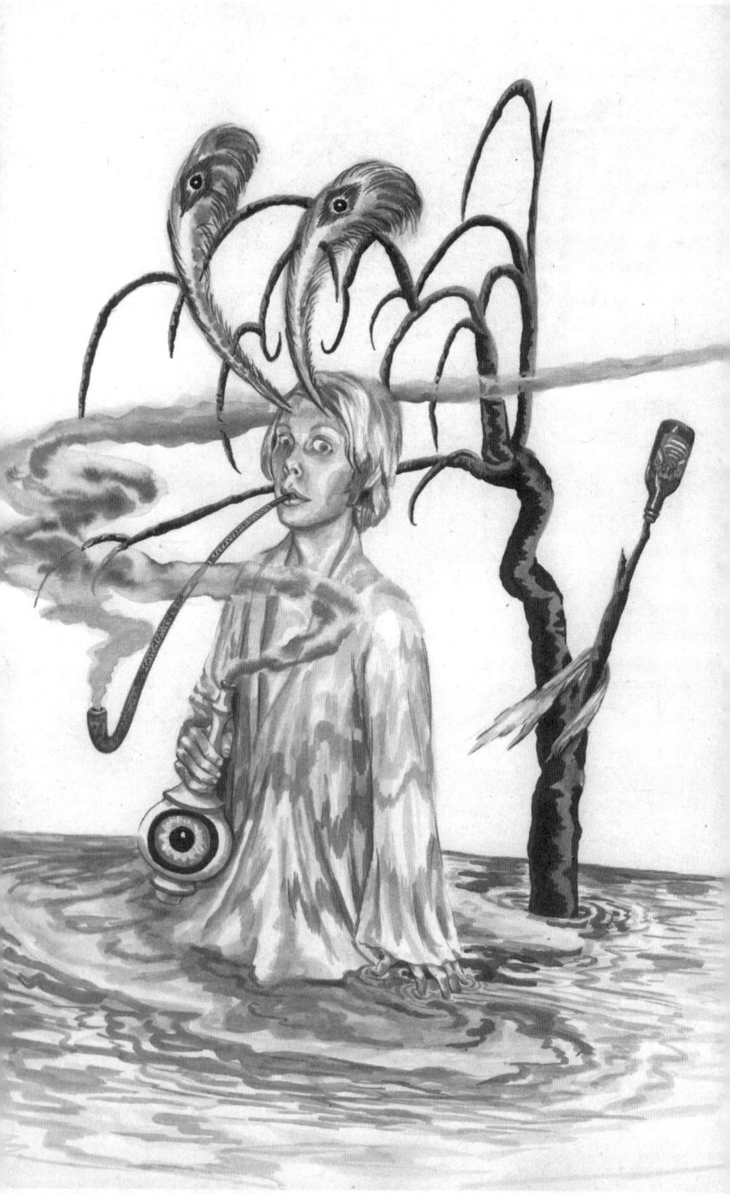

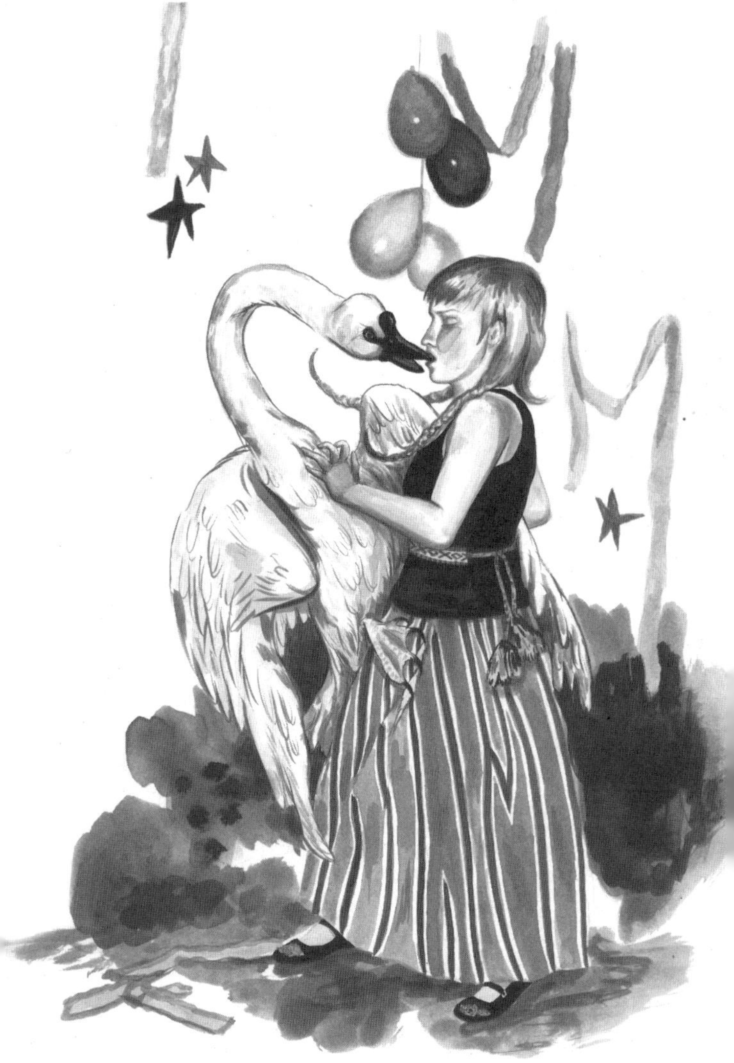

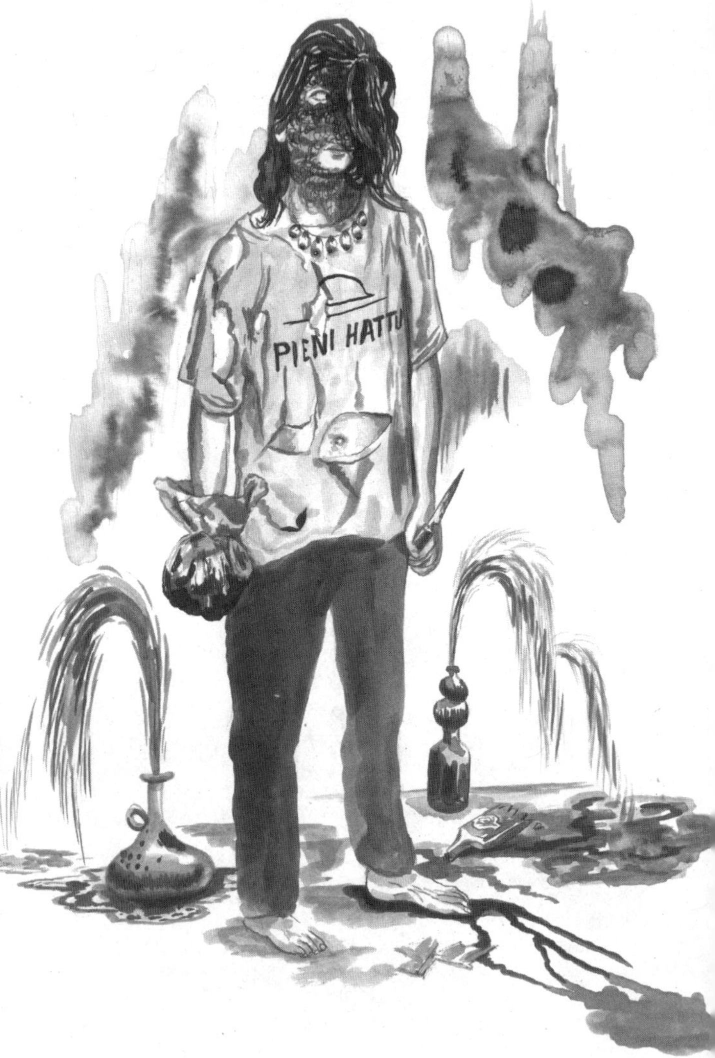
PIENI HATTU

MAYA MERRICK
from The Hole Show

1966

They say if you've put it in right you can't feel it, and they're right, you can't, not really, but she knows it's there, up there inside her, up there, down there, whichever it is or whatever it's called, it's there and she knows it. She once told her best friend that she loved it. Love what? Angelina had asked. My, you know, time of the month, she'd said. You love it? Angelina'd asked, her eyes going round. Well, yeah, she'd said. Oh, no, Dahlia, nobody loves it, Angelina had explained. That's why they call it The Curse. You can't love it, I don't think. Nobody does.

But Dahlia does. She walks around all day with her cotton secret, a secret planted in her by no one but herself. A secret thing she does to herself, and carries around in her, not at all like the furtive handstrokes she's gotten from boys, not at all like the ones she gives herself sometimes, those are over. Those disappear. This, this is something else. This she can feel.

*

Dahlia's moving into her sister's old room. Her sister has gone to *Visit her Aunt in Maine*. This phrase is always spoken in italics, in a loud whisper, whispered by Dahlia's mother's friends as they sit sipping tea in the kitchen. Dahlia overheard them one day and loudly pointed out that they don't have an aunt in Maine, but Dahlia's mother just told her to mind her business. Dahlia wonders about her sister, wonders what really happened to her. Dahlia would like to find her and thank her.

Dahlia's new room is much nicer than her old one.

*

If she pees onstage it's Mrs. Haversham's fault. She told her
she didn't want to do this. She told her she'd do something else,
anything else, make up the credit somehow. She tried everything.
But no. Mrs. Haversham just said, "Angelina's doing it, Dahlia,
it'll be fun for the two of you. Besides," Mrs. Haversham said, "it's
required. Do you want a black mark on your permanent record,
with graduation coming in a couple of years and you with such a
good chance at getting into a good school? Your father would be
very disappointed, Dahlia. Do you want to break your father's
heart?" Dahlia doesn't, but she doesn't know why. So.

She's wearing a baby-doll nightie, in shimmering blue, with
a pair of wire-framed wings strapped to her back, the nylon
bands digging angry red tracks under her armpits and leaving
wide, itchy trenches next to her brastraps. They've been tied on
so tight they pull her shoulders back in a strange, aching position, pushing her tits out front for all the world to see. She tries
to huddle back into her regular slouch but she can't. She shoves
her glasses up on her nose, as she's been doing manically every
ten seconds for the past hour.

"Dahlia! You look wonderful! Are you excited? I'm excited!!!
Are you excited?!" Angelina Morretti comes boucing up, her
Mrs. Claus outfit tucked up into her Mrs. Claus wide black
patent leather belt until the hem of her skirt barely covers her
cheeks. She is positively squeaking with pressurized glee.
Angelina and Dahlia are best friends. They sit next to each other
every recess and every lunch. They walk to school together
every morning, and home each afternoon. They have sleep-
overs and try on each other's outfits. They draw faces on each
other and pout into the mirror. They talk to each other on the
phone at least ten times a night. They are, as their mothers say,
inseperable. Two peas in a canoe.

"Oh, so excited. I can't wait for this to be over." Dahlia's
folding her arms over her chest and frowning towards the floor.

"Oh, Dahlia! Don't be silly!" Angelina shoves Dahlia play-
fully. "I got flowers!!! Did you get flowers???"

Dahlia didn't get flowers. Her mother is currently leaning heavily on the arm of a man out there in the crowd, possibly the only man who came to this thing alone. Her mother can always find them, men alone. Dahlia's father is working late. Another man alone. Dahlia wonders who might be finding him, right now.

"Oh, my daddy sent me some but they're at home." Dahlia smiles this creaking stretched smile at Angelina. She smiles so hard she almost believes it. She tilts her head up and casts her eyes to the ceiling, looking, she thinks, dreamy. "The bouquet was just too big to bring here. But they're really pretty." Angelina cocks her head to one side and bobs it up and down. "Pink," Dahlia adds, before Angelina gives her a great big smile and one last bob of her head.

"Wow! Well, good luck out there!" Angelina gives Dahlia a brief, spare hug that might as well be from across the room. "Boy, Dahlia, I sure wish I had a part like yours! It must be great not to have to remember any lines!! And you're sure to be the only angel with glasses!!! You'll really stand out!!!" Angelina catches someone's eye and makes her way over, waving to all the pretty angels and blowing kisses to all the elves. Dahlia shoves her glasses up on her nose, then crosses her arms even more tightly over her tits and wonders if she has time to run to the bathroom for just a second.

Mrs. Haversham is running around madly pinning costumes together, patting rouge on rogue elves who think themselves far too manly for makeup, and tugging the errant Mrs. Claus skirt back over Angelina's far too visible ass. Dahlia walks over, hugging her tits to her chest and trying her best to breathe.

"Mrs. Haversham?"

Mrs. Haversham is trying to squinch down Loretta's overly ratted hair, always the tallest hair in class.

"Yes, dear?"

Loretta is rolling her eyes and tapping the toe of her black ballet slipper impatiently. Loretta smokes in the bathroom and carries a switchblade in her garter. Loretta dates university boys and carries a safe. Loretta is fast. Loretta is smirking and quietly giving Dahlia the finger. Dahlia sighs and walks away, shoving her glasses up on her nose one more time.

"Nothing," Dahlia mutters, to no one.

It is bright, brighter than any place she's ever been before. She can't see anything, anyone, even though she decided at the last second to wear her glasses. With her hair she can hardly hope to go unnoticed, whether she's wearing her glasses or not. But up here it doesn't matter, nothing matters, nothing at all. No one else is there, at all, at all. And she can just kind of be invisible up here, away from everybody else, where everyone can see. Dahlia blinks and gets this feeling like maybe she's found a big secret, like maybe that blinding light can make her into something she never even knew was anywhere, let alone somewhere inside her heavy glasses and white hair and big tits and weird nervous peeing. She forgets her steps and gets shoved by the angel behind her. She stumbles through it, her first minute and a half onstage, and makes it offstage and into the bathroom before she even really knows what happened. She locks herself in a stall and starts to laugh, until her fake lashes come loose and crawl down her face, their million million black legs tracing scratchy trails down her cheeks and leaving the only evidence that she was ever even there. Onstage.

1971

And here comes Dolly, weebling toward him from across the smoky bar. She's got her war paint on tonight, slick hair-thin lines painted around the base of her neck, on her elbows and wrists, all her joints articulated in browns and pinks over her powdered glue-white skin. She leans up against him and flutters her caterpillar eyelashes.

"Hello there Hicklin. Buy me a drink?" She talks slow and quiet, a tired, sad old song, words coming out whole with her lips barely moving. Her hair spills red over her shoulders, tumbling perfect over either side of her cold white neck. Shiny red head-band, wide like Alice's. Her mouth is glossy and red, matching the headband, sort of blinding. Hicklin wants to touch her mouth, wants to see what's under that paint, what's under that shiny shiny red. Something white, something pink, something else alto-gether, something maybe he's never seen before, something fresh that's never ever been touched by daylight. He looks up into her scary violet eyes, the whites too white, the colour inhuman, sur-rounded as always by their armed guard of fake lashes, extra extra long, what else?

"Sure, Dolly. Whatever you want."

She leans her head on his shoulder, puts an arm around him all slow. "Thanks Hicklin. You're a good kid you know. A good kid." Her lips barely moving, her words coming out whole from her sad, shining mouth.

He doesn't know for sure, but he's heard that Dolly is younger than he is. She runs this thing called *Les Sucettes*. Suckers.

"You got a show tonight, Dolly?"

She looks at him with those gleaming, glassy eyes. Opens them wide and looks at him, putting her chin down so he's sur-rounded. Lashes everywhere.

"Yeah. You want to watch?"

Her drink arrives, two fingers of whiskey with a speared cherry, floating. He pays with the last of his birthday money.

"Can't," he shrugs. "No money."

She squeezes up close to him, her crinoline crunching between them. Her dress is shiny red too, strapless. She's added childish, poofy sleeves out of an almost matching fabric. They've fallen down, stripping her shoulders bare. Hicklin can see the thin lines she's drawn around her shoulders there, so her arms can move. He wonders if they are all drawn in, around her hips and everywhere?

"Come with me. You won't have to pay for anything if you're with me. Come on. I like you." Dead cold lips not smiling she tugs at him. "C'mon." He looks down at her hand, tugging at his sleeve. Her fingernails are creepy pink, buffed to a brand new shine. Her pale white makeup has left tiny prints all over him, prints of her cheeks, her fingers, her neck. He looks at her. Doesn't look like any of the makeup has come off at all. She cocks her head at him, coyly, not smiling. She blinks her lifelike eyes. He gets up off the stool, and follows her to the back of the bar.

*

At first he thinks it's Flannery, that she's forgiven him and come back.

Hicklin's sandy head next to a curly red one, just as it was, for so long. But. Skin pale, paler than human, and these funny lines all over the girl. Beau thinks maybe it's the blue light that makes her look that way, like skim milk, a cataract, the inside of a cow's eyeball.

They tried to find Hicklin, all over the city, went to trashy bars and strip clubs and all the little holes he likes to drink in and: Nothing. Maybe he was here the whole time. It's the only place they didn't bother to check.

Beau takes a slow step into the room, the floor groaning low under his weight. The girl shifts slightly, rolls over, curling into herself, away from Hicklin. Beau can see from here that Hicklin is wearing at least a shirt, a dress shirt, dirty white, still buttoned. Hicklin doesn't move when he sleeps. Sleeps on his back with his eyes shut tight, performing some weird kind of penance. Beau takes another step in. Crosses as soft as he can, bends down until his face is level with Hicklin's.

Big eyes closed, eyelids unwrinkled but still not smooth. Not a crease on his face, a baby beard just starting to grow in, sandy as the rest of him.

"Hicklin," Beau whispers, "Sorry about your birthday."

There is a smell, a smell like Christmas, a smell like the home outside him. A girl falling backwards in gold dust. Beau puts his hands out, trying to touch without touching, his fingers not finding anywhere to be.

"Hey." There is a whisper from across the bed. She is looking at him with these scary violet eyes, smudged from sleep and the whites a little red, but the colour so bright, he's surprised they can blink. But they do. "You okay?"

"Yeah." Beau nods his head, once.

"But you're crying." She speaks softly, a crinkle coming out like you hear on old records. Raspy, worn with a needle. Beau rubs a finger around under one eye. Comes back wet.

"So I am," he whispers back, and gives her a weak grin. "S'been a long night, I guess."

"Come to bed." She doesn't return his smile, just folds back the edge of Hicklin's holey army blanket and squinches over a bit to make room. She is wearing a red cocktail dress with tattered sleeves. Beau stands. "Come on there's room. Come to bed."

There is white powder dusting the blankets and pillows, there is white powder everywhere. She is still holding open the blanket for him. Still not smiling.

"You always this friendly?" Beau asks quiet, climbing into the bed, sheet slightly shifting.

"Always," she whispers, forever not smiling, closing the covers right over him, slow, with an arm that smells of Christmas. He turns away from her and she curls right up around him, her breath coming slow on the back of his neck. He can't see her face anymore but she holds him slowly, tighter and tighter, crinkling with crinoline, until he falls asleep.

1966

Dahlia lies awake in her bed, listening to her parents arrange themselves into separate rooms, patterns of shifting, their feet clomping (Dad) and tikking (Mom) away from each other down the hall. Their voices come soft through the floor, strained, almost silent. She hears her father say please and her mother say simply, goodnight. She hears the door to the den shut softly. No more clomping. There is a tik tik tik, her mother taking three steps, then stopping. Two soft thuds, duk, duk. A soft padding follows, through the kitchen, down the hall, up the carpeted stairs. Past Dahlia's bedroom, not stopping. Her mother's bedroom door is opened, quietly, then shut. Click.

Dahlia waits. She winds her bedside alarm clock, as her grandad told her to when he gave it to her, not too much, just enough to keep it running. She winds it a bit too tight, she can feel the springs start to give. Start to buckle. She forces herself to put the clock down before she sees how much further she can turn the key. Bathroom noises come muffled through the walls, water splashing, a medicine cabinet opening and shutting, a toilet flushing. Dahlia's mother has her own bathroom, off the master bedroom. Dahlia shares the downstairs bathroom with her father, when he is here. Usually, he is not.

Her mother's bed barely creaks. Dahlia listens to her mother reading in another room. At 10:00 PM precisely by the hands of Dahlia's Baby Ben she hears her mother switch off her reading lamp. Dahlia waits.

She has scissors in her bed. Tucked under her ass, in case any one had come in to say goodnight to her. She didn't really need to worry, though. No one did.

*

The kitchen in the morning is uncommonly full. Her mother and father are there, eating toast. Sunlight streams through a pot of homemade (though not by her mother) marmalade, this golden, perfect light shining out from the heart of it. Dahlia wonders did Abigail ever see such a thing? She shoves her glasses up on her nose and takes a step, down the stairs. Another. All they can see is her feet, for now. She creeps down, slower, and quieter, her bare feet finally landing on the linoleum, golden and green.

She crosses the floor, silently. Her father reads the paper, her mother makes a list. Like every, every morning ever. Before.

"Hey, Kitten!" her father says to the paper, "How's tricks?"

"Dahlia, I had a most disturbing conversation with Mrs. Lovecraft the other day, did you know — what on earth have you done to your head?!!?"

Dahlia says the only thing she can think of to say.

"They said I had lice."

Which was a lie, because they didn't. She cut it off curling in long pale strands, filled her pillowcase with it. All the ends looked back at her with these tiny, wee eyes, accusing her.

"I'll keep you, don't worry. You won't have to die." Tied up the open end of her pillowcase and cut everything else as short as she could. The scissors slipping out of her sweating hands. Her nightgown off, blocking the light under the door. All these tiny bits of hair, too many to count. Cut to the shape of her head.

Swept them up as best she could, into the toilet, dumping a wad of crushed Kleenex on top and flushing. Turned off the bathroom light, opened the door, quiet creak. In the light from the hallway when she opened the door, her eyes huger behind her glasses than she ever remembered, her head she'd never seen swimming back at her. Under ten minutes, as she'd promised herself.

"Lice? Who has lice in this day and age?" Her father slams down his paper and strides over to peer at the top of Dahlia's head. "My father had lice! I had lice! All my brothers and sisters too! But my daughter should not HAVE LICE! What are they doing over there? Can't they keep the place clean? Or don't I pay them enough! Who can I call, Sissy? Who?" Throughout this tirade he is pulling at the tufts of hair still sprouting from Dahlia's head, pulling on them with his fingernails, examining the results underneath. "Sissy, I can't see a damned thing, get me my glasses, would you? And what kind of half-blind nincompoop cut your hair, anyway? Jeezus, don't they have to call before they butcher your child's head? Keeerist!"

"Oh, Albert, settle down, dear. I'm sure they had their reasons and that they got the best person they could to cut the children's hair. There must've been a lot of them. Isn't that right, honey?"

Her mother looks at her sweetly, vacantly. Her father is still yanking at her head. Dahlia is staring at the floor, making pictures from the spots and scuff marks on the lino. There is a man wearing a monkey for a hat, riding a puffy bull. He is drawing an arrow through a huge, huge bow. She can't see what he's aiming at, as her father has a pretty tight grip on her head right about now. A tiny bird laughs from the man's shoulder.

"Honey?"

"What? Um, no... it was only me."

"What? Only you? What kind of a Mickey Mouse operation is that place anyway? They haven't heard of tar shampoo? Good lord! Sissy, I still can't see a damned thing, where the hell are my glasses?!!"

"Oh, yes. Sorry, dear." Dahlia's mother rises to fetch the glasses from down the hall, from the dish near the door. Dahlia made it out of cheap grey clay, painted it gold and green to match the lino. When the floor was new, when the house was new, when she was little and they'd just moved in. Her father tugs at her head, scratching her scalp with his big, blunt nails, moves her view to a new spot on the floor. There's a high heeled scuff mark down there, shaped like a tiny horseshoe. Driven down deep, and dark. Dahlia's mother only wears shoes with a low, wide heel. At home she wears flat, soft shoes. Like slippers. She broke one of her vertebrae diving when she was young. She was supposed to go to the Olympics. She's never worn high heels. She can't. Dahlia stares at the tiny heel mark, such a deep hole in such a shallow thing. The lino is only this thin, how can that hole go down so far? She can't even begin to see the end of it. Who could wear shoes that make holes like that?

Her father is still muttering away, pulling at her hair. Her mother is coming back down the hall, her feet softly creeping.

"There you go, Albert."

Her father lets go of Dahlia's head, to put on his glasses.

Dahlia turns and stares at him. What is he even doing here, pretending like things are normal? He doesn't even live here. Do they think she doesn't know?

"Thank you very much. Now! Let's take a look at this 'lice', shall we?"

The glasses on his face. His fingers going up to his eyes. There was someone they never talked about, a tramp. That's what her mother called her. Would a tramp wear shoes like that?

He's peering at her head now, tsking. "Dahlia, I don't see a damned thing on your head that could even be related to lice. You want to tell me the truth now? You want to tell me just what the hell is going on?"

Her mother looks slowly from Dahlia to Albert. "No lice? Dahlia, what is going on? Who did this to you?"

Dahlia takes a deep breath. Maybe she should just tell them, just say it out loud. But Abigail wouldn't, would she? Abigail would keep her secret safe. She opens her mouth and says, "Momma, you don't have any high heels, do you?"

1971

"You terrible bitch!"

"What?"

"You ratted on your Dad to save your own ass!"

Dolly pauses and considers this, rolling her big scary eyes ceilingward as an aid.

"I suppose I did. I guess I am a terrible bitch." Another pause, a long shrug from one black-sleeved shoulder. "What the hell. He deserved it. Rat bastard."

Hicklin enters the kitchen, still wearing his ragged white shirt from the night before, his hair sticking up all over, in places gone white from Dolly's dust. Beau and Dolly are sitting at the table, sharing a cigarette and drinking coffee from jam jars. Dolly is wearing glasses. Dolly is bald. The stubble is so pale it almost hurts to look at it. She's wearing Hicklin's old skeleton print T-shirt and nothing else.

"Hicklin, have you heard this story? This little tart ratted out her daddy to save her own sweet ass! Can you believe it? She's wonderful! Where did you find her?" Beau rises to give Hicklin a hug. "Sorry about last night, sunshine. But we got you a special breakfast!"

Dolly rises ceremoniously, lifts a dishrag from a plate, does a sweeping thing with her arms like those spangled ladies on daytime TV, the ones who show off your crappy prize.

"Oooooh," goes Beau, in a suitably awed tone.

On the dish: two May Wests, unwrapped, nubby candles slanting sidewise. A jam jar of something clear. Six bananas, a bowl of honey, and a pear. Squishy cheese and a long loaf of bread.

Beside the dish: as Dolly lifts her arms to present these wonders, a peep of pubes. Pale as ghosts, ghosts of the screaming squiggle of his one true love.

Hicklin bends and picks up the jam jar, trying his best to look anywhere else. Even those ghosts have the power to make him fall down. The smell of whatever it is in the jar, though, isn't helpful for standing.

"Pah! What the hell is this?"

"It's alcool, baby! Cheaper than gas and twice as good!" Beau takes up the jar and sips. "Achhh!" he sputters, "Smoooooooooth!"

Dolly fixes them with a grave stare, and reaches for the jar. A finger disappears down her throat. Then another. Licks her lips and hands it over. "It's still your birthday Hicklin. Have a drink."

Holding the glass just to his lips and feeling them burn, his eyes watering from some vicious vapour. Sips. Being burned alive from the inside, in a cozy way. Warming. Like rage.

"Oof... geezus...."

"Ooo, oooh! Can I have another?"

"Well I don't know," sighs Dolly, a little almost cheery lilt in her voice. "What kind of day do you guys wanna have?"

Illustrations by JOE OLLMANN
Story by WAYNE GLASS

Three Ladies and Jesus

A PARTIAL EXCERPT OF A LETTER, CONSISTING OF A STORY INVOLVING THREE WOMEN AND A MISTAKEN IDENTITY CASE INVOLVING JESUS HIMSELF.

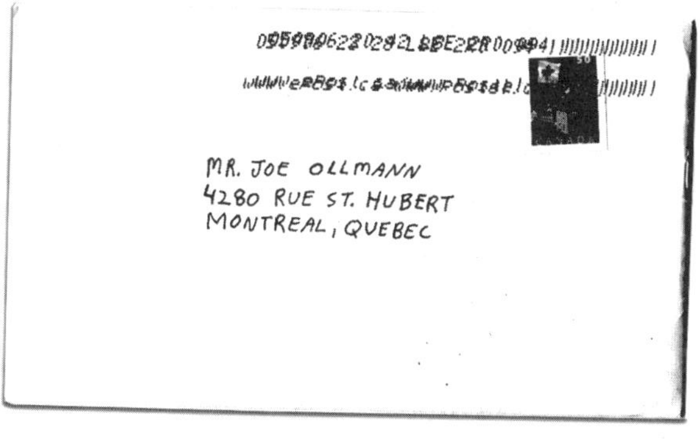
MR. JOE OLLMANN
4280 RUE ST. HUBERT
MONTREAL, QUEBEC

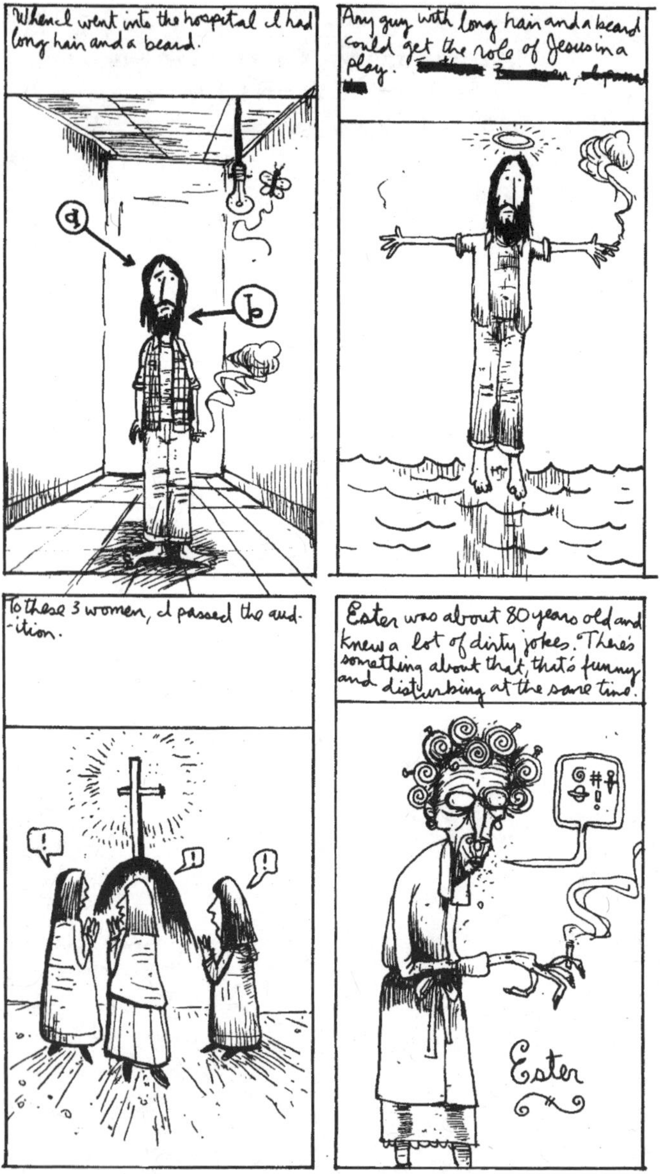
When I went into the hospital I had long hair and a beard.
Any guy with long hair and a beard could get the role of Jesus in a play. [redacted]
To these 3 women, I passed the audition.
Ester was about 80 years old and knew a lot of dirty jokes. There's something about that, that's funny and disturbing at the same time.
Ester

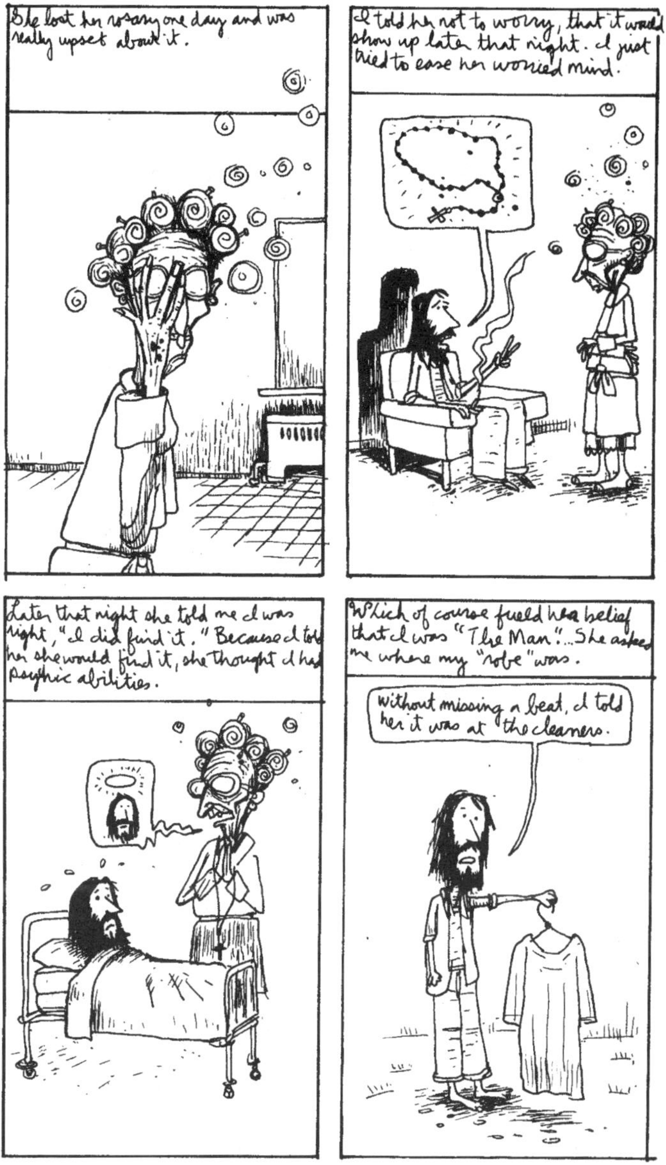
She lost her rosary one day and was really upset about it.
I told her not to worry, that it would show up later that night. I just tried to ease her worried mind.
Later that night she told me I was right, "I did find it." Because I told her she would find it, she thought I had psychic abilities.
Which of course fueled her belief that I was "The Man"... She asked me where my "robe" was.
Without missing a beat, I told her it was at the cleaners.

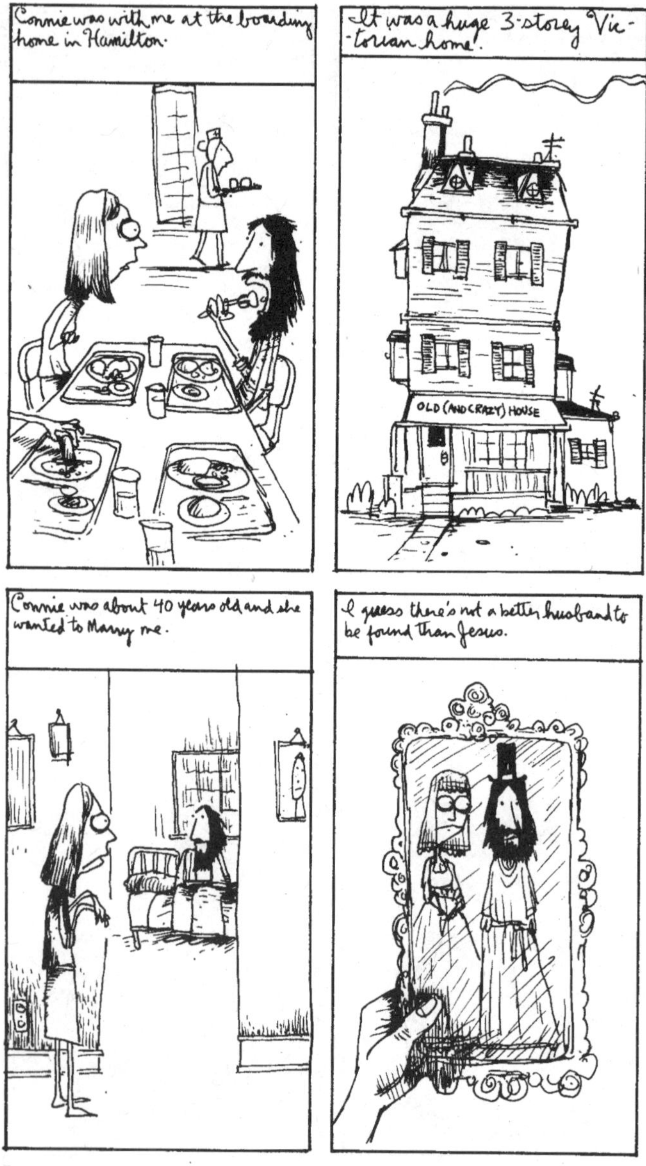
Connie was with me at the boarding home in Hamilton.
It was a huge 3-storey Victorian home.
OLD (AND CRAZY) HOUSE
Connie was about 40 years old and she wanted to Marry me.
I guess there's not a better husband to be found than Jesus.

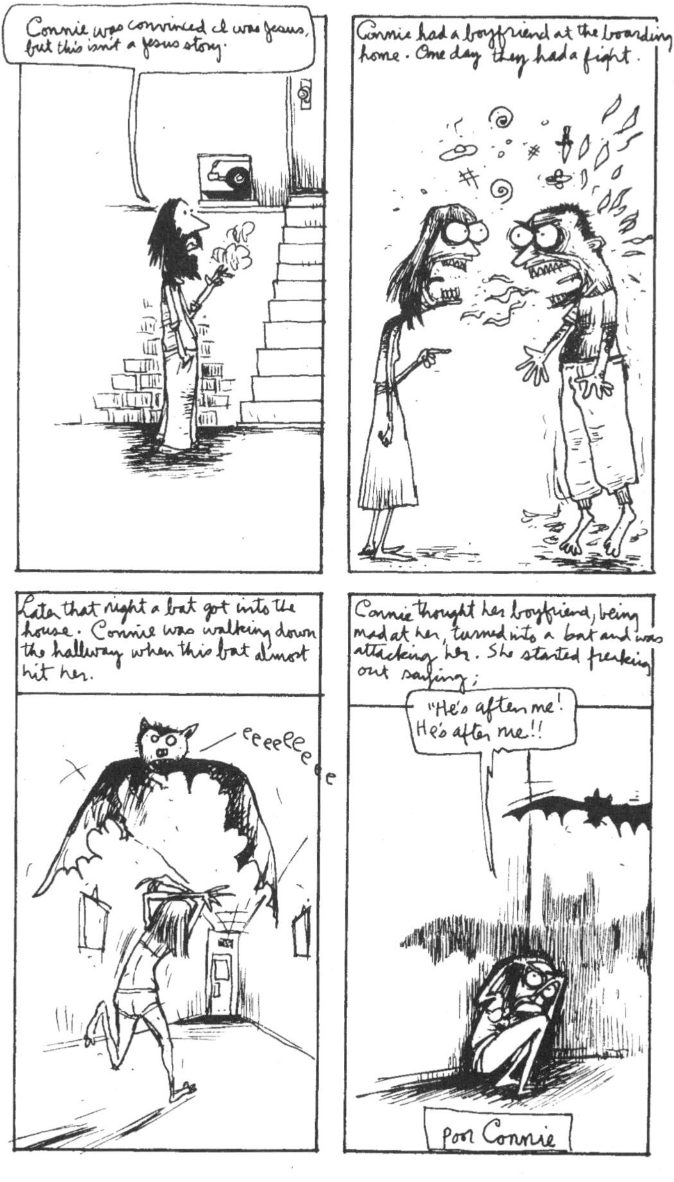
Connie was convinced I was Jesus, but this isn't a Jesus story.
Connie had a boyfriend at the boarding home. One day they had a fight.
Later that night a bat got into the house. Connie was walking down the hallway when this bat almost hit her.
eeeeeeee
Connie thought her boyfriend, being mad at her, turned into a bat and was attacking her. She started freaking out saying;
"He's after me! He's after me!!
Poor Connie

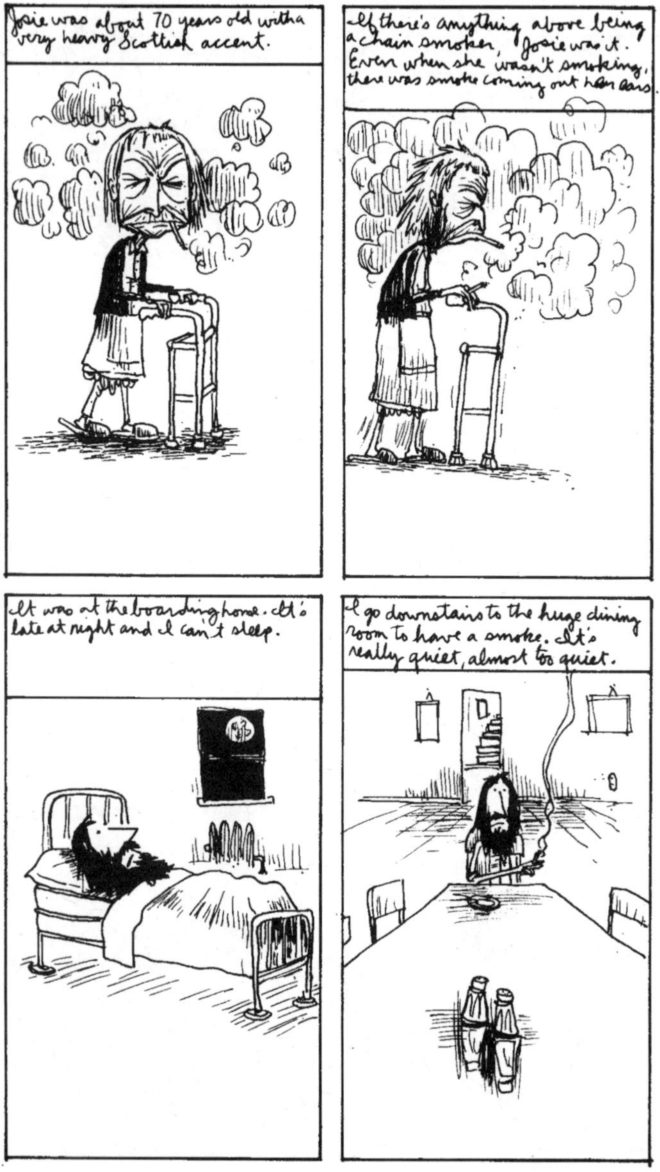
Josie was about 70 years old with a very heavy Scottish accent.
If there's anything above being a chain smoker, Josie was it. Even when she wasn't smoking, there was smoke coming out her ears.
It was at the boarding house. It's late at night and I can't sleep.
I go downstairs to the huge dining room to have a smoke. It's really quiet, almost too quiet.

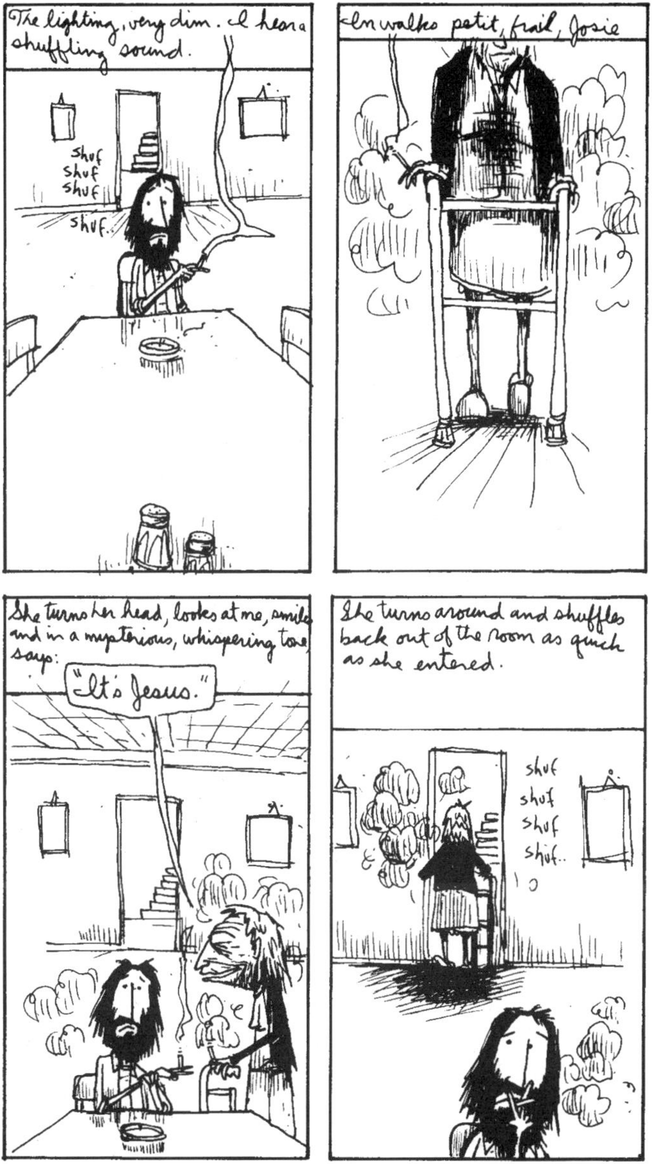
The lighting, very dim. I hear a shuffling sound.
shuf
shuf
shuf
shuf..
In walks petit, frail, Josie
She turns her head, looks at me, smiles and in a mysterious, whispering tone, says:
"It's Jesus."
She turns around and shuffles back out of the room as quick as she entered.
shuf
shuf
shuf
shuf..

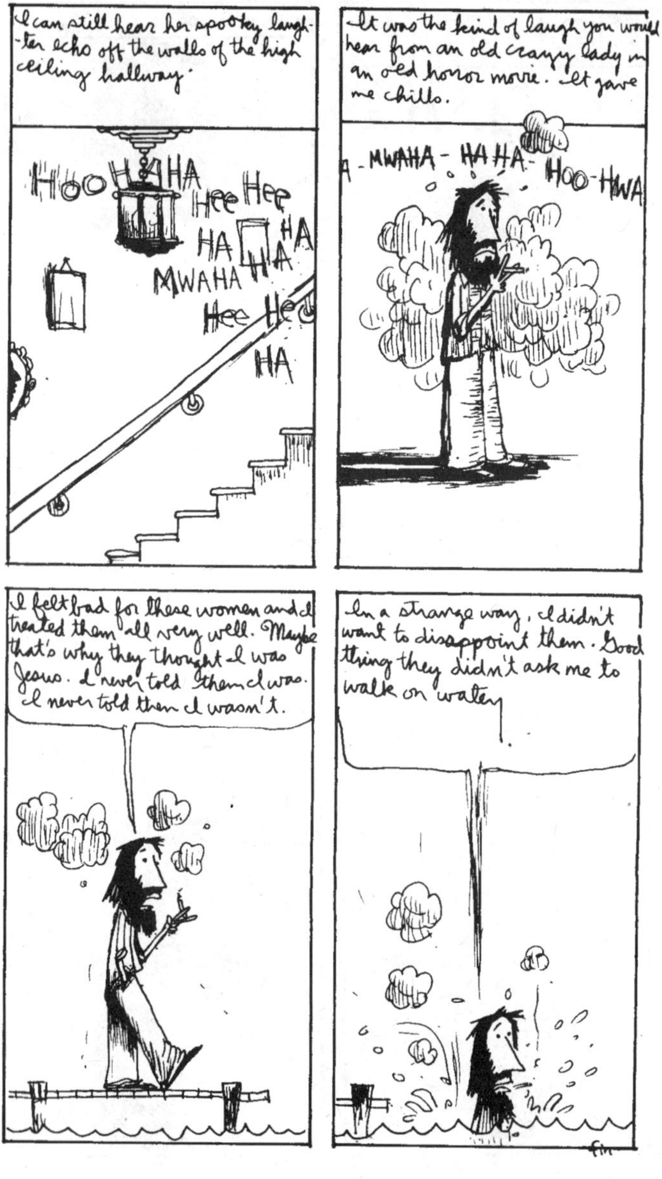
I can still hear her spooky laugh-ter echo off the walls of the high ceiling hallway.
HOO HA HA
Hee Hee
HA HA HA
MWAHA HA
Hee Hee
HA
It was the kind of laugh you would hear from an old crazy lady in an old horror movie. It gave me chills.
A - MWAHA - HA HA - HOO-HWA
I felt bad for these women and I treated them all very well. Maybe that's why they thought I was Jesus. I never told them I was. I never told them I wasn't.
In a strange way, I didn't want to disappoint them. Good thing they didn't ask me to walk on water.

fin

NATHANIEL G. MOORE
from Legends of Welfare

*W*elfare *recipients in Ontario may face mandatory drug tests under a new plan unveiled on Wednesday by the Ontario provincial government. But an even newer twist in welfare culture may see some recipients back to work faster than you would imagine possible under the old system. The latest faction of social services is already facing criticism by morality groups and some MPs have called it "demeaning, dangerous, degrading, disturbing and in poor taste." What's all the fuss? Legends of Welfare program insures you get your money quicker, but with a catch. Your caseworker may end up crashing on your couch.*

Office Hours

Perry Oaltch sat in the office of the municipal social services for District C-5, filling out a three page *LOW* questionnaire with a hangnail of a writing instrument, a stubby well-worn number 3 pencil *sans* eraser. As he did, two Legends scuttled past in their matching navy blue trench coats and sunglasses, carrying a tray of lattés and two paper bags filled with fresh bagels.

You get your money quicker eh? said an unwashed shadow in a chair beside him. *But they monitor you like you wouldn't believe. I can't lose 'em,* the dirty beard said, as Perry continued to scan the application pages in his lap, and ignored his surroundings, dreaming the bagel waft would return.

Perry inhaled the teasing aromatics of the waning breeze, brushed his greasy brown hair from his hazel eyes with confident gusts of taco breath, as he forced the comical plastic wrap for the treat deeper in his jacket pocket. He had been quick at the corner snack stand, spending what seemed like the last paper bill of money to his name. He was desperate, without hope, twenty-two-years-old, unable to return home, and completely muddled in fantasy.

The reality was, he couldn't stay with his aunt anymore, he

couldn't return to school, he couldn't go anywhere but the strange economic netherworld known to most as a welfare state. He licked his lips and tried to clean his breath with several nervous swallows. Each teaspoon of saliva contained 56 grams of cornstarch. *Meeting Keegan after this*, he thought to himself, obsessed with his new 'gang'.

"Fare-well," he laughed, looking at the word. *Welfare*. This was some moment, some sinister removal of innocence and hope. He closed his eyes and daydreamed of being simultaneously bludgeoned and embalmed while his body lay twitching on the academic blood slab. Academic suspension due to lack of funds. Lack of scholarships, planning. Lack of good luck. This was some end.

Just lend me the fucking money, now! That's what he wrote to his parents. His grandparents. His senile uncle. His dead grandparents.

Perry was thin, pale and moved with awkward and cluttered gestures.

Of course, eight months earlier, in late August, you would never have recognized Perry Oaltch. He was a top academic prospect, a student among students, slowly getting hopped up on the unsettling notion that he could recast himself in Graham Greene's *Brighton Rock* with the nod of a fedora. He read from it obsessively, had copies of the book stowed away in washroom stalls and tucked seamlessly under friend's couch cushions. He even conjured up his own gang within the web of his dysfunctioning social life. The work-in-progress gang was comprised of four core members, who Perry would write about on index cards, assigning tasks, descriptions and roles within the gang.

"Of course you never show the cards to anyone, right?" his caseworker asked.

"No. I don't know what this has to do with my going on welfare."

"Oh, it has plenty, you'll see."

Perry wrote obsessively about his gang, until he finished the outline for their demise.

"I don't understand why you need to know about these things," Perry said.

"We want to know how you have been spending your time," the caseworker offered.

"But more importantly," a second worker added, "how you plan to spend your time."

"On welfare," the duo said simultaneously.

He would get through the nasal inquisition, he would overcome the landslide of paperclips and carbon copy signatures, obtain an instant income, meet up with fellow gang member and heavily medicated associate Keegan Keeley, crash on his couch and call it a day. And what a day, for Perry Oaltch. He was assured, pending any unforeseeable conflict, his first welfare cheque would be hand delivered on Monday morning. That gave him two days on the lam, eating out of imaginary troughs and cleaning his socks in the sawed-off washrooms of food courts and abandoned bagel factories.

"Hey, let's meet up," Perry said, leaning creepily and twirling at a crusty payphone.

"Sure. Where?" Keegan said in a low monotone voice.

"Your place. I've got nothing remember?"

"Five," Keegan said, maintaining a deadpan voice, groggy and forced. He coughed and sighed, as if each breath was a push-up. "Come over then."

Keegan hung up the phone. He was working afternoons at the library, shelving books, trying to put his medicated life back in order, and Perry was now a part of it, a deep and muddled but all too real hallucination. Keegan worked slowly, one book at a time, sometimes losing his count, forgetting which section he was working on, even with a giant list and fluorescent marker in front of him. He was muddled in the dirty and deep-trenched world of pharmaceutical roulette; his stomach was a fertile garden of dangerous toxins, burbling through his veins and altering his states of mind and consciousness, the quicksand effects of the always in fashion Cogetin and Epival, voted best supporting pharmaceutical in a nervous breakdown. *Perry,* Keegan thought, *what does he want me to do now?*

Hostility & Carbohydrates

The sinister black van pulled up in front of the bungalow, noting a tattered woman adjusting a piece of paper on a vacuum cleaner with the dedicated movements of an art dealer.

"This must be the place, there's an old woman adjusting a sign on an orphaned vacuum cleaner," The Legend said, setting his watch with his partner. The camera crew in the van prepped for the invasion, their garb a big black net of dark Velcro and rayon.

The well-worn couch cushions were not protective sandbags but roots that secured the Barringtons to the unsuspecting migration of irritants. For these fatigued limbs there would be no way of preparing; the driveway was unusually alit with radiant car lights. The Barringtons thought the additional light was odd, mainly because everyone was inside the house and none of them drove. There was no family car.

As the lights breathed their final riot into the front window before dimming, as each family member helped finish off the remaining pretzels and cheese puffs, they took unscripted turns wrenching their necks.

"I'm not counting anyone's cankers this time; that was a one time thing with my cousin's family on their fishing trip," The Legend said to his partner. "And as far as actually eating with these people goes," The Legend stated, "I'm not actually going to eat boxed pasta with that flare orange cheese powder. You can film it going into my mouth but then we're using a welfare stunt double."

"And you?" the director asked.

"Naw, I'll eat it," the other Legend said, combing his hair back behind his ears, adjusting his ball cap to fit tightly around his round head.

"Of course you will. You're vile," the first Legend mewed

from his slightly more narrow face.

The hush was intolerable. The unsuspecting Ontario family sat, barely giving in to physical reaction. Instead, in a symphony of eye rolls and nostril flaring, they pivoted when the door began to rattle open.

"Yeah, okay so we need a shot of them coming in, hold on, I'll have to get them to sign the waiver before we start rolling."

The kitchen clock twitched twenty minutes to eight, Eastern Standard Time. The sitcom was moments away from returning to its due course; the commercial break was weakening. There were other moments at stake: a piece of processed cheese was about to escape the folds of its plastic prison and land on an over bleached slice of white bread, a dirty tea towel tumbled against a foreign pair of sports socks in the dryer, while a thirty-second mpeg of pornography poured into an unnamed desktop folder in a teenage girl's laptop, snug behind her locked bedroom door.

The hullabaloo came running through. There was no knock, just two forms. One wore candy beads around his wrists. The other tried other, less teen idol modes of fashion. The house needed a boost of energy: paint was fading, plants were drying up, dogs were shaving themselves in hopes of being mistaken for a slab of smoked meat, ready for the deli window – and, with the exception of a collective mouth-drop that seemed ten seconds too late, the Barringtons welcomed them in with the clichéd shuffling of newspaper, up off the couch, *Who is it Dear*, ah, the Barrington household was rewired in anxious horror.

The first to speak was the beaded one, citing an appreciation of the décor and the choice of light sources. Sonja Barrington was on her way into the shower when the men entered the home. *Mom, what the fuck are they doing here! Is this an intervention? I don't want people to know we're on welfare! Mom, I hate you.* The current was real, raw, unhinged. These men came to inspire, these two over-suburban men known as 'The Legends' entered the house with a camera crew, two bags of chips and Popsicles spraying their hyena-affected laughter.

Using inappropriate social material, the job of the two guests is to ruin the balance of harmony in the welfare state, thus causing the sloths to go out and get jobs. "It's hostile, but so is life," says a *LOW* board member.

With this new initiative, look for more and more welfare families to get out of the house and find work. "Even if it's yard work, it's a breath of fresh air," says Ministry of Social Services Justine Beatlehoven. "We've found two men whom society really doesn't get along with, but at the same time, are no real threat. They're just really annoying." The unidentified men were screened after 425 applicants attempted to become 'Legends'.

Videogame masturbation

Like, well, uh, what would you have done? I'm a girl okay, I was totally horny and bored. It was innovative like those 3M commercials, a part of our heritage thing. The controller started vibrating in time to the music, what else was I going to do? We were just sitting around one night, not like we were being filmed or something. I moved the controller into my lap and the rest is masturbation history.

"So anyway, I stopped going to my therapist. I think he's a serial killer," The Legend said, extinguishing his cigarette with jittery eye and finger movements.

"Why?" the second Legend asked his partner.

"He stares at the wall when I talk to him. He said I was narcissistic. I said, *Thanks.*"

The Legend's neck darted around, mouth open, then closed, unable or unwilling to speak in the moment. He wanted to, but was captivated by the actions of the subtle Sonja, their new sister-in-welfare who was comically positioning the videogame controller at her crotch. This was not the subtle Sonja he had earlier poured a bowl of cereal for… this was something daring.

"I'm bored," Sonja mouthed to The Legend. The other Legend continued, unaware of the off-camera exchanges.

"I said that I wanted to talk about my childhood and he said,

You don't need to do that. Yeah, I came home one night when I was sixteen and my house was on fire," The Legend said.

His partner nodded. He had heard the fire story many times. Sonja was beginning to laugh at their jokes, which didn't seem like jokes so much as horrible moments endured by humans told with a sort of malicious deadpan, subjecting the audience to rashes of guilt.

Now, let me confess that this is not the first time that I've used a game component to, er, stimulate myself physically… said Sonja, the seventeen-year-old daughter of the Barringtons, who has been getting along great with The Legends. *Ever since they invented the whole rumble pack vibrating technology in controllers, it's been a huge part of my lifestyle.*

"I'm not going to judge you," said The Legend shrugging indifferently to the entire revolution.

The Legend signaled for an interview and took the camera operator into an adjacent hallway.

Day One of *Legends of Welfare:* "I feel honoured…. It's a way to give back to a system that helped me, and also gives my friend and me a place to play videogames and enjoy a fine meal with a real family. Family is the key. In 2004, the average North American family spent 43.2 hours a week together as a unit, that's down from 86.3 hours a week just ten years ago. And you'd think on welfare, families would be spending more time together, but they're not. We're hoping these Legends will help penetrate the secret world of the welfare recipient. Imagine two strangers invading your life, and having to share food and time and energy with you. We live in a world of privilege, and our tolerance as a society is in jeopardy of becoming obsolete. So many countries live in fear of total devastation. The fact that so many people already have a problem with the *Legends of Welfare* program shows how our society has lost its sense of community. If individualism is the new conformity, welfare is the new reality television."

Animal Morphing in the Post-Starbucks Art World

Dear Canada Council, I require $14.53 for fish food for my new project.
And some tennis shoes would be nice too. Signed, Golden Cheetah Six.

"What do you think?"

"No way, this artist makes way too much money. No way he's in the program," The Legend told his supervisor.

"What's his application doing here then?"

"I dunno. I didn't file it. Must be a clerical error."

"Who is it?"

"Ah, he's this artist Geoffrey Pugen, obsessed with turning into an animal, and he is the subject of a new reality show called *Dear Canada Council* which focusses on his exploits. Oh it's not controversial at all. *A future-based corporation that offers the global insider a sixteen-level metamorphosis program allowing users to finally realize the freedom held within their inner animal in both mental and corporeal form….* That sounds fine, if you have time to commit to that sort of program. I'd quit my job in a minute if it meant I could really become a shark. This narrative assumes a panacea in which primal urges are filtered through a cognitive objectivity, wherein the consumer actually 'buys' into their own natural make-up and replaces it with a pure animal-based spirituality and identity. Through this metamorphosis, the consumer is set free, returns to nature, and discovers true love. All negativity subsides, and concerns such as environmental apathy are foreign."

"It says here Geoffrey Pugen was born and raised in Toronto, Canada. Throughout his education one of his main focuses was competitive tennis. After high school, Geoff obtained a full scholarship to Coastal Carolina University in South Carolina for Tennis NCAA division 1. Once in a university setting Geoff was exposed to parts of the unwashed Parkdale community of the arts and felt drawn to collaborating and making work in digital and electronic based mediums. Geoffrey Pugen has a degree in Theatre Arts from the University of British Columbia and is a graduate in Integrated Media from the Ontario College of Art and Design. He worked in the bulk foods section of the pet store on Dolphin Avenue. In 2002 he and Nathaniel G. Moore met and hated each other because they were both dating the same house plant."

"He's not *Legend* material."

"What's that?" the supervisor asked, pointing to a sketch in the folder.

"A T-shirt logo," The Legend replied.

"What does it say?"

"WHAT MORPH DO YOU WANT?"

"I think we should move onto the next case. Who's next?"

"James Mills. He claims to work at a bookstore but he's still getting a welfare cheque."

"I'll get the car and my sleeping bag. Get all my calls transferred to my cell."

"Don't forget his folder."

"Thanks."

Amputee Sexual Repression Guilt

The early morning erections scattered and were scratched at… the Barrington household was slowly waking up to the Legends' obnoxious banter, recalling some of their dreams and thoughts from their over-suburbanized scripture.

"Hey, last night you were talking in your sleep," The Legend said, tossing a box of cookies into the air.

"Really? What did I…?"

"What did you say? You said some fucked up shit about Jenna, that girl from 1998 that you were obsessed with, the one you said was an alien."

"What was I saying?"

"You said, "I'm stuck with Jenna, she has no legs.""

"I wish I could remember that dream."

Your dream was a physical manifestation of a fear cavity. A stalemate has been issued in your creative gene; you have a consuming fear to let go of this girl who symbolizes an era of innocence. I am not exactly sure, I can't get into it, really. Your guilt or memory is so outdated, your obsessions are cutting off their legs in protest. Your mind is tired of carrying the images around in your subconscious as well. Your mind wants you to feel exhausted by these memories and discover new ways of thinking.

The Legends darted into the driveway while the camera interviewed Sonja about adjusting to the Legends. When asked who they could be compared to, she balked. "There's really nothing there," Sonja said. "I think the closest comparison is with Popsicle Pete. His power stems from a concentrated emptiness."

Just as Sonja began to open up, The Legends walked into the frame. "We have to talk to you about the videogame problem. There are late fees for some of the games, but more importantly, Blockbuster won't rent out additional controllers anymore, so we have to buy one. But now we have to buy two, because one member of this household keeps using it to gratify her teenage lust. But I'm not naming names."

Multiple-Orgasm Forgery

The forestry industry has a lot of splinters. Wear gloves. Termites will come in your mouth if you're not careful.

"Can I call you *Timber?*" Nathaniel asked.

"Sure," Emma said.

Chew on sawdust salads, try not to sneeze while you fuck each other in the woodshed, in the wood barn, teeming with beams and bark and pieces of freshly plucked timber. Pull the splinters out of her ass and suck up the blood.

"Timber!" Nathaniel shouted. "Are you allergic?"

"To coming?" Emma asked.

"No, to wood or sawdust?"

"I don't want to talk about it, I just want to feel you inside me."

"But you're a forest creature."

"No, a co-worker. Don't start up about your forest fetish again. I hate that hillbilly voice you put on, don't even start or I'll dry up right here."

"I made a recording once when I was about eleven. The year was 1985, it was March or December and we were having a wrestling match in my basement with cups of water because we were working up a sweat. My friends Eric and Andrew and I took turns doing play-by-play. At one point during the playback, you can hear Andrew scream: "OH MY GOD HE'S GOT A SAW BLADE. HE'S JUGGLING WITH A SAWBLADE."

"So what?"

"So isn't that interesting? Like, even back then, I knew that I'd be working with wood and how interesting it is that we all live in houses that are structurally reliant on the forestry industry and once again we cut down trees and destroy so we can create, sleep."

"Or fuck."

"Right. Fuck. Okay tree slut, let's go."

It didn't happen this way but it's how Nathaniel remembers things. "It was so funny to be screwing (in front of) this terrifyingly generic audience of extras," Nathaniel said last week to a man pirouetting in front of the James Joyce pub.[1] As for any sequels or the sarcastic nature of romantic grocery habits, he muses: "I'm just pretending that nothing bad has ever happened."

The girl's name wasn't even Emma. Nathaniel acted alone.[2]

---

[1] In Toronto, crusty 84-year-old men have two choices: scratch retail employees and say "Tough!" when the workers complain of physical assault or do ugly pirouettes in the hopes of being gang-beaten when the bar closes.

[2] Right hand, stage left.

ELISABETH BELLIVEAU

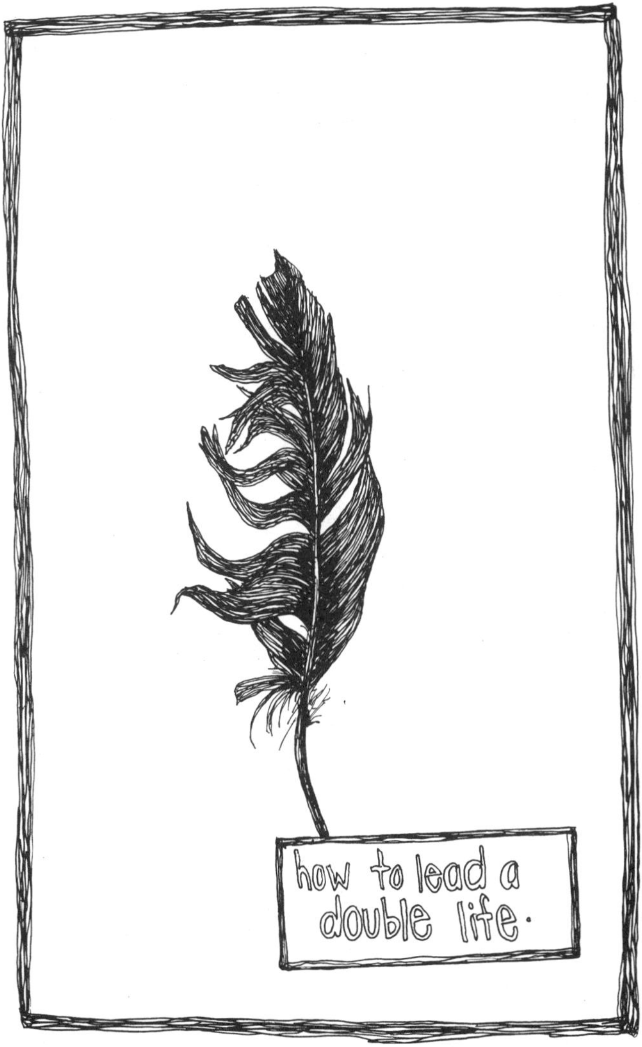
how to lead a
double life.

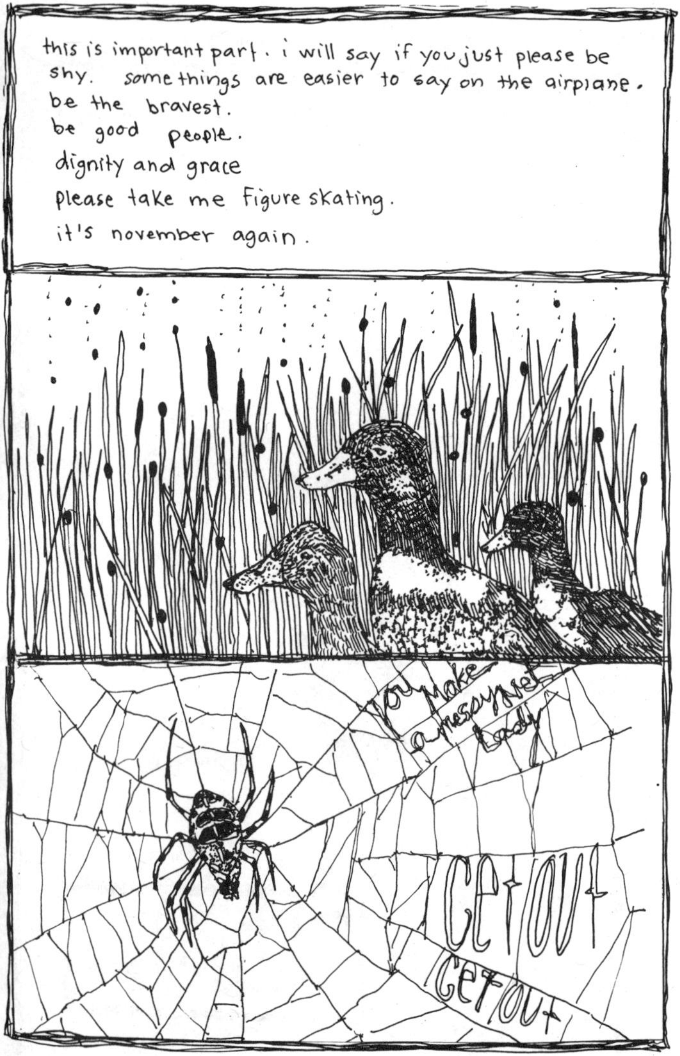
this is important part. i will say if you just please be shy. some things are easier to say on the airplane.
be the bravest.
be good people.
dignity and grace
please take me figure skating.
it's november again.
you make a messy net badly
Getout
Getout

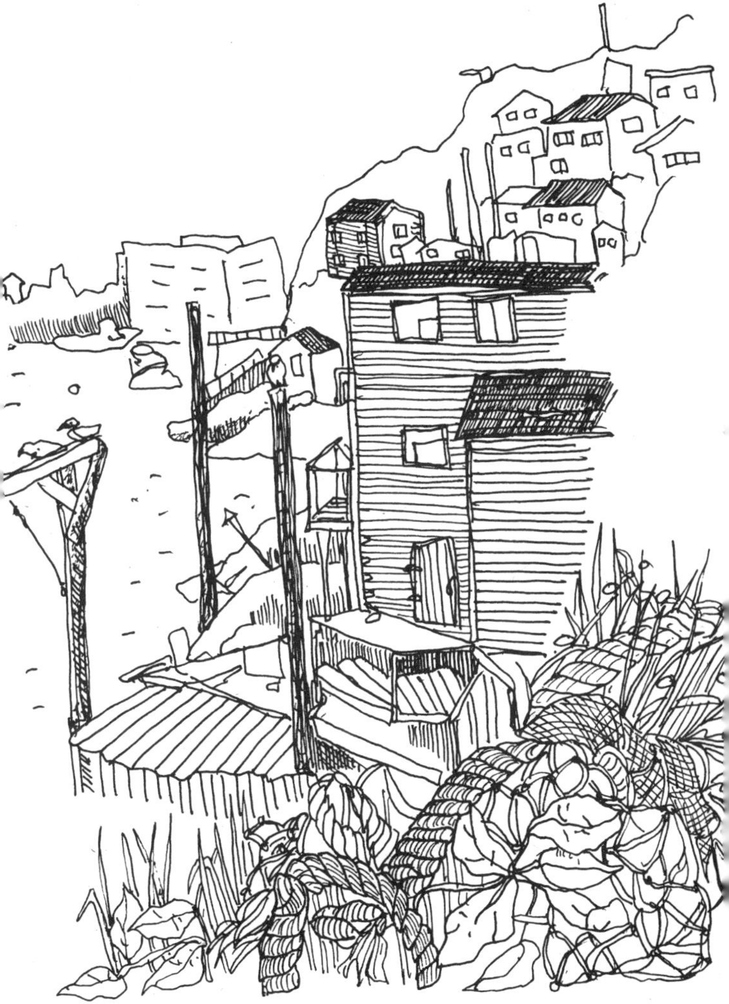

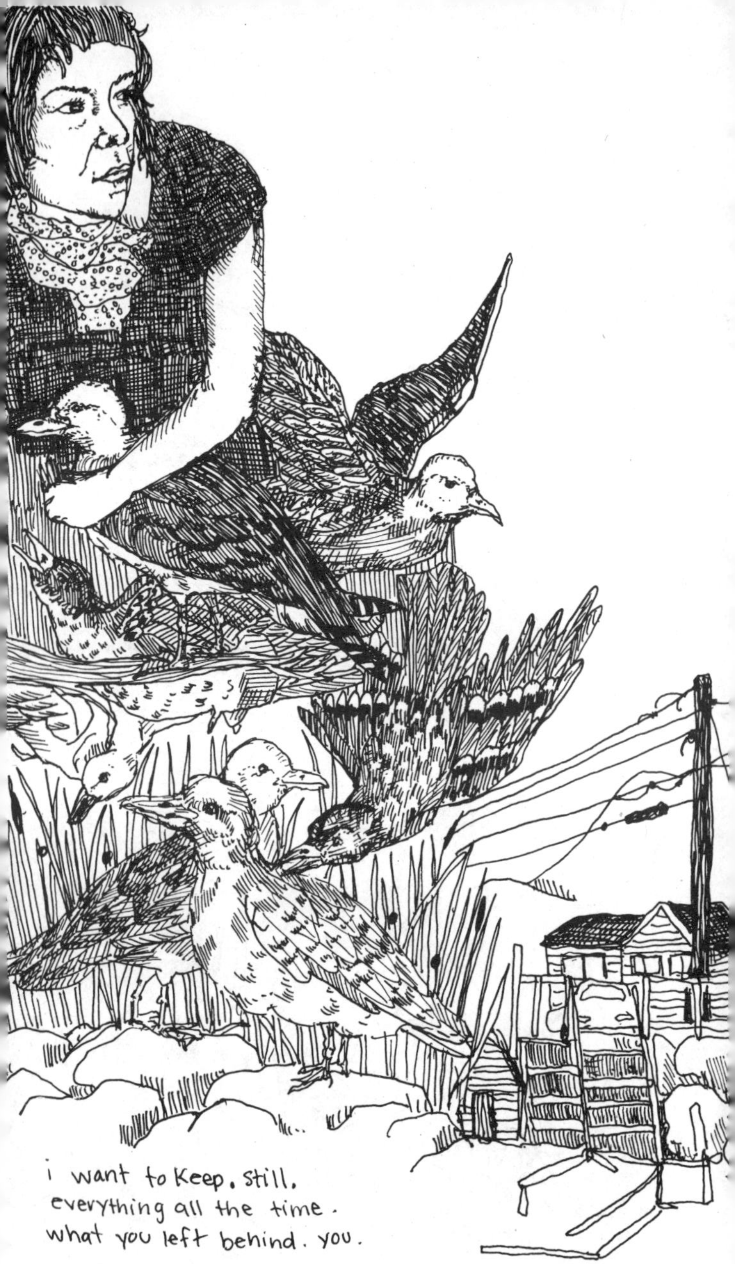
i want to keep. still.
everything all the time.
what you left behind. you.

break habits. break hearts. no.

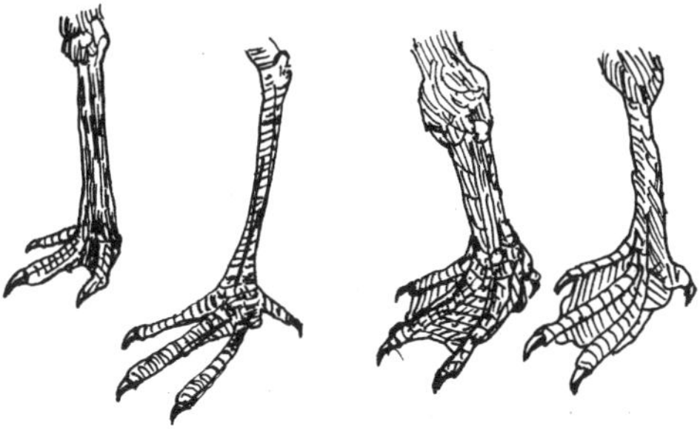

feats of love.

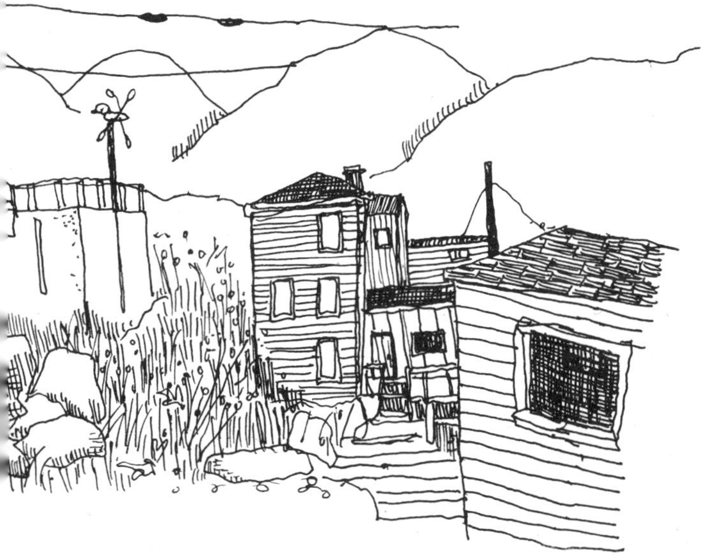

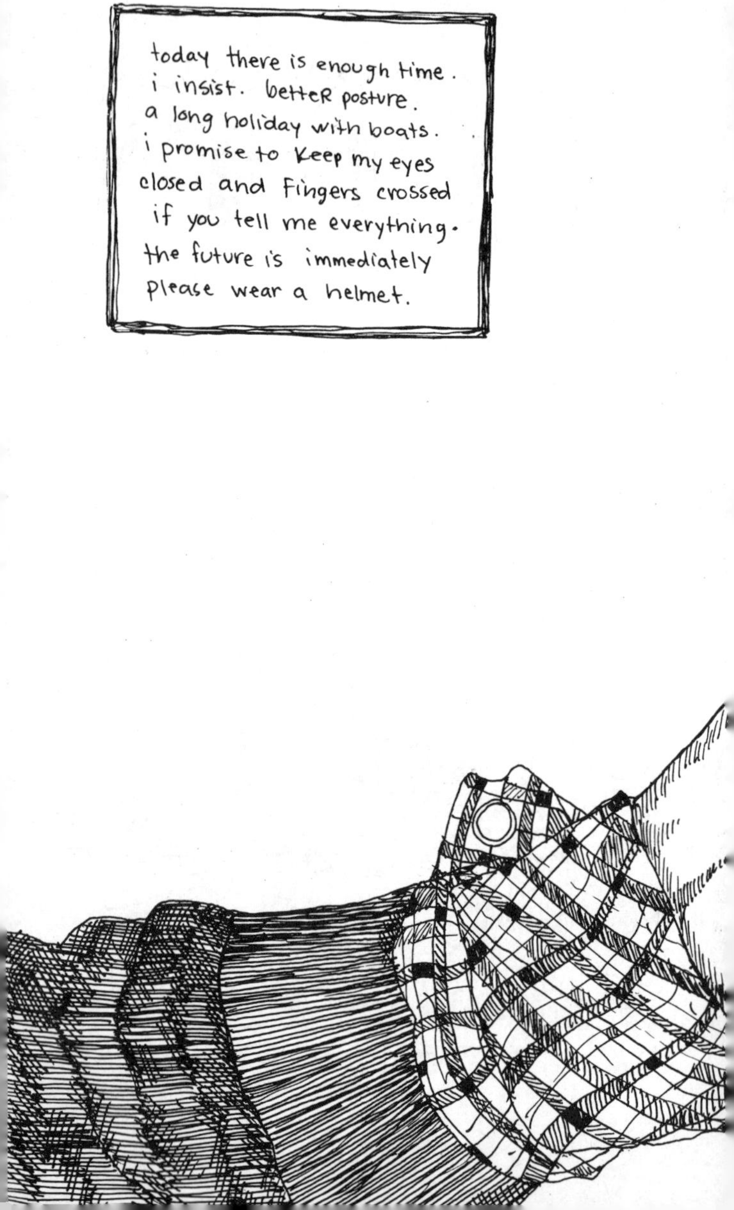
today there is enough time.
i insist. better posture.
a long holiday with boats.
i promise to keep my eyes
closed and fingers crossed
if you tell me everything.
the future is immediately
please wear a helmet.

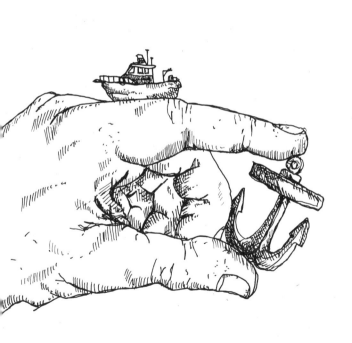

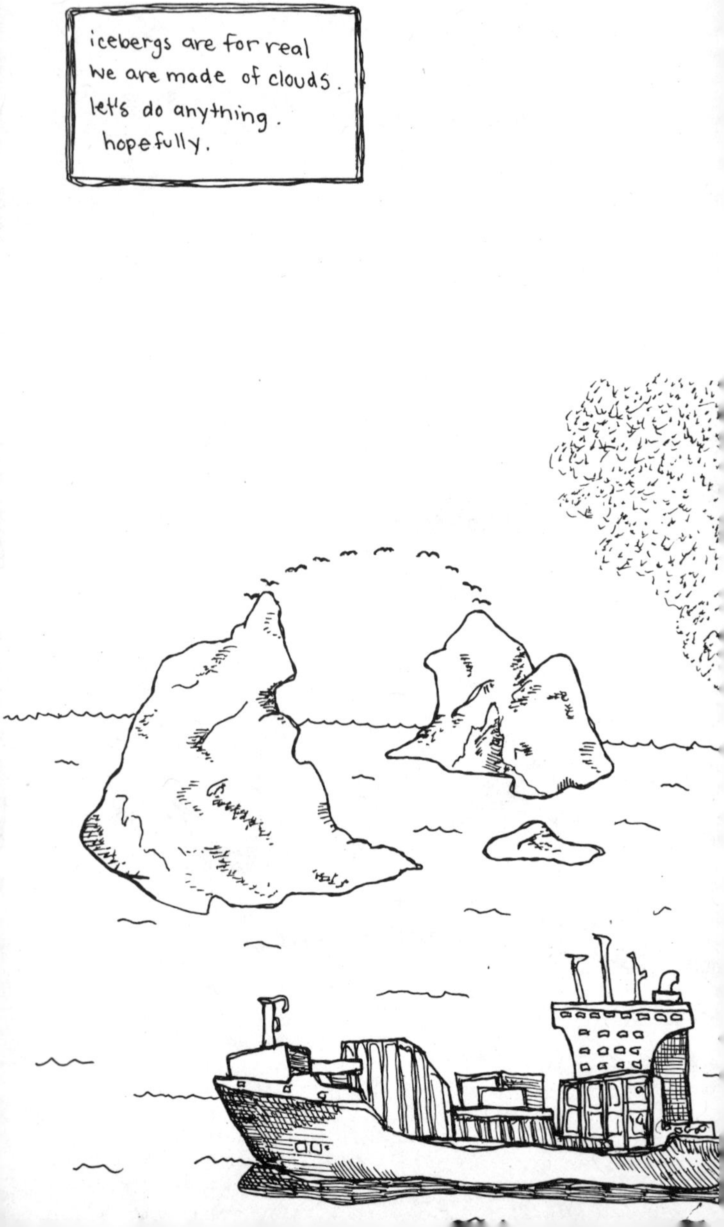
icebergs are for real
we are made of clouds.
let's do anything.
hopefully.

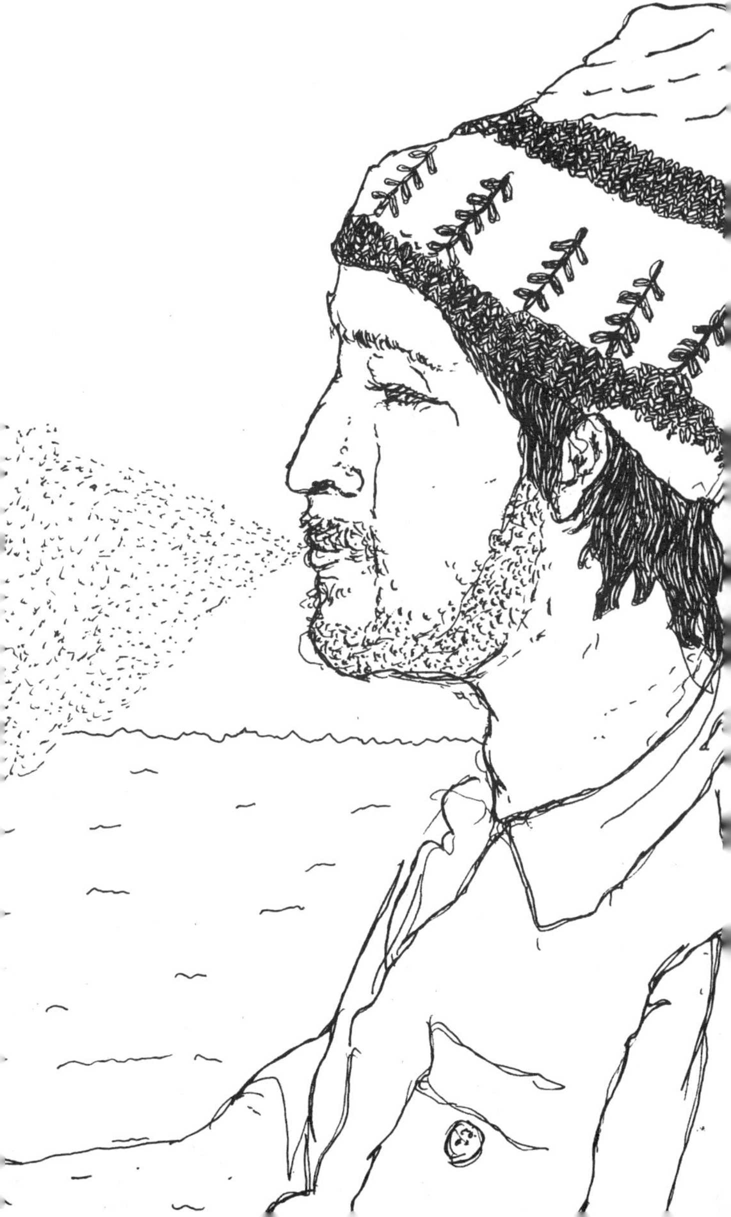

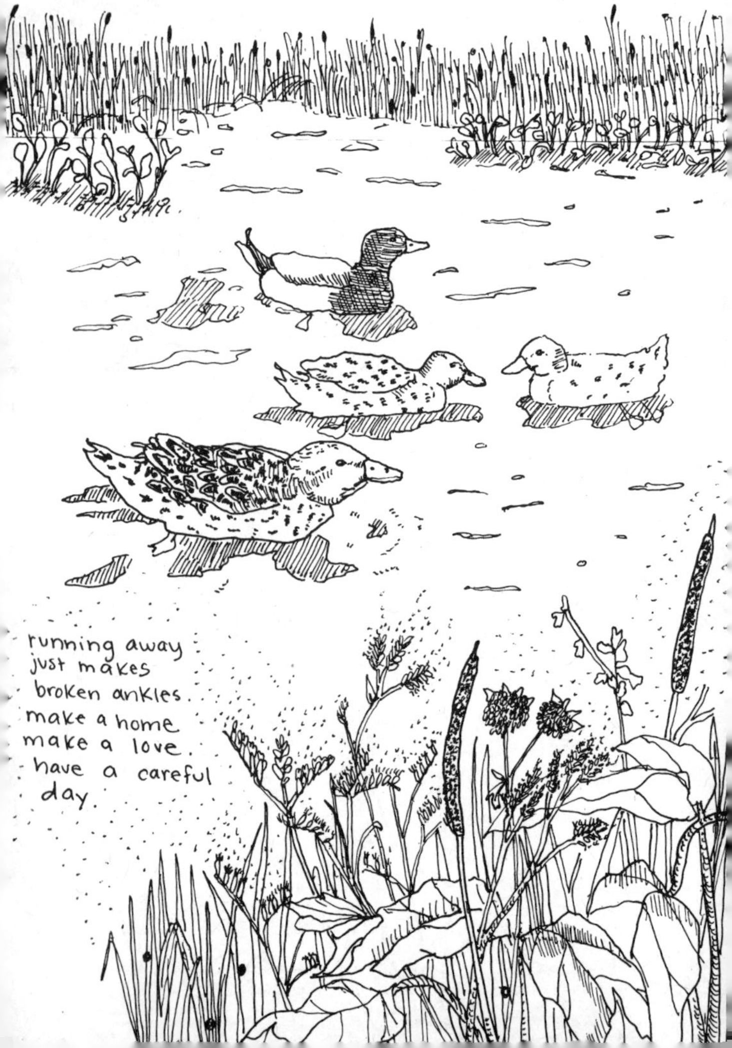
running away
just makes
broken ankles.
make a home
make a love.
have a careful
day.

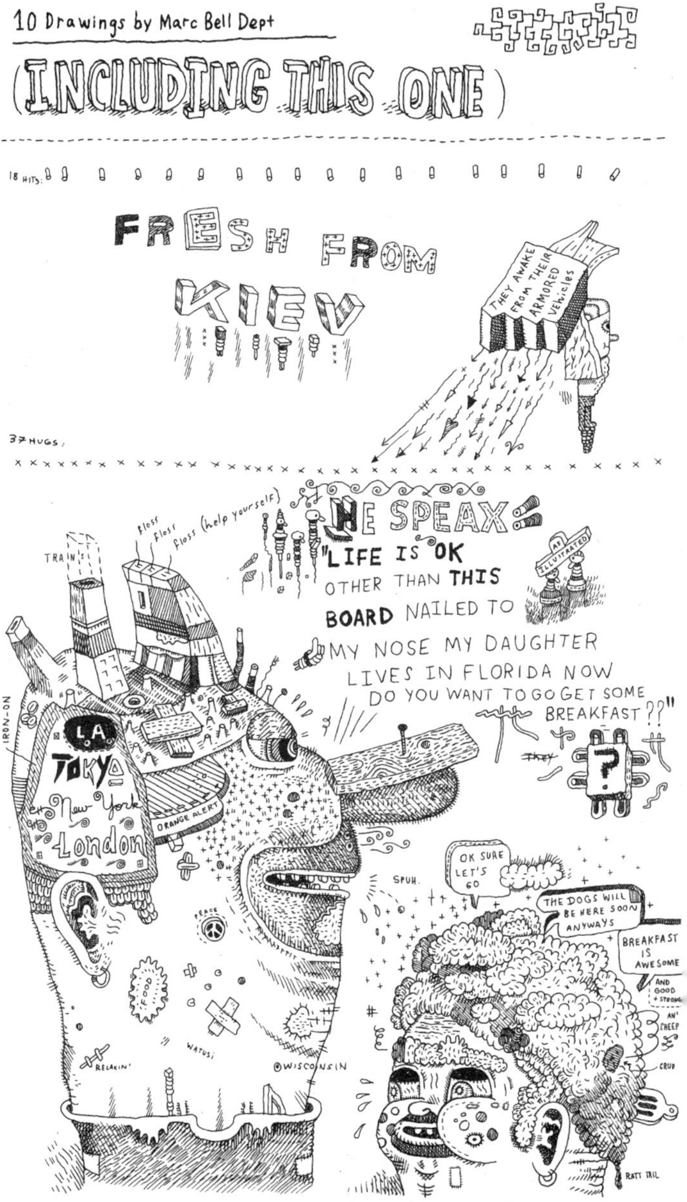
10 Drawings by Marc Bell Dept
(INCLUDING THIS ONE)
18 HITS:
FRESH FROM
KIEV
THEY AWAKE FROM THEIR ARMORED VEhicles
37 HUGS:
HE SPEAX
"LIFE IS OK OTHER THAN THIS BOARD NAILED TO MY NOSE MY DAUGHTER LIVES IN FLORIDA NOW DO YOU WANT TO GO GET SOME BREAKFAST??"
AS ILLUSTRATED
TRAINS
floss floss floss (help yourself)
IRON-ON
LA
TOKYO
New York
London
ORANGE ALERT
OK SURE LET'S GO
SPUH.
THE DOGS WILL BE HERE SOON ANYWAYS
BREAKFAST IS AWESOME
AND GOOD + STRONG
AN' CHEEP
CRUD
PEACE
FOOD
WATUSI
RELAXIN'
@WISCONSIN
RATT TAIL

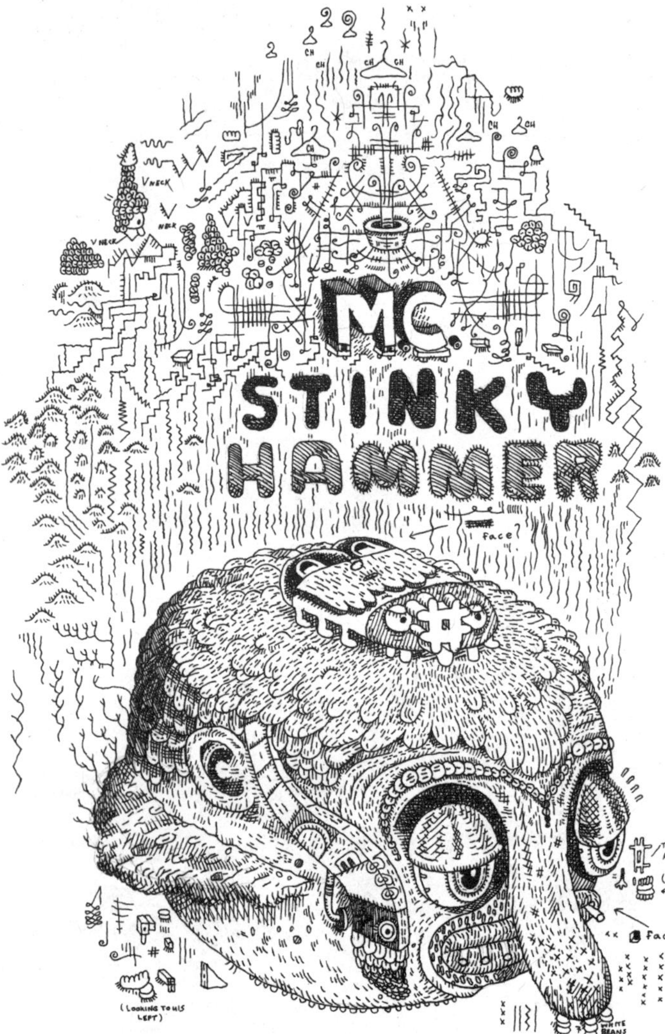
MC.
STINKY
HAMMER
V NECK
V NECK
V NECK
CH
CH
CH
CH
CH
CH
CH
face?
THINKING ABOUT
(ABOUT)
face
(LOOKING TO HIS LEFT)
WHITE BEANS

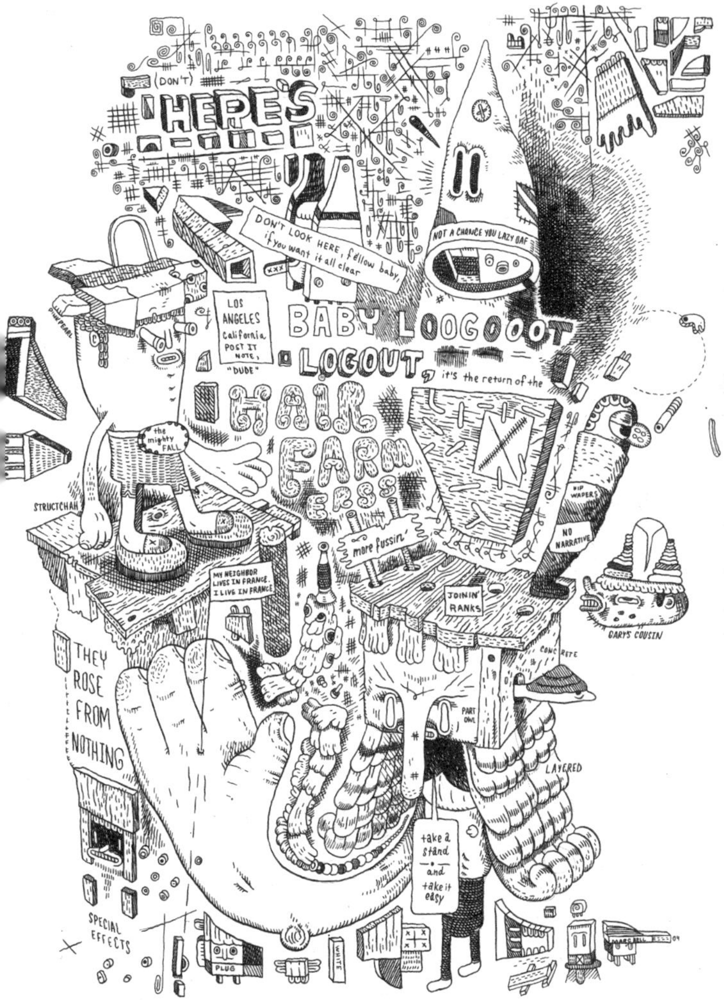
(DON'T)
HERE'S
DON'T LOOK HERE, fellow baby, if you want it all clear
NOT A CHANCE YOU LAZY OAF
LOS ANGELES California POST IT NOTE, "DUDE"
BABY LOOGOOOT
LOGOUT, it's the return of the
HAIR FARMERSS
the mighty FALL
STRUCTCHAH
more fussin'
MY NEIGHBOR LIVES IN FRANCE. I LIVE IN FRANCE
JOININ' RANKS
NO NARRATIVE
GARY'S COUSIN
CONCRETE
THEY ROSE FROM NOTHING
PART OWL
LAYERED
take a stand and take it easy
SPECIAL EFFECTS
PLUG
WHITE

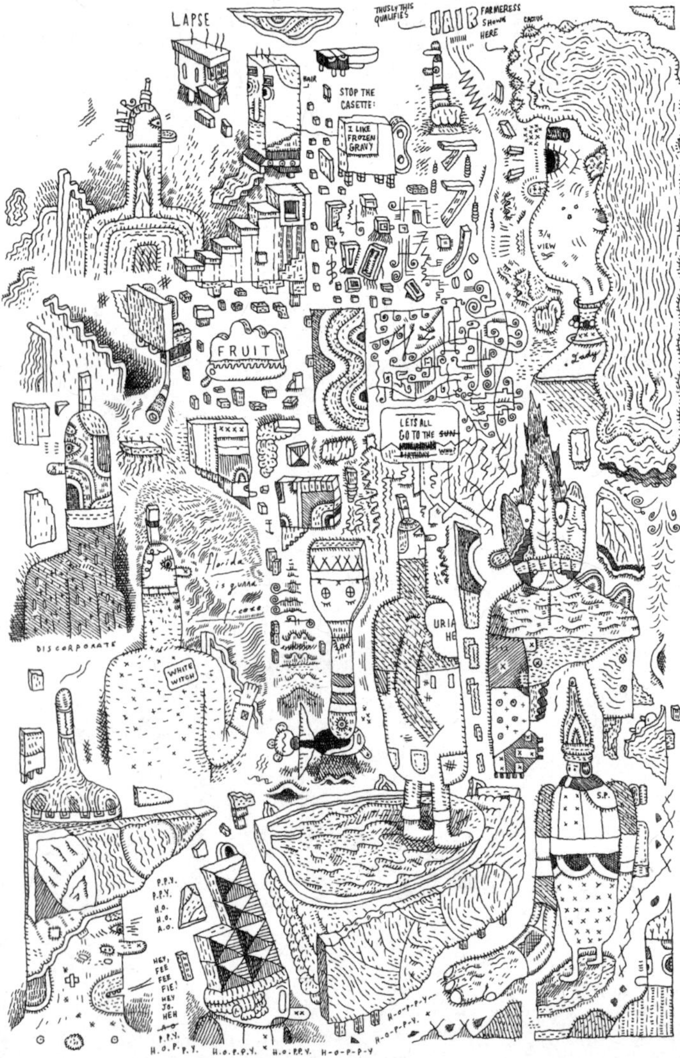
LAPSE
THUSLY THIS QUALIFIES
HAIR
FARMERESS SHOWN HERE
CACTUS
HAIR
STOP THE CASETTE:
I LIKE FROZEN GRAVY
3/4 VIEW
Lady
FRUIT
LETS ALL GO TO THE SUN
BIRTHDAY
florida is gunna freeze
URIA HE
DISCORPORATE
WHITE WITCH
S.P.
P.P.Y. P.P.Y. H.O. H.O. A.O.
HEY, FEE FEE FIE! HEY JO. HEH A.O. P.P.Y.
H.O.P.P.Y. H.O.P.P.Y. H.O.P.P.Y. H-O-P-P-Y
H-O-P-P-Y
H-O-P-P-Y.

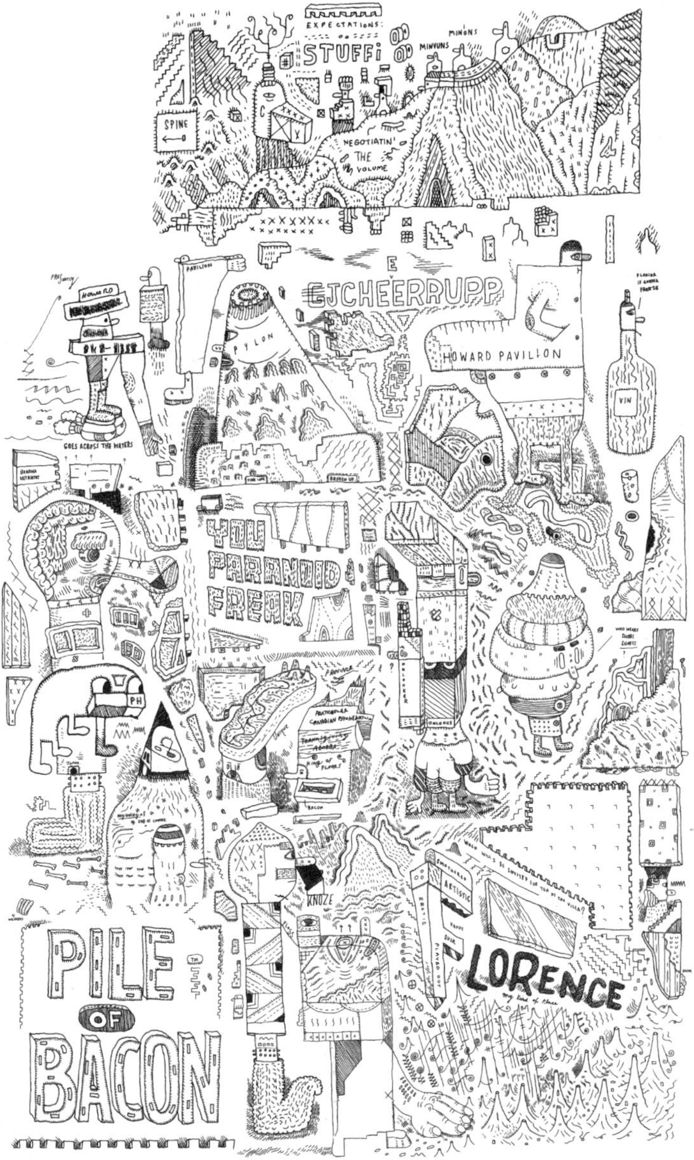

EXPECTATIONS:
STUFFI
MINONS
MINVUNS
SPINE
NEGOTIATIN' THE VOLUME
PAVILION
HOWARD
PYLON
HOWARD PAVILION
FLORIDA IS GONNA FREEZE
VIN
GOES ACROSS THE WATERS
YOU PARANOID FREAK
ONLOOKER
PH
BACON
WHEN WILL I BE INVITED FOR TEA AT THE VILLA?
KNUZE
SMOTHERED
ARTISTIC
EROTIC
PLAYED OUT
LORENCE
PILE OF BACON

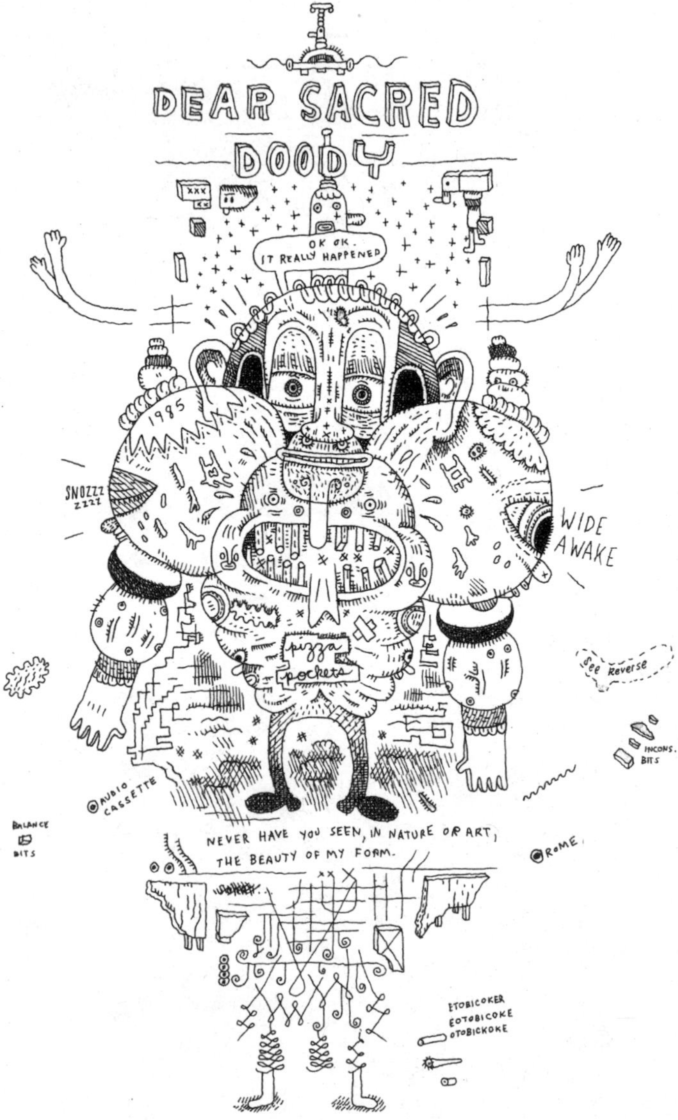
DEAR SACRED DOODY
OK OK. IT REALLY HAPPENED
1985
SNOZZZ ZZZZ
WIDE AWAKE
pizza pockets
See Reverse
INCONS. BITS
AUDIO CASSETTE
BALANCE BITS
NEVER HAVE YOU SEEN, IN NATURE OR ART, THE BEAUTY OF MY FORM.
ROME
ETOBICOKER
EOTOBICOKE
OTOBICKOKE

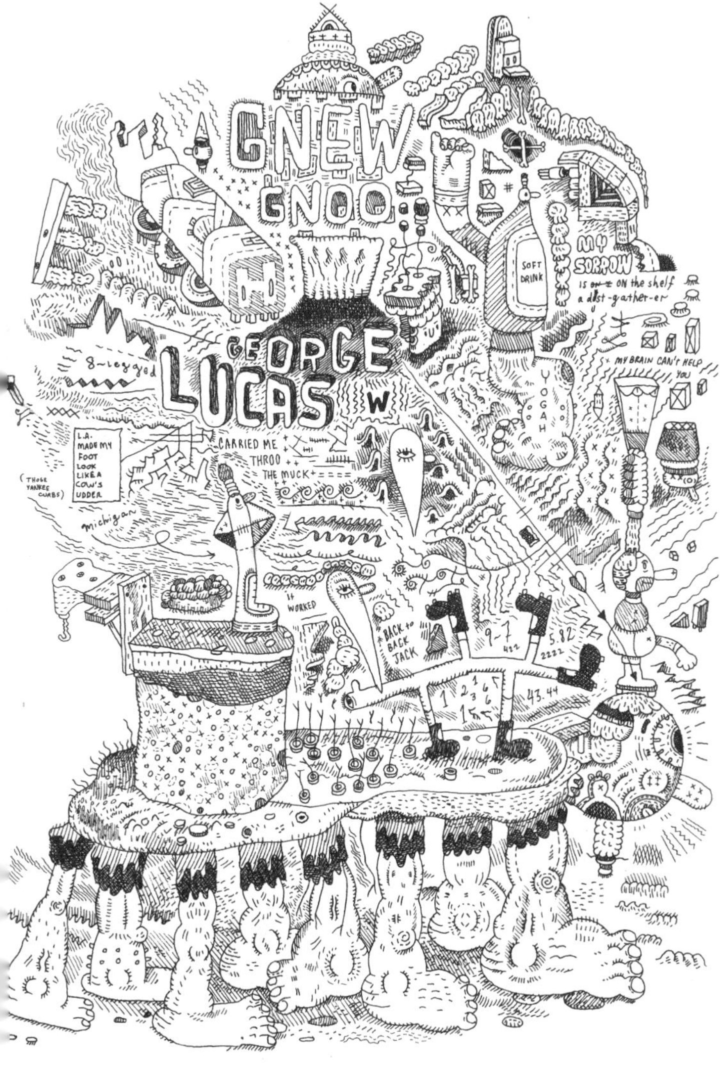
GNEW
GNOO
GEORGE
LUCAS
W
MY
SORROW
is on the shelf
a dust-gather-er
SOFT DRINK
8-legged
MY BRAIN CAN'T HELP YOU
YOGAH
L.A. MADE MY FOOT LOOK LIKE A COW'S UDDER
(THOSE YANKEE CURBS)
CARRIED ME THROO THE MUCK
michigan
it WORKED
BACK to BACK JACK
9-7
5.82
2222
43.44

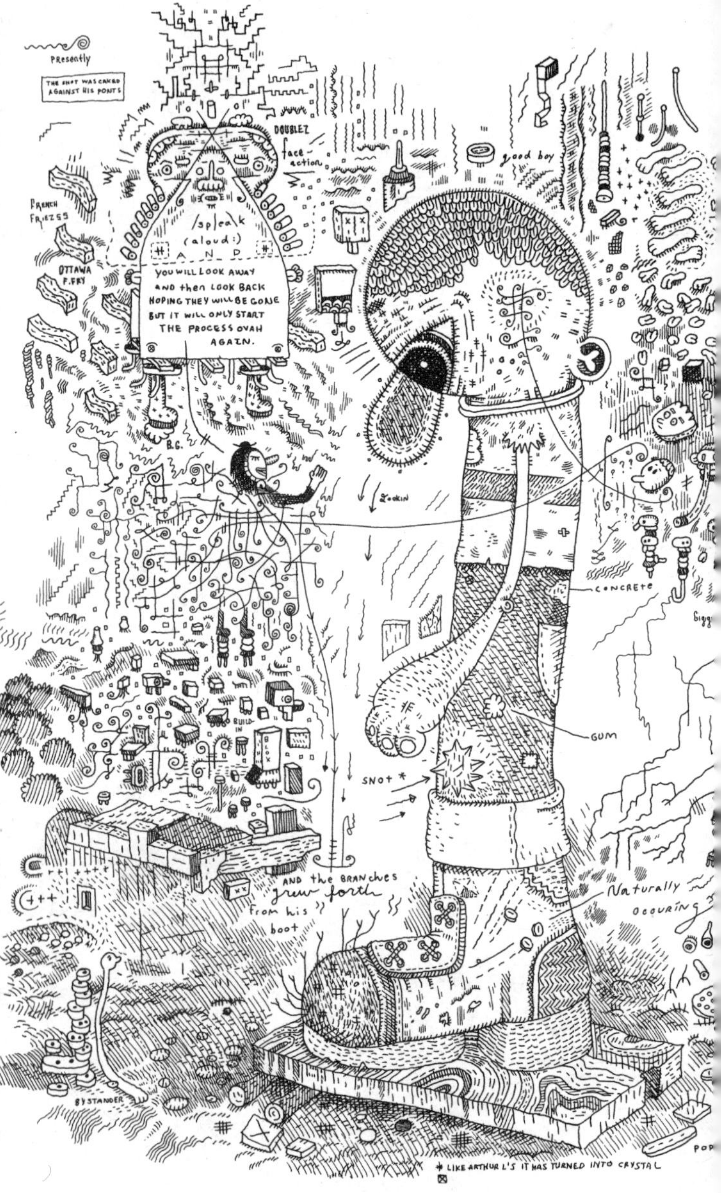

Presently
THE SNOT WAS CAKED AGAINST HIS PONTS
DOUBLEZ
face action
good boy
FRENCH FRIEZSS
OTTAWA F.FRY
/sp|ea|k (aloud:) AND
YOU WILL LOOK AWAY AND then LOOK BACK HOPING THEY WILL BE GONE BUT IT WILL ONLY START THE PROCESS OVAH AGAIN.
B.G.
Lookin
CONCRETE
GUM
SNOT *
BUILD-IN
BLOK
AND the BRANches grew forth from his boot
Naturally occuring
BYSTANDER
POP
* LIKE ARTHUR L'S IT HAS TURNED INTO CRYSTAL

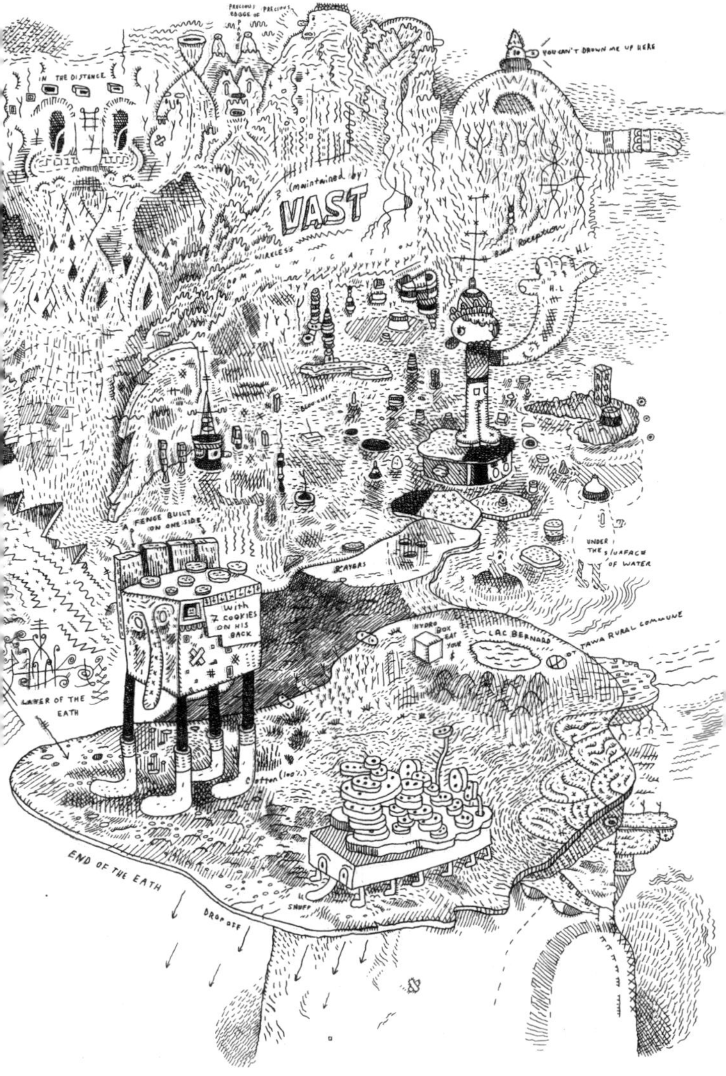
PRECIOUS EDGGE OF PAGE
PRECIOUS
IN THE DISTANCE
YOU CAN'T DROWN ME UP HERE
(maintained by)
VAST
WIRELESS
COMMUNICATIONY
Bad Reception
H.L
H.L
BLOO-CHIP
LAYERS
UNDER THE SURFACE OF WATER
A FENCE BUILT ON ONE SIDE
with 7 COOKIES ON HIS BACK
HYDRO BOX EAT YOUR $
LAC BERNARD
OTTAWA RURAL COMMUNE
LAYER OF THE EATH
Cotton (100%)
END OF THE EATH
DROP OFF
SNUFF

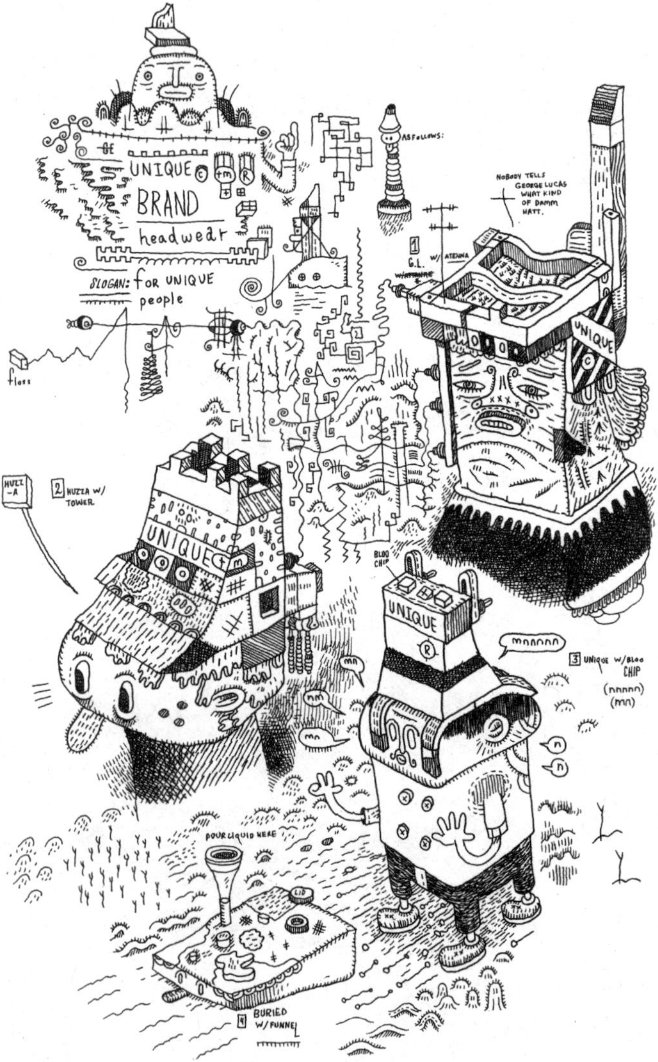

UNIQUE © tm R
BRAND
headwear
SLOGAN: for UNIQUE people
floss
AS FOLLOWS:
NOBODY TELLS GEORGE LUCAS WHAT KIND OF DAMM HATT.
1 G.L. W/ ATENNA
UNIQUE ©
HUZZ-A
2 HUZZA W/ TOWER
UNIQUE tm
BLOO CHIP
UNIQUE R
mnnnnn
3 UNIQUE W/BLOO CHIP
(nnnnn)
(mn)
mn
nm
mn
n
n
POUR LIQUID HERE
LID
4 BURIED W/FUNNEL

ROBERT ALLEN
from The Journals of Irony Jack

Prologue: Montreal, December 1999

It was a dream and I knew it, but it seemed more than real. I was at Giorgio's, reading the newspaper and eating a Greek salad. I seemed to have feta stuck in my throat, no matter how hard I swallowed, and I was trying to get my horoscope into focus. As with all Libran forecasts it was balanced right in the middle of the three columns. It didn't start off well, *You are down to your last fish head and bones.* This was clearly not true, I thought, but when I looked down for my Greek salad it had become a fish carcass. I saw then that it was true, and the lump of feta was me just swallowing hard as I tossed in my afternoon bed, asleep and dreaming again, at 3:00 PM.

I lingered in the dream long enough to toss aside the newspaper and light my last cigarette – the last cigarette in my dream – and I did this because I knew that when I woke up I would be faced with an empty pack and an ashtray overflowing with butts too short to smoke. Hanging on in dreamland I downed a bourbon on ice, then another, but the illusions disappeared before I had the satisfaction of feeling the booze bring a flush to my cheeks and a familiar warmth to my thoughts.

And then I was awake. I would have ransomed what days of my sunny life were left me for a real bourbon and a cigarette, but at the bottom of a well, looking up, I could make out nothing but a narrowing shaft and its hanging star of light. In the immortal words of Nick Charles in *The Thin Man*, it was too early for breakfast but just the time for a drink. Whisky with a splash of soda from one of those spritzers you see in old movies was Nick's drink. I preferred Jim Beam twelve-year; or, failing that, my second choice – anything else.

The imaginary cigarette had gone straight to my head, as the first always does, so I did not panic, but then I began to feel desperately thirsty, as if I had swallowed a dust devil on a long dry afternoon, and when I swallowed down the balance of the dreamy smoke my whole body shuddered as though rigor mortis already had a foot in the door. I took a long draught of Montreal tap water. I was beginning to despair that the world – my second floor walkup part of it, anyhow – had acquired enough of a hue of hatefulness for the frail afternoon hours to bear, and I thought I had better turn my thoughts to getting some money and putting myself right enough to think about writing my column.

I called my agent from the bar phone at Don Giorgio's. Don Giorgio always called me 'Professor', with an old world bow, and let me use the phone and sit and drink coffee all afternoon. Today he just waved, shouted, "Hello, Professor," from the kitchen, and went back to counting the lunch receipts. He was the only one allowed to touch money in the restaurant, meaning that the quality of the help was generally low, and did not always rise to the knowledge of what a dish or a fork was for, or how language worked in the relationship with a customer. The current waitress got quite a few sympathy tips, which she was frightened to touch, and which Giorgio collected and changed for her, rounding down to the next lowest five dollars.

By the time she brought me a cup of coffee I had got through to my agent's executive secretary, who made a big deal out of accessing my file, as if she didn't know, or didn't want to know, who I was. Anyway, nothing was new. For months there had been talk of selling my last novel to Grolier, a small publishing house in Boston, but I was beginning to wonder if this was not just fate's transparent device to keep me alive and hoping. Probably Grolier just hadn't finished laughing yet, if there was a Grolier and it wasn't a client firm of some vast media and publishing conglomerate, like Bertelsman or MGM – or were they the same company now? Somebody had acquired somebody, I vaguely remembered ranting about in my column the Friday before. To tell the truth I had got a hold of a bottle of now-legal absinthe – well, legal in Belgium or someplace – and I can assure you its mind-wasting properties weren't exaggerated by Gide or Rimbaud, or whichever Left Bank types touted it. One thing it did was knock about one week of short-term memory out of the loop and replace it with another, whether from past or future I can't tell yet. It's like wearing someone else's body: it performs, but you just can't quite figure out how, or what impels it. It was a vibrant dissociation of the kind Frankenstein must have felt from time to time, at once immersed in the universe and apart from it, in the way you are apart from a page of quadratic equations that are said to be as beautiful as an Italian sonnet. Anyway, not to go on raving, the absinthe had dissolved some of my recent intellectual substance. Luckily right now I was a city columnist for a Montreal daily, not an especially challenging task, even for a poet and novelist at the end of his creative rope.

Giorgio's coffee, gratefully on his cuff, did little to give me pleasure. He would sometimes slip me a plum schnapps, but not today, and as I exited the restaurant into the dark December afternoon I set myself to brooding.

I am not always a pleasant man when I brood, and I probably take my troubles out on others, as my first wife used to like to point out. I walked slowly back to my room on Ontario Street, over a sex shop, and kicked the ginger cat out the door. She wasn't mine, just a fellow traveler with nary a fish head or bone, and a skinny garden path of vertebrae down a scrofulous backside. A walking carcass, really.

I looked around for something to pawn. The TV had already been cashed in, and so had my laptop, which had been an endless source of trouble to me anyway – a friend had reprogrammed the error messages to haikus, which is why, in the middle of a column and in the shadow of a deadline, I read one day:

> A crash has reduced
> Your expensive computer
> To a simple stone

I looked at the upright Remington manual, which I'd been using for the last few weeks to write my column... five bucks at best; a half litre of red wine in a screwtop bottle. Tomorrow's column stared up at me from the typewriter – about six words and some items of punctuation. It was supposed to be in by nine tonight, hand-delivered since I now had no computer or modem. I wondered how long I could continue sweet-talking the girl at the security desk into typing it up on her computer and sending it upstairs. Christ, that girl could type – a whole column in about four minutes, which is what it should rightfully take me to write the damn thing, given the level of thought and language we're encouraged to aim for at *The Fount*. Founded by Ben Franklin, they say. Owned now by another of those vertically integrated media conglomerates with its fibre-optic tentacles on everything. Making everything even harder to take was that it was payday, and the tax department had garnished my wages so I wouldn't see a penny until doomsday. Any cash I managed to get was under the table stuff – freelance and such, or even 'errands' for Jimmy Firfishkin, a local entrepreneur whose business required him to operate in either hard currency or severed fingers.

After a few moments of reflection I ripped the column out of the Remington and carted the cast-iron monstrosity, along with a sardine can full of pennies and nickels, down the road to Sid's Surplus, where I stood blowing on my freezing fingers while Sid viewed it from several shrewd angles and offered me four bucks. I was too dispirited even to haggle, and I took the money, bought cigarettes and a glass of red wine at Viola's Dance Bar, tipping the preternaturally cheery and dreadlocked bartender with the last of the nickels and pennies, and sat down at a corner table to think.

Beyond the darkening window, with its winking and reversed neons, the Montreal night unfolded like a picture book of Dickens' London. A grainy snow blew in zigzags, whorls and other chaotic patterns, rapidly clearing the street of anyone likely to want to saunter. A big girl in tights, a roll-necked sweater and fingerless gloves ploughed north on the Main on her one-speed, suspended seemingly while the dark buildings across the road scrolled South and the sky, like a glass paperweight, shook complex confettis on the few shoulders visible to me and on the curiously unfashionable knitted hats with their Peruvian swirly colours or laced-up earflaps, putting a wintry end to all those Montreal fashion myths of halcyon fall and summer. In truth, when winter gets its icy boot in the December door we're pretty much indistinguishable from Edmonton.

Taking the wine (red, boxed) in slow, acid sips, I let my mind mull over the last few years in my adopted city. Montreal hadn't been half-bad, especially when I'd fallen in with the burnt-out cases at Viola's, who mingled freely with the starry-eyed young artists and writers come to live in Canada's Paris. For a time it appeared the city would become the golden place it had once thought it had been, but Toronto was where we all went to make money or publish our books, and no rebirth had occurred, or if it did was quickly adopted by Toronto and taught to speak in the right accent. What Montreal now had was a movie-set old city, lots of movies shooting in it, summer festivals and winter alcoholism, and a newly-merged urban government, modelled after those of medieval petty kings, circa 1300 – oh, and Irony Jack Curtis, novelist and poet, whose contemplation may have spun this gothic nightmare out of gossamer thought, but who, on the off chance that both the city and his own sorry plight were real, was trying to contemplate in something more than historical generalities, so as to find a way out before the millennium turned. This was in a mere fifteen days, according to one set of measurers, who would have liked to burn at the stake those who wanted to put the party off while an extra year rolled by. I have a hunch more people have died over mathematical than religious quarrels, though scant difference that makes, I know.

All these thoughts spent a second or two in transit, then exited my head. What I can't remember is just what I was thinking before Imogene appeared, while I dragged deeply on a *Gauloise* and insulted my palate with another tiny sip of Viola's *ordinaire*.

It was a minute or two after five, in that stomach-turning interval of not quite complete black, before the balm of the night had quite descended. I was between my second and third cigarettes, but the gulf between my life as it was and as it was supposed to be yawned even wider. For a second, and subliminally, I lived a post-mortem life as a writer for the ages, a man loved and respected and feared by all the poetasters – and then, cravenly backing off even from imagined death I wondered for a split second if there was any chance in hell the dull gaze of the public might light on me for an instant, if only to decide I was a solid, decently inventive minor writer of a minor national literature, and deserving of a few dollars a day for food and wine and cigarettes, and maybe some nice clothes and a loft on the Plateau. And a nice car – I may have been thinking of the car, in fact, when Imogene showed up.

Those dreams, vivid as they were, carried no sense they could be cashed in, but like those curlicued faux cheques from The Publishers' Clearing House they were palpably frauds. Instead of writing and living above the poverty line I was working for a sorry-ass journal no one with any taste bought or read, writing gossipy city columns for a pittance, which was then snatched away from me by a government with more sympathy for my bankers than for me – I had signed some creative checks, in order to finish my last novel, for sums which I described to my bankers, reasonably enough, as 'involuntary venture capital', or some such thing. This predictably enraged them, though I'm certain it would not have if I had engaged in something my bankers approved of, like the slave trade.

So there I was, at the lowest point of the curve, a swashbuckling, epicene, bunch-backed muse of twistedness and spite, all sweetness and light in print, all venom and gall up close. Dolled up at clubs, my deformity cloaked in a loose white tropical suit, my lips rouged and luscious on an oversized head, I'd been a match for anyone – man, woman, little, big. The boys and girls in their genderless guises flocked around me for my

poetry, my jibes and japes, my malign epigrams... but that was
so long ago it could have been on another planet. Four wives and
a snake-swarmed sargasso of booze, and suddenly I was on the
street, fighting a rearguard action against whole regiments of
landlords and bailiffs, grey-suited teasers with such a honeyed
way about them I wanted to throw myself into their commodi-
ous arms, even as they took me for every cent and every scintil-
la of self-respect I had left.

Imagine, then, me stripped of everything, fallen lower than a
snake's belly, sitting disconsolate at Viola's Dance Bar looking for
an affordable exit from life's troubles. Imagine me smoking the
second *Gauloise* almost to the filter and lighting the third from the
glowing tip. Imagine a man who once had everything and now
didn't have a pot to piss in. Imagine my fifth wife, Imogene, alight-
ing like an angel, or devil, at my table, shouting greetings to me
that I didn't hear because her voice hadn't yet followed her here
from the twenty-fifth century, where she was employed as a literary archivist at the Irony Jack Centre for the Study of Twenty-first
Century Fiction. All this I learned later, of course, and I was not
to marry her for a month yet, some three hundred years before
she was born. I used to think of all those hundreds of years separating us whenever we were having sex, which I gloriously redis-
covered, along with my writing. But I am ahead of myself. Right
now, regard Irony Jack Curtis – contemptible hack at a third-rate
city rag, who reached rock bottom one early winter night only to
see his lucky star twinkling up above, unaware that fate was now
ready to lift him up and make of him John Curtis, the early third
millennium's most celebrated man of letters.

Imogene, soundlessly greeting me from the background gar-
ble of traffic noise and low bar conversation and lottery terminal
electronic anthems, materialized across the corner table in about
five incomprehensible seconds and offered her hand. It was slim,
almost bony, of a sandy, unblemished white, and well-mani-
cured. The hand could be taken to represent all of her, in fact –

neat and well packaged, dressed in that tasteful way that makes you forget completely there's flesh and blood underneath. Her smile betrayed teeth that suggested a genetic perfection unrelated to the slapdash of human reproduction. Except for the half-smirk of intelligence and a tiny mole on the curve of her neck, below the chin, I could have been looking at the shiny page of a magazine. I felt abashed, conscious of my rotting yellow teeth and glaring, jaundiced eyes, my diminutive size, and the bunched-up shoulder that made me look forever on the brink of sidling out of sight.

She wasn't the slightest put out, apparently. She shook my hand firmly and said, "Montreal, late nineteen nineties... it's the two-cheek kiss, isn't it?"

I meant to say something funny or endearing, but words failed me. I nodded, feeling my mouth twitch.

"I'm Imogene McCloud. Sorry for popping into thin air like this, but the machine's finely calibrated. I could just as easily have fallen into your arms."

"Who are you?" I blurted, one question behind.

She had the grace to ignore this. "I'm doing a book on your work – more than one actually. The Irony Jack Institute is putting out a four hundredth anniversary edition of your works – variorum, with commentary. I'm an expert on your later novels, early next century, and I decided to come back and see if I could meet you. This instrument" – she gestured vaguely with one of those cursor-clean hands – "is relatively new, and I have a pass. My aunt is a technician. You see, about five years ago, my time, we figured how to go back and forth in time without wreaking havoc with things. It's simple really, you just find a CTC and ride it back into history like a child's slide. That's how they explained it to me. I'm not –"

"CTC?" I said, still behind.

"Closed timelike curve. In areas of gravitational deformation a worldline – that's the line of your life – can close on itself, forming a loop. Or you can just rip or bunch the fabric of time-space yourself if you have the know-how, aiming your worldline where you like."

She paused, letting me take all this in. Down as I was to less than pocket change, I decided to take her at her word. Maybe I just didn't see her come through the door, which she had entered like any other mortal, out of the snow, seeming to appear out of nowhere. She wouldn't have been the first of my friends to possess this ability lately, when I let distraction or booze flip randomly through the pictures in my head. As far as I knew, I was in a familiar place, darkened and aromatic, letting the movie of life flit across the window to the accompaniment of my restless reflections.

"You come from the future," I finally said, pausing to relight my cigarette and sending a fresh plume of toxic intoxicants into the stale air. "And there's an institute devoted to studying and preserving my work... you mean the Irony Jack columns?"

She laughed. "No, of course not. That's why I don't study your early work. Your juvenilia are quaint and naive – charming even. Your middle period was – is – a mess, frankly. You drank far too much and couldn't put a sentence together for the longest time. That's now, by the way. We decided it would be less disruptive if I talked to your during your lost years."

"My lost years? How many of them are there, these lost years?"

"Oh," she said, "I couldn't tell you that."

I changed the subject. "Do you have any money?"

"Oh, lots. They gave me this." She pulled out a roll of hundreds and thousands, colours I had dreamt but never seen. "All I need is for you to sign."

She reached over the table to take my hand. For a second I thought she would pull me to her, that I was in one of my more elaborate fantasies, but I checked myself. I could smell my own breath. With a rush of self-hatred and anger I attempted to pull my hand from hers, but her grip was firm. She touched my fingertips to a small plastic pad and suddenly the money was in my other hand. "Let's have a drink," she said.

That was how it began with Imogene.

While she was off in the washroom and two double scotches were delivered from the bar, I counted the money three times over. There was over $10,000, all in colourful mint-fresh bills, dated and signed in the 1990s and too real to be real. Nothing smaller than a fifty, whose glowing red colours I decided I was in love with. The hundreds were a crisp dun, the thousands a crayola purple – two of them – which I folded carefully and put in my back pocket. The rest, folded, made a bulge in my side pocket. I patted it. Flush.

When she came back we started drinking. The scotches kept coming. Alcohol was apparently a novelty for Imogene, and she quickly began to show the effects, becoming the slightest bit unravelled round the edges, so I got to feel quite cozy. I plied her with drinks and questions, and gradually the awful truth began to reveal itself: somehow I would sober myself up, regain my powers of poetry and language, and go on to compose the three greatest novels of the twenty-first century, at least according to the critics of the twenty-fifth. While she painted this ravishing picture I watched my two hands. One held a cigarette, the other a drink. Both shook. I was barely able to contemplate writing my name, let alone a great work of fiction.

The conversation ebbed, as she reached the end of her ability, or willingness, to fill me in about myself. The lights dimmed, as late evening took hold. There were three or four people playing pool, another at the bar, four college students talking loudly over a pitcher of beer. This was all the way it ought to be, but when Imogene paused, obviously thinking she might be going too far with explanation, I found my head spinning with the possibility of it all.

"When will I write these great novels?" I tried to casually say, not wanting her to stop. The drinks had unbent her. There was no talk in the bar at all, no clicking of pool balls. The air assumed an unlikely lucidity.

Imogene smirked. "Oh, I can't tell you that.... What are you writing now?"

"Well, I was... what's the name of my first great novel?"

She considered. "I guess there's no harm in that. It's called *The Real-Time Adventures of Johnny Firfishkin.*"

"That's what I'm working on," I lied. It's sort of my autobiography, displaced though... isn't it...?" I suddenly remembered that she had read it and I hadn't. Luckily, as a teacher of literature, I was used to talking authoritatively about books I'd never read. I shrugged, making a wavy motion with my hand, signifying, I hoped, some post-modern uncertainty principle. "Kind of a fictional system of analogues," I added lamely.

She looked at me oddly. "Well, in the grossest sense... a kind of biography of a lost soul, a drug dealer and petty thief. I think you must have read Genet – oh, I love the way Shklovski puts it in the last chapter... let's see.... Art is not the object, but the vision of the object. It does not organize the world conceptually, but disorganizes the forms through which the world is customarily perceived.... That's just before Johnny gets a knife in the liver."

I sat stunned. The words seemed a river of beauty to me, doubtless due to the scotch, but I was sure I had struggled for years to articulate this thought, been on the very edge when it fled like a dream, skateboarding off the brink of consciousness. Why couldn't I write something like that? The whole world seemed sweet at that moment. "I said that?" I uttered wonderingly.

"Well, you will – or Shklovski will, and he's your character."

"Yes he is – he's my character... is he Russian or something?"

Imogene smiled, fondly I thought. "No, but he takes on the name when he's beaten up by the cops and has to spend a night in jail with a sexual sadist, who forces him to recite nursery rhymes – ooh, I'm telling you too much – because he loves the Russian formalists." She stopped talking and began to run her foot up my calf.

I caught just the last phrase. "The Russian formalists.... Good, I'll have to read them again." The truth was I hadn't read a Russian formalist in my life and wouldn't know one if it came up and offered to stand me a drink. "What else?" I asked her, trying to keep the craftiness from creeping into my voice. I was conscious suddenly of how much this might mean to me and how unfitted I was to impress. Still, if she was not completely delusional, just being Irony Jack might be enough, notwithstanding the pathetic stagger I was doing across the dance floor of discourse in a vain attempt at getting the tone right.

I surveyed my plight desperately, while Imogene happily lapped up twentieth century booze. (My joke was I was feeding her Nick and Nora Charles style scotch and sodas, but the joke was on me apparently, since it later turned out I had borrowed both the drink and the trope for my characters Rolly and Jade in a novel not yet even conceived, and Imogene happily took the drinks for my private emblem and – in this case – charming gracenote.)

I think you can see the problem: I had to get around this critic from the future far enough to find out what it was I had written that was so earth-shattering, so I could at least start thinking about how to go about writing it. All I had so far was the name of a character and the title of a book – which itself contained the name of a man I knew. That was something, but hardly enough to get me writing. I cast back to the last one, a pretty good novel, I thought, even though one reviewer had called it incomprehensible and, Lana, my editor had made a big thing of checking the Help Wanted ads one morning when we were having breakfast at Beauty's. She wanted to suggest in some subtle ways that her living depended on writers like me selling, and not being lionized for their literary qualities and never read. Another subtle hint was ordering the cheap breakfast, without the freshly-squeezed orange juice. I sincerely hoped she wouldn't be representing me when I hit it big, so that, walking past Beauty's on a Sunday morning in search of a croissant and latté, she might see me slurping oysters and champagne, the oyster juice and bubbly running prodigally down my chin and staining the silk handkerchief tucked into my shirtfront.

I'll wave, Lana. Wave back....

RICHARD SUICIDE

Monsanto II

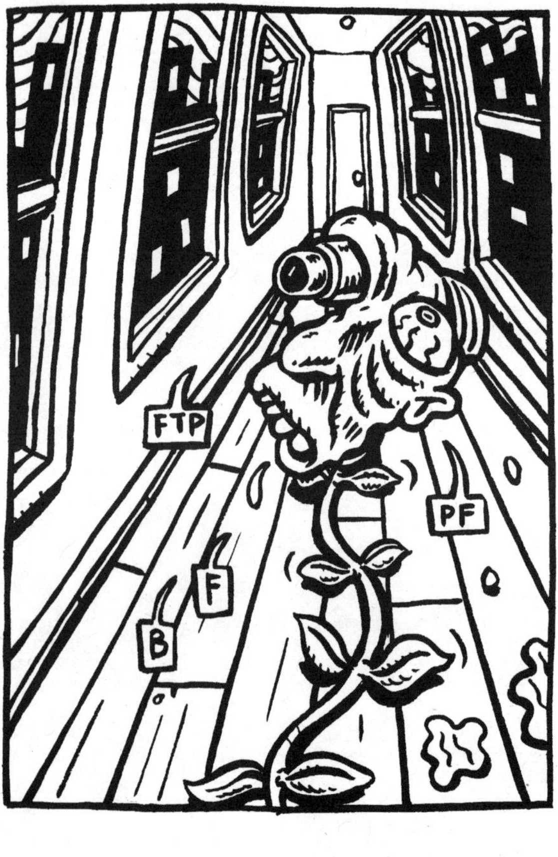
FTP
PF
F
B

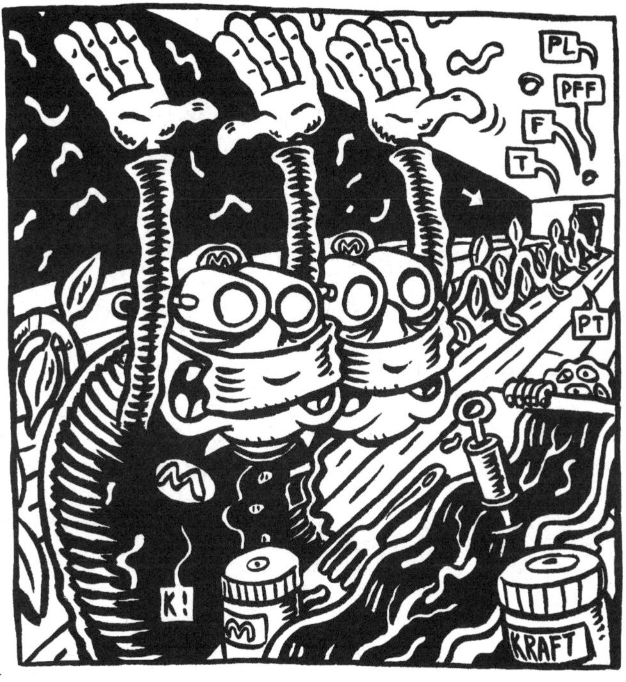
PL
PFF
F
T
PT
K!
KRAFT

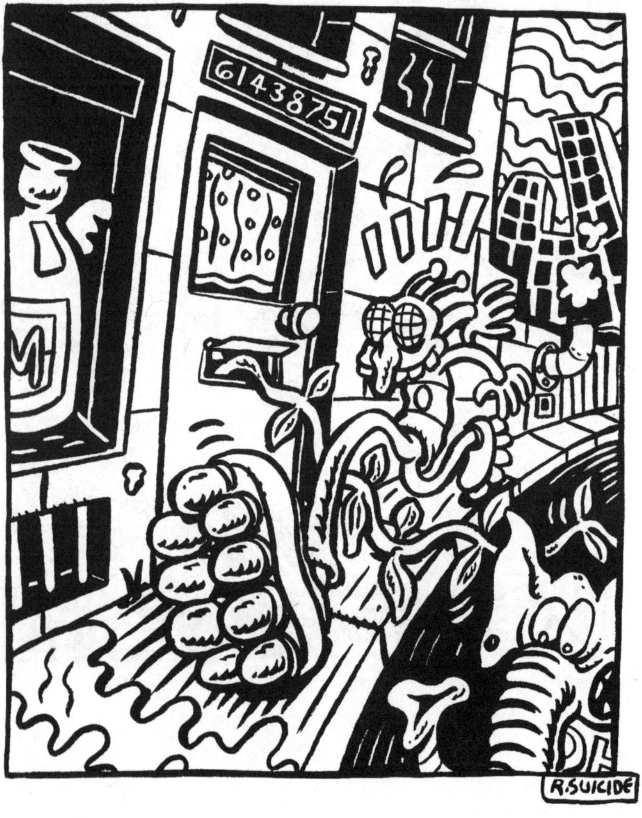
61438751
R.SUICIDE

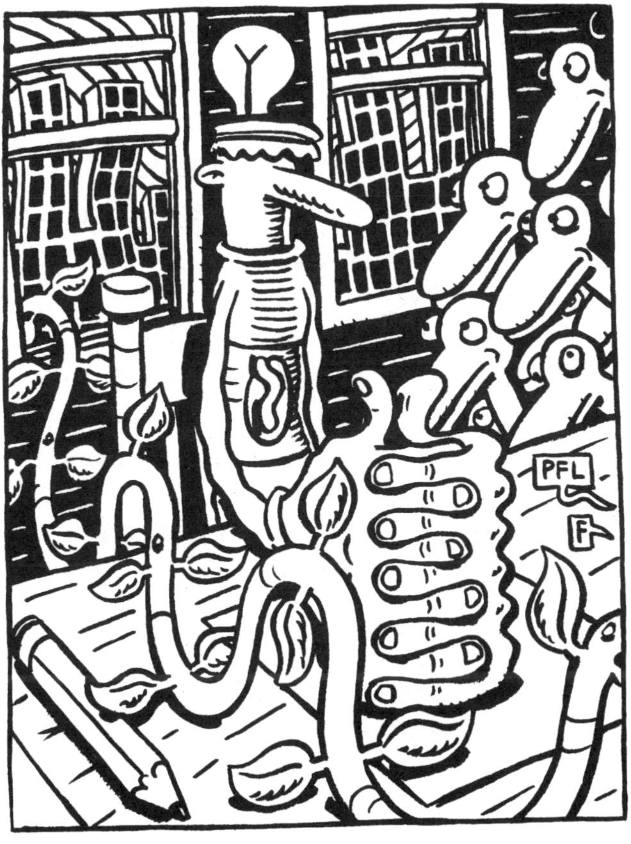
PFL
F

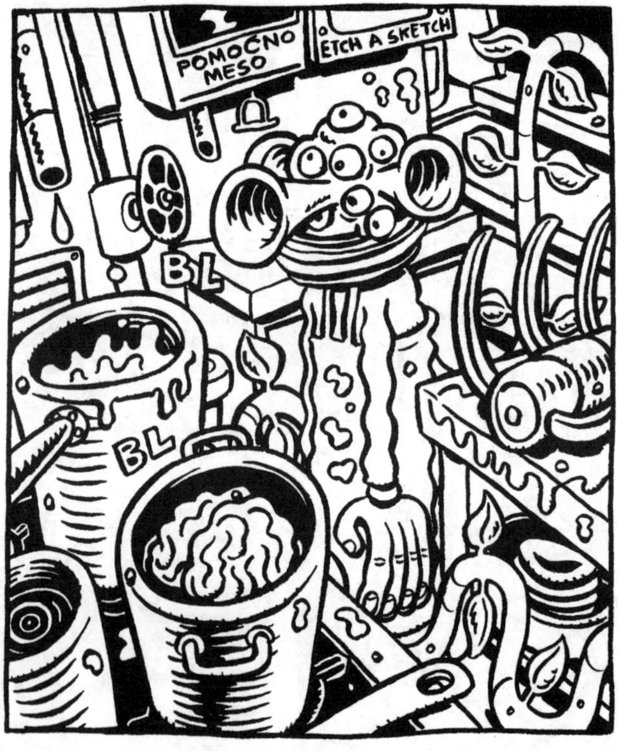
POMOČNO MESO
ETCH A SKETCH
BL
BL

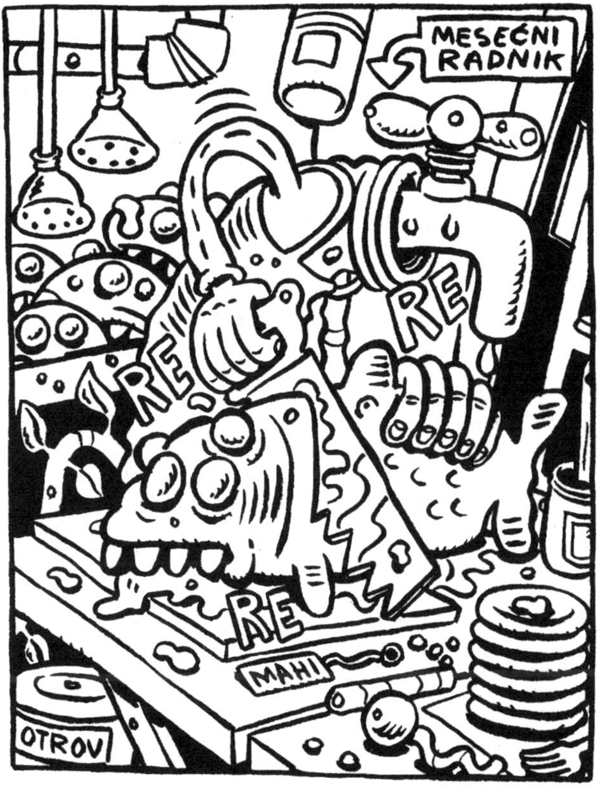
MESEĆNI RADNIK
RE
RE
RE
MAHI
OTROV

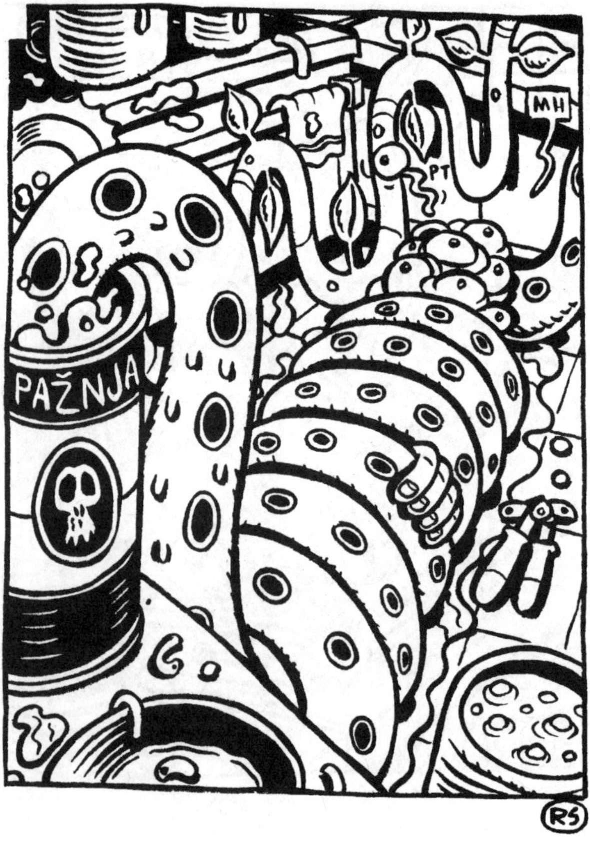
MH
PT
PAŽNJA
RS

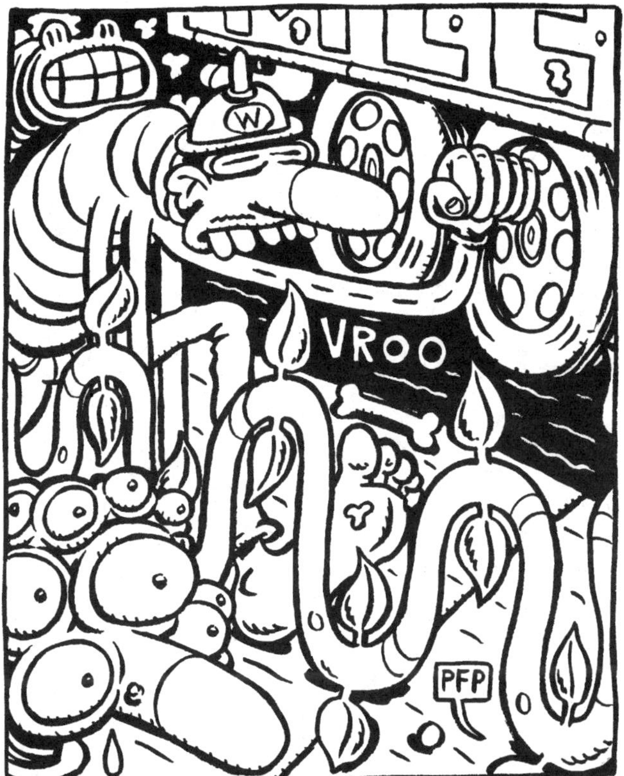
VROO
PFP

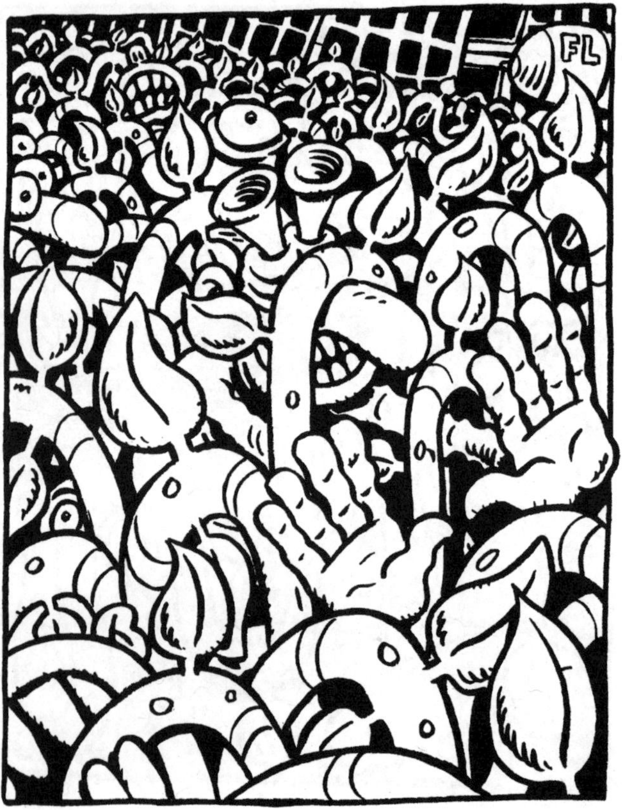
FL

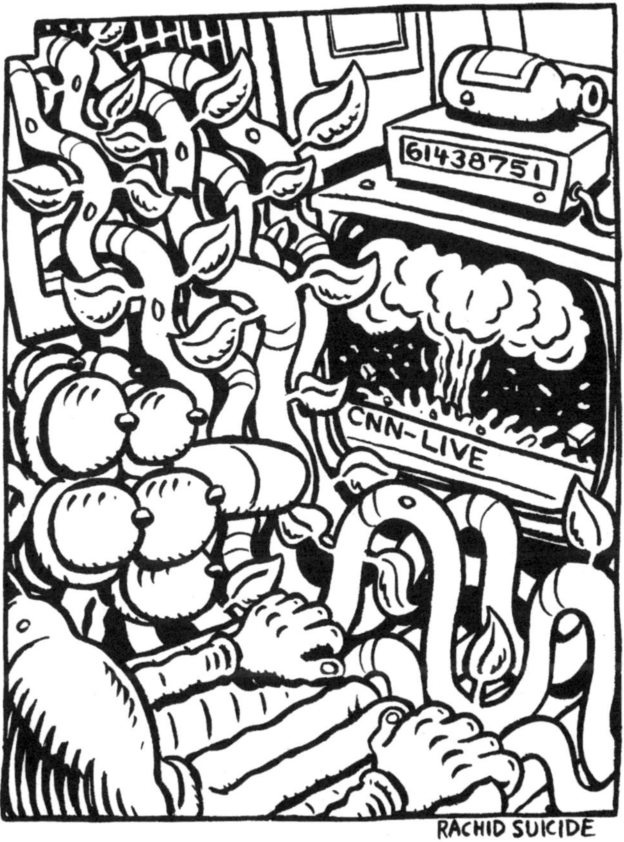
61438751
CNN-LIVE
RACHID SUICIDE

JILLIAN TAMAKI

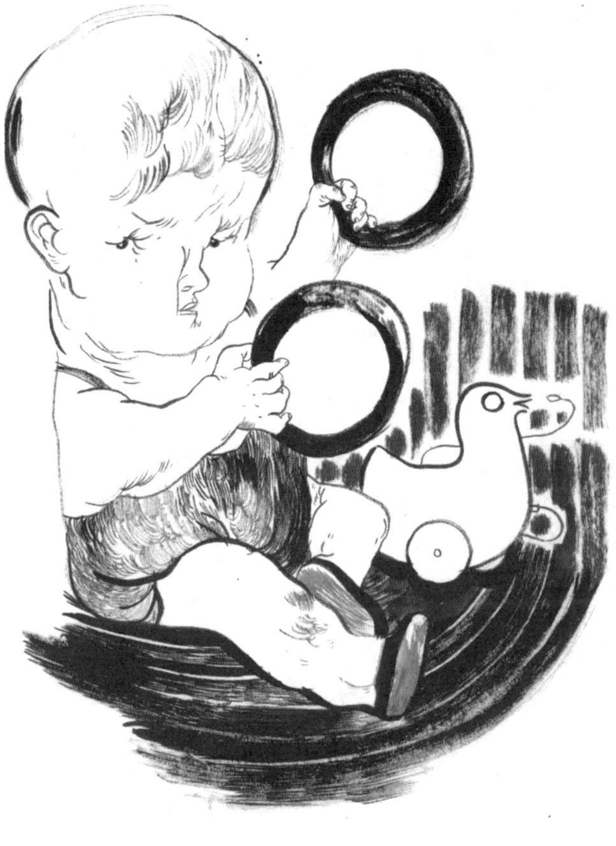

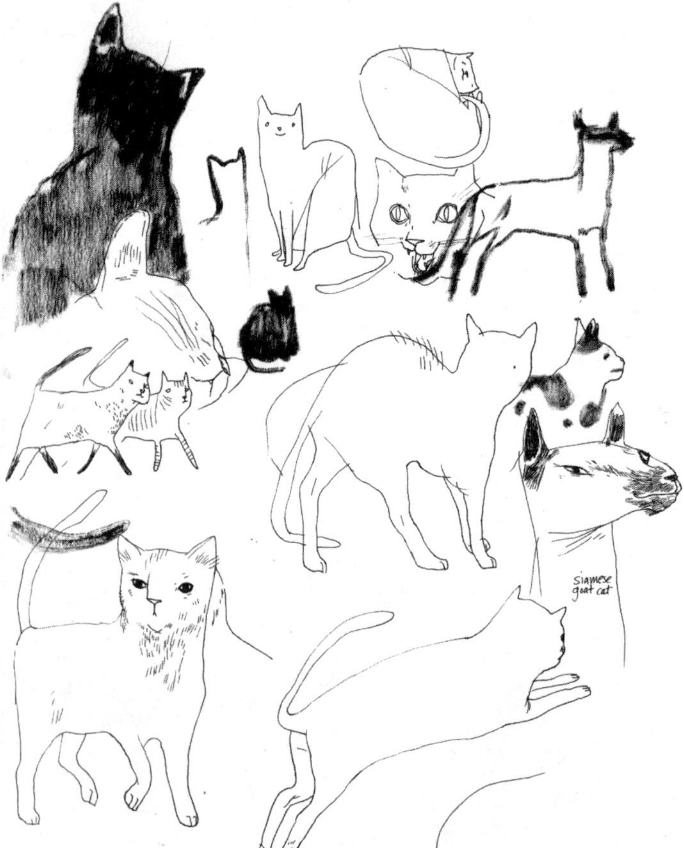
siamese
goat cat

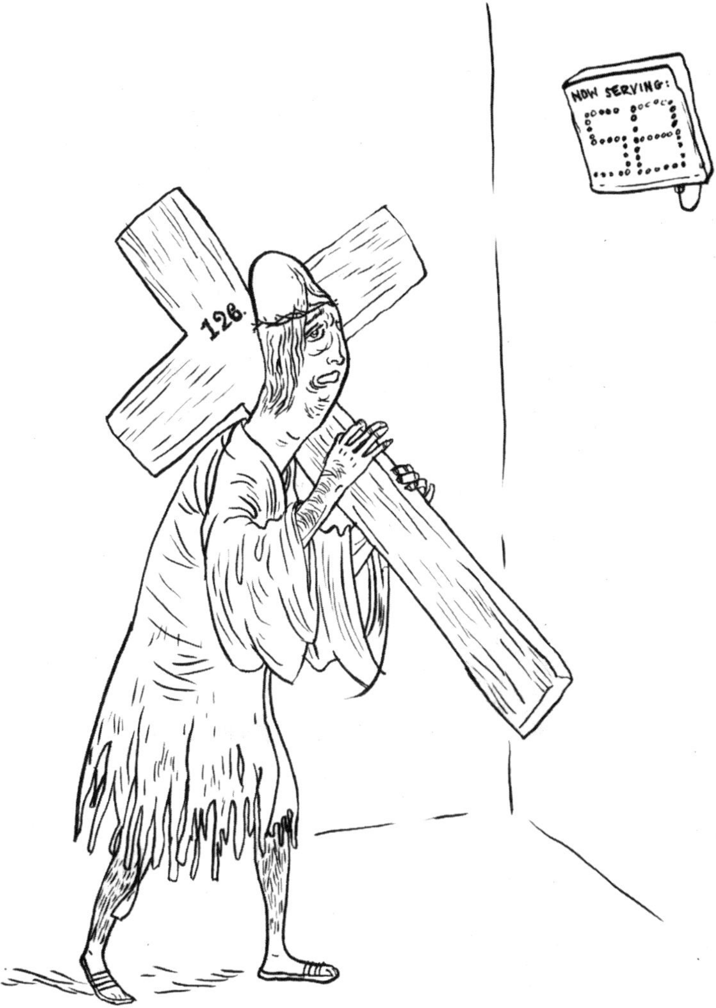
NOW SERVING:
58
126.

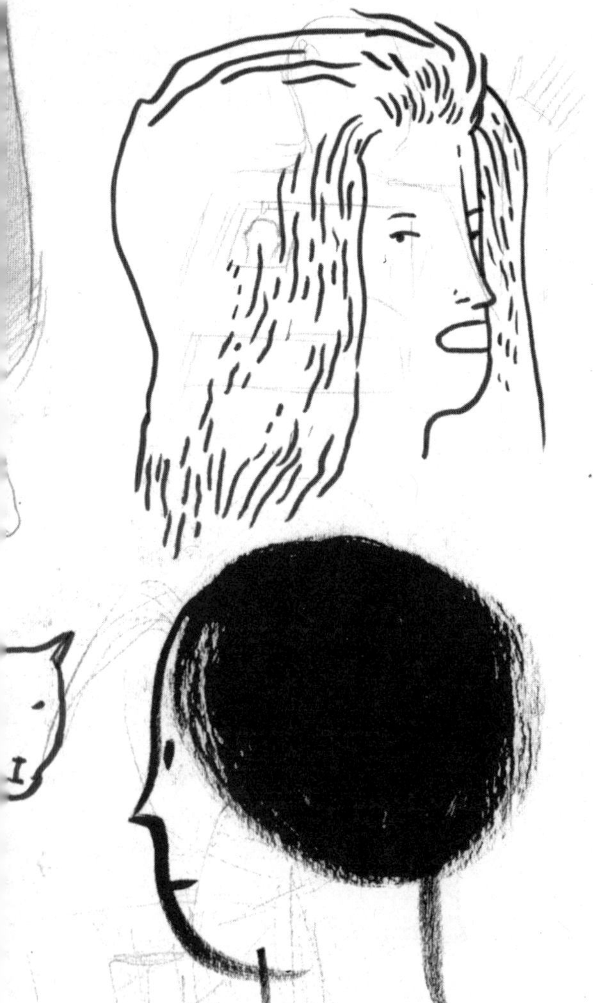

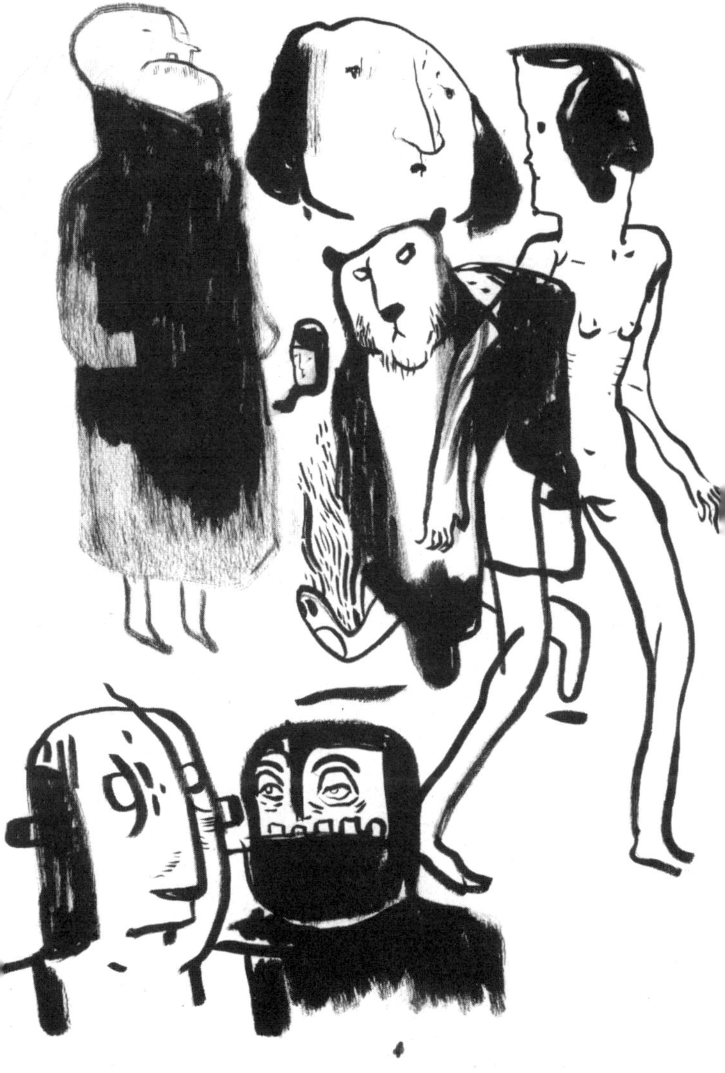

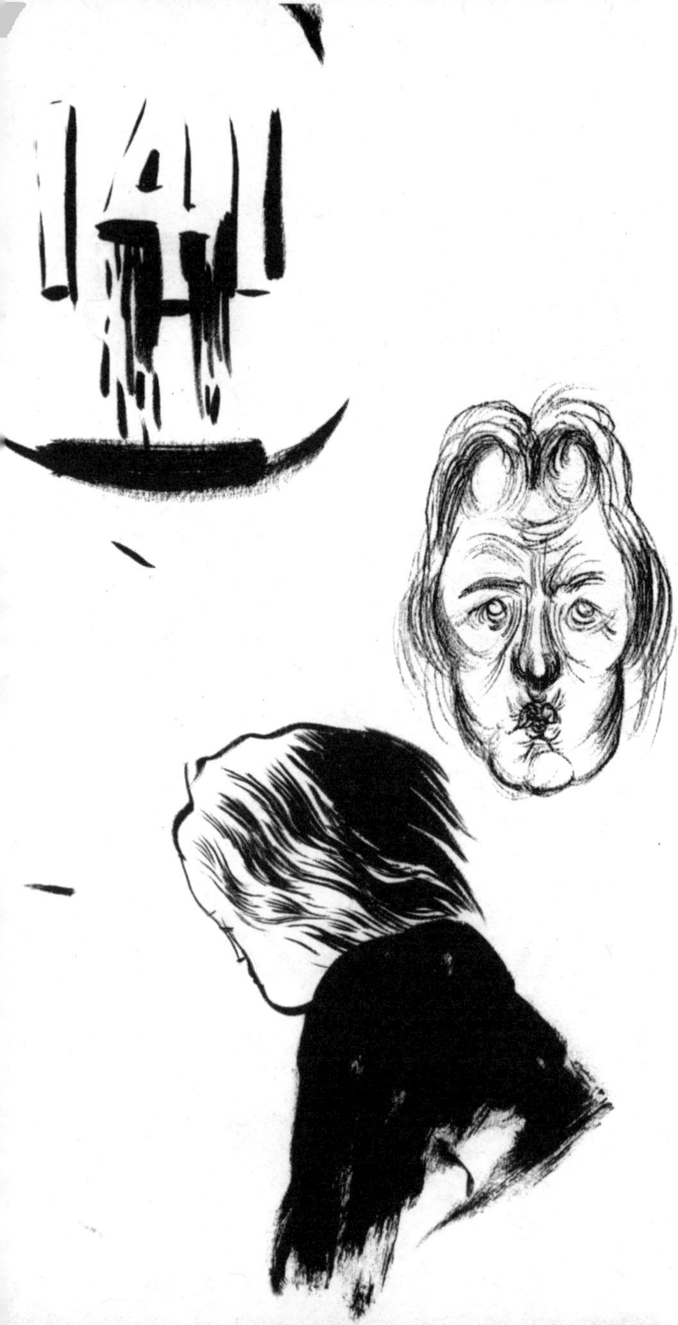

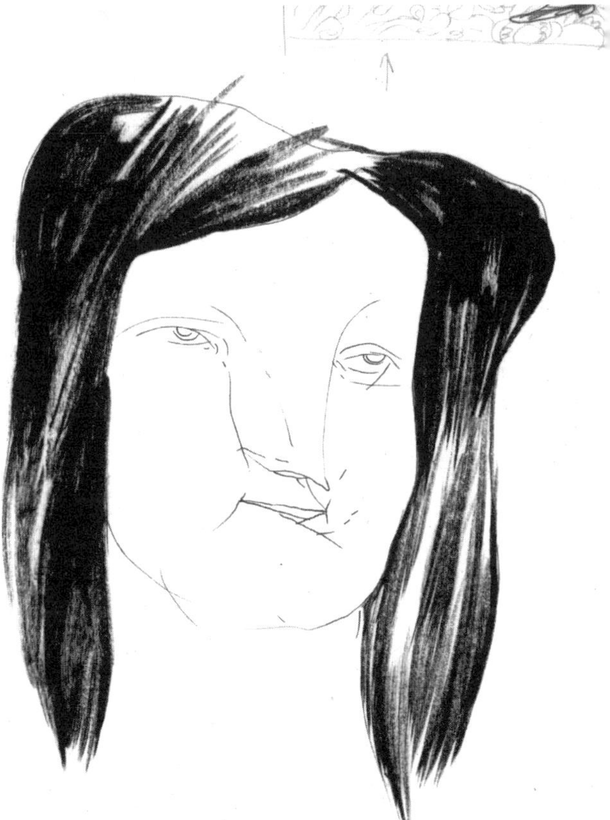

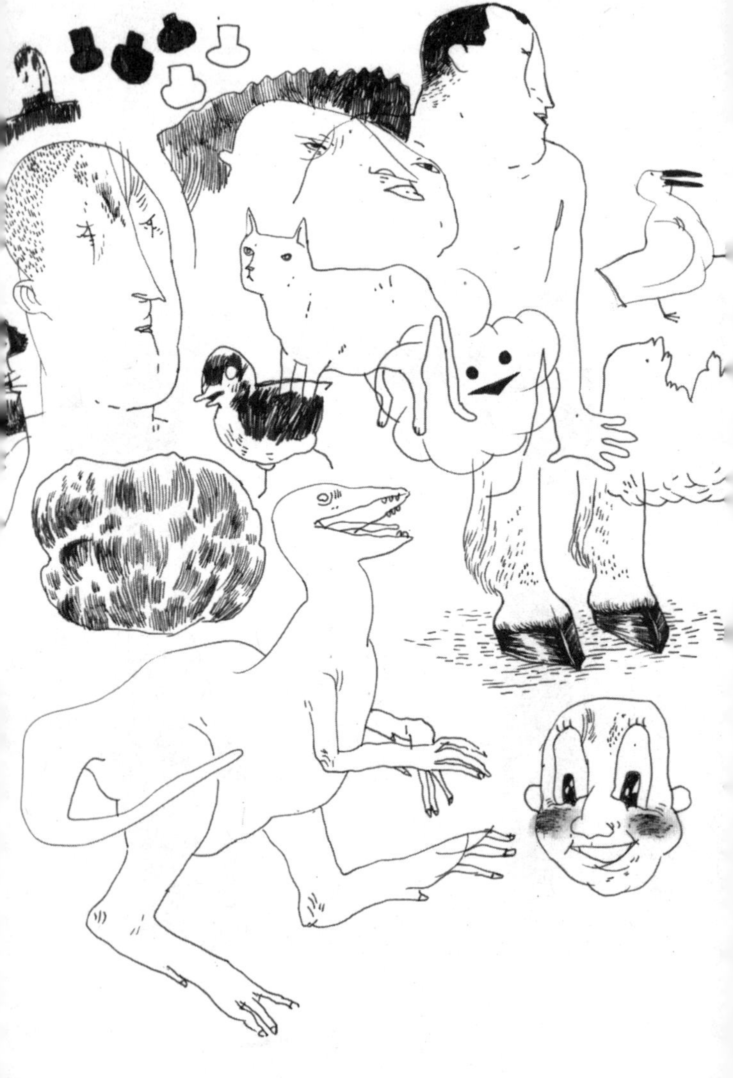

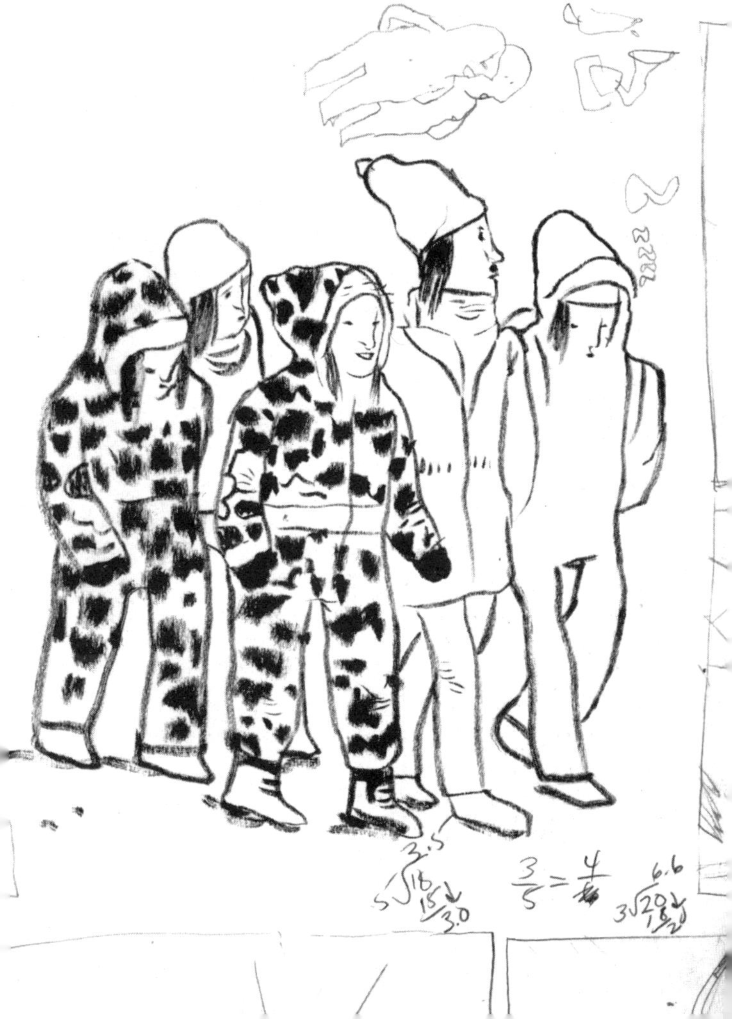

APPENDIX

conundrum press launch posters

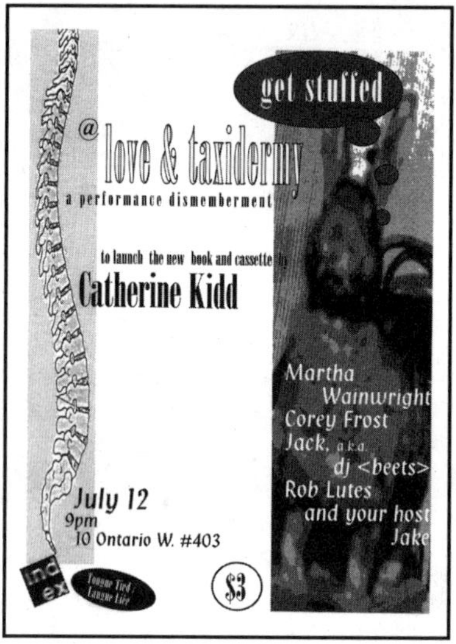
get stuffed
@ love & taxidermy
a performance dismemberment
to launch the new book and cassette by
Catherine Kidd
Martha Wainwright
Corey Frost
Jack, a.k.a. dj <beets>
Rob Lutes
and your host Jake
July 12
9pm
10 Ontario W. #403
$3
index

The event that started it all. One of two versions of the launch poster. The stuffed rabbit was on loan from the local Deli. Corey flew in from Japan. Many events were held in the lofts in the pre-condo 10 Ontario. Very early performances from Martha Wainwright and Rob Lutes. My early attempt at QuarkXpress.

Anne Stone thought my chapbook *Sleeves Sewn Shut* deserved a launch so she kindly organized one. I didn't realize I was expected to read! I stubbornly refused. The book itself was made from the scrap paper of *taxidermy*.

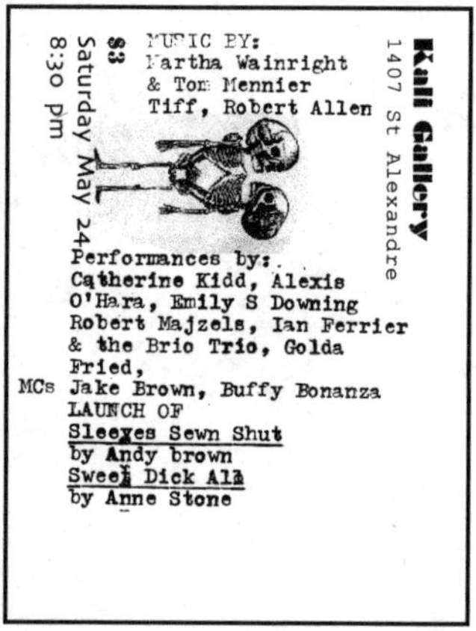
Kali Gallery
1407 St Alexandre
MUSIC BY:
Martha Wainright
& Tom Mennier
Tiff, Robert Allen
$3
Saturday May 24
8:30 pm
Performances by:
Catherine Kidd, Alexis O'Hara, Emily S Downing
Robert Majzels, Ian Ferrier & the Brio Trio, Golda Fried,
MCs Jake Brown, Buffy Bonanza
LAUNCH OF
Sleeves Sewn Shut
by Andy brown
Sweet Dick Ala
by Anne Stone

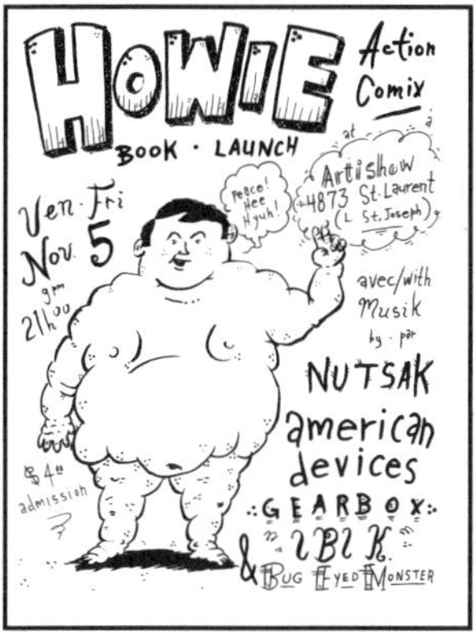
HOWIE
Action Comix
BOOK · LAUNCH
at à
Artishow
4873 St-Laurent
(L St. Joseph)
Peace! Hee Hyuh!
Ven-Fri
Nov. 5
9pm
21h00
avec/with
Musik
by · par
NUTSAK
american devices
GEARBOX
& IBI K.
BUG EYED MONSTER
$4.00
admission

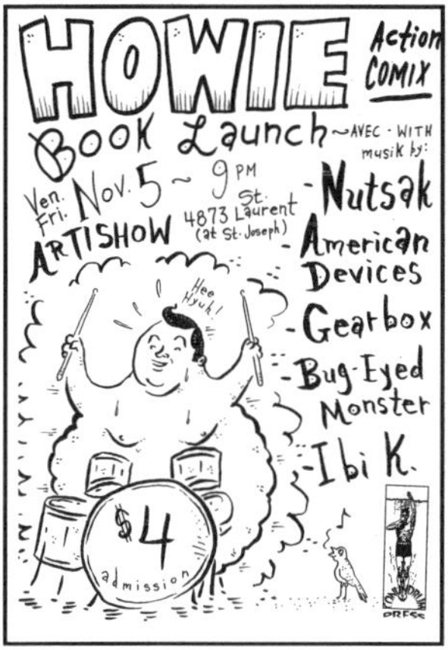
HOWIE
Action Comix
Book Launch ~ AVEC · WITH musik by:
Ven. Fri. Nov. 5 ~ 9 PM
ARTISHOW
4873 St. Laurent
(at St. Joseph)
Hee Hyuk!
-Nutsak
-American Devices
-Gearbox
-Bug-Eyed Monster
-Ibi K.
$4
admission

The poster for the poster book. Held in Corey and Dana's loft. Sam Shalabi played oud. Lots of old school punks. The book was printed by a Greek 'uncle'. The book only represents half of Billy's legendary output from from those years.

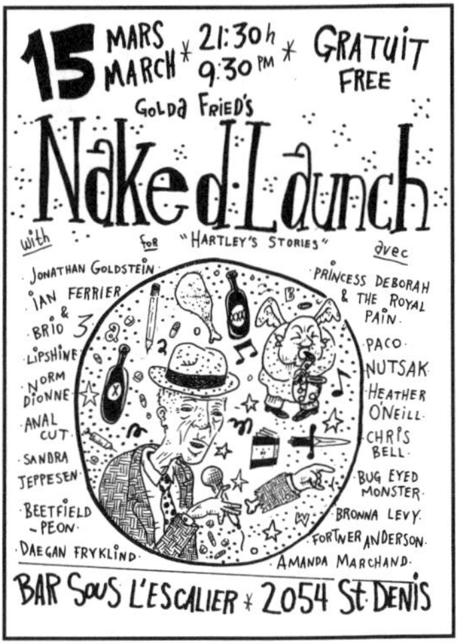
15 MARS MARCH * 21:30h 9:30 PM * GRATUIT FREE
GOLDA FRIED'S
Naked Launch
with
for "HARTLEY'S STORIES"
avec
JONATHAN GOLDSTEIN
IAN FERRIER & BRIO
LIPSHINE
NORM DIONNE
ANAL CUT
SANDRA JEPPESEN
BEETFIELD - PEON
DAEGAN FRYKLIND
PRINCESS DEBORAH & THE ROYAL PAIN
PACO
NUTSAK
HEATHER O'NEILL
CHRIS BELL
BUG EYED MONSTER
BRONWA LEVY
FORTNER ANDERSON
AMANDA MARCHAND
BAR SOUS L'ESCALIER * 2054 St-DENIS

Two variations on Howard's launch poster. Artishow was in the space that is now Casa del Popolo. You had to buy beer from some guy in the basement. Also the Howard drawn poster for Golda's launch.

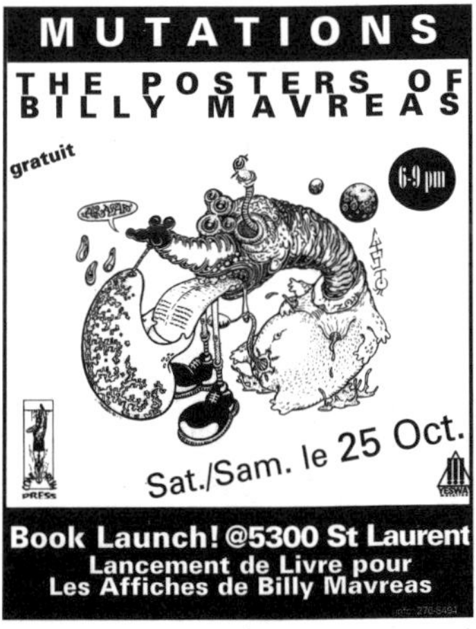
MUTATIONS
THE POSTERS OF BILLY MAVREAS
gratuit
6-9 pm
Sat./Sam. le 25 Oct.
Book Launch! @5300 St Laurent
Lancement de Livre pour
Les Affiches de Billy Mavreas

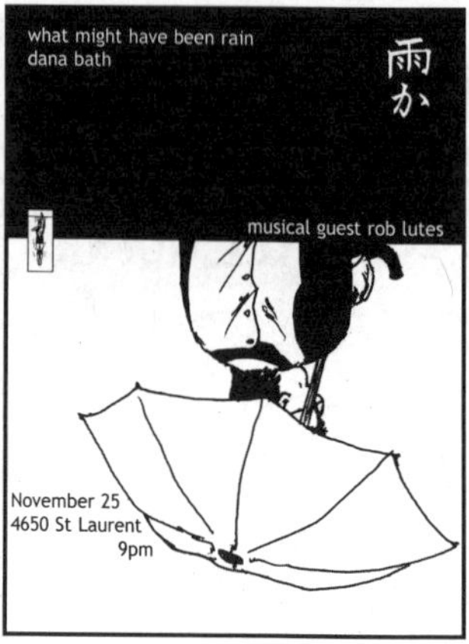
what might have been rain
dana bath
雨か
musical guest rob lutes
November 25
4650 St Laurent
9pm

Two variations on Dana's launch poster. At the old Sergeant Recruiter with excellent music by three Robs and a Tony. The kanji mean: Rain. Question.

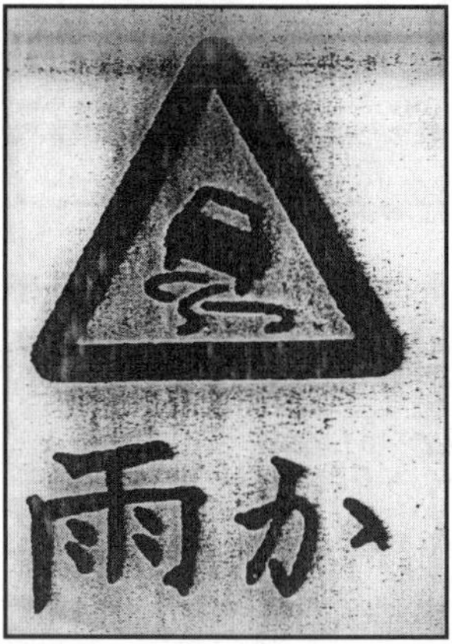
雨か

After hours Charles Chalmers slide show. Notice the conundrum logo is still more oval than pill shaped.

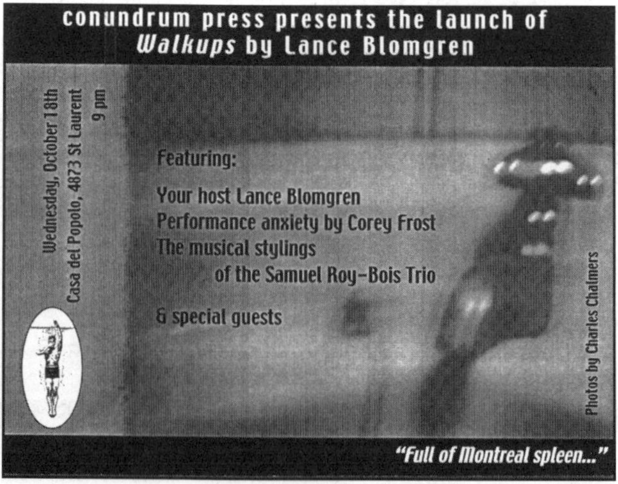
conundrum press presents the launch of
Walkups by Lance Blomgren
Wednesday, October 18th
Casa del Popolo, 4873 St Laurent
9 pm
Featuring:
Your host Lance Blomgren
Performance anxiety by Corey Frost
The musical stylings
of the Samuel Roy-Bois Trio
& special guests
Photos by Charles Chalmers
"Full of Montreal spleen..."

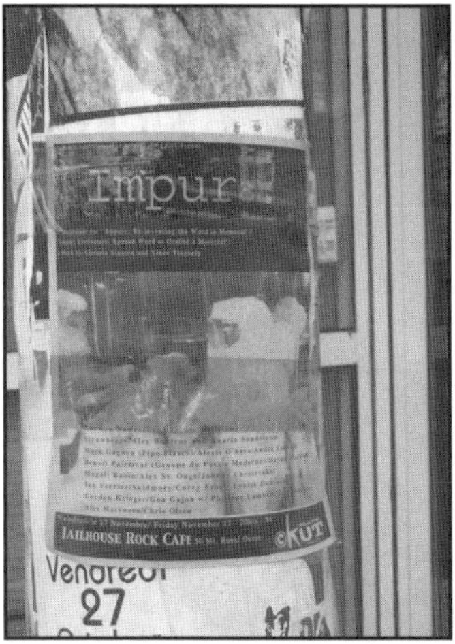
JAILHOUSE ROCK CAFE
CKUT

The benefit poster that was the beginning of my commitment to conundrum. The *Impure* manuscript was almost complete at this stage, and seeing all the incredible performers helping to raise money for Vince and Victoria to keep working on it made me realize debt was in my future.

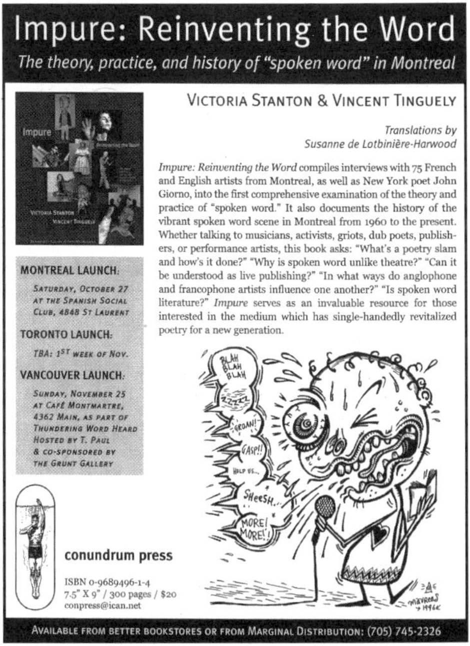

Impure: Reinventing the Word

The theory, practice, and history of "spoken word" in Montreal

VICTORIA STANTON & VINCENT TINGUELY

Translations by
Susanne de Lotbinière-Harwood

Impure: Reinventing the Word compiles interviews with 75 French and English artists from Montreal, as well as New York poet John Giorno, into the first comprehensive examination of the theory and practice of "spoken word." It also documents the history of the vibrant spoken word scene in Montreal from 1960 to the present. Whether talking to musicians, activists, griots, dub poets, publishers, or performance artists, this book asks: "What's a poetry slam and how's it done?" "Why is spoken word unlike theatre?" "Can it be understood as live publishing?" "In what ways do anglophone and francophone artists influence one another?" "Is spoken word literature?" *Impure* serves as an invaluable resource for those interested in the medium which has single-handedly revitalized poetry for a new generation.

MONTREAL LAUNCH:
SATURDAY, OCTOBER 27 AT THE SPANISH SOCIAL CLUB, 4848 ST LAURENT

TORONTO LAUNCH:
TBA: 1ST WEEK OF NOV.

VANCOUVER LAUNCH:
SUNDAY, NOVEMBER 25 AT CAFÉ MONTMARTRE, 4362 MAIN, AS PART OF THUNDERING WORD HEARD HOSTED BY T. PAUL & CO-SPONSORED BY THE GRUNT GALLERY

BLAH BLAH BLAH
ZZZZZ
GROAN!
GASP!!
HELP US...
SHEESH...
MORE! MORE!

conundrum press

ISBN 0-9689496-1-4
7.5" X 9" / 300 pages / $20
conpress@ican.net

AVAILABLE FROM BETTER BOOKSTORES OR FROM MARGINAL DISTRIBUTION: (705) 745-2326

This was more of a press release but check out the early cover design. Fantastic Billy Mavreas Yawp poster drawing. There's the pill logo too. Thanks to Peter Paré for vectorizing.

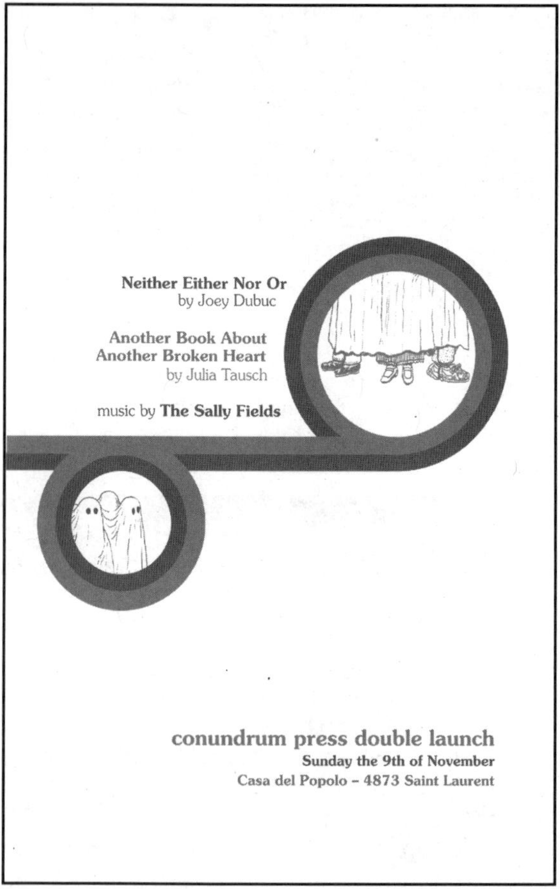
Neither Either Nor Or
by Joey Dubuc
Another Book About Another Broken Heart
by Julia Tausch
music by The Sally Fields
conundrum press double launch
Sunday the 9th of November
Casa del Popolo - 4873 Saint Laurent

Beautiful silkscreened poster designed by Joey and printed by Studio Alphonse Raymond. On the way home from picking up the posters from the studio the borrowed car ran out of gas in the middle of a busy intersection. Jesse Bochner happened to be passing and helped push. This event was very notable for the onstage kidnapping of Joey, who was blindfolded and handcuffed until the audience rebelled.

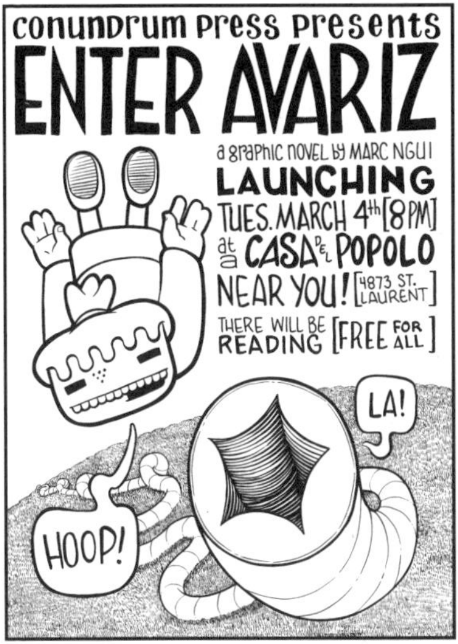
conundrum press presents
ENTER AVARIZ
a graphic novel by MARC NGUI
LAUNCHING
TUES. MARCH 4th [8PM]
at a CASA DEL POPOLO
NEAR YOU! [4873 ST. LAURENT]
THERE WILL BE READING [FREE FOR ALL]
LA!
HOOP!

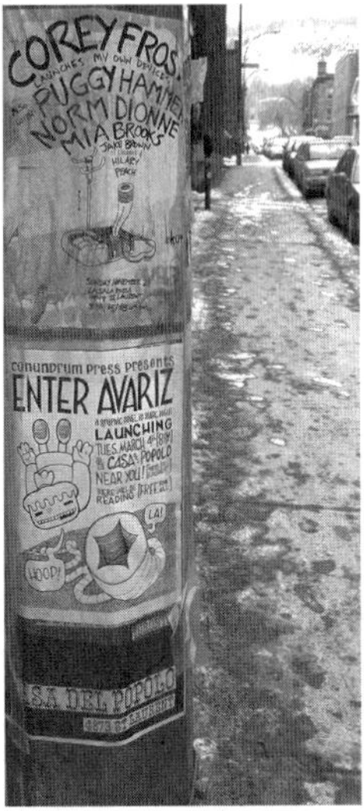
COREY FROST
ENTER AVARIZ

These events were more than three months apart yet advertised on the same lamppost on Duluth. Corey's is my attempt at lettering Marc Bell's device drawing. Marc Ngui shows how it's done above.

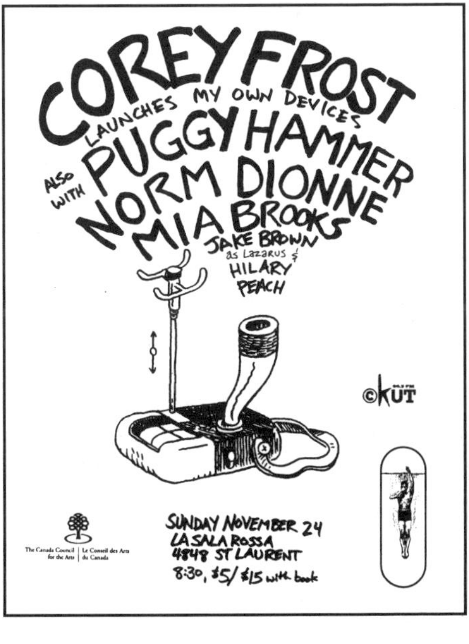
COREY FROST
LAUNCHES MY OWN DEVICES
ALSO WITH PUGGY HAMMER
NORM DIONNE
MIA BROOKS
JAKE BROWN as Lazarus & HILARY PEACH
CKUT
The Canada Council for the Arts | Le Conseil des Arts du Canada
SUNDAY NOVEMBER 24
LA SALA ROSSA
4848 ST LAURENT
8:30, $5/$15 with book

Launch Party for Lance Blomgren's

Corner Pieces

Thursday April 7
80 St. Viateur E. B1
10 pm, free

Lance was in Vancouver when Meg and I went out on the streets of Montreal with the ball of frayed rope Lance had been storing at our apartment. After the photoshoot we abandoned the rope. Lance came in for the launch at this underground loft. The Vancouver launch of *Corner Pieces* at The Whip was notable for the attempted robbery.

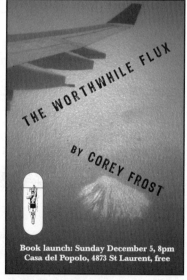

THE WORTHWHILE FLUX

BY COREY FROST

Book launch: Sunday December 5, 8pm
Casa del Popolo, 4873 St Laurent, free

Classic Corey Frost airplane photo. That's Mt. Fuji. This could have been the cover of the book.

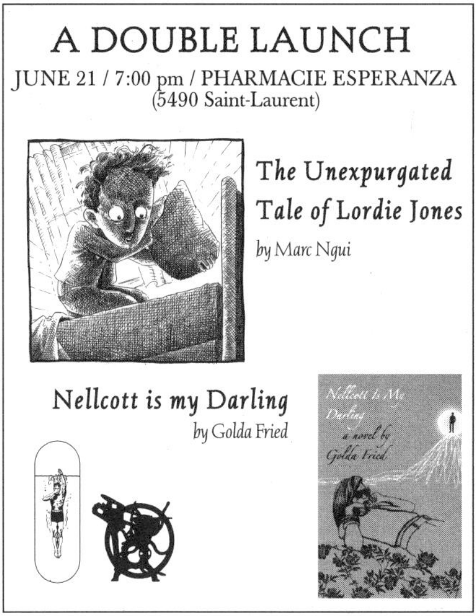

A DOUBLE LAUNCH
JUNE 21 / 7:00 pm / PHARMACIE ESPERANZA
(5490 Saint-Laurent)
The Unexpurgated Tale of Lordie Jones
by Marc Ngui
Nellcott is my Darling
by Golda Fried
Nellcott Is My Darling
a novel by Golda Fried

A co-launch with Coach House and the return of Golda Fried. A hot night. Notable in my mind because Meg was very pregnant and in fact went into labour the next day!

One of my favourite all time posters because Joe totally nails the caricature of me. Strangely enough, at the actual launch we played out this scene without realizing the irony.

buy a book from this man
(and make his publisher hap-hap-happy)
I thought you said your friends would buy books.
they'll be here … snif…
monday, october 17
10:00
at Korova
3908 st. laurent
(above the copacabana
the big book of WAG!
book launch for the Big Book of Wag!
cheap drinks, multi-media extravaganza, the sound of vinyl disks spun by the lovely jace & the smashing olga, the chance to buy this book, fourteen years in the making!
Bring $$, or bring excuses…
conundrum press, www.home.ican.net/~conpress/
www.wagpress.net

CONUNDRUM PRESS
COMPLETE BIBLIOGRAPHY

1996: *everything I know about love I learned from taxidermy,* Catherine Kidd. 7x5 inches, 52 pages, 500 copies. Cassette produced by Jack Beetz at The Swamp.

Sleeves Sewn Shut, Andy Brown. 6x3.5 inches, 16 pages, 300 copies. The first in the 'single story books for a single dollar' series.

June Makes a Friend, Amanda Marchand. 6x3.5 inches, 16 pages, 200 copies. A single story book for a single dollar.

1997: *Hartley's Stories,* Golda Fried. 5.5x4.25 inches, 16 pages, 300 copies. A single story book for a single dollar.

Mutations: The Posters of Billy Mavreas, Billy Mavreas. 8.5x11 inches, 80 pages, 250 copies signed and numbered, letterpressed, saddle-stitched. Introduction by Jake Brown.

Phelton Turns Twenty-Five, Peter Paré. 5.5x8.5 inches, 8 pages, 100 copies. A single story book for a single dollar.

Booked into the Wartime: Literary Figures Adopt New Careers, Andy Brown. 5.5x8.5 inches, 16 pages, 150 copies.

1998: *Ten Cent Packs,* Liane Keightley. 4.25x11 inches, 8 pages, 100 copies. A single story book for a single dollar.

what might have been rain, Dana Bath. 8x10 inches. 5 blueprinted posters (18x24 inches), 200 copies.

Machines that speak of distance, Andy Brown. 5.5x8.5 inches, 32 pages, 100 copies. Poetry chapbook with wraparound cover and each page laser printed.

psittacine flute, Catherine Kidd. 5.5x8.5, 16 pages, 100 copies.

1999:   *Howie Action Comics #1*, Howard Chackowicz. 5.5x8.5 inches, 32 pages, 200 copies. Cover silkscreened by Mille Putois. Guest writer Jonathan Goldstein.

   The Coincidence, Andy Brown. 5.5x4.25 inches, 24 pages, 100 copies. Mini-comic.

   How Do I Look?, Meg Sircom. 5.5x4.25 inches, 24 pages, 100 copies. With flip book drawings by Meg Sircom.

   I can see you being invisible, Andy Brown. 4.25x5.5 inches, 16 pages, 50 copies. Drawings.

   How to Build a Wall in 12 Easy Steps, Andy Brown. 5.5x4.25 inches, 32 pages, 100 copies.

2000:   *Walkups*, Lance Blomgren. 5x7.75 inches, 112 pages, 500 copies. First perfect bound book.

   Book du Jour: Montreal Literary Book Crawl 2000, Connie Barnes Rose, Kit Brennan, Esther Delisle, Marie Gray, David Homel, Debbie Howlett, Byron Rempel, Rachelle Renaud, Ray Smith, Joel Yanofsky. 5.5x8.5 inches, 24 pages, 100 copies. Collaborative chapbook created in three different bookstores over the course of one day (April 27) and launched the same evening.

   My Girl, Meg Sircom. 4.25x5.5 inches, 16 pages, 50 copies. Mini-comic. Reprinted for Distroboto imprint, 3.25x3.5 inches, 50 copies.

2001:   *All Day Breakfast*, Valerie Joy Kalynchuk. Distroboto imprint, 3.25x3.5 inches, 24 pages, 50 copies. Reprinted as part of the perfect bound *All Day Breakfast,* 5.5x5, 60 pages.

   as if from the mountains, Golda Fried. Distroboto imprint, 3.25x3.5 inches, 24 pages, 50 copies.

   Intruders, Andy Brown. 5.5x8.5 inches, 24 pages, 25 copies.

   Impure: Reinventing the Word: the theory, practice and oral history of '*spoken word*' *in Montreal*, Victoria Stanton and Vincent Tinguely with translations by Suzanne de Lotbinière-Harwood. 7.5x9 inches, 288 pages.

The Overlords of Glee, Billy Mavreas. 7x10 inches, 76 pages. Co-published with Crunchy Comics.

2002: *Enter Avariz*, Marc Ngui. 6x9 inches, 120 pages. 8 foldout pages, 22x9 inches.

My Own Devices, Corey Frost. 5.5x7.5 inches, 162 pages.

Simultaneous Brazil, Corey Frost. 5.5x3.25 inches, 32 pages, 100 copies.

Downward Facing Dog / Tale of the Horse Leech, Catherine Kidd. Mini CD for Distroboto imprint.

Sea Peach, Catherine Kidd. 5.5x5 inches, 80 pages. Includes CD.

2003: *Cyclops: Contemporary Canadian Narrative Art*, Marc Tessier and Hélène Brosseau editors. 7.75x10.75 inches, 224 pages.

Howie Action Comics #2, Howard Chackowicz. 3.5x4.25 inches, 46 pages, 100 copies. Distroboto imprint.

Sapphic Traffic, Suki Lee. 5.5x5 inches, 196 pages.

Another Book About Another Broken Heart, Julia Tausch. 4.25x7 inches, 168 pages. Metro series.

Neither Either Nor Or, Joey Dubuc. 4.125x6.875 inches, 104 pages. With 25 illustrations by Joey Dubuc.

The Andy Brown Project, Andy Brown. 3.5x4.25 inches, 32 pages, first printing of 50 copies for Distroboto imprint. Second printing of 550 for *Maisonneuve* subscribers.

2004: *Cherry*, Chandra Mayor. 4.25x7 inches, 128 pages. Metro series.

Mac Tin Tac, Marc Tessier and Stéphane Olivier. 6.5x10 inches, 160 pages. Each chapter illustrated by a different artist.

Caleb, Andy Brown. 3.5x4.25 inches, 24 pages. Distroboto imprint. Drawings by Marc Bell. Text and images from 1996.

Witness My Shame, Shary Boyle. 6x8 inches, 160 pages.

Corner Pieces, Lance Blomgren. 6x8 inches, 112 pages. Hand embossed cover and one rounded corner.

The Worthwhile Flux, Corey Frost. 5x7 inches, 144 pages.

2005: *The Unexpurgated Tale of Lordie Jones,* Marc Ngui. 7x7 inches, 80 pages.

Sextant, Maya Merrick. 4.25x7 inches, 260 pages. Metro series.

The Big Book of Wag!, Joe Ollmann. 7x8 inches, 192 pages.

Bowlbrawl, Nathaniel G. Moore. 6x9 inches, 192 pages.

Something to pet the cat about, Elisabeth Belliveau. 6x8 inches, 176 pages. Rounded corners.

2006: *bipolar bear,* Catherine Kidd. 6x7 inches, 88 pages. Includes DVD.

Beauty is a Liar, Valerie Joy Kalynchuk. 4.25x7 inches, 128 pages. Metro series.

The portable conundrum, Andy Brown editor. 4.25x7 inches. 312 pages. Ten year anniversary anthology featuring 34 contributors.

CONTRIBUTOR BIOGRAPHIES

Catherine Kidd has produced four titles for conundrum press including the first, *everything I know about love I learned from taxidermy* which came with a cassette. Her book / CD *Sea Peach* won a MECCA award for best new text in 2003 and her latest book, *bipolar bear*, includes a DVD. She has performed all over the world including Oslo, Bavaria, Edinburgh, Vancouver, Minnesota, Toronto, Singapore, and Montreal. One of her stories was nominated for a Journey prize. She lives in Montreal.

Andy Brown is the founder and sole employee of conundrum press. He is a founding organizer of Expozine: Montreal's small press, comic, and zine fair, and the art director of *Matrix* magazine. His book of stories, *I can see you being invisible* (DC Books), was released in 2003 and his novel, *The Mole Chronicles*, will be released later this year by Insomniac. He is originally from Vancouver but now lives in Montreal.

Amanda Marchand is a writer / photographer originally from Montreal but currently living in New York by way of San Francisco. A recent MacDowell fellow, she has exhibited her work in numerous group and solo shows, and is represented by Traywick Contemporary in Berkeley. She is the author of the conundrum chapbook *June Makes a Friend* which was reprinted as part of her book *Without Cease the Earth Faintly Trembles* (DC Books) which was selected as Critic's Pick in *Now* Magazine.

Golda Fried's first book was the conundrum chapbook, *Hartley's Stories*. She also contributed to conundrum's Distroboto imprint with the story *as if from the mountains*. Her latest novel *Nelcott is My Darling* (Coach House) was recently nominated for the Governor General's Award. Originally from Toronto she attended school in Montreal and now lives in Greensboro, North Carolina.

Billy Mavreas created many of the posters for spoken word shows in late 1990s Montreal. Conundrum press collected many of them into the book *Mutations*. Conundrum then collaborated with Crunchy Comics to release his first book of comics, *The Overlords of Glee*. His comics and drawings have appeared in zines and anthlogies world-wide. Currently he provides a regular comic strip for *Matrix* and *Ascent* magazines.

Peter Paré is the author of the conundrum chapbook *Phelton Turns Twenty-Five*. He recently completed a design program at the Emily Carr School of Art. He lives in Vancouver where he plays poker on-line as well as face-to-face.

Liane Keightley is a Montreal writer and the author of the conundrum chapbook *Ten Cent Packs*. She is a graduate of Concordia's Masters of Creative Writing program and has attended the Banff Center's Writing Workshop. Her stories have been published in *Matrix*, *You and Your Bright Ideas, Ribsauce*, and *The Moosehead Anthology*.

Dana Bath wrote the stories which made up *what might have been rain*, an art book published by conundrum in a limited edition. Some of these stories were reprinted in her Arsenal Pulp book, *Universal Recipients*. Her first novel was *Plenty of Harm in God* (DC Books). She has won the Short Grain Writing Contest, has twice finished in the top three in the 3-Day novel competition, and has been shortlisted for the ReLit Award. Bath is originally from Corner Brook Newfoundland and now teaches at Vanier College in Montreal.

Howard Chackowicz was nominated for a Harvey Award for best new comics talent in 1993. Since then he has published two conundrum comics, *Howie Action Comics* #1 and #2. He currently works at a used bookstore, plays drums in the band Nutsak, and is a regular contributor to the CBC's "Wiretap".

Meg Sircom is the author of the conundrum chapbook *How Do I Look?* as well as the mini-comic *My Girl*. She has also been published in *The New Quarterly, You and Your Bright Ideas,* and *Matrix*. A graduate of the Concordia Creative Writing Masters program she now teaches at Vanier College.

Lance Blomgren presently lives in Vancouver where he works as the co-director of the Helen Pitt Gallery. He is the author of conundrum's first perfect bound book *Walkups*. He recently completed the Informal Architecture Residency at the Banff Centre for the Arts where he wrote much of his recent book, *Corner Pieces*, which was shortlisted for the Relit Award in 2005. To *The portable conundrum* Lance contributes pieces which originally appeared in Vancouver's *Terminal City* newspaper.

Valerie Joy Kalynchuk is a regular contributor to *Matrix*. Her work has also appeared in *Geist, The Original Canadian City Dweller's Almanac, Fish Piss, Career Suicide,* and *You and Your Bright Ideas*. Originally from Winnipeg, she currently lives in Montreal. Her first conundrum book was *All Day Breakfast* and her new novel is called *Beauty is a Liar*.

Victoria Stanton and **Vincent Tinguely** were founding members of the performance poetry troupe Fluffy Pagan Echoes during the 'spoken word explosion' of the nineties. Since then they have performed either solo or collaboratively across the globe, launching their conundrum book *Impure: Reinventing the Word: the theory, practice and oral history of 'spoken word' in Montreal* in Montreal, Toronto, Ottawa, New York, Vancouver, and Melbourne. Stanton is the founder of The Bank of Victoria and is active in the performance art community. Tinguely writes about spoken word for *The Montreal Mirror* and creates chapbooks and cassettes. They co-host a radio show on CKUT.

Marc Ngui is an artist whose work is firmly rooted in DIY / zine culture. Ngui has also published the graphic novels *Enter Avariz* and *The Unexpurgated Tale of Lordie Jones* with conundrum. He spent the 2004-2005 season learning about the media machine as the Toronto DIY arts correspondent for ZeD Television on the CBC. He is currently traveling while trying to balance an over-whelming surge of technology inspired optimism with an under-standing that the polar ice caps will no longer be frozen in the winter by the end of this century.

Corey Frost has toured his multi-media performances on the Perpetual Motion Roadshow in Canada and the US, and in Europe and Australasia. Most recently his writing has appeared in *The Walrus* and *Matrix*. His most recent conundrum book, *The Worthwhile Flux*, collects his performances and was shortlisted for the ReLit Award in 2005. In fall 2006 conundrum will release a new expanded edition of his first book, *My Own Devices*, which was nominated for the ReLit Award and QWF First Book Award in 2003. Currently he is pursuing a PhD and lives in Brooklyn, NY.

Marc Tessier has collaborated with Alexandre Lafleur on *Theatre of Cruelty* (Fantagraphics) and the *Abinagouesh* series (Delacourt). He is a frequent contributor to *The Comics Journal*. He is the author of the conundrum graphic novel *Mac Tin Tac* and the co-editor of the *Cyclops* anthology.

Hélène Brosseau is the co-editor of *Cyclops*. Her comics and draw-ings have appeared in numerous anthologies. She works at the comic shop Fichtre! in Montreal. She contributes drawings which originally formed a small silkscreened accordion snapbook as part of the Collection Panique from Editions Alphonse Raymond.

Suki Lee is an Ottawa-based fiction writer, columnist and world traveller. Her fiction has been widely anthologized, most recently in *With a Rough Tongue: Femmes Write Porn* (Arsenal Pulp Press,

2005). *Sapphic Traffic*, her debut collection of short stories, was published by conundrum in 2003. Suki has an MA from Concordia University's Creative Writing and English Literature program. A contributor to the CBC and the *Ottawa Citizen*, Suki is also the literary curator of Westfest. Her website is www.sukilee.com

Julia Tausch is the author of the conundrum title *Another Book About Another Broken Heart* which won a Mississauga Arts Award. She completed her MA in Creative Writing at Concordia University. She won the J.C.W. Saxon Award for playwriting in 2001. She lives in Toronto.

Joey Dubuc is a writer and visual artist from Montreal who wrote and illustrated the popular book *Neither Either Nor Or* for conundrum. Since receiving his MFA from York University he has shown his work in galleries in Vancouver, Toronto, Montreal and Australia. His written work has appeared in *The Walrus* and *Alphabet City*. He currently lives in Vancouver.

Chandra Mayor is a Winnipeg writer and editor. She won the Carol Shields Winnipeg Book Award in 2005 for her conundrum novel *Cherry*. Her first book, *August Witch: poems* (Cyclops), won the Eileen McTavish Sykes Award for Best First Book in 2003. She is the recipient of the 2004 John Hirsch Award for Most Promising Manitoba Writer, and is currently the poetry co-editor for *Prairie Fire* Magazine.

Stéphane Olivier teaches graphic design in Montreal. He recently finished the graphic novel *Le Clairon* and is editing the next book in the Cyclopes series. He was the co-director of the conundrum title *Mac Tin Tac*. With his design partner **Gilles Boulerice** he won the Graphika award for cover design for the conundrum *Cyclops* anthology as well as a Concours Lux prize for best cultural illustration.

Shary Boyle has worked and exhibited in Berlin, Paris, Los Angeles, Chicago, New York, Nova Scotia, Vancouver and the Yukon. Boyle also collaborates with musicians such as Peaches and Feist, creating 'live' drawings which are animated and projected onstage alongside the performance. Her work has been published in magazines and books such as *The Story of Jane Doe, The Walrus, The National Post, Starship, Maclean's, Toro, Saturday Night, Kramers Ergot,* and *Girls Who Bite Back.* Her bookworks were collected into the conundrum title, *Witness My Shame.* She lives in Toronto. Visit www.sharyboyle.com

Originally from Vancouver, **Maya Merrick** presently works as a barmaid in Montreal. She appeared as an invited guest at the Word on the Street festival and at Canzine in Toronto. Her work was recently seen in *Matrix* but her conundrum novel *Sextant* was her first publication.

Joe Ollmann is a cartoonist who had a monthly comic strip in *Exclaim!* for four years and is now a regular graphic columnist for *Matrix* magazine. His animation has appeared on America Online, The Comedy Network and at the Canadian Comedy Awards. His first graphic novel *Chewing on Tinfoil* (Insomniac) received rave reviews. Conundrum collected the best of his long running series of mini zines into the book *The Big Book of Wag!*

Nathaniel G. Moore is the author of the instant cult classic *Bowlbrawl* (conundrum). He lives. Visit www.bowlbrawl.com

Elisabeth Belliveau is a visual artist and animator based in Montreal. After graduating from the Alberta College of Art and Design, she attended artist residencies in Banff, Charlottetown and the Yukon. She continues to exhibit her sculpture and installation work across Canada and is currently producing claymation animations and learning how to tattoo. Her zines were collected by conundrum into the book *Something to pet the cat about.*

Marc Bell's work has been serialized in many periodicals including *The Montreal Mirror* and *Vice Magazine* and his own *Worn Tuff Elbow* (Fantagraphics) as well as appearing regularly in such book publications as *The Ganzfeld* and *Kramers Ergot*. Drawn & Quarterly published his book *The Stacks* in 2004. Bell, originally from London Ontario, now lives in Vancouver, BC. He is represented by the Adam Baumgold Gallery in NY. Bell's work will be appearing extensively in *Nog A Dod*, a collection of (previously) self-published Canadian 'Psychedooolick' bookworks from conundrum.

Robert Allen teaches creative writing at Concordia University, is the editor of *Matrix*, and the author of fifteen books of poetry and prose including the novel *Napoleon's Retreat* (DC Books) and the recent book of poetry *Standing Wave* (Véhicule). Conundrum will publish his epic long poem *The Encantadas* in its entirety in 2006. He contributes an excerpt from his novel in progress.

Richard Suicide is the Robert Crumb of Quebec. His underground comics and paintings have earned him a reputation in the francophone comix milieu. He is also a regular contributor of illustrations to the *The Montreal Mirror*. Conundrum will publish a collection of his work in translation called *My Life as a Foot*.

Jillian Tamaki is the artist behind the future conundrum title *Gilded Lilies* which includes her mini comic *City of Champions*, a stream-of-consciousness ode to Edmonton, plus other comics, illustration and sketchbook work. Her work has appeared in the *New York Times, Entertainment Weekly, The New Yorker* and CBC Arts On-line. With her cousin, Mariko Tamaki, she's currently expanding the comic *Skim* into a graphic novel for Groundwood Press (an imprint of Anansi). Raised in Calgary, she graduated from the Alberta College of Art and Design in 2003. She currently lives in Brooklyn, NY. You can visit her on-line at www.jilliantamaki.com

NOTES